TRAIN

>> *to* <<

OBLIVION

TRAIN

≫ *to* ≪

OBLIVION

a novel

MOIRA MILLÁN

TRANSLATED BY CHARLOTTE WHITTLE

AMAZON **CROSSING**

Text copyright © 2019, 2024 by Moira Ivana Millán
Translation copyright © 2024 by Charlotte Whittle
All rights reserved.

Previously published as *El tren del olvido* by Grupo Editorial Planeta S.A.I.C. in Argentina in 2019. Translated from Spanish by Charlotte Whittle. First published in English by Amazon Crossing in 2024.

Published by Amazon Crossing, Seattle

www.apub.com

Amazon, the Amazon logo, and Amazon Crossing are trademarks of Amazon.com, Inc., or its affiliates.

ISBN-13: 9781542034968 (paperback)
ISBN-13: 9781542034951 (digital)

Cover design by Mumtaz Mustafa
Cover images: © Vibrands Studio / Shutterstock; © Michieru / Getty

Printed in the United States of America

TRAIN

≫ *to* ≪

OBLIVION

Contents

PROLOGUE

My name is Llankaray. I am a Mapuche woman. What does it mean to be Mapuche? I will tell you: *mapu* means land, and *che*, people. People of the land. But it is not just the idea people usually have of the land. It goes beyond that. It is the tangible world, the visible world, the world beneath our feet, and also what is above, that which is all around us. The mapu is alive. It is a force, a *newen*. What a beautiful word, don't you think? Newen: energy, force, every single form of existence that creates and feeds the magic circle of life.

I was born and have always lived in Patagonia. My language is Mapudungun. Speech of the land, that is what we call our ancient tongue. I am a warrior for my nation, a *weychafe*. I come from a line of brave and long-suffering women. One of these women, perhaps the bravest of all, is the one who showed me the way and left us an inheritance—her medicine, and a lesson: never give up. And a promise to never forget. Her name was Pirenrayen, and she was my grandmother. From her, I learned of all that happened to us since the Wingka invaders arrived.

These last few days, memories have crowded into my mind, as if I had been riding the wind and it had carried me into the past. Winter, its fingers trembling with cold, has confined me to an unceasing pause, lit by the warmth of the fire that lulls me with crackling logs. Time has drawn out my grandmother's tales from a warm alcove in my soul, as if each were a patch of the tattered memory of my people. So often when

I was a child, I tired of hearing the same stories over and over, and now that I am seventy-five, they seem vital and full of spirit. To keep them inside me and silence those voices would be to kill the truth of my essence, my origin.

Many things are now said of my people. Those who speak of us have evil thoughts and intentions. *Weshakeche*, evil, is what they are. Yet there is no vengeance in the heart of my people. There are no words. Great silences are there, unfurling like the arid plains of my Patagonia. The southerly wind whispers names, events, injustices. The age-old mountains preserve our memory. The rivers sing the truths of the past. The forests cry out the wounds of the present. But the Wingka does not know or see; he cannot, will not, speak the language of the land, open the doors to consciousness, and meet with his own heart.

Despite everything, the seed of a new humanity is starting to blossom in the fertile meadows of hope. There are new flowers of many colors beating in a single earthly heart. In this new present, women and men walk and wonder about the truth, seeking in the memory of the territories the hushed voices of ghostly figures past, so they can reveal to them their true stories. Without lies, without glory, with neither winners nor losers, neither evil nor good. Invaded and invaders seeking a place in history, on the land, and in a fleeting present that allows us to seize from injustice the names of those we will honor with the truth.

This is why I tell our stories. This is why I speak.

PART ONE

PART ONE

Chapter 1

A Fleeting Peace for Our People

My grandmother used to say that the old-timers remembered the Desert Campaign with tears. Those who survived the genocide were pushed to the south, detained and tortured in concentration camps, forced to walk thousands of miles in deadly deportations. They were taken to work in the sugar harvest and other forced labor in the northern territories. The governors of Tucumán and Salta sent for hundreds of Mapuche and Tehuelche slaves. Whole families were split asunder, unable to ever find one another again. Mothers lost their babies forever; men would never again hear word of their wives or children. It was a time of pain and darkness, so our elders told us. If they did not die of hunger, they died of sorrow.

In the Puelwillimapu, today known as Patagonia, they herded us onto small plots of land. Rural-Indigenous reservations, the Argentine state called them. They began to limit us to the most barren regions, infertile, lacking water, places where all resources were scarce. Gradually, hunger took over our lives. Not even those communities friendly with the Argentine state were spared the government's plunder and tyranny. My grandmother was born on one of those reservations in 1900, during the second presidency of General Roca. She was the daughter of Kalfurayen, my great-grandmother.

Kalfurayen was the only daughter from the marriage of Fresia Coliman and Naweltripay, my great-great-grandparents. They were already older when they married. Fresia had been widowed with five children. Her first husband was captured on the outskirts of a fort, and there he was tortured and murdered. Naweltripay was a cacique, though the correct term is *longko*. Cacique is what the Wingkas called him. They meant the one in charge, who made decisions and gave orders to his people. But they were wrong; that is not what our world is like. A longko is someone who uses his wisdom to seek consensus, keeping to the ancestral ways, organizing the life of the community with respect for the elders' teachings. He does not give commands; on the contrary, he obeys the natural cosmic order. Longko Naweltripay has always been remembered for his integrity and his wisdom.

How did my great-great-grandparents meet? Fresia's first husband was Naweltripay's nephew, and the two men were the same age. Naweltripay had married, at almost the same time as his nephew, a girl much younger than he was. Antupray was her name. Ever since she was very young, she had been close to Fresia and viewed her as an older sister, and Antupray reaped the benefits of Fresia's medicine. Fresia's humble heart touched Antupray, who came to love her a great deal. My great-great-grandmother's gifts as a healer helped Antupray in childbirth and in treating her children and even her animals.

Antupray was saddened and anguished by her friend's widowhood. She was a joyful person, and highly sensitive. Her husband could not bear to see Antupray weep for the pain of others. He did all that he could to please her and showered her with attention, but even then, he was unable to make her happy. Those times in the aftermath of war had tinged the soul of my people with ashen sorrow.

The custom of marrying more than one woman lasted well into modern times. Even though the longkos no longer had many animals or food in abundance, they continued to take on the widows, and also married other women who were to their liking. So when Fresia Coliman was widowed, Antupray asked her husband to take her as a second wife, since in this way, Fresia would be cared for and protected. When Antupray confessed the idea to her friend, Fresia was displeased that she had spoken to the longko without first consulting her. Initially, she refused since it did not seem fair to her that the longko should have to care for and feed her five children. And there were many widows and few men who could take care of them all.

Fresia felt strong despite her pain. Many women went to her, seeking advice and support. Although she knew how hard it would be to care for her children in times of hunger and scarcity, of persecution and death, she kept her freedom and solitude as a shield from an uncertain future and a present full of trials. Her task was not remotely easy. The Argentine government, along with the Vatican, had resolved to do away with medicine women, our priestesses of healing, the machis, and the herbalists whom we call the *lawentuchefe*. The government considered them to be enemies of the Christian faith and the security of the state. Too much power, too much vision, too much wisdom dwelled in the bodies of women.

The machis are the only carriers of spiritual language, which connects them to the forces of the beyond and brings them visions, words, and recipes for healing the bodies and spirits of the people. Meanwhile, the lawentuchefes are the carriers and guardians of herbal knowledge. They speak to the plants, asking them for their medicine, and they know when these will attain the necessary curative properties. In Wingka culture, shaman women and warrior women are neither valued nor accepted. They want only ornamental women, women with a fertile uterus and an enslaved body. That is how it has always been in that ruthless, patriarchal culture. Now, today, looking at the women of the world makes me smile, because I no longer find grief in the feminine spirit. There is rebellion, there are dreams, and there is courage, too.

All this happened around the middle of the year 1880, the time when my great-great-grandmother was widowed. So Naweltripay had no choice but to accept the responsibility of protecting his only lawentuchefe. His beloved wife's affectionate pleading had done its work. The *mafün* with Fresia was decided. The mafün is the ceremony in which a man and a woman are united, and the couple celebrate their union before the *lof,* or community, and the ancestors. They ask the machi to present them before the *pu newen,* the forces of nature with which they will coexist. From them, a new energy will be born, dual and complementary.

One morning, with all the preparations made, a large party made up of wise elders, a machi, Naweltripay, and his wife, children, grandchildren, brothers, sisters, nephews, nieces, and all kinds of relatives, set out on the journey to Fresia Coliman's house. They took several draft horses loaded with saddlebags of food; a cart pulled by oxen, with woven blankets, earthenware pots, and other utensils; a few sheep; and silver Mapuche jewelry as offerings for Fresia.

Naweltripay spoke to her at length of her deceased husband's bravery and how Naweltripay admired and thought highly of him. My Mapuche people are golden tongued; our speech, the *pentukun,* is a sophisticated art, the art of uttering long, ceremonial speeches on important occasions. Longko Naweltripay had to take great care with his words. Although everyone knew that the mafün had been agreed upon and that Fresia's decision was to accept, Naweltripay's pentukun must still be most profound and correct. When the groom had finished his speech, those present also spoke one by one, emphasizing the groom's attributes and defects, and the bride's virtues and disadvantages. Among our people, adulation and falsehood are considered repellent. We seek truth in order to be reconciled with life.

Fresia listened in silence, and when everyone had finished speaking, she thanked them and accepted the proposal, but she asked not to move, since she wished to stay there in her *ruka.* She had built it with her own hands, with the help of her sons. There was love and honesty in those humble walls made of adobe and thatch. She felt that the house was her being; the adobe clung to the walls with the same solidity and bond with which, despite everything, Fresia clung to life.

So when summer came, a mafün was held. Antupray was thrilled and grateful to her husband. She felt relieved to know that Fresia, her dearest friend, would no longer be alone and that they were sisters now.

Longko Naweltripay loved his first wife deeply. He used to complain about her capricious and girlish behavior, but her goodness and her sweet nature made up for her temper. He was captivated by her beauty. While his second marriage allowed him to grow his family, which was always a reason for joy and celebration, he experienced it with great discomfort. He admired and respected Fresia, but it was difficult for him to desire her. He accepted the marriage only as a responsibility. Love is often mysterious and unpredictable. He knew he must face his situation as a new husband and consummate the marriage, but he postponed the encounter with his new wife by making excuses about important tasks that awaited him. So no sooner than the mafün was over, Longko Naweltripay left to round up animals on the other side of the mountains.

The elders remembered the time of my great-great-grandparents' marriage as a period of fleeting peace, which allowed them to overcome the famine with good harvests and an excellent breeding season. The Argentine state always interfered in the lives of my people, announcing government programs with deceitful names that legitimized our death. They developed a population-management program through which they arbitrarily decided the number of youths and families that should make up our communities, the quantity of animals allowed, and the kinds of crops that could be grown. They quantified our goods and decreed by law that no Mapuche families should prosper, justifying their policy as the prevention of a threat to the new state's power and sovereignty.

The government argued that our potential economic prosperity could threaten the young country's future. If we bred a large number of animals, the frontier unit came to our land, rifles in hand, to kill the new lambs and calves. Our young men were herded like livestock toward the estates and towns where the Wingka families needed slave labor; they used us as if we were objects that could be owned. We were auctioned off and distributed. The aristocracy did not consider us human beings; we were in the same category as animals.

The Bullriches, a prominent family of the time, became the wealthiest slave merchants. They used public auctions, which at the time were legal. They set up a platform in the courtyard at their offices, still named for them to this day, where they displayed us half-naked, offering us up for any kind of work.

A sorrowful event has endured in the memory of our people that, despite this sorrow, is told with euphoric enthusiasm because of the bravery the story contains. They say that a Mapuche man, whose name and origin are unknown, escaped from that platform in the middle of the courtyard where they lined up the men, women, and children captured by the Argentine Army. This man was handcuffed and had shackles on his feet but was so strong and sturdy that he managed to break the chains, and even with his strong arms trapped by the grim metal around his wrists, by kicking and shoving, he beat several of the scrawny soldiers guarding him. His freedom lasted no more than a few yards. He was felled by the weapon of a stranger in the audience, and those gathered applauded the murderer fiercely. Our people remember this event for the Mapuche's bravery. He must have known that if he escaped, death was inevitable, but he would rather die in the attempt to recover his freedom than die as a servant on some estate. I ask myself, What is the point of life without freedom? And how many more lives will it take for freedom to take root in our people, our land, and our lives?

Each new integration policy meant more poverty and more hunger for us. They turned us into the ghosts of a glorious past—famished, persecuted, and humiliated. The "noble" patrician families were the most murderous, meting out a genocide with neither jails nor justice, fattened on arrogance and impunity. When we were conquered, our people never knew peace again. The possibility of seizure, eviction, capture, and death threatened our existence at every moment.

Naweltripay was a longko with great wisdom and strength of character. He did not believe in the Wingka's word. He did not allow himself to be deceived. He sought the advice of the elders and could find answers to his questions in the whispering of the wind. When problems and anguish besieged him and clouded his mind and spirit, he would mount his horse and gallop without stopping until he reached Fresia's ruka. She would see and welcome him with fondness and respect. She took pains to care for him, and she listened to him. He asked for her advice. Many things were said about that woman's power and wisdom. Perhaps that was what made him withhold his manly instinct to touch her. His desires clashed with an icy mass of admiration and fear.

Fresia was a serious woman, and somewhat homely, but she created an atmosphere of great peace in her steps and her movements, which could transform the longko's anguish and worries into a state of harmony and tranquility. Naweltripay used to stay at Fresia's ruka until late, but they did not share a bed. Neither had any intention of touching, exploring, or knowing the other in that way. As time passed, the visits became more frequent until, in the end, Naweltripay was a daily presence. She enjoyed his silences and his words; she longed for him to arrive, and each day he went in search of her. Driven by need and habit, he went to her with neither intentions nor expectations, given over to the spell of wholeness.

One night, Longko Naweltripay arrived with silence dwelling inside him. The weak light from the stove in Fresia's ruka assured him that she was still awake. She seemed to intuit his heart. The dogs betrayed his presence, and Fresia saw him arrive. When he drew near the fire, its light revealed an expression of profound sorrow on his face. She felt that any word she uttered would be clumsy in that moment as he unburdened himself. She fed the longko and wrapped him up warm. They sat by the fire, and she stroked his hand, not saying a word. He accepted her strong, worn, calloused hand firmly, and pulled her toward his body. They embraced and wept for the sorrows accrued over centuries. They wept in anger, too. Each tear seemed to bleed from the lives torn away unjustly. Naweltripay had just lost his eldest son. Antupray was keening and wailing alongside her mother when he took his horse without thinking and, in the reddish sunset of a muted sky faintly streaked with orange, galloped without pause until he was cloaked in stars on a freezing night of gloom and sorrow. Again, strange illnesses were spreading death. He told Fresia the news, and she cried in silence and embraced him lovingly. As they cried, they caressed, explored, and found one another. The kisses were salty, but this time it seemed as if the tears were sweet. They shed their clothes, and between their pain, sighs, and sobs, they watered a love that grew from a seed to a deeply rooted, fragrant, and eternal flower.

The longko experienced a different kind of love. This time, his mind and body were not consumed with passion. This love revealed itself to him, deep and calm, a love that had steadily walked toward the knowledge of the most hidden chambers of that magical woman. Their hands touched the skin cracked by hard times, their flesh drooping with years, their bones heavy with living. He stroked her full breasts, beginning to sag. She kissed his face, his mouth, the back of his neck; she traversed with kisses the whole map of his body. Together, they entered a land of pleasure and desire to heal their wounds.

There are loves that have nothing to do with skin, though skin might become the touch of the soul. These loves graze against other folds, other delicate, complex, ancestral layers. They deeply intertwine invisible threads of a fabric woven between two people and the cosmic forces. Sometimes that magic is destroyed with fleshly contact, while other times it is fed even more and turned into something sublime. But it is difficult to distinguish the line between love and passion, the spiritual and the carnal, the superficial and the profound. This is just what happened to Fresia Coliman and Longko Naweltripay.

They awoke in an embrace, and before dawn brought the light of day, they prepared to attend the funeral. They set out early. Fresia carried *lawen*, sacred medicinal herbs, to strengthen Antupray's *piwke*, her heart. In her own chest, she felt the grief of her friend, her *lamngen*. Her sister Antupray was suffering, and she felt a deep desire to help her. She harbored neither rivalry nor jealousy in her heart or mind. Both women loved the longko, and the longko loved both women. In those days, love was a newen and not a shackle that trapped you, turning you into a piece of property.

Chapter 2

The Land Tells Us Who We Are

In my great-great-grandparents' era, the government used colonial policies against the Indigenous peoples. The few plots of land we had left were reduced due to the peoples' lack of the Spanish language, which allowed merchants, landowners, sad bureaucrats, and the usual nonentities to play all kinds of tricks and scams to take over our land and our animals. There was no one we could complain to; the criollos' methods of acquiring land were socially accepted and legally allowed. This meant that the longkos and other Mapuche authorities accepted certain agreements even though they were unfavorable to our people.

In 1885, the year my great-grandmother Kalfurayen was born, a large community political assembly was held. We call these assemblies *futa trawun*. In this space, our communities examine our new reality and make decisions. We have never stopped holding them. That's how it was then and how it is now. I should admit that I detest the word *community*, since we are not units held together by something in common, like a cog in some kind of machine. We are more transcendent. We are *lofche*, the space in which people also live. This gives the idea that there are many others who coinhabit with the human and with whom we must agree upon the art of inhabiting. And so, if you'll allow me, in what remains of my story, I will use that beautiful word: lofche, or sometimes just lof.

Naweltripay invited Fresia to accompany him. He was convinced that the flow of her wisdom would contribute to good decisions. The place for that great meeting of Mapuche authorities lay two moons away on horseback. Fresia felt moved because she was returning after many years to the land where she had been born and raised. She took her little girl, Kalfurayen, only a few months old. Everything had changed. The fields of good pasture with their wooded hills no longer belonged to them. There wasn't a single Mapuche family there; these were now the lands of settlers and criollo landowners.

They arrived exhausted, but the sight of thousands of Mapuches together, from all the territories, revived them. The next day at dawn, there was a ceremonial offering to the mapu. They offered *muday*, a fermented drink made from wheat, quinoa, and pine nuts; grain; and tobacco. And they asked the ancestral spirits for strength and wisdom. To begin the speeches, a longko from the Guluche territory, today known as Chile, rose to his feet. He was well recognized among the Mapuches on both sides of the mountains. He gave a long speech in Mapudungun, and I will translate his words: "Our ancestors knew a time of joy and prosperity. There was no illness, no hunger or sorrow, no borders or property. Now, everything has changed. We have been divided, displaced. They have stolen our territory, they have stolen our children, and they have stolen our women. The Wingka state has invented borders between us. Now we must choose whether to be Chileans or Argentines. What is it to be Chilean? What is it to be Argentine? We are people of the land. Do they want to know who we really are? Does the Wingka even know who he is? The land recognizes us; she tells us who we are. Does the Wingka state want to know who we are? Let them ask the mountain who we are. Let them ask the river, let them ask the wind, let them ask the forest, and they will answer. Today we are speaking of sending our children to the Wingka school. And I am not in favor of this. I, Longko Paimun, assure you that it will

be a great error to send our children to the Wingka school. There, they
will tear from the children our language, our culture, our spirit, and our
thought. Let us care for our children, let us teach them our customs,
let them not forget our language. This is the last chance left to us to be
true on this earth."

Longko Nancucheo was also there, and he spoke and said:

"Feley may así es pu peñi ka pu lamngen," he began, in respect to
Paimun. "But we cannot go on without knowing the Wingka's weapons. They come with their Spanish, and we do not understand them.
They learn our Mapudungun so they can lie to us, and we should know
their language so we can learn the truth of their thoughts. We should
demand that the Wingka let our children learn Spanish, that they learn
their knowledge. If our children know the Wingka's thoughts, they will
know how to defend our people. We have not been able to do this, and
they have won the war. What good to us is our culture, our spirituality,
if it gives us no power to confront the Wingka? There is hunger among
our people because there is no longer land. Everything belongs to them.
We should send our children to school. So that they can recover what
the Wingka have stolen, with the same weapons."

In this way, they debated for days, until they agreed that they would
ask the Argentine state for at least the sons of the longkos to be educated
in their schools. Later, Mapuche girls were also admitted. But what
they believed would be a strengthening process for our people, for the
establishment of our rights, became an overwhelming force that would
violently sweep away our memory, our language, and our identity.

That was when Fresia and Naweltripay had their first major argument. Fresia supported Longko Paimun. She believed that it was not
a good idea to hand their children over to the Wingkas, that these
schools would damage them, separating them from their families, but
Naweltripay thought differently and held fast to the opposite position.
Something changed within Fresia that day. She would no longer view
her husband with the same eyes of admiration and trust as before.

Now that I am old, I understand how their hearts were paralyzed, because in times of war and resistance, either love is weakened and quickly evaporates or it takes on an immense strength. My great-great-grandparents suffered the whirlwind of both. They vacillated between mistrust and blind dedication, disillusionment and admiration, coldness and passion. Yet despite all this, they gave balance to each other's lives until the end of their days. Naweltripay was one of the first longkos to send his sons to school. He and Fresia argued a great deal over this decision. She never agreed.

Naweltripay was already old by the time Kalfurayen was born. Fresia loved to play with her. She knew that she would not be a mother again, and she enjoyed her little girl's early years perhaps even more than she had enjoyed those of her sons. She valued life so much, despite the troubles of the era, and though the times were overshadowed by poverty and violence, she felt grateful for the existence of each of her children. She was grateful, too, for the love of Longko Naweltripay, her sisterly link to Antupray, and especially the gift of healing, and of finding her most loyal friends in plants. She liked to wander and lose herself among the hills, dunes, and mesas with her daughter, finding the shoots of the neneo, that spiky Patagonian bush with yellow flowers. The mint growing at the water's edge helped her calm a feverish stomach, and she also chewed it to fragrance her breath. From the petals of the charcao flower, she extracted an effective medicine for weak vision. Many elderly men and women had hearts full of gratitude for that woman, who was able to return to them, for a long time, a renewed picture of the universe. Muted colors regained their intensity, and blurred shapes acquired their true dimension. Those tiny drops extracted from such delicate petals served as magical tears in eyes that were worn out from so much living.

As the years went by, Antupray lost the twinkle of joy that used to show in her eyes when she laughed, but she remained clever and talkative. She and Fresia visited each other often. She never stopped advising her friend to leave her small house and move to the one the longko had built for her; it was larger, and very near her own. Antupray had chosen the spot. One sunny afternoon, she'd gone out walking and noticed a soft, slightly elevated ridge, offering a good view of the territory. It was ideal for spotting plants and animals that came there to drink. To the right, a spring emerged, camouflaged by a bright-green carpet of moss and grass. In the end, Fresia gave the house to one of Antupray's older daughters, the first one to marry.

Naweltripay was an excellent husband to both his wives. The day his spirit decided to depart, he knew that his time had come. It was a summer full of color and fragrance. He asked his older sons to saddle his horse and ordered them to slaughter two calves and tie the oxen to the cart, which they loaded with food and drink. In this way, accompanied by Antupray and his children and grandchildren, he arrived at Fresia Coliman's house, just as he had years earlier to ask her to be his wife.

He looked as if he had little strength. When she saw him arrive, Fresia felt in her breast a sweet and heartrending pain. She knew that she had to let him go, and that he had chosen to share his last moments with her. There was roast meat and abundant food, and the women sang, sometimes together and sometimes one after another. The longko also offered an age-old *ül*, an improvised song, which at first was joyful, but which was gradually transformed into a melancholy song. In it, he sang to life, to his sorrows, to love, to his people, and to his wives. It was a sad melody, and his voice faltered and cracked. The character in his song became a nocturnal bird brought by the evening star and that rose to the *wenu mapu*, the world above. From there, it would light the way of the *wenülfu*, the brightest star in the night sky, called the evening star.

At dawn, they held a small ceremony of gratitude and made offerings to the mapu. They shared several days with Naweltripay until he breathed his last. Finally, as he sat on a rough-hewn wood bench beneath the midday sun, his spirit abandoned his body. He seemed to be asleep; his peaceful expression gave him an air of serene contentment. His grandchildren, not noticing what had happened, kept playing around him. Suddenly Fresia, who was working in the vegetable patch, felt a warm breeze that embraced her and entered her body through her ear, as if exhaled by some powerful being. Antupray was separating wheat from chaff in the kitchen when she realized that he had died, and the ears of wheat fell and scattered across the floor. She called Fresia with desperate cries. Fresia threw down her tools when she heard her and dashed from the vegetable patch to the house. She raced and panted, not stopping until she arrived. There she saw him and understood that he was gone. For a long time, the widows embraced and cried for their husband. Then they prepared to arrange his funeral.

The news spread quickly across the territories, and friends and relatives came from different lofches to say goodbye. Naweltripay's oldest son ordered the funeral, the *eluwün*, and prepared the place where it would be held. It was a wide pampa. They went in carts pulled by oxen, and many traveled on horseback. All those who came brought gifts for the longko's close relatives, expressing their care and affection for the family of the deceased. The gifts were animals, food, and warmth. Shelters were built. In a great circle, each mourner lit a fire; there they prepared abundant food and drink, which were shared out among the guests. The body was placed on a wooden cart, wrapped in woven blankets, alongside his most-used possessions.

Naweltripay had a great many grandchildren. At that time, Fresia's older sons with her first husband were already parents; she, too, had several grandchildren. Kalfurayen, who was still very small when her father died, would not remember his face or his voice in the future.

Fresia was now a widow for a second time. No pain dwelled inside her. Only the melancholy that our loved ones leave when they depart, the empty space in our lives that can be occupied only by their embodied spirits, which are irreplaceable. Nostalgia, too, filled her heart, fed by memories and experiences, the kind of yearning that makes us tremble when a vision of the past comes into our mind.

Fresia was busy, helping with every task. She lit her fire along with her children and grandchildren. Her branch may have been the most numerous. She was a beloved and respected woman, and she made sure that Naweltripay's farewell was full of songs and sacred dances. One of the longko's sons arranged for an *awun*—moving in the shape of a sacred circle—so many of the men present mounted their horses and galloped around the shelters surrounding the coffin. The cries of hundreds of riders made the ground shake powerfully. The cries were thunderous, strong, and victorious. All the people cried out an *afafan*; "Yayayayaaa," they proclaimed. Their throats seemed to emerge from their mouths, so great was the effort they made with their cries. There was laughter and joy. They played *palin*, an old ball game played with sticks, which these days is known as *chueca*.

When dusk fell, when the sun had almost said goodbye, an elderly storyteller, a *wepife*, who held many memories, made the funeral speech. It was a profound and moving speech. This kind of speech seeks to give a truthful account of the life led by the deceased, his virtues and flaws, his wise choices and his errors. All this is told in beautiful poetry, in the wepifes' style of speech. Thus, the feats of the longko, my great-great-grandfather, were remembered, along with the naivete and the foolishness of his later years, when he made agreements with the state that confined him and his people to small reservations of land.

On the day of the burial, the morning sky was cloudy. Kalfurayen, my great-grandmother, was taking her first steps. Her brothers watched her while her mother came and went, carrying out all kinds of tasks. As they prepared the cart to carry the deceased to his final resting place, the sky began to shed the tears it had been holding back. Fresia remembered her baby and went to the shelter to find her. When she arrived, she saw her sons alone.

"Where is your little sister?" she asked them.

Only then did they realize that the little girl was gone. Each of them blamed another. Fresia chided them in her fury and ordered them to help her search. There were many people there. They asked at all the shelters, but there was no trace of the girl. Fresia began to despair. She did not understand how the girl could have disappeared, and her anguish was great. Word soon spread of what had happened, and dozens of people went out to search. The burial was delayed. The sky closed its eyes and darkened with tears. It rained so much that the ground quickly turned into a bog that was difficult to cross. Fresia moved farther out, guided by instinct. She fell several times, tripping on the hem of her long skirt. Soaked and covered in mud, she cried for her daughter. Then she began to weep and to beg the spirit of Naweltripay to help find her little girl. Fresia Coliman knew how much Naweltripay loved his tiny daughter, and as she implored him to help, she stumbled upon her. There she was, sitting on a high rock, as if someone had lifted and placed her there. The most startling thing was that beside the little girl stood a *nawel*, a jaguar, like a puma but with a thicker coat and with black and tan spots stretched across its lustrous fur. It swayed its feline tail, long and thin, hypnotizing the girl.

"Naweltripay! Do not take our daughter! Leave her with me, please!" she begged, and cried desperately, choking on her tears.

The animal gazed at her, then fled in fear and disappeared among the high bushes.

Fresia cried with joy and took her daughter in her arms, drawing her close to her chest. Then she checked her all over to make sure she was not hurt, and went with her to bury her husband.

That was the last time she saw him, transformed into a jaguar. They say that every so often, he appeared among his people to help or to punish them, depending on the reason he'd been invoked. Even today, I sing his *tahiel*, his sacred song, and I speak to him in the hills, in the mountains, and among the lakes. I have felt his presence, like a furtive shadow among the leaves of the forest. I say to him, so he will not be frightened or hurt me, "Naweltripay, it is I, your descendant. I carry your blood in my veins. I keep the memories of your deeds, and I honor your teachings."

Each time I say these words, I feel peaceful, guided by his goodness, and shielded by his spirit.

Chapter 3

THE SPIRITUAL FORCES OF NATURE

Kalfurayen's five brothers loved her dearly and spoiled and protected her like a sapling born in the snow. Her mother admired her gentle and kindhearted nature. She was about eleven when the authorities appeared along with the director of the local school, an Italian priest who came to chastise Doña Fresia Coliman for refusing to send her daughter there. The priest had come to Patagonia after being expelled from his homeland for certain improper practices that led to his trial before a council and expulsion. Here, though, his past was unknown. The church had concealed his abuses and sent him with great recommendations in the knowledge that in fact they were punishing him. He was convinced that if he managed to preach effectively to the "savages," he would soon be pardoned and restored to his previous role.

Patagonia was seen as a barbaric region, untamed and hostile, a prison that allowed the enclosure of all that was abject and abominable within its bounds. They doubted that we had souls. "They are surely creatures created by God, but they are definitely inferior," said the church. This is why the abuses perpetrated by the government authorities mattered little or not at all, just like those committed by any other whites. There was no one to ask for justice. Inequality was their order; unlimited greed, their civilization.

Giuliano Pirinello was the name of this Salesian priest. He was tall and ungainly, had a prominent nose, and was loquacious but unfriendly. The youngest girls were his weakness. He was half a century old. He did not remember when it all had begun, but an evil force had taken hold of him with ferocious power and eventually became impossible to control. That evil tempted him to possess the defenseless bodies of the most innocent creatures.

Fresia Coliman greeted the men with her sons. She did not invite them in. She did not speak Spanish, so one of her sons served as interpreter and translated what the Wingka authorities said. The priest warned her in a threatening tone that she must send her daughter to school; otherwise, not only would the girl be taken by force, but Fresia would be imprisoned, just like all Indigenous mothers and fathers who failed to comply with the laws of the state. Fresia had already been in scenarios like this one as her sons grew and reached school age. Her struggle against this obligation was becoming more and more difficult. School interfered with the Mapuche way of life, since the school year began in spring, which was the breeding season. For Fresia Coliman, that obligation was doubly painful, not only because it took her children far away and subjected them to colonization, but also because she was left without any help with her work, and it was impossible for her to do it alone.

She did not doubt the threats. She knew very well what the Wingkas were capable of. So that very spring, she took her daughter to school. As they walked gently along the path that led to the town, she felt her chest swell with invisible sobs that burned with anger and sorrow.

When she said goodbye, she had a sense of foreboding. Perhaps it was because her sons had told her of the punishments and mistreatment they'd received, or perhaps it was because Kalfurayen was the youngest, and her only daughter. She could not rid herself of this overwhelming feeling of pain and doom. But when fall came, her dread dissipated when she saw Kalfurayen and nearly all her children return. The two eldest sons had to stay in the town, both as workers at a sawmill that had been established a few months earlier.

Kalfurayen was pleased to be back with her mother. She had outgrown her shyness and chattered excitedly, laughing and sharing the chores with her mother from early in the morning. She went with her to the riverbanks to look for medicine. Sometimes they had to climb high, rocky mesas, from which little flowers, roots, or creepers emerged. Rounding up the animals and taking them to the corral, feeding the hens, taking grass to the milking cow. In the evening, when the sun went down, she helped her brothers bring in the sheep. She breathed in the smell of the sheep's dung with sublime satisfaction, as if it were the most delicious perfume. The autumn brought flurries of leaves she liked to play in, finding in them bright hues and fascinating shapes. Childhood in the countryside is magical, an enchanted time of simplicity and imagination that brings delight and awakens all our senses.

That winter, Kalfurayen had managed to weave her first *pelera*, a woven blanket used like a saddle on a horse's back. Fresia had helped her set up the loom and taught her the secrets of weaving with love and patience. Kalfurayen wanted to give her first weaving to her *laku*, Antupray. The two loved each other very much. When the little girl was born, Fresia had asked her friend to be her daughter's laku. A laku is a lof member who lovingly accompanies a child as they grow, with good advice, teachings, and attention. Antupray always had some gift for Kalfurayen, and the girl liked to stay with her for several days at a time. They would laugh heartily at the stories and gossip that her laku shared with her.

When Fresia and Kalfurayen went to visit Antupray, they found her very sick; her lungs were consumed by an aggressive tuberculosis. Not even Fresia's medicine could save her. Antupray left this world covered in a thick blanket of snow. A musical fluttering of small black birds accompanied the farewell song that her friend sang amid her tears. Fresia's voice echoed in the deathly silence of the snowy mountain; nothing could be heard, only her voice sending up the tahiel for her dearest friend. Twelve years had passed since the death of Longko Naweltripay, and now, once again, it was time to bury another loved one.

Kalfurayen felt the loss of her laku keenly. But winter slowly drifted away, and spring stroked the earth, giving fragrance to the days and rekindling life and hope. It was time for her to return to school with her brothers, but the end of her vacation filled her with weariness.

The boarding school was a building of medium size, a kind very common in Patagonia. There are still a few of them left. In those days, education was provided by the church. There were schools with nuns for the girls and schools with priests for the boys. There was never enough staff: the director, two nuns (one of them being the vice director), two cooks, a guard, and a caretaker. The students cleaned, chopped wood, and did laundry. Seventy girls were strictly educated in this school. The boys' school, not far away, had more students, around a hundred. Men were prioritized in their process of assimilation and Christianization. Rigor and discipline were the backbone of the school's authority.

The mission entrusted to the "educators" was to erase from the children's minds and behavior any trace of their savage past, so that they would adopt "good Christian and civilizing habits," among them, speaking Spanish. If they were caught speaking Mapudungun, they were forced to hold out their hands and were caned mercilessly. These measures were not applied exclusively to Indigenous children but were used with all children in the country, a pedagogical practice of the triumphant civilization. Students were strictly forbidden to laugh, talk among themselves, and look the adults in the eye. All their heads were shaved, and some girls wept in silence when they saw their long black braids fall to the floor. For us Indigenous women, the longer our hair, the more sensitive we become to our surroundings; our hair is like a fine fiber connecting us to the mysterious, inaudible voices of our ancestors. The vice director, a Spanish nun, complained, "These lice-ridden Indians send their children with hair like a horse's mane. It's impossible to tidy hair that coarse. It's better to shave them; it's the only way to impose a shred of decency."

At school, Kalfurayen, like nearly all the other girls, became a different person, like a shy little animal, tamed with beatings. At night, when the lights went out and the staff had withdrawn, sobs could be heard from the youngest girls, and the older ones comforted them. They set free their Mapudungun—forbidden during the day—by whispering it at night. Kalfurayen seemed fearful and overcome with silence and was nimble at the tasks she was charged with. She did not learn easily, seeming always to be lost in thought, in a distant place where no one could reach her. Sometimes the teacher brought her back to reality with a slap; then, ashamed and in pain, her eyes glistening with tears, she struggled to hold back her sobs.

One afternoon, the girls were playing and running around in the courtyard when Kalfurayen tripped and bumped into a classmate, fell to the floor, and fainted. She soon discovered that she had a heart condition. Once every four months, a priest who was also a doctor would visit the Salesian schools to check on the boarders' health. He came at around the time of Kalfurayen's fall. After examining her, the doctor concluded that she had hypertrophic myocardiopathy, an illness that many women in her line would inherit. That very night, in bed, she felt pain throughout her body. The next morning, she discovered a strange moisture that seemed to come from between her legs. She ran to the bathroom and examined herself in terror. "I'm bleeding!" she told her friend. "I'm wounded inside!" she cried amid desperate tears.

Kalfurayen received neither advice nor explanations, just a few cotton pads she was ordered to always wear. She wondered if she would ever stop bleeding. Later, she learned that the blood would flow from her only a few days each month. The nuns reported the news to the director that the student Kalfurayen, whom they decided to name Paulina, had become a young woman. The priest, Pirinello, soon convinced the vice director that Kalfurayen should live in his house so that she could help him with domestic chores and he could teach her to read. And they would not risk her escaping with a boy from the other school, as had happened with some students. Kalfurayen thus had only one full year of schooling; the remaining three, she became an unpaid live-in domestic servant in the priest's house.

Each winter, Fresia Coliman came to the school to ask for her daughter, and she always received the same answer, the promise Giuliano Pirinello made to her in a cutting, irritated tone: "The girl is fine. She is studying in my house, and I am teaching her good manners. Soon I will manage to bring her closer to God. Next winter she can leave."

Until one autumn day, to Fresia's surprise, Kalfurayen finally returned. She arrived at her community beaten and bruised, and in a sea of tears. The vice director, a veteran nun of Basque origins, had in recent days begun to suspect the priest. His habit of locking himself in his office with little girls had convinced her of his immoral deeds, though she had never dared to denounce him. Troubled by her regrets, she could no longer bear to keep silent and went to the priest's house one night. She found the door unlocked. As if possessed by a decisive force, she strode straight to the sitting room, where she found the priest beating and whipping Kalfurayen, who was stark naked, disheveled, and crying.

"Stop in the name of God! What are you doing?" the nun cried in horror.

Giuliano Pirinello turned abruptly in fright and alarm. His bulging eyes and trembling body betrayed the arousal possessing him.

"What are you doing, entering my house without permission? You have no right to burst in at this time of night!" he bellowed in fury.

The nun did not know how to answer, but she managed to cover the girl with the shawl she was wearing. She took her away from the priest's house without a word, wrapped Kalfurayen up in warm clothes, and took her to the school, which lay about a half mile away. When they arrived, she bathed and dressed her. And the next day, she set out with her for Fresia's house.

As they were nearing my great-great-grandmother's house, the nun dismounted and helped the girl down from the horse. Then she excused herself, saying that she could not stay, that she must return immediately because the director was furious. With a shy smile that had a hint of kindness about it, she gave Kalfurayen a stroke on the head. The girl looked at her absently. It was an empty, spiritless, lifeless gaze. The nun took from her saddlebags some food and offered it to Kalfurayen, who took it hesitantly. Then the woman left, making her cowardly departure in shame, with no further explanation.

When she caught sight of her daughter, Fresia went swiftly to greet her. The girl was unrecognizable. They embraced and cried. Kalfurayen, her voice faltering between sobs, confessed to her mother, "I'm going to die, I'm very sick. He beat me and did horrible things to me."

Her mother took the girl's face in her hands and said, looking into her eyes, "No, my daughter. You will not die. He will pay for what he has done. I will heal you."

My great-great-grandmother Fresia immediately laid her daughter gently down on a blanket. After her long period of confinement and slavery, Kalfurayen rested. She never wanted to tell the story of that cruelty. After a few days, her mother noticed the vomiting and the exhaustion. The girl spent all her time dozing. Fresia suspected what had happened. She gave her a glass jar and told her to pee into it. Then she went to the sacred tree, where she sought wisdom for her healing work. There, she spoke to the spiritual forces of nature and read the urine against the sun's rays. That was how she learned that her daughter was pregnant, and that she was terribly unwell. She did not need Kalfurayen to tell her what had happened; the oracle knew it all. That golden liquid had revealed the rape, the rapist, and its consequence. Fresia prepared the cure, the lawen, imploring the spirits to help as she gave it to Kalfurayen to drink.

The days, weeks, and months went by peacefully. Kalfurayen's belly grew little by little. Spring began to paint bright colors onto the mountain. Migratory birds from the north brought their vibrant feathers and song, embracing the leaves of the willows that brushed the river's surface. Their wings flapped in the breeze, fragrant with mint, which gave the surroundings a heady air.

Fresia Coliman waited patiently for spring, when she would exact her revenge.

The hens began to lay. Pirinello liked to drink a mixture of eggs with sweet wine each morning. The townspeople knew his tastes because when the hens at the school stopped laying, the priest asked the students' parents for a dozen eggs each week. That spring, an unknown epidemic decimated the hens at the school. Not even the rooster survived, and Pirinello once more asked the parents for eggs. Fresia knew this, and prepared a basket with enormous, beautiful eggs. She added a sweet, late-harvest wine she had received in an unfair trade of several pounds of spun wool for a quart of wine. Of course, it wasn't just any wine; it came from Málaga, a land of excellent wines. All the eggs and the wine formed part of a special ceremony on the night of a new moon. What did Fresia add to them? We'll never know, but one morning, the priest found the basket on his table. How did it get there? Another great mystery, though it is rumored that Avelina Rupallan, who worked for the priest and did his laundry, was outraged by his cruel and indecent ways and offered to help Fresia one afternoon when she went to see the lawentuchefe in search of medicine for her aching legs.

When she arrived at Fresia's house, Avelina Rupallan saw Kalfurayen with the child in her belly; she had always seemed to her such a good and gentle girl. After her treatment, she sat down to drink maté and talk to Fresia, and she saw the noble woman's eyes fill with rage and sorrow as she described the dreadful state in which Kalfurayen had returned home. It is said that she did not hesitate to help her. But there are no witnesses, or anything to prove that she was the necessary accomplice in this act of revenge.

And so it was that when he drank his mixture of eggs and wine, the rapist was left impotent and shriveled up. First, the phallic dagger with which he had plunged Kalfurayen in sorrow and darkness began to shrink. Dismayed to see it grow smaller and smaller, the priest consulted specialists in the large cities in search of a cure. But the puzzled doctors, who had never before seen any such illness, could not diagnose him and sent him away, assuring him that there was nothing they could do. And his member went on withering until it was reduced to a pitiful, puckered bump in his groin. In desperation, convinced that this could be none other than divine punishment, he tried prayer and self-flagellation to win God's forgiveness and his own.

In search of an answer, he even visited a healer, a fortune-teller who was famous among the settlers. She read his palm and dealt his cards. A profound silence gripped the half-lit room. The fortune-teller lifted her face and stared into his eyes.

"I cannot save you. This is a powerful curse brought upon you for a great evil you have done. I can do nothing to help you, Father. But if you wish to take revenge, it will cost you two cows and their calves," she declared.

The weakened priest declined, believing that in this way he would placate God's hatred. Soon afterward, he died. Fresia Coliman's ire was not to be placated. Pirinello had penetrated her daughter's pure soul with his evil, and a dark and watery texture had indeed spread through her womb.

Fresia fought death relentlessly. She longed to protect the lives of both her daughter and her new granddaughter, but she could barely sustain the breath of life in the new baby that was born. Though it was spring, an icy sheet still unfurled over the rolling green carpet of Patagonia, which seemed intent on embracing pure beings, like the mother of that little girl, with death.

First, Fresia occupied herself with life: she cut the umbilical cord and washed the baby. Her beloved daughter lay dead, stretched out on the faded woven blanket. Her last whimper merged with the cry of life; the two sounds met and kissed as they vibrated in the air. Mother and daughter greeted each other a single time, one giving her welcome, the other lamenting her departure. Fresia was certain that not only had Pirinello's rape and injustice killed her daughter, but also her revenge. Lan, death, had killed the offender, but had also claimed the life of the innocent girl.

The new grandmother took pains to care for her tiny granddaughter, who demanded the proper attention with her powerful lungs. Fresia washed, swaddled, and rocked the baby in her arms until she was soothed.

When the baby fell asleep, she buried her daughter. She did not want a wake like the ones Christians held for their dead, or a funeral, as was the custom in those days. It was a private act, with just the two of them. Her daughter was ascending to the wenu mapu, where she would meet Longko Naweltripay and her dear friend Antupray. She sang Kalfurayen's sacred songs, offering each tahiel sprinkled with tears; she spoke to her daughter of her virtues and chided her for her flaws; she cooked her favorite food; she wrapped her in a colorful blanket that she had loved, that Fresia was planning to give her when autumn came. She spoke to her with a broken heart: "My daughter, you have departed so soon. You have left your little girl in my care, and I don't know how well I will be able to tend to her. I am growing old, and my strength is slipping away. I am alone, without the help of your brothers. Now you are leaving like this, in such a hurry, for the wenu mapu. Your father will surely be waiting for you there, for you to ride together along the path of the stars you loved to gaze at with me."

When she finished digging and burying her daughter, a brightly colored butterfly perched on the tomb. Fresia smiled and said, "Welcome, Kalfurayen. How beautiful you are, turned into a butterfly!"

Chapter 4

The Ancestors Watched Over Them from Above

My grandmother was born in the spring of 1900. My great-great-grandmother called her Pirenrayen, which means snow flower, because she was the first flower of a snowy spring.

In those years, the British aristocracy was at the height of its economic success in our territory. During the second presidency of Julio Argentino Roca, the English exerted a strong influence on the Argentine government in international and commercial affairs. Roca was a staunch enemy of our people. He was indebted to the English bankers for their economic support during the Desert Campaign. He paid off the debt with land, and vast swaths of territory passed into the hands of the British. My grandmother grew up in an atmosphere of continual tension with the government. The reductions of our territory were ongoing; arbitrary obligations were imposed on our goods and even our lives, and not a single right was recognized in our favor. My great-great-grandmother swore to herself to protect Pirenrayen from all dangers, but especially from the worst of them all: the Wingka.

At first, Fresia managed to slake her granddaughter's hunger with sweetened water, but the little girl soon began to cry so piercingly that she decided to visit Chekeken, a young widow whom she had helped in childbirth two summers earlier. This young first-time mother had borne a son, and her breasts were generous and full of milk. Though her son was soon to reach his second solstice, she was still nursing him. Fresia saddled her chestnut mare and prepared food to carry with her, which we call *rokiñ*. She took charqui, which is a dried, salted meat cut into strips, and filled a leather pouch with cooked and toasted quinoa. She took gifts and set out on the journey with her granddaughter in the *kupalwé*, a wood baby carrier that her husband had made her to carry Kalfurayen. Chekeken's ruka was not far away. Pirenrayen cried all the way until she fell asleep.

Chekeken welcomed them fondly. She had heard the news of what had happened to Kalfurayen, and the two women fell into a wordless embrace. Sometimes words must be silent so only an embrace can be heard. An embrace can say things that language still has not learned. They sat down in front of the fire. As Chekeken stoked the flames and fed them with cypress logs, she asked, "How are you, *ñaña*?"

Fresia sighed and wept when she tried to answer. They took refuge again in silence. Chekeken made some maté, and her young son woke up crying, which woke Pirenrayen, who felt her hunger again. Fresia remembered the reason for her visit and said to Chekeken with no further ado, "Sister, can you feed my granddaughter? The poor thing won't stop crying with hunger. I need you to take her as a *moyolufe*. Can you?"

"Don't worry, Doña Fresia, I will feed her as if she had come from my womb."

"I am deeply grateful, sister. What have you named your son?" Fresia asked with a smile.

"Linkoyan," Chekeken answered proudly.

Fresia put her granddaughter in Chekeken's lap while Linkoyan played. Pirenrayen began to suck immediately. The young mother felt her breast fill, not only with milk, but with a deep love for the little orphan girl.

Doña Fresia had to stay and live for a long period in that house. Together, the women bathed Pirenrayen for the first time, preparing the water with healing plants. The grandmother had kept Pirenrayen's umbilical cord in her small medicine pouch when it dropped. That day, as she dried off the girl's tiny body, a hen came into the ruka and began to cluck nearby. Then it left, as decidedly as it had entered. "This hen has laid a wind egg. Bring it here, my dear," Fresia said in amazement.

Chekeken went to find the egg. It was still warm when she brought it in. Fresia took the egg with a delicate, solemn gesture, as if showing a powerful object.

"Every once in a while, a hen lays a wind egg. The egg has only a white, but this white is powerful and can assure a good birth. You must spread the white onto the baby's hips. That way, my granddaughter will have no pain or suffering when she gives birth," she said, teaching Chekeken the secrets of her magical medicine.

The young woman watched her in admiration and curiosity, like an apprentice watching an expert surgeon. My great-great-grandmother was full of secrets and knowledge, and she shared them generously with other women among my people. Fresia's heart was deeply grateful to the spirits for having provided the medicine to prevent pain and even possible death for her granddaughter in the vital work of increasing their lineage. So many times she had helped birthing women, had helped bring so many lives into the world, and on so many occasions she had come face to face with death. But none was as painful as that of her daughter, Kalfurayen.

Death, always unwelcome, unpredictable, premature, reaching its long and delicate fingers, gripping the wombs that shelter tiny lives. Sometimes, death waits until they are ready to leave the womb, then Lan snatches them away mercilessly. Lan, death, has walked in the world since time immemorial. Sometimes, it imposes its rule, while at others, it is life that asserts itself, laughing heartily and painting colors of passion and survival. Lan admired Fresia for her strength as an adversary. She fought to outsmart it with wisdom and skill and was able to conquer it many times. Lan knew that life emanated from the hands and warmth of that woman, and so it respected her. With death, one

35

must also build reciprocity. Lan is part of the cycle of life. If we respect it, it will respect us. Because Lan is not the end of existence for living beings but the portal to another kind of life.

Pirenrayen grew up loving these two mothers. One, her forebear—strong, wise, and unwavering. The other, her caretaker—generous, gentle, and understanding. They were a loving dyad who nurtured her in knowledge and values, who shaped her as she grew into a woman.

In the time of my grandmother's birth, an emissary of the British Crown arrived in Buenos Aires to lay claim to the many hectares of land that had been promised in return for English help received during the Roca government. This fact was to have a decisive influence on my grandmother's life and destiny. The English had spread their estates throughout Patagonia with total support from the Argentine government, which deployed troops of ragged and poorly fed soldiers to take care of British interests.

Workers' uprisings, attacks by rural bandits, and cattle rustling were the estate managers' main concerns. Thousands of heads of livestock were spread across the green and rolling lands of Patagonia crossed by the Chubut River, which cut through a valley of high pastures, watered by natural springs, streams, and waterfalls that bathed the fertile ground. But the English landowners felt threatened. The Argentine government was questioned about the return of Mapuche who were determined to recover what had been snatched away from them. Policies of assimilation were established to erase our identity and our memory. Not only was education a strategic tool for this, but also health.

Cruelty wielded against us was the law; the English easily held sway over a wealthy, prosperous, and abundant Patagonia. Sad, gray, time-serving officials, mostly sent here as a punishment, wanted only to return to their homelands with riches and prestige. Patagonia was offered as the dream of immediate wealth. Here, it was a free-for-all; the adventurers who came wishing to take everything in exchange for nothing had no moral scruples. But life was not easy. The vast expanse of territory was like a ghostly plain of solitude and wind. The harsh winter climate, the lack of roads and transport, and the scattered settlements that would one day become major towns made up the map of the "inland," as the military of the era referred to our Puelwillimapu, Patagonia.

The English preferred to hire Irish, Scottish, and Welsh workers; but for slaves, they had the different Indigenous peoples: the Wichí, the Qom, and the Mocoví in the north, and the Mapuche and Tehuelche in the south. The Irish were a minority. They came fleeing war and famine, and soon managed to amass their small fortunes.

In those days, the country's progress and development were believed to be associated with the whiteness of the population. The more we looked like Europe, the more opportunities we would have in international trade. All kinds of measures were therefore taken during this period to colonize our lands. Of course, not all immigrants were welcome. The presence of anarchist or ideologically dissident immigrants caused concern among the privileged ruling classes since their revolutionary ideas might jeopardize their comfort. Roca approved the Law of Residence, through which unionist and activist immigrants were expelled without trial. There was also a move to consolidate nationalist sentiment. The use of the Argentine flag both with and without the sun was approved in public establishments, and monuments were erected to the military figures who had contributed to the genocide of the Indigenous people.

In the national consciousness that the regime of liberal criollo oligarchs dreamed of, there was no room for us, the Indigenous people. Not even by force were we going to achieve a trivial scrap of citizenship that would allow us to rebuild our traditional world in the territory bequeathed to us by our ancestors.

This was the setting in which Pirenrayen grew like a flower, watered with longing for justice, opening petals of dignity and hope. That little Indigenous girl was destined to make history.

Summer came. Fresia's younger sons had deserted the school and had stayed with their mother to help her. Many hands and arms were needed to prepare the annual ceremony where the community renews its pledge to live in harmony with all the forces of the cosmic order. This is our most important ceremony, and we call it *kamarikun*.

The Argentine government had not authorized its celebration, so everything had to be kept strictly secret. Only a few lofches had been granted permission. Yet despite the restrictions and in some cases prohibitions, our Mapuche people kept our spirituality alive. Some communities received authorization for the kamarikun and were forced to raise the national flag when the ceremony was held. The frontier police came to enforce the presence of the Argentine flag, and any unauthorized activity was considered a conspiracy against the sovereignty of the state. But not all Mapuches were obedient or fearful of the government. Demands for land and freedom of movement were constant. The idea of property, with its metallic threads trapping the earth, was something so alien to our life that we could not understand it. Borders? We have never understood what they really are. Boundaries for the world or boundaries for people? Can a guanaco or a bird of prey comprehend barbed wire or divided skies? Can a seed know where to sprout, on what border line? Our people are a tree that knows where its roots grow, but not where its branches will end.

The Argentine government, pressured by the landowners of the Rural Society, used various forms of punishment against us. To disobey it was sometimes a way to protect our private collective existence. This is why, in Fresia's lofche, the kamarikun became not only the most important moment of dialogue with the mapu—where we asked the forces of nature to strengthen all forms of life in the territory and pledged to live harmoniously and with respect for all forms of life—but also the greatest social event of our people. It was the moment when all the family members scattered by the conquest gathered again. They came from many different places, even those farthest away. Once a year, they were summoned by the call to this celebration.

Our secret spirituality saved us from oblivion, madness, and desperation. We learned how to take advantage of distance and prudence and to be careful in our preparations; in this way we could carry out the ceremony without the Wingka officials' notice. This is what our elders told us; this is how they remembered their feats of resistance. Heroes and heroines without plaques, without names written on street signs. Thanks to their intelligence and courage, here we are, still alive to walk the path of our history.

At the kamarikun, there is a great deal of eating and drinking. Not alcohol. There is no alcohol, just muday, which Doña Fresia and the other women prepared. For us, muday is a symbol of celebration. It nourishes the body and brings joy to the spirit. The wheat harvest had been good, and the sacred drink was fermented so that it could be offered to the mapu. Despite the impoverishment of our people, collective effort ensured that on this occasion, food was plentiful. Fresia received a visit from her older sister, with all her family. It was a poignant reunion, with tears and laughter. They loved each other dearly and had lived through so much fear and pain amid the harsh events of the war.

The place where the ceremony was held was a pampa surrounded by gentle hills that allowed the carts easy access. Shelters were raised with branches of laura, a kind of pepper tree with plentiful leaves whose boughs made an excellent sanctuary from the rain. The structure acquired a circular form. In the middle of the circle, the *pillanketral*, the sacred fire, was lit, and behind, at a short distance from the fire, twelve bamboo stalks were placed. On their tips, two flags were raised, one yellow and the other blue. This altar is called a *rewe*, which means place of purity.

On the first dusk of the four days of the ceremony, when the moon, still not quite full, lit the temple of pampa and ivy with its whitish light. The formal greetings began, in strict and meticulous pentukun, long welcome speeches delivered by spiritual and political authorities. They spoke still mounted on horseback, greeting one another and telling the latest news. Often, midspeech, the men wept as they told of the hardships they had suffered since the Wingkas' arrival. Many had lost their families and knew nothing of the whereabouts of their daughters, wives, fathers, and mothers. It was known that there was a large prison where the most important longkos and their families were confined. Martín García Island had become the largest concentration and extermination camp.

It was a time of great pain, of great sorrow, of hunger and solitude. Only the kamarikun revived the strength and unity of the Mapuche Nation. Perhaps this was why the Argentine state often banned these ceremonies.

This kamarikun was especially important for Fresia since it was the first she celebrated without her daughter, and the first she attended with her granddaughter. On the initial day, the sacred fire was lit. Bamboo sticks were driven into the earth facing east, toward the *Puelmapu*, where the sun rises. Over the four days, two girls and two boys were responsible for receiving and transmuting the spiritual forces that descended to the rewe. The *pullu*, the spirits, come to us to listen, to heal, and to bring strength and harmony. For those four days, the children must stay there until they have performed their task. The *kalfumalen* are small, sacred maidens chosen for this task; they must be pure, meek, obedient, and highly spiritual. They are dressed in blue, since *kalfu* is the sacred color, and adorned with shining silver jewelry. The *rutrafe*—the jeweler—embeds in each piece the philosophy and spirituality of my Mapuche people. The *kalfuwentru*, blue boys, were boys with the same qualities who wore on their torso a woven sash covered in rattles and a headdress with a rhea feather on their heads. The girls were wrapped in a woven blanket with a blue fringe called an *ulkilla*, a shawl. The boys wore a *makun*, a poncho made with guanaco wool, which was later replaced with sheep's wool.

They presented two horses that were placed before the rewe. There they were painted, one white and the other black. Drawings were made on their heads and hindquarters. Animals were also offered, which were slaughtered at the beginning of the ceremony: horses, sheep, and cattle.

After the pentukun, well into the evening, all those present gathered in a great semicircle before the sacred fire. The yellow and blue cloths placed on the sticks waved like flags in the wind. Amid calm and silence, the *kultrun* burst forth like a thunderbolt. I have always felt the kultrun's power; it is not merely a musical instrument. At first sight, it is simply a kettledrum made with a large wooden bowl taken from a healing tree trunk, but for us, the Mapuche, the kultrun is the heartbeat of the earth. Each beat marks the time of life, in the heavenly space we inhabit and that inhabits us.

A musical dialogue began with the *trutruka*, that simple yet powerful trumpet we use to enhance the music that emerges from the kultrun. Its pipe is hollow, and the bell at the end gives it a deep and strident sound. The women's voices joined in, rising, opening the cosmic doors with their sacred chant, communicating with the ancestral spirits.

Then the sacred dance, the *purrum*, was held. For four days, we dance around the fire. This is how we danced to the wind, the rain, and the earth, and we still dance in this way today.

The next morning at dawn, hundreds of men mounted their horses and galloped around the rewe. A ring of dust began to rise, covering the sacred circle, the awun. This is a ritual still practiced in these ceremonies, and it brings us the strength and freedom of our forebears. Their cries were thunderous and seemed to shake the surroundings, spreading the voice of a people who refused to disappear.

On the third day, the men, covered in feathers from the rhea bird that we call *choike*, brought their skills and beauty to the sacred dance of the *choikepurrun*. The seminaked men wore loincloths, their faces painted, their torsos also decorated, with a headdress on their heads called a *trailongko*, to which they added a crest of choike feathers and a makun, a woven wool poncho that imitated the bird's wings. In this

41

guise, they danced gracefully in front of the women, shaking their rattles to the rhythm of the kultrun. Then the women, grateful for the men's gallantry, answered with their tahiel, the sacred song. This was how many men and women fell in love, and joy and hope once again dwelled inside them. And not only human voices conveyed that deep feeling. The fire spoke; it expressed itself and brought revelations. The wind whispered the proximity of rain, and when the ceremony ended, *mawun*, the long-awaited rain, would come. Mawun is the baptismal force that cleanses us, bathing us in prosperity. She would arrive with her wet, grayish sheet, enveloping everything. At first, she caressed the earth with scarcely perceptible drops. Then the children born during that time were presented to her. The mothers and fathers rushed to carry their babies in their arms and dance around the fire.

Fresia danced the purrum with joy, her granddaughter in her arms. Pirenrayen's big, dark eyes were wide open, and she enjoyed the sway of the dance. Linkoyan danced clumsily, holding his mother's hand and tripping often. He would whine and then keep dancing. Another young woman with her baby bound to her chest also danced; the little boy slept, oblivious to the dance, the rain, and the people.

That was how the mapu welcomed them. That was how the ancestors watched over them from above.

When they returned home, it rained for the whole journey. That was a good summer, with no drought. And thanks to hard work and the earth's generosity, the hunger that had ravaged our people would become a nightmare of the past. But this good fortune wouldn't last long.

Chapter 5

A Muffled Cry of Sorrow

That summer, after the kamarikun, Fresia's last sons decided to leave for the nearby towns in search of work. The hunger had persisted, and as it had for many other young men in the community, it drove them away from their homes. Not far from there, they met a team of mule drivers who, on seeing their disorientation, offered them food and work. Fresia's sons were pleased. A young longko was their guide. He belonged to a distant lofche and told them the details of the work. They were driving cattle from Puelmapu to Gulumapu, from the Argentine Patagonia to Chilean Patagonia, as they are known today. Many heads of livestock were in their care, and many were the dangers they would have to confront.

Fresia was left alone with her granddaughter, who was too small to help. Chekeken, knowing Fresia's situation, offered to stay with her for a while. Both women set about building a room next to the kitchen. Adobe, wood, and stone mixed harmoniously, becoming solid walls crowned with a roof of cane, wood, and thatch. They took delight in building the rooms where Chekeken and Linkoyan would spend the winter. Chekeken was big and strong, and any task was easy for her.

One night, they woke to Linkoyan's cries. He had a fever and was wailing in desperation. Fresia intuited straightaway what might be happening. She lit a fire, took out her medicine, and filled her clay pipe with dried wineberry leaves. She drew close to the little boy and smoked his ears. And as she smoked them, she asked the newen to bring healing to that little body. Suddenly, a peregrine falcon, the kind we call a *peuco*, crashed into the window of the ruka and fell to the ground. At that moment, Linkoyan fainted. The boy's mother was afraid and began to cry. Fresia brought in the dying peuco, laid it on a woven blanket, carefully stretched out its wings, and gently rubbed its cartilage with her fingertips. Then she relit her *kiltra*, the pipe she always used for her powerful smokings, and exhaled the herbal smoke onto the moribund bird. Fresia closed her eyes and began to sing. She sang with sorrow, but as she repeated the same tune again and again, a force seemed to radiate from her lungs and throat that rose and enveloped the surrounding space.

The peuco gently fluttered its wings, and the boy began to wake. At first, the bird's efforts seemed useless, but in Fresia's magical hands, the bird came to life. Yet she kept singing until she was certain that it was time to pluck a feather from its breast. She did this with such care that the peuco did not resist. That night, she did not let it leave the house; but the next day, she took the bird in her hands and pressed it against her chest, went to her sacred tree, and there, as she sang, she let it go. The bird flapped its wings in bafflement like a fledgling learning to fly, then rose up high and vanished into the misty winter dawn. Linkoyan recovered that very night and never fell ill again. Fresia made him a pendant with the feather, which he wore until it disintegrated over time. From that day on, a small part of his spirit dwelled in the peuco, and its newen strengthened and guided him for the rest of his life.

Linkoyan and Pirenrayen played constantly, always looking for each other as soon as one lost sight of the other; if one cried, the other did, too. They seemed to have been conceived by the same mother. They merged into one peal of laughter and gave themselves over trustingly to pleasure and mischief. When they were a little older, they told each other secrets under the shelter of the tallest, leafiest tree.

Chekeken came from the Patagonian plateau. She was a girl from the Aónikenk people, also known as the Tehuelche, who had married a young Mapuche, a great jeweler. He had arrived in Tehuelche territory trading blankets and jewelry for salt and animal skins. The languages of the Mapuche and the Aónikenk differed greatly, but the two nations lived harmoniously in shared territory. In the old days, on the shores of the Colorado River, great bartering gatherings were held, which my people called *trafkintu*. These bartering meetings were famous all over the land. Not only the Mapuche and the Tehuelche participated, but peoples from even farther away who came with their crafts, their grain, and all kinds of food and animals to trade, especially for salt and meat.

Chekeken was there with her family when Pichiliempe saw her. He had heard many stories about her; her great height gave rise to all kinds of legends—they say she was extraordinarily large. The tallest man among her people reached only to her shoulder. She was shy. Her beautiful smile captivated Pichiliempe. Her hair was long and thick; she wore it loose, held at her brow with a woven band. Her copper skin gleamed; she seemed to have been burnished like a fine clay vase. Her back was broad and her arms strong. Her breasts were voluptuous and rose up like mountains. She was indeed a beautiful young woman, still a girl in many regards, yet no man dared love her since her great height inhibited them. She had learned the art of tannery to perfection. She had a collection of sharp scraping tools that she and her younger brother made, sometimes with rock and sometimes with bone. In her hands, fur blankets made from guanaco or puma hides turned out as soft as the petals of the firetree flower.

Pichiliempe was a cheerful, strong, and brave young man. On his travels, he had learned a few words of the Aónikenk language, and though he did not speak it well, he could make himself understood. Many carts and people had gathered there to exchange goods. They came from all over, hoping to return with the precious salt they needed so badly, or certain animal hides that were harder to obtain. Without knowing, Pichiliempe and Chekeken were witnesses to the last great trafkintu, since after the Conquest of the Desert, these events would be over forever, along with other social events that these peoples had enjoyed so much in the time of freedom.

He had arrived there with the firm decision to meet the Tehuelche giantess and make her his wife. He approached her with determination. Holding his head high, lengthening his neck like a guanaco, he said, "Little big woman, what is your name?"

"Chekeken," she answered shyly.

"Which of these pieces of jewelry do you like?" he asked, showing her the silver jewelry he had made from coins.

She picked out a hoop that he had carelessly pushed aside and, looking at it with a sweet and girlish smile, said, "This one."

She took the *chaway*—an earring—in her large hands and walked away, pressing it to her chest.

When the war with the Wingka broke out, some Mapuche longkos and Tehuelche chiefs had agreed to join forces against the invader. But there were many chiefs, perhaps the most important among the Aónikenk, who believed in the word of the Argentine government and joined forces with the white state. They believed that this was their only chance at survival. But they soon realized their mistake when the Argentine military betrayed them.

Pichiliempe married Chekeken when the war was nearly over, at the end of 1887. He decided to remain at the camps with her, and for a long time did not return to his lof or have news of his family. At first, he stayed with his father-in-law, who had given him a *weralka*, a fur blanket that, among other things, was used to cover the frame of a tent; it was a pelt like leather, and very warm. As their first full moons passed, they enjoyed the freedom of the hunt and community life. But winter soon came, and they could no longer store as much food as they usually did, since the area was now controlled by the enemy, who every day advanced farther, shifting the frontier as they came.

One cold, damp dawn, when the first glimpses of winter were showing, the ground began to shake with such force and intensity that everyone awoke with fright. An army of hundreds of soldiers was approaching. They had almost no time to gather their belongings or shield their children before the butchery began amid swords and bullets. Pichiliempe took Chekeken's hand, and without a word, they escaped together. He ran toward some mesas with immense caves that were home to red pumas. There, he hid Chekeken, then returned to save her parents. She cried in anguish for her family's fate and, fearing that her husband might die, soon left her hiding place to search for him. At that moment, some soldiers spotted her. They were so startled by her great size that they froze before her. Suddenly, from among the bushes, the captain, who had dismounted to pee, appeared. He loudly commanded them to capture her. They threw her down and tied her hands then and there, as if she were an animal.

They took her far away, along with some other prisoners. Their destination was the city of Buenos Aires. It took them months to arrive, and Chekeken almost died during the pilgrimage. The soldiers were afraid of her, which was precisely why they treated her with more cruelty. They abused her in the most callous ways to let her know who was in charge. They wanted to tame her as if they were training a ferocious beast. Once they reached the city, the prisoners were taken to the army barracks, which served as temporary accommodations until the captives' fates were decided. The army had stations in Chacarita, Retiro, and Palermo. These were enormous premises with stables, corrals, immense storehouses, paddocks, offices, and a racecourse. There the prisoners spent several days underfed, cold, and anguished, with no news of their loved ones. Everything was uncertain.

Chekeken was separated from the rest of the prisoners. They shut her in a room of adobe and stone, with a sturdy wooden, padlocked door. The room was adjacent to the inner courtyard of the offices. The floor was paved with flagstones and was terribly cold. Every so often, distinguished men arrived to negotiate with the officials in charge of the general command of the armed forces about the places and uses the Indigenous prisoners would be destined to. Many were especially interested in the giantess from Patagonia, but the official in charge of the expedition, who had discovered her, sold her at an excellent price to a criollo magnate who was well connected in Paris; he planned to put her on display in a human zoo.

They chained her to a wood column supporting the ceiling in her room. Chekeken had wounds on her wrists and ankles from the constant rubbing of the handcuffs and shackles and the weight of the chains. Each time a soldier came into the room, she could guess what was coming. First, the man would watch her as he summoned his courage; then he would drag her by the chain until he had forced her down to her hands and knees. Once she was on the floor, he would mount her like a mule and, whipping her with a riding crop, force her to move about the small room. When the ordeal was over, the soldier left satisfied, just like the colleagues who had gone before him, telling his cronies that he, too, had ridden the giantess. "She smells worse than a pig," the soldiers complained.

One morning very early, several of them entered with buckets of water, soap, and a brush with a long wood handle of the kind used to shine horses' coats. They stripped off her clothes and began to bathe her. She cried out and sobbed desperately while the men joked and larked about. When they had finished, they left her naked on the floor with bleeding hands. She had hurt the tips of her fingers by trying to remove her chains. Naked and shivering from the cold, she wanted to die.

When dusk fell, an older man came in and covered her with some blankets. He pitied her, collapsed and defenseless.

"Poor creature," he said in a friendly voice. "Are you cold?"

She did not answer.

"Are you afraid of me?"

As he questioned her, she remained sunk in a gloomy silence, staring at the floor and not saying a word, not only because she did not understand the man's strange language, but because her sorrow and fear had devoured even her cries and groans. Yet there was something about that man that brought her a kind of peace.

The next day, the man arrived with his servants, who dressed Chekeken in garments especially made for her, and took her away. He was the one who had bought her, and he had everything ready to ship her off to Paris.

When a blanket of silence fell, and all the land had become a muffled cry of sorrow, when there were no longer wails or voices, when the sky and soil were teeming with vultures and other carrion birds celebrating their own banquet, Pichiliempe, covered in wounds, bleeding and suffering, returned for his wife. She was gone, and he assumed the worst. He was so bewildered that he set out in search of her immediately. He was confident in his skills as a tracker.

Pichiliempe learned what had happened from a man he took prisoner, a cowardly young corporal whom he'd found crouching behind some rocks, and who shrieked and cried and trembled with fear when he was discovered. As soon as he saw the man, Pichiliempe questioned him in his broken Spanish. He listened to his tale of what had happened, and half understood. Though he was skilled with languages, since to trade and sell he needed to know how to speak to his customers, he had a certain resistance to learning Spanish. The corporal, for his part, knew a little Mapudungun, and with gestures and signs, he explained how Chekeken had been taken by the soldiers.

We will never know this corporal's name, but his exploits are still spoken of today. The truth was that this young man had no desire to be in the army, but had ended up joining the ranks due to the foolishness of his father, who believed him to be a troublemaker and a thief and had handed him over personally to the sergeant. It seems the unfortunate youngster had a good friend who liked to bet on fighting cocks. The friend played the money that his boss had entrusted to him for an investment and lost it all. When the boss found out, he went in search of his employee, intending to kill him, but the young man who was to end up a corporal defended his friend and took the blame for him. He begged for mercy and offered to pay his friend's debts with hard work. Touched by the gesture, the boss accepted the excuses, punished his worker with lashes, and withheld his pay for a year. He spoke to the young man's father, persuading him to enlist his son in the army and distance him from bad influences that could lead him to ruin. That was how he ended up a corporal.

When they came down from the high, rocky mesas, they headed downstream, following the river's edge. There they met with a view that neither man would ever be able to erase from his memory. It had been a Tehuelche settlement, and bodies were scattered everywhere. Some were partially devoured, others charred, but all were destroyed. They could not identify a single whole corpse to bury in a *chenke*. The Aónikenk buried their dead shrouded in a weralka. Above the defenseless body, they laid earth and rocks until they had raised a visible mound, and this grave was called a chenke.

They stayed there, staring for a long time at that terrible sight. A river tinted with blood, a red river of pain. The wind came to sweep away the sickening stench in the air. There were no words or tears or any human gesture that could express the shock, the helplessness, and the sorrow that overwhelmed them. Pichiliempe and the corporal looked at each other with their eyes moistened—Pichiliempe's with rage and despair, the corporal's with shame and contrition. Pichiliempe looked at his prisoner and was startled to see the tears pouring down his cheeks. The young man did not speak for a long time, moving a few steps away and collapsing onto the ground. He rested his face on his knees, hiding between his legs, and wept in silence. Pichiliempe let out a piercing howl, crying out his pain like a clap of thunder breaking onto the rocks. When the explosion had risen from his chest, he took a deep breath, closed his eyes, and spoke in his mind to Chekeken: *Guide me to you, my love. My beautiful girl, do not stop thinking of me, so that I can find you.* Pichiliempe had loved the young giantess at first sight.

Chekeken was no more than fifteen when they married. She was a little girl trapped in a giant body. Only he could see in her the gentle young girl she really was.

Pichiliempe decided to trust the corporal's directions, and they began to climb the steppe. They needed another horse for the prisoner urgently, since carrying the man on his own horse's rump slowed him down. He wanted to reach the soldiery that had kidnapped his beloved as soon as possible. He suggested that the corporal steal a horse from the first ranch they encountered, promising him that as soon as they spotted the military camp, he would be freed. The young man accepted and remained loyal; at no time after stealing the horse did he try to escape.

The two horsemen galloped for days and slept little. They even traveled by moonlight. Pichiliempe fed and cared for his prisoner gratefully. Gradually, their relationship became friendly, and they even became accomplices. Finally, after several weeks, they came upon the squadron. The young man no longer wished to abandon Pichiliempe in his mission; he had grown to admire and respect him. He asked to stay by his side to help him, and Pichiliempe accepted and gave him a beautiful knife, whose handle he himself had covered in silver. They mingled with the soldiers. There were Indigenous men in uniforms among them who acted as interpreters and trackers, so Pichiliempe stole a soldier's jacket and donned it straightaway, and dressed like the Indian collaborators in their sandals, chiripa trousers, and military jackets, he entered the camp unheeded alongside the corporal. Not a soul noticed the presence of the two intruders.

There were hundreds of prisoners. Chekeken was constantly guarded; it was impossible to get close to her, much less to free her. They would have to wait until they reached Buenos Aires. The pilgrimage across the pampa took another month. During that time, they plotted in detail their plan of liberation and escape. To this end, they recruited other soldiers who wanted to desert and longed to flee far away to begin another life. The arrangement was land and livestock in exchange for help. In those days, land and livestock obtained from the reductions of our people's territory were always handed over to the criollo oligarchy and high-ranking officials in the armed forces. An ordinary private was never going to be rewarded for his efforts. Pichiliempe promised them a new and better life at the encampments of the friendly Rankülche chiefs, who inhabited this territory.

They arrived hungry, parched with thirst, and dressed in rags. Captives and captors alike looked like ghostly figures as they stepped out of a wild and fearful desert at the end of the world.

The whole time they were in the city, Pichiliempe never once glimpsed Chekeken, but he was filled with hope that soon they would be reunited.

Chapter 6

Journey to the Center of Patagonia

Once the eccentric millionaire had Chekeken in his house, he decided to present her in public by giving a soiree the night before her departure for Paris. He wanted to show his peers how mistaken they were in their desire to exterminate the Aónikenk. He claimed that they were defenseless creatures and that if they were domesticated, they could become even more effective servants than the Africans due to their immeasurable physical strength. He decided to dress Chekeken as a lady of the era. She had a charm that he found unsettling. He felt for her a mixture of fascination, fear, desire, and repulsion.

During her captivity at his ranch, Chekeken had spent many hours locked up each day. A few days after her purchaser took her away, he had discovered her gentle nature and decided to free her from her chains and shackles; but each time he visited her, he brought a whip, like a tamer who does not trust his beast. He spoke and read to her, and even brought a phonograph to play music for her. She was so distraught that she remained crouched in a corner of the room, staring blankly. Gradually, he grew bolder, until one day he came so close that he could brush against the skin on her cheek. His heart raced with fear and pleasure. Chekeken remained undaunted, until he tried to lower his hand to her neck. She stood abruptly, and the man stepped back in fright and fell to the floor. He saw a furious expression on the young woman's face and fled the room.

Yet when he closed the door and breathed in the mellow air outside, he laughed joyfully: the episode touched him. In the eyes of that woman, he had seen the gaze of any other who would not allow herself to be touched. She was less of an animal than he had assumed. That day, he ordered the servants to clean the room and place in it a large bed, a table, and a chair. He had decided to civilize the savage.

During that time (she could never say exactly how long it had been), my great-grandmother Chekeken was fed, washed, and forced to sleep in a bed. An Aónikenk woman who worked on the estate served as her caretaker and interpreter. Her name was Aiken. She had been a captive since early in the war and had learned Spanish by force of the whip. She was gentle and wise and took care of Chekeken with great tenderness. She was her friend during the time she remained there.

Aiken was obliged to notify their master once everything was ready for Chekeken's daily bath, when he would come to watch her as if she were putting on a show. The task could not begin until the master was seated comfortably before her. He sat before the bathtub into which Chekeken stepped naked, with a puzzled and fearful demeanor. Two women performed the task of bathing her, Aiken and some other who was free from her work in the mansion. The man liked to watch the water trickle over the skin of that voluminous body. Her broad back, her wide face, her ample breasts, and her firm and muscular legs caused him an arousal he did not disguise in front of the servants, and as they bathed Chekeken, he touched his private parts. The ritual was accompanied by Tchaikovsky; "Dance of the Sugar Plum Fairy" was the soundtrack to these encounters. And so it went every day. Then they would dress her and take her out for a walk so that her bones would not stiffen. Despite his predilections, the master never touched Chekeken again. He supervised her diet himself and made sure she was kept warm and comfortable. Each morning, he got up and went to see her. At night, he had terrible nightmares in which he saw her escape from his arms. She was in his thoughts when he awoke and when he went to sleep again.

Finally, the day of the soiree arrived. The estate where the party was to be held was thronged with people and opulent carriages in picturesque, orderly lines in front of the mansion. A fleet of elegantly dressed servants in stiff gloves slid silently and skillfully through every corner of the house where guests milled around, relaxed and happily clutching flutes of champagne, while a string quartet played a sweet and joyful symphony. All signs seemed to indicate success, yet the host was unaware of the fragility of his luxurious world. Accustomed to organizing functions and festivities, he had no idea that things do not always go according to plan.

In the darkness of night, five men hid in the gardens, plotting. Pichiliempe and the young corporal, who by then was his friend, divided the tasks of their plan between them. The corporal would act inside the mansion, while Pichiliempe would remain hidden with the horses, ready for flight. He had obtained a big, strong horse for Chekeken. Two of the recruited men stayed beside him; their job was to get the attention of the guests and of course the owner. The corporal and a fugitive slave named Juan, who had joined them in recent days, infiltrated the party dressed as servants. The other man had obtained servants' clothes from a girl who worked as a kitchen helper in the house, whom he knew because he had seen her buying spices with the cook at the local market. They had taken a liking to each other at first sight and began to see each other in secret. He promised to take her with him that night. His task was to go inside the mansion and find the room where Chekeken was being held. When they found her, they would take her out through the library door, which led to one of the inner courtyards; they had chosen this door because it was almost unused. They would also take the chance to steal some valuable jewels belonging to the mistress. The girl told them exactly where the mistress kept them and gave them the keys to the small chest containing the treasure.

For all this to happen without any surprises or mishaps, the men needed to cause a major distraction from outside. As soon as they had their hands on the jewels and had located Chekeken, one of them must give the signal for the escape plan to be set in motion. The jewels were easy to find: the girl's instructions had been so accurate that they had no trouble at all. But the search for Chekeken, though intense and meticulous, turned up nothing. Not knowing what to do, they decided to go to the busiest place, thinking that perhaps she would be part of the decoration and the party's attraction. They were back in the main room when the music paused and the master of the house began to speak.

"Dear friends, the most important moment of the evening has arrived. Those of you who know me know of my fondness for oddities, for strange creatures unique among their species, that demand our attention. In my youth, I became interested in felines, and later in snakes. I came to have a collection of butterflies of more than five thousand species from all over the world."

The audience applauded.

"But now it is humans that interest me, those races lost amid inhospitable regions. Dangerous, even cannibal races. I have seen men and women so tiny they could fit into the palm of my hand."

The man spoke excitedly. At times, his speech was so booming the audience trembled; at others, he spoke so quietly he could scarcely be heard. He made theatrical gestures, fully embracing his role. His loquacity kept the audience in breathless suspense.

"I have seen men with hunchbacks like camels," he went on, "women with ears so large they looked like elephants, but nothing has amazed me or awakened my scientific curiosity so much as the tribe of the savage giants of Patagonia."

No sooner had he said this than a heavy velvet curtain slowly drew back. There she was, sitting on a wood platform, in an oak chair made especially for the occasion: the terrified, sad giantess, dressed in a long blue skirt with many ruffles and a white blouse with tiny blue flowers. Her hair was gathered into two braids. She stared at the floor. She was lit by a chandelier made of dozens of golden candelabras that hung just above her head, which cast an even more elongated shadow of her body behind her.

The audience expressed its astonishment in unison. Then the host and master of ceremonies ordered Chekeken to stand. She obeyed, and the people, dazzled by her height, applauded the spectacle. The man approached the platform and drew near Chekeken. He touched her braids and her hands, addressing the audience.

"See how harmless this creature is. Of course, it has not always been so. When she was found in the lands of the south, she was a wild and aggressive beast. She ate the flesh and blood of any animal or human; her whole tribe eats in this way. Hundreds of men were needed to control her fury. She destroyed the chains placed on her hands and feet. Thus she was brought to the city. But when I learned of her existence, I bought and decided to tame her, and she has become gentle and obliging. I am convinced that these giants would be the best servants and workmen we could have," he said, turning to observe Chekeken. Then he looked back at the audience and continued, "Behold her. Do you really see in her a savage? The giants of Patagonia can be our property, and we can even export them. Many people would pay a fortune to be waited upon by giants. Let us not allow their extermination. It would be a great shame if this race of giants were to disappear from the face of the earth."

The audience clapped in excitement, and he bowed in gratitude for the ovation. When the applause subsided, he proposed a toast and announced his departure the next day for France. The giantess would travel with him to participate in the International Exposition of 1889, where there would be a human zoo. He was certain that his Patagonian giantess would be received with vigorous acclaim.

While those inside stood, champagne glasses in hand, outside, cries and explosions were heard. The men went out to see what was happening. To everyone's surprise, the stables and an immense barn close to the mansion were ablaze with bright and leaping flames. Suddenly, shots rang out. The women scattered from the hall in alarm. The master of the house and his wife tried to calm the guests' nerves but could not prevent the stampede. They knew that this was the work not of common outlaws, but of the repressive forces of the radical opposition urging the people to topple President Juárez Celman, and that they were now coming for the guests, his allies and friends.

Fate had decreed that this was also the night of the prelude to the Revolution of the Park, where radical forces and other dissidents organized to protest fraudulent elections and an oligarchic regime that cared only for its own privileges while the people went hungry. Suddenly, around the mansion appeared dozens of men on horseback, armed to the hilt. Amid the whistle of bullets and cries for liberty, they shot at the windows of that sumptuous house. Inside, men dressed in elegant tailcoats hid behind columns and anything else that provided protection. The few that were armed hid in the colonnade encircling the house, in spots that allowed them a good view to take aim at the rebels.

The host went in search of weapons, and some men mustered the courage to join him in the defense. The millionaire distributed all the rifles he had and some revolvers that were collector's items. The gunfire was relentless. Pichiliempe and his two companions were trapped between the two lines of fire. They improvised barricades. They needed to find a way to get out of there and get to the mansion and rescue the others. The corporal and his companion soon took advantage of the confusion to search for Chekeken, but in a moment of carelessness of the servants, she had already escaped. The corporal searched blindly, desperately for her, to no avail. A few steps away, the other man was also searching, when he felt a warm hand take his own. It was the young servant girl, who had recognized him by the light of the few weak candles from the candelabras along the hallway. Aiken also appeared, took a candle, and guided them through the long corridor to the kitchen. She had been the one to rescue Chekeken from the gunfire.

The girl explained to Aiken who the men were and their purpose. She understood it all and translated what they said for Chekeken to dispel her doubts. The corporal took from a bag the beautiful scraper made of bone that Chekeken had given to Pichiliempe and that he always wore around his neck. This way, she could be sure that her husband was outside, waiting to rescue her. Aiken embraced Chekeken to say farewell, knowing that they would not see one another again.

They left the kitchen quickly and headed for the library. Now they had to get past the bullets. Inside the house, everything was pitch dark. The incessant gunfire had hit some of the priceless chandeliers lighting the rooms. They came to a large window, and one of them opened it. It was about ten feet from the ground; they would have to jump out of it and then emerge into the park, where they would meet Pichiliempe. Chekeken was the first to jump. Once she was on solid ground, she waited for each of them to place their feet on her shoulders so she could gently help them down. The cries, wails, and rushing made the situation all the more chilling.

Once outside the house, they trusted that Pichiliempe and the other two men would be waiting for them close by with horses. Of course, they did not anticipate that their accomplices wouldn't be able to escape from the place where they'd hid, since the invasion of the rebels had happened at the same time.

Pichiliempe had decided to cross the firing line, armed only with a bow and arrow, a knife, and a slingshot that we call a *wutruwe*. The other two men each had a shotgun and would cover him. They started to run with several draft horses, all at a gallop, but the gunfire was such that one of the riders covering him was wounded; his horse bolted, and he fell to the ground. The man tried to drag himself along, but someone finished him off, and the same gun shot at Pichiliempe, who nevertheless kept going. He and his companion managed to reach the place where their friends were waiting. They were only about three hundred yards away when Chekeken spotted them. She was the first to see them arrive. She had recognized Pichiliempe from the way he rode. She ran to him, disregarding the danger. When he saw her coming, he was filled with joy. He dismounted quickly and rushed toward her, and they embraced and kissed tenderly. She lifted him in her arms as if he were her little boy; he looked so tiny by her side. At that very moment, a booming shot rang out, which came from the place where their friends awaited them.

"Let's go and see what's happening there, but be very careful. If we're seen, who knows if we'll be able to get away," Pichiliempe said to the men. Then he looked at Chekeken and said lovingly, "My little flower, you stay here with the horses so they don't take you away from me again. I will come back for you. We will never be parted again."

She flung her arms around him in anguish, and for a few seconds that seemed eternal, she refused to let go of him. He kissed her hands passionately. Chekeken hung the scraper that she had given him in answer to his marriage proposal back around her beloved's neck. Pichiliempe smiled, and she quivered again to see that beautiful sight, his white teeth, his thick lips, and the subtle curve at the edge of his mouth. He was the strongest and most handsome man any woman could love, she thought. She stayed there waiting quietly, with the servant girl, just as he had asked.

Slowly, almost imperceptibly, hidden among groves of trees and thickets of brush, they drew near the place. Later, Juan and Pichiliempe would tell Chekeken the details of all that had happened there. Some armed men with torches came out from among the trees. There were many of them, and they were emboldened. They ordered them to lay down their arms. Pichiliempe's companions agreed and threw them to the ground. As the men were preparing to pick them up, the corporal managed to intercept one of them and overpower him, taking his weapon. He used the man's body as a shield, sparing himself the bullets. Pichiliempe began to shoot well-aimed arrows, and his two companions took the chance to beat and disarm some of the gunmen. As the bullets whistled back and forth, the corporal battled several men at once with stabs and punches. They say he fought like a wild animal, but just when it seemed the battle was won and they had felled all the gunmen, a man who lay on the ground like a corpse snatched up a revolver and, with what little strength he had left, fired an infallible shot at the corporal, who crumpled and fell down forever. Pichiliempe wanted to take him with them, but his body would impair their flight. There was pain in his heart, a bitter sorrow that made his throat burn and that stifled tears that wanted to flow like a waterfall. His friend had died valiantly. All that was left were his memory and the stories Pichiliempe would tell his family over and over, especially to Chekeken, stories that would be passed from generation to generation, and which I treasure as relics of my past.

When they passed through the gate of that property, they all felt free. The air seemed lighter, and they took deep, gulping breaths, filling their lungs with life. They rode all night, and when the sun announced the beginning of a new day, they bid each other farewell. Juan and his beloved set out for the northeast; they wanted to reach Brazil and search for their families. Meanwhile, the other soldier, who had survived so many things, with hope for the promise of land and refuge in the Rankülche encampments, asked Pichiliempe to honor his word, and he did so, taking him to Longko Epumer's camp. There, the man stayed. My great-grandparents also remained there for a brief time.

Autumn had tinted the grasslands of the pampas with yellow and ocher when my great-grandparents began to travel south. They wanted to arrive before the winter set in. Several moons passed as they made their long journey to the center of Patagonia. They went hungry, and at times feared assault by bandits. As if this weren't enough, Chekeken's heart flooded with sorrow when she learned that her parents and siblings had been murdered. Of the other members of her community, she knew nothing, but later she would learn that many of her people were split among different ranches, and some were even taken to museums. As they traveled, they had to avoid the military camps that were erected along what had once been the salt road.

Finally, they managed to cross the Colorado River. They were surprised to see little towns arranged around small plazas, in which poplars had been planted and stood weakly, trembling in the wind. They did not enter these settlements, despite their hunger, for fear of persecution and imprisonment. They drew closer and closer to the Negro River. When they reached its shores, they camped there for days, then later took the path into the high mountains.

They moved deeper into the thick mountain forest. They came to an enormous lake that shone like a mirror. The intense cold had turned its water to glass. That day, Pichiliempe managed to hunt a pudu, a deer native to the region. They ate it, savoring every part with fascination. Chekeken seemed to recover her strength, and the spirit of life took root again in her soul. That night, Pichiliempe made love to her sweetly and desperately. He wanted to fill her whole being with life, to enter her with longing for them to merge into a hopeful future. She received him tenderly at first, but then a fire burned through every inch of her skin and pores, and she gave herself over to desire and passion.

When the shadow of death lurks near, brushing against our bodies and spirits, we humans exorcise it with embraces and caresses, with the deep penetration of our vital senses, which lets us perceive the corporality of our existence. In this way, my great-grandparents welcomed the dawn locked in an embrace. And in this way, the whole winter passed.

Chapter 7

Our People's Defeat

One white and silent dawn, Chekeken woke in the embrace of a dream she had forged during the long night in the shelter of her husband's fiery body.

"Pichiliempe, Pichiliempe, wake up! I must tell you my dream," she said in her sweet, almost girlish voice, which was now tinged with hope and joy.

Her husband opened his bleary eyes and gazed at her in bewilderment. Chekeken, his little big flower, had cried so much. There were days when she refused to eat, when she only wanted to die, and now she awoke with this gleam in her eyes, full of life and appetite. He smiled and caressed her face.

"Of course, my little big flower. Tell me your dream."

Still lying among the blankets, Chekeken encircled her husband in her arms and told him her dream as tenderly as a mother would tell a tale to a child, because that's how they say she was; she was pure maternal instinct.

"It was a very lovely dream. You and I were climbing the mesas of my homeland. When we reached the top, you could see a river and a bright-green forest. The waters of that river were crystal clear, and a cool wind chilled my face and whipped through my hair. I don't know why, but I had an urge to open my arms, and my arms grew feathers, and became wings. And you also turned into a bird, and we were part of a flock of many birds crossing the sky. There was no pain or solitude. I was light, I felt free, and I was happy. What could this dream mean? What were the spirits telling me with this dream, Pichiliempe?"

He gazed at her and caressed her face again, running his fingertips softly over her lips, and answered with a smile, "Your ancestors came to console you, to tell you that our pain will soon be over and that we will arrive safely to where we are going."

She interrupted him, asking, "And where are we going, Pichiliempe?"

He answered with a sigh, "We are going to search for our loved ones, for my people, Chekeken, who will also be yours."

A few days later, they continued their westward pilgrimage. One cold midday when they were very weary, they came upon numerous encampments of Mapuches who were heading south. To his great surprise, Pichiliempe found his family among these people. First, he saw his brother, then his father, his mother, and many others. There were cries of delight and rejoicing. They had heard news of what had befallen Chekeken's community and had assumed that the couple, too, were dead. There was a feast. They ate roast meat and drank muday. There were also potatoes in abundance, some of them long, purple, and sweet, a variety known as *meñarqui*, and ground pine seeds.

Chekeken and Pichiliempe, my great-grandparents, stayed there until the end of spring, until a messenger from the northern territory brought them bad news. The army was on its way to that area. The agreement signed by the longkos of the south and the Argentine government had once again been betrayed by the state. Rumor had it that they must leave in search of other lands to settle. There was a *trawun*, a parliament, and before the soldiers arrived, they decided not to leave. Several spokespeople, or *werken*, were designated to travel to Buenos Aires and ask officials for total respect of the agreements.

Our people's defeat and the creation of the republic in our territories turned us into pariahs, with constant displacements pushing us farther and farther away. The removals came one after the other, and nothing could be done to prevent them. And so my great-grandparents and their whole community were exiled.

The army arrived before our werken reached Buenos Aires. One dismal dawn, they were forced to leave.

During the southward crossing, Chekeken began to feel unwell. She could not keep down any food. The vomiting left her weak, and she felt a tremendous urge to go to sleep and never wake up. Her mother-in-law realized that she was pregnant and felt sorry for Chekeken. How ill-timed was this renewal of life amid dispossession and persecution. Her body was demanding rest at the most agonizing moment, when all of them were forced to keep going without a break. The blazing sun was already warming their bodies, and they paused only to eat and drink. The nights were very short, yet despite the harrowing pilgrimage, the men and women gave each other brief moments of repose, and around the fire crackled the stories of yesteryear, mixed with anecdotes of the journey, which drew out laughter. We have always been able to survive as a people because, somehow, we have managed to smile.

That night, under a starry summer sky, Chekeken announced her pregnancy to her husband. He embraced her with joy.

By the time the due date drew close, Chekeken's life and those of the whole community would be irrevocably changed. Their wandering path in search of faraway places that could not be reached by the Argentine Army was plagued with hardships. Yet they never gave up, and they managed to find a patch of land and peace in what is now the province of Chubut, a settlement authorized by the Argentine government. There they stayed and built houses, began to raise livestock and to plant wheat.

But an unknown illness soon reached the reservation. They called it smallpox. It had entered these lands along with the invaders, like so many other evils.

Pichiliempe was racked with pain all through his body, and a freezing cold took hold of his bones. No matter how warmly he was wrapped, his shivering could not be calmed. His legs were weak. He collapsed on the ground as Chekeken called out to his mother in fright. Together, they positioned him by the fire and carefully prepared a range of remedies. But that illness unknown to our people was so powerful that it could not be overcome. It triumphantly carried away the lives of thousands of our people, among them, that of Pichiliempe.

During his dying days, Chekeken was constantly by his side, and she neither slept nor ate. She stroked his hair, spoke to him, and cried in silence. In the freezing dawn, she performed *ngllipun*, spiritual ceremonies, begging the ancestors to help and heal her husband.

Barely a handful of people survived that cursed illness. They buried the dead, and then they moved on.

They decided to head southeast, and so it was that they came upon our lof. My great-great-grandfather, Pichiliempe's father, welcomed them in solidarity. It became hard to reorganize life in the lof with the ongoing arrival of refugees. Not only did it mean adjusting to living with strangers, but also adapting to a new territory, getting to know it little by little, and gradually building a connection.

The Mapuche people relate to nature and build our identity based on it, strengthening our spirituality. Even today, the Wingka state does not like us to speak of the lof. The category of "community" has been imposed upon us. As I said at the beginning of my story, this idea belittles the perception of life, tears us away from the strong, invisible threads that connect us in brotherhood to the rivers, mountains, and lakes, the forests, and all forms of life. To believe that humans need only one another, or that only humans can love and hear one another, is a mistake. We are lof; we are humans interacting reciprocally with nature.

As time passed, the growing lof strengthened; it found its rhythm, its friendly voices, its daily routine. Those details that root us to a space, to what we call home, and define us as part of a world.

Chekeken was loved and treated as another sister of the lof. All the residents treated one another as family. They helped each other, and no one failed to be involved in collective tasks. There were several *ruka-tuns*: a rukatun is a way of building dwellings in community. That was how the stone and adobe houses were built, solid houses that offered a permanent home to the new arrivals. That was how my great-great-grandmother Fresia Coliman met my great-grandmother Chekeken.

The young Tehuelche girl, pregnant and without her husband, felt disconsolate. Fresia accompanied her and adopted her as a daughter, attending her baby's birth. The night of the delivery, Chekeken was sub-merged in the world of dreams. She saw herself as a girl again, walking toward the sea with her tribe. She could feel the fragrant, fresh, salty air enter her nose; she saw herself with her siblings and parents; hundreds of Tehuelches walked there with her. She wanted to run and meet the sea, which roared in fury. But an unknown elderly hand held her back. When she arrived, there were hundreds of fires in rows all along the beach, just as she had seen in her childhood when she went with her parents to the annual ceremony of her people. There she danced with her ancestors, heard them sing, and saw them take little steps in a gentle dance to the song's rhythm. Their feet moved from left to right, right to left, as if swaying along with the sea.

That was what the ceremonies of her people were like, skirting the sea, dancing and singing, and that was how she dreamed it that night.

We Mapuche call a revelatory dream a *pewma*, something that appears to us as a mystical language between the world of the spirits and our own. The dream speaks to us, warns us, reveals its secrets to us. In that pewma, she saw herself with hundreds of people. Suddenly the sea began to swell, and from its depths emerged a giant whale that opened its mouth, and thousands of different people emerged from it and climbed onto its back. They gathered in a circle around something Chekeken could not see. Out of nowhere, the same wrinkled hand squeezed hers again. She looked and saw that it was her grandmother, who took her firmly and led her to levitate above the sea. Her feet grazed the water, and it felt warm. She smiled at this surprising marine caress. They both reached the back of the whale and saw a tree sprout up. The creature wailed in pain, and Chekeken felt pain in her abdomen. No one did anything to uproot the tree. She was determined to do it, but her grandmother stopped her.

"That tree is yours," she said. "You planted it there. These people came out of that tree. The whale will live on as the root of that tree. If you pull the tree up, the whale will die."

Then she asked the old woman through her tears, "Why did I do this, Grandmother? Why did I do it?" And she embraced her disconsolately. The grandmother answered in a quaking voice, "Little girl, you did not do it. They did."

Chekeken's grandmother pointed to the beach, where all her people were being massacred by white men in uniform. The girl called to her mother in despair. The grandmother looked into her eyes and said, "There is nothing we can do, but you are saving us all. They will never be able to find the root of this tree, because it lives inside this whale, and they will never be able to sever it."

Then she began to cry and woke up drenched. Her water had broken, and her legs and feet were wet. The child did not take long to arrive. Fresia took him in her arms, washed him, and placed him at Chekeken's breast. The little boy had navigated the sea of dreams, crossed it with its ancient tree branches to get here. The tree sprouted another branch, and just as the dream announced to Chekeken, she was never alone again; from that son, a great lineage issued and multiplied on Earth. That is where I come from; I have Tehuelche blood in my veins. The Aónikenk are also my people.

I will continue to tell you everything, so that the truth is known. I, Llankaray, have not forgotten. Memory dwells inside me, bringing me the voices of the past in my dreams. My father and mother did not allow me to forget Chekeken, or the story of those who went before me. I give it to you so you can treasure it in your memory, and so this will not be a land of oblivion and pain.

Chapter 8

WILL WE BE STRONG ENOUGH?

Winter was a favorable time for Fresia to teach Chekeken the art of weaving. The young woman was silent. She had kept the loving sound of her mother tongue inside her heart and was gradually incorporating Mapudungun. She spoke the bare minimum and received acceptance and respect among her new family. In Mapudungun, lamngen is used to express sisterhood among women. It is a beautiful and profound word, since it transcends us. It means, united in our essence. That recognition of spirit and cosmic force brings us close together.

Chekeken admired and respected and felt affection for Fresia. She had watched as Fresia's hands seemed to fly like a *pilmaken*, a swallow, over the warp and weft on the loom. The threads seemed to give in without resistance to the magical flexibility of her fingers, whose precise strokes drew a symbolic world in her weavings. Fresia and Chekeken forged a deep and lasting friendship. It was not necessary for the girl to ask to be her student. Fresia noticed the attention she gave to the work she carried out.

The first step was to prepare the pieces to set up the loom. Chekeken chose the wood under Fresia's supervision. One of her brothers-in-law, Huentemilla, cut and polished it vigorously. Huentemilla was the youngest of Pichiliempe's brothers, and the most beloved by Chekeken's departed husband, so she felt attached to him. Whenever she needed anything, she would tell Huentemilla, and he was always ready and willing to help. Chekeken cared for him as if he were her own brother. They had wandered across vast expanses of land to finally settle there. It was a difficult, arduous journey, and it had brought them together, Mapuches and Tehuelches, in search of an opportunity to keep on living.

After lunch, Fresia and Chekeken set about building the loom.

"You must always pay attention to the weaving, ñaña. If you get distracted, the threads can slacken or get tangled up," Fresia recommended maternally. As she arranged the sticks, she went on with her advice.

"First, we will make sure the side sticks are standing nice and straight and steady. These are called *wichalwichalwe*. They must always be straight, one alongside the other. They say the wichalwichalwe lead from the earth to the sky. You must choose strong rags to knot them, not just any rag. They have to be strong, ñaña. If you use just any rag, they get frayed, they break, and then the weaving comes apart. These threads will knot the whole structure of the loom together. We have a habit in life of thinking that there are parts that are important and others that are useless, but that's not how it is; even the tiniest details matter to achieve good work. That's how we make mistakes, ñaña, tying our lives together with just any old rag. That's why when I was widowed the second time, I decided to stay alone. Why tie myself down with any old rag?" Fresia said, and they both laughed heartily. She went on, taking the thickest sticks.

"These, ñaña, are called *klow*, and you put one above and one below. They must be nice and straight, both of them, and together, but separate at the same time, as if they were both strapped to the same animal that will take them to the same place. They cannot be twisted, that would be like leading a twisted cart. Where would the poor oxen go? So these sticks go together. First, put the one below, on the ground, and then the one above, the *wenu*. These are going to mark the length of the piece you're going to weave. The klow is very important because you are going to bring the threads over that piece of wood. You and I are the klow. Our children are the threads; they will be weaving on this loom. What wood are we going to be made of, lamngen? Will we be strong enough, sister?"

And as she spoke this way, my great-great-grandmother Fresia Coliman tied the cross sticks firmly. Then she took a very thin one, and explained, "This is called *rañilelwe*. Where I am from, we used to use bamboo, but there isn't any here, and this stick Huentemilla has found is pretty, and nice and straight. With this, you're going to start dividing the warp in half. You must lay it crosswise." She put it in its place.

"There should be a rañilelwe for the heart," said Chekeken sadly. "Then you could keep living with pain on one side and happiness on the other, without them mixing so much all the time inside you. Sometimes I don't even feel like living."

Fresia challenged her.

"How can you say that, ñaña? You have to live because that is what your ancestors want, and your little boy, and Pirenrayen, and what I want, too. I love you so much," she said, and embraced her tenderly. Chekeken shed a few tears.

"Let's keep going, night will soon be here. Hand me the white wool on the bench, we'll use it as *tonon*. This wool is for crossing the weave, it must be eye catching and different, so you won't get confused between the warp and weft." Fresia gave Chekeken a tender look and said with a complicit smile, "Sometimes it isn't a bad thing to be tonon. Being different allows us to weave our life better. My fate was to be tonon lamngen, and I am content with my destiny."

"And that stick where you put the wool, does it have a name?" Chekeken asked.

"Yes," Fresia answered. "It's called a *tononwe*."

They finished building the loom and sat down by the fire to drink maté and talk. Fresia said, "We weave when we have dreams, when the pewma comes to tell us that we should draw. The ancestors guide our hands and our fingers. As soon as we choose the wool we are going to spin, we can be sure of the fate of the fleece. To weave is also to preserve our memory, sister, our past. We women weave to wrap ourselves up and to shelter, to preserve. We have saddlebags that will carry food or medicine, we weave the world where we walk and where we want to walk. We draw it, and in this way we make it, little by little, and by paying attention, looking carefully, and passing on our knowledge to others."

Chekeken watched her with eyes glistening with light, eager and full of joy. Outside, dusk was falling, blushing and beating with sounds. The bleating of the sheep returning to the corral, the birdsong, the Patagonian wind all offered their music to the living and to life—the life that was spun each day, tinting everything with color in a time of whiteness imposed with bullets and blood.

Around that time, Pirenrayen fell sick with vomiting and fever. The fever lasted several days. In desperation, Fresia asked the spirits for guidance. She fasted, and sang and sang all day long with her kultrun at the foot of an *aliwen*, a broad and ancient tree, where she used to place the urine of the sick and make an offering to the mapu to ask for insight and wisdom. The spirits would come down to the dense treetop and, from the branches open like arms, would whisper their most precious medicinal secrets through the rustle of the leaves in the tree's abundant boughs. That tree was no simple aliwen but an oracle, a guardian of the *küme alwe*, the good spirits that came down to reinforce life, to balance, protect, and heal. But their visions were not for just anyone; only the lawentuchefes or the machis could read in its trunk and branches the shamanic language it spoke. This was how Fresia once again learned with certainty the medicine that she should dispense to her granddaughter. With no time to lose, she went inside and asked Chekeken to help ready her horse. She told her that she was going to search for the remedy that Pirenrayen needed. She left her granddaughter in her charge and gave her advice to lower the fever while she searched for the sacred medicinal plants.

She headed in the direction of the river, skirting its shores. As she went, she spoke to the *leufu*, asking permission to harvest the medicine. That day, a ferocious, frigid gale shook the plants mercilessly and swayed the river's waters, giving it a doleful roar. It was difficult to walk, whipped this way and that by the violent wind. She tried to wipe the dust from her eyes to see the plant that held the cure her granddaughter so badly needed. She had sand in her eyes, nose, and ears. Everything was turning to sand.

Kurruf, *the wind, is jealous,* Fresia thought. *He will sweep this place clean of obstructions,* she said to herself.

She realized that searching there was useless and that she should leave the river. She made her way toward the mesas. She noticed that, up above her, bushes of a considerable height were growing and convinced herself that the powerful plant she was searching for would be there. So she began to climb. Suddenly, the stone on which her feet were resting came loose and fell, rolling to the ground. Fresia was left hanging. Clinging to a rock with her hands, she looked around for a foothold but could not find one. She stayed there a long while, wondering what to do. Her hands could not support the weight of her body much longer. Farther down, though, there were some long, large rocks that looked like steps. She would have to let go and trust that she would land near them. She was uncertain that her body could manage it, and this troubled her mind. She had only one choice: to let go and jump, then scramble halfway down the mesa, rounding it on the other side. This annoyed her, since she had been trying to reach the top, where she believed she would find the *ñankulawen,* a medicinal plant with great healing powers. But she did find it. As she reached the steps, she noticed a bush growing among the cracks in a rock. She steadied herself on the ground, studied the plant, and cried gratefully. It was the ñankulawen she was looking for. Now all she needed was the *pañil* and the *akachan-lawe,* but these were easier to find. She spotted them on her way back, near the river. She mounted her horse and galloped on.

While Fresia was away, Pirenrayen could not stop crying. Chekeken sang and paced back and forth holding the child, until she was overwhelmed by fever and exhaustion, her cries waned, and she fell into a deep sleep. Chekeken had great faith in Fresia and was sure she would arrive with the medicine at any moment, and that once again, her miraculous hands would revive the patient, restoring her strength. Chekeken had seen Fresia achieve this so many times. How could she not do the same for her granddaughter? With these thoughts, she put Pirenrayen to bed.

When Fresia arrived, she rushed into the house and saw Pirenrayen asleep. She came close, touched her brow, her little hands, and told Chekeken to put water to boil on the fire. She took the plants in her hands, went to the sacred tree, and spoke.

"Here I am, speaking so that you can hear me. Sacred forces of this healing tree, ancient woman tree force, ancient man tree force, young woman tree force, young man tree force, I beg you to hear me. My heart is suffering, my granddaughter is sick. She is pure and full of innocence. Her mother is dead, and I must take care of her; she is my strength and my joy. If you heal her, I will teach her everything I know so that this knowledge will not be lost. She will also speak to you, she will offer her life to you, she will always care for this sacred tree, and she will honor the memory of our ancestors."

Fresia cried, watering the feet of that noble aliwen with her tears; the tree watched over her, shading the tired body of the medicine woman who kept speaking as she knelt, as the sun went down, indifferent to her sorrow, her tears, and her longings.

She went back into the house, relieved. With her mortar, she ground the plants and prepared a poultice for the little girl's belly, one for her chest, and one for her back. She made a concoction with the ñankulawen and gave this to her granddaughter to drink. Soon, the fever and vomiting vanished. After a few days, the girl was laughing and playing. She felt slightly weak, but soon afterward, she was fully cured.

Not only did the plants reveal to Fresia their healing secrets, but they also taught her the power of love and that the more we sacrifice on the way to healing, the more effective the medicine. She had noticed how her mood interfered with her medicinal concoction. *Love is more important than medicine,* she thought, and she smiled in satisfaction as she finally understood the order of the world of healing and clairvoyance.

She was a lawentuchefe; she had a special gift for speaking to the plants and gleaning their medicine. She also had occasional visions. In general, these visions came to her when she observed her patients' urine. She never wondered why they came to her and not some other woman. She accepted her newen, that mysterious and wonderful gift, wanting to learn a little more as each day passed.

They say the plants no longer speak as they did before, that they grow now without spirit. Many humans also grow in this way, never meeting their own souls. The magic pills sold here and there will never be able to banish our deepest pain, no matter how much we pay for them.

For Fresia, the joy that Pirenrayen and Linkoyan radiated when they laughed and played together was a soothing balm. The little girl's first two years were accompanied by the constant presence of Chekeken and her son. But then Chekeken's mother-in-law fell ill, and for a time, they had to return to their own settlement. Fresia Coliman was left alone with her granddaughter.

Chapter 9

The Spirits Know Our Pain

In those years, the Argentine state became fully established. The victors implemented cruel policies against my people. All kinds of atrocities were committed daily, with no exceptions made for children or the elderly. That was why the way our children were raised and educated changed. Severity replaced comprehension, and violence, gentleness. The priests taught them these things in Spanish. They "civilized" them with beatings and other dreadful physical punishments. They whipped the men who worked on the land, shackling them, and displaying them in public to teach the rest of the community a lesson.

It was common for criollo landowners to place Indigenous servants in the stocks. The rape of Indigenous women was considered natural and even essential, so that all the landowners' manly needs would be fulfilled. And so it was deemed necessary to harden my people's temperament and crush their spirit for them to survive these horrors. Of course, this suffering was not exclusive to us; these were cultural ways of the time, brought from Europe. There, abuse and oppression, invasions and slavery had been going on for centuries and were later wielded against us.

Yes, there was no doubt civilization had arrived, and a new world would be imposed upon us. We would witness how all that had once existed on this mapu was swept away like dead leaves on the winds of oblivion.

But Fresia did not allow herself to be swayed by these new ideas, instead enveloping her granddaughter in an aura of profound tenderness and love. This was how she had been raised and taught, and this was how she must go on. Fresia used to tell Pirenrayen that we are not born with fear, that fear is a Wingka illness and that it must be cured. She fed her granddaughter with the hunted meat of the bravest animal, making her drink its blood and sometimes eat its heart. The night was an ally, not an enemy. In the night world dwelled sounds that fell silent with morning's arrival; at night, life took on other forms, and other newen emerged that walked in the darkness, weaving shadows and opaline lights that would take their leave at dawn. That moment, on the faint, fine line of time when night softly kisses day, is the moment of the highest concentration of healing forces, cosmic energies; for this reason, our people hold ceremonies at dawn. *Liwen antu*, we call them. So Pirenrayen grew up brave, without doubts or fears. She accepted everything her grandmother told her with conviction.

In summer, they used to go to the mountains for the animals to graze, and spend the season in the forests there. The little girl loved that landscape.

"Grandmother, why don't we live here all the time?" Pirenrayen asked eagerly.

"Because the winters here are very hard. Snow covers the mountain, the animals have no food, the leaves on the trees dry up, there are no mushrooms, and the animals go down the slopes in search of something to eat. We would not be able to hunt or plant anything here. It's better to stay where we are," Fresia said, as she brushed the little girl's hair.

"Grandmother, why don't you bring the sacred aliwen here? If you did, you could take care of the sick here," Pirenrayen suggested cheerfully.

Her grandmother kept brushing her hair. "Because sometimes, the trees get tired and no longer want to walk; they only want to give birth to themselves as roots. That way, they are in peace, always growing under the same sky, the same moon. And that tree is very special because it was born a long, long time ago, and it followed me, walking a long way, searching for me to offer me the vision and the pewma of the spirits of our ancestors, who know how to heal and guide us. And that's how they keep doing it, they come down to that tree to meet me and tell me what's coming or what's happening that I cannot see. The spirits know us, and they know our pain, our sorrows, and our desires," she said.

"Grandmother, how did you know that tree was the medicine tree?" Pirenrayen asked.

Fresia sat down and sighed. "Sit down, and I will tell you," she said.

The granddaughter obeyed and sat on her knee, and Fresia began her tale.

"It was a long time ago . . . In those days, I was a girl, who knows how old I would have been. I liked to wander around exploring, climbing trees, scrambling up hilltops. Everything called out to me. In those days, the Wingkas did not dare come here. We all lived in peace, with no barbed wire and no danger anywhere. I always took any chance to go out and walk alone. In the middle of the forest, I found a high meadow and a great pampa. There was just one lone tree that was sad and dying. I felt sorry for it, and moved close. Its branches were brittle and broke as soon as I touched them. I had an urge to climb it—I wanted to get to the highest branch in the treetop—but a strong wind stirred, and the tree shook. I fell down and scraped my knee. I cried a little and felt like hugging the tree's trunk, as if it, too, had been hurt." The grandmother laughed in delight at the memory. "I stayed there a long time speaking to it. I couldn't stop talking. New words came into my head, my thoughts, and came out of my mouth, and I couldn't stop them. It was summer, and I had an urge to pick strawberries. It was the pampa, and a lot grew there. Suddenly I needed to pee, and I thought it would be good to go under the tree. When I got up, I saw that the leaves had begun to sprout bright green. I had accidentally watered its roots. *How strange,* I thought. And I kept picking strawberries. The sun was high in the sky by then, and I felt weary. I lay under the tree to sleep a little and awoke in the world of the pewma. The darkness surprised me. I thought I had slept all day and that night had already fallen. *How long have I been asleep?* I wondered. *They're going to be angry with me. Maybe the animals have already gone back by themselves.* Suddenly, a door opened, and I realized I was in a windowless ruka, as if night had swallowed it up. When the door opened, a white light flooded in, as bright as the sun. I felt blinded for a moment, and when I rubbed my eyes to see, it was worse. And when I blinked, do you know what happened to me, my dear?"

The girl shook her head, and Fresia went on with her story.

"There was a very wrinkled and short old woman, like I am now, at my side," she said, laughing again. "She took my hand and smiled, and she took me flying. We were like little birds. We saw everything from above. The mountaintops were beautiful, high, and touching the clouds. My little heart tingled, and we both smiled happily. I remember I could even feel the wind on my face. I wanted to stay there and live in the sky like a little bird, but the old woman squeezed my hand tightly, pulling me through the air, and forced me to go down and land on a giant, flat rock like a table. There were many others, like this one or larger. Some looked like people, others like animals, as if many beings had turned into gigantic stones. They were all red, and beautiful. There, the old woman spread out a colored blanket, and trees and plants sprang up. The forest unfurled and covered everything. I was alarmed because the plants grew enormous, and they spoke to me. Some even chided me! These were the plants I had picked because I liked their fragrance. The trees also grew angry. They told me to take care when I climbed, because it hurt them; they said it made their branches suffer. It pained them, but there were also flowers and bushes that thanked me for having cared for them and for not having trampled them as many children did. I learned what they were called, where they lived, and what illnesses they cured. There were other plants that called to me because they had lights of many colors, but they did not speak to me. The grandmother told me that I was still too young to have the power to name them, to call to them and speak to them . . . and when she said this, I awoke.

"I told the people my dream, so the next day at dawn, we went to hold a *gllelipun*, a ceremony. We made offerings of quinoa muday and maqui smoke. From then on, whenever anyone fell sick, I went to the aliwen to ask for help. When the Wingkas arrived, I did not want to leave. I knew they would kill us if we stayed, but I couldn't bring myself to abandon my tree. I cried a lot, and I even fell ill when we left, but my *ñuke* told me that the tree would find me. I did not know that trees could walk—"

Pirenrayen interrupted, brimming with curiosity.

"How, Grandmother? How do they do it? They don't have feet like us!"

"Come, my dear, come closer," Fresia ordered, and together they looked out of a small glassless window. "Do you see those birds?"

"Yes, Grandmother," the girl answered.

Fresia Coliman went on with her explanation. "Those are the trees' feet. The other animals, too, the bigger ones who walk more serve as legs and feet so that the trees can walk. The wind is their wings that carry their seeds all over. One day, I found it there, where it still stands. I felt such joy when I saw my old friend again!"

Fresia finished braiding the girl's hair. Pirenrayen stood up and suddenly embraced her grandmother.

"Thank you for your story, Grandmother. I promise I will always, always take care of your tree."

The grandmother stroked her little head, answering with a sigh.

"Of course, my little one. I know you will take care of me, of the tree, and of our medicine."

They remained with their arms around each other for a long time, wanting the moment to last forever. So much love did not fit into even a million embraces.

Fresia devoted herself to teaching her granddaughter about herbal medicine. She felt that Pirenrayen had a special sensitivity. Her little hand was light and deft at harvesting plants, and she had learned their names and uses with ease. Pirenrayen learned to hunt, to weave on the loom, to spin. She watched her grandmother closely. Not only was Fresia a good harvester, hunter, and fisher, but she could also wield a knife confidently, quickly butchering the animal and tanning its skin, using it to make all kinds of objects for use in their home.

They needed nothing from the Wingka government. Their pots and dishes were made of clay, with Fresia's own hands. She made the clothing they wore. She preserved the essential seeds for cultivating the land and stored a substantial amount of dried meat. There were still wild potatoes, and food was plentiful in this soil. But barbed wire was erected throughout the territory to enclose the land, and along with this came rifles to guard it. "Indian hunting," as the state called it, never ceased; this criminal act was supported by laws on the violation of private property. For this reason, food was no longer easy to obtain, nor could they simply depend on nature's generosity.

At that time, bartering increased with the Welsh and other settlers who had recently arrived in the area. Not all of them were honest. Some, abusing our trust and our cultural belief in the value of another's word, swindled us and took our land. Some of them came with Ottoman passports from different parts of the Middle East, but all of them were referred to as Turks.

Fresia Coliman was a shrewd businesswoman who did not allow herself to be easily deceived. Furthermore, the absence of a doctor and her essential skills meant that the lives of many were in her hands. A seasoned judge of character and spirit, she knew perfectly with whom to do business and how much to trust them. New products our people had never consumed until then became key necessities. Fresia grumbled about these dietary changes. People came to see her with all kinds of ailments, but in time, she, too, adopted the new goods.

Fresia did not drink alcohol or eat sugar, but she had inherited two vices from her life with Naweltripay: tobacco and yerba maté. Each time the longko had returned to her arms, he brought yerba and tobacco. Over time, it became a loving ritual for them to smoke together in the warmth of the fire, from a clay pipe that she would make and polish, and later burn. She cured the pipe with wineberry and peppertree leaves, and the tobacco took on a rich flavor. They smoked in the afternoon, gazing at the sky. At night, before they slept, with the glowing flames of the hearth, the ritual of pipes and words was repeated. The yerba maté, on the other hand, they drank spontaneously: in the morning, in the afternoon, when a visitor came, or simply when they felt like stopping their work to drink maté for a while, to gaze at each other and talk.

Fresia therefore needed a trustworthy peddler. And she found one in a man who had come from faraway lands, who was not only the grocer who provided her with all that was new in the culinary market, but also her friend and confidant.

Chapter 10

Rituals of Survival

His name was Roig Evans. At first, Fresia was suspicious of him. She knew that his Welsh countrymen took advantage of their special treatment by the Argentine state to encroach on Mapuche territory, pushing us back toward the high mountains, where harsh winters decimated our animals and crops. But with time, Roig Evans came to occupy an essential place in her life.

The Welshman used to visit her for trafkintu, bartering. Welsh immigrants arrived in our territory around the end of 1800. They settled first on the Atlantic coast of what is known today as Chubut. Then a faction moved inland to the cordillera. Most of them were friendly but opportunistic. They had no complaints about the Argentine state's inhumane treatment of the Mapuche and Aónikenk peoples; on the contrary, they accepted their own privileges gratefully. There were other Welsh settlers who acted as hired criminals; they were authorized to kill "Indians," to conduct "territorial cleansings." In this way, swaths of countryside were prepared for the settlers and their families. Many were cowards and did not speak out against the genocide. Even today, there is a local holiday in Chubut to commemorate the so-called riflemen. But their weapons and bullets, blessed by the oppressor and wielded in the name of progress, could not erase from our mapu the life of a people that walks with the feet of Patagonian giants and knows how to listen to secrets whispered by the wind, a people that can unite with the earth to endure through time. That knowledge saved us from disappearance.

Roig Evans never felt at ease among his countrymen. He was drawn to the Mapuche people first by curiosity and then by fondness. He held socialist beliefs and had been driven out of his country for his antimonarchist conduct. As a young man, he had been involved in conspiracies and minor skirmishes against the English. It was nothing serious, but enough for the British forces to be on alert. He felt that his heart had no homeland, but rather an immense humanity that stirred his thirst for justice. He was a skilled ropemaker and knew the blacksmith's art to perfection. The main thing he traded with my people were horseshoes, a custom adopted by the criollos in the early 1900s. His affable and cheerful nature awakened affection in the heart of my people.

Roig Evans and Fresia Coliman met thanks to an absurd and fortuitous accident. Nawelpangui, Fresia's youngest son, was working for him as an apprentice ropemaker. Evans used to go out hunting with the men from the lofche, who would go away for a time in search of the herds of wild horses that could be heard neighing all over the territory. Those unbreakable colts, scattered across Patagonia, were coveted as much by Mapuches as by settlers. It was a great and joyful adventure to go out and scour the country for them, then bring them back to be broken in. Each day, Roig learned from my people the secrets of horse taming and the sacred language of respect for the cosmic order. Back in Wales, he had heard it said that the "savages" of Patagonia were the most bloodthirsty, that they were even cannibals, that the settlers must be sure to avoid them lest they be murdered and gobbled up. But when he came here, reality showed him a very different picture. He saw that, on the contrary, the Mapuches were friendly, hospitable, and vulnerable to the invaders. He also knew that when the voice of the oppressor speaks ill of the oppressed, it is because he fears them, since he has not managed to destroy their dignity and rebelliousness.

Once he was here, Roig Evans began learning a few words in Mapudungun. When he thought he was ready, he loaded his saddlebags with tools, utensils, and food and set off into the wilderness without saying goodbye, determined not to return. He soon found the first Mapuche villages. He was young, strong, adventurous, and curious. He offered his services and was accepted. He settled at the foot of the mountains to live, staying there until his death. In time, he married a hardworking, young Mapuche woman, and they had eleven children. That is why many Mapuches have a Welsh last name—they come from that line. They were neither rich nor poor: Roig promised himself that his family would never go hungry.

This peculiar Welshman adopted all our customs, taking pains to perfect every new piece of knowledge he acquired. But there was one thing that was difficult for him to understand and that only at the end of his days did he comprehend: that knowledge is not a human but a cosmic matter and that it is necessary to close the door of reason to open the door to perception, to magic; you must let yourself be carried along without resisting. Evans learned this when, almost like in a legend, he discovered the existence of a fierce old horse with a shiny coat, dazzling like the full moon and black as the darkest night. His obstinacy left no room for any advice. He insisted on searching for it, capturing it, and making it part of his herd.

My people were getting ready for winter. The first strokes of autumn showed us how the winter would come. The main food was made from dried horse meat. The hunt was viewed as a ritual of survival, in which two species fought respectfully for their right to life. The most untamed animals were freed. Through a ceremony, permission was asked of the *ngen*, the protective spirit, the essence of each species. Then the journey was undertaken. At dawn, in the last folds of the fabric of night, they set out toward the east. Fresia saw them pass the crest of the hill. She had seen Galensho (this was her name for Roig Evans) on few occasions, but they had spoken enough for her to realize what kind of person he was. Fresia was amused by the way he rode his horse, with all his tools

85

loaded on his saddle, which forced him to open his legs very wide. Our people rode bareback and simply hung on to the horse's mane. Fresia also saw her son Nawelpangui among the men riding east.

The first days of the search were long and fruitless. All the tales of the hundreds of free and wild horses grazing in peace and awaiting capture turned into myths, probably sprung from some men's imaginations. Here they were, and they had seen not even a trace of those herds. They had no idea where to go next, so they decided to camp near a gully with a stream passing through it. It was a steep and arid place, and their animals could drink from the stream's cool waters, since the narrow gully was hemmed in by stone and the animals would be well corralled.

The next morning, they awoke to a howling wind. The sand lashed at their skin and got stuck in their eyes; they could hardly see, and it was difficult to move forward. At times, the horses refused to go on, so they stopped, guided by the animals' instinct. Suddenly, they felt the mapu shudder with subterranean energy. It was the wild horses. There were hundreds! They appeared as the wind vanished, as if the horses were challenging it, pushing it far away with their strength. The animals were fat, had shiny coats and long, lustrous manes, and neighed thunderously. The men organized themselves quickly: first they must wear out the animals and spur them on to the end of the gully, where they would corral them; then they would choose their captives at random, lassoing them and rounding them up. They launched into a gallop, determined to take possession of a splendid herd. Some of the men were accustomed to riding in droves of horses. Despite his tender age, Nawelpangui was an expert. Since the time he was very small, Longko Naweltripay had taken him out to catch horses. Roping them was a task for two or three men. Nawelpangui was the strongest and most skilled in the matter. In addition to strength, skill was required, since the horses were strong and put up a lot of resistance. Once the goal was achieved, the most challenging task was left: to trap the lead stallion and enclose him in the corral.

The animal was immense and strong, with a jet-black coat. He stood out among all the others. Evans tried to capture the horse, but he couldn't manage alone. He called out for help, and three strapping youths galloped toward him. They tried to surround him, but the stallion reared on his hind legs, defending himself in desperation, delivering blows with his front hooves. One of the men, watching the display from a distance, drew closer and told Evans to stop torturing the horse, that it was an exceptional stallion and that it must have been chosen by nature as the principal stud to keep that line of *kawels* from dying out. But Roig Evans chose not to listen and, coveting the animal without calculating the risks, approached and decided to lasso it. He twirled his rope with determination and held it firmly. Gradually, the animal gave in and seemed ready to be rounded up. But like the most brilliant strategist devising a plan to escape his captors, the stallion made everyone believe that they had subdued it, and just as they were about to herd it into the corral, it began to buck, pulling Roig Evans off his horse and leaving him tangled in his rope. The price was a fractured arm and a dislocated ankle. That place is still known as Fofo Kawel, Crazy Horse. That was how Galensho learned that you can't have it all, and that human beings are just people and not proprietors.

That curious man was Pirenrayen's first adult friend. The girl would await him eagerly, since beyond the usual provisions, he would always surprise her with something sweet. Pirenrayen would devour it in secret since Fresia disapproved of Wingka fare. Pirenrayen's grandmother was convinced that the new illnesses appearing in the bodies of her people were caused by those strange foods. Galensho told her highly amusing tales from a faraway world so different that the girl couldn't imagine what it was like. Pirenrayen would ask him to sing. There was something in his voice and the way he sang that captivated her, and he liked to teach her the songs of his homeland. She grew up with the advice and company of this great friend.

Friendship has no borders, no language, no age. It occurs spontaneously, free of speculation and selfishness. It is fed by the joy of small and simple shared moments. Its memories make pools in the soul, becoming clear and present. Even when those friends are gone, each memory evoked summons them to the heart, bringing them back to life over and over, since the heart knows no forgetting, nor does the spirit know absences. Friendship is a gift that life brings us when we least expect it, a gift we should only be grateful for.

Pirenrayen felt surrounded by a world of love and joy. Her days were empty of sorrows; these were unknown to her. She knew nothing of rage nor anguish. She was familiar only with the laughter of games, races with her friend Linkoyan, dances made up to the rhythm of her friend Galensho's accordion, and his little gifts. Chekeken's kindness, adventures with her uncles, and the warm company of her grandmother. She never regretted not having a mother or father. That little world of affection, and all that the mapu gave them, made her the happiest girl in the world.

Sometimes she would go to the stream all by herself to gaze at the little fish. "Where are you going, little fish?" she would ask them, or "Is there another river beyond?" All the cleverest questions that occurred to her were made of each element of the mapu, each force or newen the little girl felt inclined to evoke. Then she would dip her chubby little feet in the stream's freezing water, and there she would sing to the sun, the sky, the clouds, all the nature surrounding her. She would lie down and dry herself off, allowing herself to be enveloped by the sun's rays.

Another great friend was her dog, who had arrived in her life as a gift from her uncle Nawelpangui. It had been bred at the English-owned estate where he worked as a blacksmith. As soon as Pirenrayen saw him, so tiny, still just a puppy, she loved him. He was black with a white patch that spread from his head to his snout. The girl hugged the puppy with joy and gratitude to her uncle.

"What are you going to call him?" he asked her.

"Kalkin!" she answered excitedly. "He looks like a black sheep. He's so pretty and woolly!" she said, kissing the animal with a maternal tenderness.

They grew up together and were inseparable. On warm summer days, Galensho always found her at the stream, splashing and playing with Kalkin, or in the company of Linkoyan.

Galensho knew all about children. His wife brought one into the world every year, and they raised them together. It was unusual in those days to see a man holding his children in his arms, feeding them, or playing with them the way that Galensho did. Years later, Pirenrayen would be at his side when his fourth child, whom they would call Nahuel, was born.

Galensho was always alert to Fresia and Pirenrayen's needs. He often came to visit with his whole family, and his older children would play with Pirenrayen. He played the accordion, and they danced to his joyful, improvised tunes. Sometimes, Chekeken and Linkoyan joined them. For both children, he was more than a friend; he was a confidant who was almost like a father, with a hand always stretched out to those who needed his help.

Chapter 11

The Happy Days of Childhood

The rooster drew back the curtain of night with its crow, opening the windows of dawn to receive the sun. Though she was not aware of it, that day, Pirenrayen was turning five. As soon as she woke, she set about getting the fire ready to surprise her grandmother. She felt unusually happy. She seemed, in every fiber of her being, to be overflowing with a colorful joy that lit up her face. Her grandmother attributed this to the spring. She looked tenderly at her granddaughter, who, as each day passed, reminded her even more of her daughter.

Usually, the girl liked to stay a while longer in bed and start the day much later than her grandmother. The old woman would rise when nature's silhouette was beginning to emerge from the fog of dawn, and night's cool fingertips were lifting its black fabric to announce the new day. She would make a fire and put the kettle on to boil, and cook over the embers. It had not been long since wheat had arrived in these lands, and she enjoyed the new flavor of bread. When the aroma spread through the small house, the chubby, sleepy little girl got up so slowly that she seemed to be performing a tortoise's morning dance. She dressed and ran out to the stream that crossed the patio of the house. There, she washed her chapped little face, raw from the cold and the icy wind.

At that time, Pirenrayen was watching for a glimpse of Galensho, who had promised her rolls of licorice on his next visit. She was helping her grandmother when Linkoyan and his mother arrived; they had come to visit and had brought the little girl a tiny orphaned lamb as a gift. How overjoyed she was! They played all day. They liked to stretch out on the grass and gaze at the clouds. They found the shapes of different animals and all kinds of figures in them; they made up adventures, told jokes, and laughed uproariously. They heard the dogs barking and guessed that they were announcing Galensho's arrival. The idea of the candy made them run eagerly to meet him.

For the first time, Pirenrayen, Linkoyan, Fresia, and Chekeken tasted chocolate. In addition to licorice, Evans used to bring them sugared candies, but never chocolate. To the little girl's surprise, her grandmother also bought some tablets of chocolate to keep, which she would later give her as a treat in a loving and affectionate ritual on special occasions. From then on, chocolate became the sweetest way to touch Pirenrayen's heart. In Galensho's saddlebags, she discovered new aromas, distant flavors from mysterious lands that came like spells to bewitch her senses and take hold not only of her body as a growing urge, but of her spirit. Although she had tried chocolate and been delighted, her grandmother, on the other hand, refused to consume those new ingredients. Sugar, for example, was an ingredient for medicinal use in her house. Fresia would burn it and then pour boiling water over it. That bubbling golden sugar was then combined with peppermint, spearmint, and paico.

Every so often, grandmother and granddaughter would take their weavings to town; there they sold them and bought food and household goods. On one of those outings, they discovered the aroma of coffee together. Pirenrayen would taste its intensity many years later, when the love of a man from a distant land would bring it to her.

Fresia was not in favor of changing her habits when it came to food; she did not wish to abandon her ancestors' teachings. She knew there were virtues and strengths in the food offered by nature, from which our spirits are also fed; so she kept hunting, fishing, collecting mushrooms and nuts, indifferent to the metal wires that loomed over the mapu, making threats about "private property." If we are what we eat, Pirenrayen was made of spearmint and honey, of strong, wild meats that were bravely hunted. Her breath smelled of wineberry and calafate berries. Her skin tasted of wild strawberries picked amid laughter and games with Linkoyan. Pirenrayen was Patagonian in body and geometry; she was a spirited maiden, fertile and fresh like the land around her. She grew up fed by the generous essence of a land where nothing but life burst forth.

When he went to visit her, Linkoyan played at challenging her to new adventures, and she accepted and passed all the tests he set for her. She could use a bow skillfully, scramble quickly up the high mesas, and ride like the best horsemen. Linkoyan laughed, thinking with satisfaction that he was responsible for this little person who had the makings of a great woman. Sometimes, they held hands and ran through a broad meadow of yellow flowers that unfurled on the other side of the stream. They chased butterflies, climbed the tallest trees so they could touch the clouds. And in the scorching summers, they went out to watch the lizards—the *fillkun*, as we call them.

"Fillkun, we're going to see your relatives," she would call to her friend, laughing.

Linkoyan would pretend to be annoyed. He would leave his task half-finished, tug sweetly at one of her braids, and run over to the rocky ground where they spent hours playing and watching them.

Linkoyan lived not only on meat and grains, but also on Pirenrayen's laughter. He gulped down her voice in mouthfuls, sucked on her tears, and when he went to sleep at night, he tasted her in his dreams.

After he and his mother returned to live near Pirenrayen and her grandmother, he went out hunting every afternoon and always came back with something for Fresia to cook. Sometimes Pirenrayen accompanied him. They had noticed that the Patagonian maras were disappearing, and wondered what was happening to them. Where could they be going, and why?

One day they were walking together along the riverbank. Kalkin set off ahead at a run. A shrill cry rang out, a wail they'd never heard before. Kalkin barked desperately. The children were frightened and hurried to catch up with the dog. Kalkin was biting an odd-looking small animal with long ears. It looked like a mara, though it was smaller. Pirenrayen leaned down to hold it, but Linkoyan stopped her.

"Don't touch it," he ordered. She grew scared. He took a long, thin willow stick and began to prod the strange animal that lay there dead. It was a hare, perhaps among the first to be introduced to the territory. They did not dare take it with them. They believed it was a water spirit that had escaped from the lagoon.

In time, the hares bred so much that they spread all over Patagonia. Once, someone hunted one and tasted its meat. They found it delicious and announced the discovery to their whole lof. Soon, the people went out to hunt in a group, and later, they discovered the virtues of the hares' pelts. Pirenrayen and Linkoyan were excited to see one leaping through the meadow and chased after it with cries and laughter. Kalkin became an expert hare hunter, and Fresia a great cook of hare stews. Whenever my grandmother saw a hare, she recalled her childhood with Linkoyan. She sighed with nostalgia for those happy days of her childhood.

PART TWO

Chapter 12

In a Magical, Unknown Land

Liam O'Sullivan was born in the glowing autumn of 1900. Dublin was dressed in its finery to welcome him, its ground carpeted with crisp leaves of crimson, orange, and yellow. His mother, Sarah Tinnan O'Sullivan, awaited him eagerly. The birth was arduous, since the baby was enormous and his mother's hips narrow, but she endured with stoicism the strong blows with which Liam fought to enter the world. That was how he began his life, making his way between pain and desire, the only child of an older couple. A teacher by profession, his mother was fond of children. Yet for many years, life had denied her a child. When she learned she was pregnant, the happy couple threw a party to announce the news. Sarah kept to her bed, ate the best fruits and vegetables, and allowed her husband and family to pamper her, until the long-awaited day finally arrived.

Niall O'Sullivan, the father, a humble baker and self-taught musician, chain-smoked anxiously as he watched the nurses' comings and goings. He had a stutter and could speak fluently and without interruption only through music. In his home city, he was famous for his marvelous tin-whistle playing. He waited for a nurse to bring news of his wife and son, feeling both thrilled and terrified. He loved Sarah so much that the mere idea of the pain and suffering of childbirth made him feel guilty, responsible for something miraculous but also excruciating. He was always on the alert, as if she were a delicate flower with glass petals that might shatter at the slightest touch. When the beautiful, bouncing baby boy was born, Niall was overcome with joy.

Niall was eighteen years old when he met Sarah. He watched her enter his father's bakery like an ethereal figure, as if she had emerged from a fairy tale. She was slender. She had reddish hair, a kind face, and intensely green eyes. They crossed paths fleetingly, long enough for him to feel that he would love her for the rest of his life. She, for her part, had seen him long before, when she moved a few blocks away from the bakery to live with her older sister, her brother-in-law, and their small son. Sarah had come to Dublin to study; she wanted to be a teacher. At a tender age, she opened herself to the world, a ferocious world, full of uncertainty, but for her, also fascinating and brimming with novelty. It was not easy for her to leave her home with so few resources. But sustained by her dreams and desires, she set out to find what she was searching for. Her story is like those of so many women all over the world.

Niall was a shy and highly talented young man. His music beguiled women with its romance and spread joy at family gatherings. He played his tin whistle in church like an elevated liturgical offering at special services. He was not gifted with words, and though he might have easily won the heart of any girl, he had reached that age single and still a virgin. His parents tried to cure his stutter in various ways, but music was the best of all, not because it really cured his stutter but because it offered him, in its place, the sound of the whistle.

Sarah decided to woo her beloved, unaware that his heart was already hers. She stopped in daily to buy bread. In those hard times for the Irish, when sales were dwindling and the English were raising taxes for the Crown to squander, both Sarah and Niall always found a way, wordlessly, one to buy and the other to sell.

Then, in the autumn of 1887, British forces furiously invaded Dublin. There were bullets and beatings. Before the terrified gaze of children who played in the streets, swords cut through many innocent bodies, giving them no time to escape. People who were walking the streets at that time were imprisoned without explanation. Amid the tumult and panic, Sarah ran desperately into the bakery. Without saying a word, she embraced Niall, who along with others, was shielding himself from the bullets.

There was no need for grandiose declarations of love or improvised poems for both to be sure that they would be spending the rest of their lives together. Three months after that episode, they were married.

Liam was the happy couple's only child. Sarah had suffered two miscarriages before Liam was born, so she considered his arrival a miracle. The baby cemented that humble, hardworking family's love. The couple felt fortunate: compared with the poverty and hunger most Irish people endured, they were well off. Niall had hired two loyal and trustworthy employees. Sarah left her job and devoted herself fully to their son. Each time she fed or changed him, she cried with joy. She prayed several times a day, asking God to protect him from any illness or pain. He was a long, slender baby. She smothered him with tenderness, kisses, and affection.

As soon as he began to walk, his father started taking him to the bakery. There he acquired a special kind of sensitivity: with his acute sense of smell, he could distinguish the aroma of different kinds of firewood and imagine which forest they came from. He loved going to the bakery with his father. The warmth of the ovens, the smell of the bread, and the sight of the fire lulled him. He used to fall asleep under the large table where the men kneaded bread as they chatted and laughed.

He grew up amid his father's brusqueness and his mother's sweetness. From his mother, he inherited his red hair and large green eyes; but his lips, chin, and mouth were classic O'Sullivan features. Friends and relatives praised the boy's beauty. His face took on certain feminine features that perplexed people and gave rise to comments that were out of place. Sarah taught him to be faithful and fair and instilled love and gentleness in him, as well as a great fear of God and a strong dose of guilt and apprehension, all of which seeped into the depths of his heart. His father observed this and forced him from a young age into hard labor and demanding sports.

His grandparents indulged him in everything, and he relished playing with the neighborhood children; yet despite all this, Liam was shy and overly obedient. On Sundays, they took the train to visit his maternal grandparents nearby. He adored those outings, and he adored the train. Niall was a great admirer of the railways and instilled this love of trains in his son. Thanks to his mother's dedication, Liam learned to read and write before starting school, while his father taught him to play the tin whistle. He began school along with his friends from the neighborhood, and they enjoyed themselves greatly together. From a young age, he shared generously with other children. He was an excellent student and helped his classmates with their studies.

Sarah tried in vain to have another child but kept losing her pregnancies. In time, she accepted her fate and decided along with her husband that it would do her good to go back to work. She returned to the classroom to teach.

Liam and Sarah would return home together at the end of their days. She from a humble school on the other side of the city, and he from his school a few blocks away from their house. When he left the school, Liam would kick tins and stones on his way, playing soccer with his friends. The uneven cobbled streets seemed to let out a wail each time the tins or stones, transformed into the highly prized soccer ball, skittered across them. When he was at his father's bakery, he waited eagerly for his mother. She was always hurrying, sweet and affectionate. Liam adored his mother. His father was quiet and sparing with words due to his temperament and his stutter. But he was also strong and energetic. Liam feared and had great respect for him. But although he loved him, communication between them was difficult.

Liam would rush through his homework so that he could play with the train his father had bought him. It was a miniature railway, with stations, an engine car, cargo and passenger carriages, bridges, railways, tunnels, and mountains. All this made up an imaginary world of adventure for little Liam, with his dreams of becoming a railwayman. His world of adventure was expanded by books. Then there was tea with his mother, who sometimes surprised him with a cup of hot chocolate, and the delicious cookies his father made at the bakery. Liam's affection for his loved ones and his exploits with his neighborhood friends in the streets of Dublin made him feel like the happiest boy in the world.

The streets of that city were teeming with poor children roaming from here to there, many of them orphans. In winter, the days were short and cold, and a good coat was a luxury few could afford. But Liam was untroubled by this; his parents made sure he lacked nothing. One day, he saw a boy with whom he had played a few times shivering with cold on the pavement outside a restaurant. He must have been the same age, scarcely six years old. The little boy was mute and had made a strong impression on Liam, who took off his coat and wrapped it around the boy. When he arrived home, he tried to pass unnoticed, but his mother realized right away.

"Where is your coat?" asked Sarah.

His father, who was absorbed in reading the paper, looked up and said, "Y-y-your mother asked you a qu-question. A-answer her."

Liam lowered his head and answered fearfully in a voice that could hardly be heard, "I gave it away."

"I ca-ca-can't hear you," said his father. "Sp-speak louder p-p-please."

"I gave it away!" said Liam, almost shouting.

His father flew into a rage, shook him violently, and forced him to admit to whom he had given it.

They went outside in search of the mute little boy, finding him in the same place Liam had left him. The little boy lay dead, and the coat was gone. He had been brutally beaten. Father and son were aghast. Liam ran directionless through the streets in desperation. When he reached the train tracks, he began to cry out with rage and burst into sobs, overcome with sorrow and heartbreak.

A peeler, a British policeman, standing guard at the train station, approached Liam with an air of harshness, wanting to toy with him.

"What are you up to so late here, boy? You shouldn't be so far from home. You must've run away. Where are you from?" he asked curiously.

Liam bowed his head and did not answer. The peeler approached him furiously, seizing him by the hair.

"I asked you a question," he insisted. "Where do you live? Have you lost your tongue?" The boy stayed silent. The peeler grew enraged, and shouted, "What's the matter with you Irish? Are you all cowards?"

Then the peeler mockingly confessed to his crime.

"You're the second mute boy looking for trouble I've found in these streets. Do you know what happened to the other little thief who wouldn't answer me? Do you want to know what I did to him?" he said as he began to beat Liam. "You're thieves, vagrants, and troublemakers, the lot of you. You need to be taught to respect us from a young age. That other boy wouldn't tell me who he'd stolen his coat from."

"Murderer, murderer!" Liam cried, attracting the attention of the few people in the station at that hour. When they saw what was happening, they tried to help him. Suddenly, from among the crowd, Liam's father appeared, brandishing his fist and felling the peeler with a single left hook. He picked up his son in his arms and took him home, Liam feeling his heart about to burst out of his chest, choking on tears and rage, bitterness and indignation.

Perhaps that was the exact moment Liam O'Sullivan grew up, the moment the sweet goodness and innocence of a child were crushed by the weight of seven hundred years of his people's colonial subjugation. He could not understand the evil, the inequality, or the tyrannical power of those who believed themselves superior. The British offered them hunger, torture, and death in return for the riches of Irish land. *Why did I give him my coat? I should have ignored him, perhaps then he would still be alive,* he reproached himself over and over.

That night, Liam had a fever and vivid dreams. His parents tried to lower his temperature, but at one point, he felt his spirit detach from his body. He saw himself in a strange land where everything was covered in snow and gave off a white light that seemed as if it would blind him. Suddenly, an enormous bird with a white ring around its neck swooped down so elegantly that he stopped to gaze at it despite the cold. The bird perched before him. Liam fixed his gaze on it, and the bird seemed to grow angry. It rose and began to flap threateningly around him. Liam looked desperately for something to defend himself with. He realized that he was wearing his pajamas and was freezing cold. He saw a stone and picked it up, determined to toss it at the bird. But just as he was about to do so, a little girl intervened. She spoke to him in a language he did not know but that, inexplicably, he understood. She told him not to harm the bird, not to kill it. He shuddered with fear. She looked at him sweetly and began to speak.

"Do not kill me if you want to live. All beings contain good and evil. For there to be day, there must be night. For there to be light, there must be darkness. For there to be joy, we must know sorrow. Your life is my flight. You are tied to me. Do you reject what you are, and what you carry inside? I come from you, and I have come to take care of you."

The girl stopped speaking and was transformed into a condor, a bird Liam had never seen in his life, and rose until she was lost on the horizon. He wanted to run after her, but his feet were buried deeper and deeper in the snow. He felt an immense loneliness and began to cry. Then he awoke.

His mother was by his side, speaking to him, putting cold compresses on his brow, and giving him water. His father was in the sitting room with a doctor who had come to examine him. After a few days, his sickness improved, but he could never forget the dream that had seemed to him so real. The little girl's face, her expression. Her speech was so distant and strange, yet so familiar and heartfelt.

From then on, whenever he found himself in danger, that little girl and the exotic bird returned to speak to him in his dreams, making him fly across magical, unknown lands.

Chapter 13

THEIR DREAMS RODE THE RAILS

His childhood was happy despite the reality that lay in wait. Liam and his friends spent hours trying to entertain themselves. Liam O'Sullivan, John Walton, Sean Campbell, and Ernest Beckett played constantly. The train tracks were their meeting place. They were all the same age, except for little Ernest, and they believed they were inseparable. They were about to turn nine when an unforeseen episode changed their lives.

Liam loved all his friends very much, but the most beloved among them was John Walton, who was like a brother to him. He was the son of a longshoreman, a widower. John was the youngest of five brothers. He had one considerably older brother who worked alongside their father, and the three others took strict care of him. He was playful, brave, sharp, and highly adventurous—qualities Liam admired. John was scarcely two months older than Liam but had taken him under his wing. He was a natural leader and sternly commanded the most mischievous gang in the port neighborhood. He was always dreaming up different things to do, all of them entertaining, to break the monotony and rigor of how the adults wanted them to spend their days.

John had met Liam through Ernest Beckett, who lived on the same block. Ernest's mother was a widow and worked as a maid at the hospital. Ernest spent long hours without his mother, playing with friends. John Walton loathed the English, was always getting into trouble, and dreamed of growing up to be a fighter in the Irish Republican Brotherhood. His uncle, while still a teenager, had followed the ideas of the nationalist leader Charles Stewart Parnell closely. When he became a man, he joined the Irish Republican Brotherhood. And though this uncle's youth was fading, he still maintained his spirit of enthusiasm and shared his ideas and dreams of freedom and justice with his nephew. He even took John to occasional meetings. That was where John's passion for the independence struggle was born, which also influenced Liam.

Liam's mother, Sarah, was cold and uncongenial with little John. She considered the friendship between that boy and her son inappropriate. John Walton lacked good manners and wandered the streets of Dublin all day. He was a terrible student. But what caused her the most anxiety was that his dreamy, adventurous spirit might lead her little Liam astray.

Despite what their parents thought, the boys enjoyed their afternoons playing soccer with friends and making trains out of tins from preserves and other discarded objects they found in the street. When Liam turned nine, his father bought him his first bicycle. With this, Liam felt like a true explorer. In the summers, they held swimming races, looking for dangerous cliffs to climb and sometimes even diving into the sea.

But without any doubt, what most appealed to Liam and his friends was playing on the trains. All of them wanted to be engine drivers. Their dreams rode the rails, with thunderous whistles announcing arrivals and departures. The smells wafting around the train yard seemed to them a sublime perfume. The aroma of burning coals and petrol mingled with the stink of the animals, both the horses that pulled the carts and the animals that were transported; the fishmongers; the greengrocers; the women selling food. It was a tremendous, malodorous wave. They went out and vied for its ineradicable memory.

Some pedestrians and railway workers felt drunk with pleasure, while others found the atmosphere repulsive and kept their noses buried in their embroidered, lightly perfumed white handkerchiefs. Liam hovered, listening to the railway's music. The rough sound of the train pounding the rails seemed to him a metallic symphony inviting him to dance, to run, to unfurl his soul. Each quaver, each note, was accentuated by the train's enticing swagger. The whistle announced the final cadence of a sonorous journey, distancing him from his imagination and returning him to a bustling, chaotic reality.

One of Liam's favorite pastimes was to go around midday to the station, just at the time it seemed bursting with people. Salesmen, relatives who'd come to say farewell to their loved ones, travelers arriving, lovers prolonging their embraces before their imminent separation. The smell of food. Newspaper boys selling the paper, crying out the latest headlines. Women loaded with baskets of flowers, selling bunches of roses and daffodils. Soldiers and workers, all hurriedly taking their place on the platform. Railway life seemed to swarm all around him.

They would run amid laughter and adrenaline from the school to the station, trying to see who could get there first. The last to arrive took care of distracting the guard while the others quickly climbed into the first carriage they saw. Then he had to find just the right moment to disappear before the guard's eyes and clamber into the train. Each day, they agreed to meet in a different carriage, from the lowest class to the inaccessible first class, where the berths were located. They knew exactly how long the train stayed at the station. When the whistle announced its departure, they waited until the train started up to throw themselves out. Sometimes they hurt themselves, but at others, they escaped with creative, athletic movements that provided an interesting spectacle for the other passengers. Over and over, they repeated the same routines, and the guards never spotted them in time to take pleasure in punishing them by throwing them off the train. John was the mastermind and the leader of this conspiracy. He gave the order to board the train and to escape. Liam trusted him blindly. He thought John was the bravest and cleverest of them all.

One sunny afternoon beneath a bright-blue sky in the early summer of 1912, they went to a railway bridge. They made bets to see who was brave enough to cross without fearing its height, a risky proposition since in some stretches the sleepers were missing. The danger gave them a thrill. They egged each other on, hugging and applauding one another as they accomplished the feat. John was the first to cross. Sean Campbell and Liam followed him, sauntering from one end of the bridge to the other. Ernest Beckett, the smallest of them, hesitated and froze with fear as he stared into the abyss. He did not want to cross, and his friends understood. He said he would sit on a big rock near the bridge and wait for them. They could see how the little boy watched them with admiration and joy from his perch.

Just then, another gang of boys arrived, led by a youth with whom they were all too familiar, a braggart who was the son of an Englishwoman and a Unionist Irishman. When they saw the defenseless boy, they began to tease him. "Coward," they said, tormenting him. John shouted at them to leave Ernest alone, but they only increased their cruelty. They started pushing and beating him. Ernest managed to slip out of the braggart's hands, but ran away toward the bridge in fright and began to cross. When he reached the middle, he came to a wide gap between one sleeper and the next. There were several sleepers missing, and he didn't dare jump. He tried to cross. As he stood there, hesitant, his friends encouraged him, crying, "Come on, Ernest, you can do it! Cross!" until a whistle warned them of a train's arrival. Ernest shuddered and was so paralyzed with fear that he could neither retreat nor advance. His friends cried for him to hurry. When the train was upon him, all he could do was hang, holding on to one of the tracks for dear life with just one hand. He closed his eyes. The train barreled over him and severed his hand. Ernest plummeted into the river, howling with pain. As soon as the boy fell, some nearby shepherds plunged into the river and managed to save him. He was alive, but he was drowning in pain and terror. The children who had been teasing him went off satisfied with the result. Some felt fear and sadness, but the oldest felt powerful and continued to mock the little boy.

At school, the empty desk submerged Liam and his friends in sorrow. Ernest lost his right hand, and then a few weeks later his forearm, which had become infected, forcing the doctor to amputate. It would be a long time before he recovered, and when he grew up, he hated the sight of his stump. For a time, all of them felt despondent and guilty.

A few weeks after the incident, John revealed a new plan to his friends. He wanted to avenge what had happened to Ernest. The boy responsible for the accident was the son of an Anglican bishop. They would venture to the forbidden end of the city under the cover of night to break all the windows of the Anglican church where the boy lived. John had it all planned out.

Liam went to bed arousing no suspicions at all, and when he was sure that his parents were sleeping deeply, he crept silently downstairs from the bedroom to the sitting room and toward the door with determination. Without making a sound, he drew back the lock softly, turned the doorknob, and went out into the street.

At first, he walked uncertainly, fearfully, but he soon sped up his pace and continued steadily to the meeting place they had agreed upon. John was already there and was pleased to see him. They had to wait for Sean, who always arrived late, usually due to his mother's strict watchfulness. It was difficult for him to slip away without her spotting him; she seemed alert to every movement in the house. But this time, like so many others, he managed to escape.

They had to walk a long way to the other tip of the city. Their progress was betrayed by dogs announcing their steps with ferocious barks. When they reached their destination, John looked at his friends and asked, "Did you bring them?"

His friends removed an abundance of stones and marbles from their pockets. With their catapults, they began shooting at the church's great windows. Their shots were so precise that the glass panes shattered into smithereens. The sound of broken glass and dogs barking awoke the neighborhood, and the church's caretaker came out to see what was going on. When they heard the ruckus, some nearby policemen ran over and caught them red-handed. They took them to the police station.

The police notified Niall O'Sullivan, John's father, and Sean's parents that their boys were in custody. They had to endure arrogant speeches from the superintendent before the boys were released. The sermon also included the parents, who were warned that if their boys were caught making trouble again, they would be sent to reform school.

Outside the police station, as they were leaving, Sean's mother began to cry. Her husband grew cross and reproached her.

"This is all I need. Don't cry here, woman!" He seized his son brusquely by the ear and told him off. "I don't just have to work all day so you want for nothing, you also expect us to watch you around the clock to make sure you behave decently!"

John's father intervened, but Mr. Campbell was so angry that he would not let him speak.

"All this is *your* son's fault," Mr. Campbell insisted. "If your son hadn't led mine astray, this wouldn't be happening. Sean told me it was his idea to go to the railway bridge."

For John, these words were like a slap in the face. He stared at his friend with disappointment and reproach. Sean blushed and hung his head in shame.

John's father exploded with anger and answered him. "Those are cowardly words. You know those other boys were responsible for the tragedy, but it's easier to take it out on John than the Anglican Unionists." He grabbed his son's hand furiously and marched off without saying goodbye.

Liam and John looked at each other as he was pulled away.

The happy days seemed to be over. It was clear that they would no longer have the freedom to be together. Liam was punished and for a time was not allowed out of his house. Sean Campbell kept going to school but was forbidden to speak to his friends. John Walton left school that year and started to work, which gave him an abrupt introduction to the adult world. The demands made of his young body in the train warehouses and carriages, carrying heavy sacks of grain and potatoes, led him to view the world through different eyes. But the playful sweetness that dwelled in his spirit never abandoned him. In time, all the boys would begin to long for those happy childhood years.

Every so often, Liam would write to his friends. He felt overcome by a dull and despondent apathy. When he tried to convince his parents to allow him to go out and meet his friends, they wouldn't let him. That year, he resigned himself to studying at home with his mother. The only one he saw often was little Ernest. His mother would accompany him on his visits to the hospital. At first, these visits left him feeling heavy with anguish, nerves, and discomfort. He relived that tragic afternoon over and over, the evil of those other boys, the reckless idea of crossing the bridge. Nothing provided relief from his guilt.

Later, as an adult, Liam would discover that no one can be happy in a world governed by evil, that children and adults are alike in their pain and fear. That injustice cuts through the fabric of goodness and innocence, wresting peace away from us. This fabric must be sewn back up inside us; but each stitch made by the needle pricks our memory, making it bleed again. Our spirit wails when the needle stabs through us, sewing our past into a single cloth with our present, because we cannot walk our path in life when it is torn in two.

We must thread the needle and stitch together our soul.

Chapter 14

The Oppressed Peoples of the World

Summer slipped quickly away with the warm breeze that came in through the bedroom window. Liam saw the trees painted with brush-strokes of yellow, orange, and ocher. Then he watched as they unhurriedly shed their majestic robes and stood naked. Winter had arrived, covering the streets with its alabaster blanket. His father took him to work at the bakery. John and Sean would sometimes buy bread from him and tell him about the news from the neighborhood and the streets.

Christmas 1913 was drawing near. Liam's parents agreed that he had been sufficiently punished, that he could now enjoy his friends' company once again. Liam convinced all their parents to let them collaborate on building a sleigh. John was the most skilled at carpentry and could be very useful. Liam argued that they owed it to Ernest and that they would make it especially for him. He was convincing, and the parents allowed their daily meetings. For two weeks, the three boys worked hard until they had built a beautiful sleigh, one that adjusted to their friend's new physical state. The Christmas present touched not only Ernest, but also his family.

They went out to try it and roared with laughter as they sledded thunderously down the streets, delighted by the gentle dips in their path. The four friends were together again and regained the joy and vitality of their earlier adventures.

But with the arrival of the war, the dawn of these boys' lives was about to be torn away like pages from a calendar.

On July 28, 1914, when the First World War was declared, John was deeply absorbed in his work. He was only fourteen, but since he had to contribute money to his household to survive, he seemed to have suddenly grown up. He no longer sought out his friends to play. He was always busy and had become a pragmatic young man and a realist. While Liam continued to be bohemian, imaginative, sensitive, and fearful, John could sometimes be brash and cold. Those things that make us sublimely human had not yet been stripped away from Liam.

My people, the Mapuche, are all too familiar with the atrocities of war. Those little things that make up our daily lives and make us feel part of a small and wonderful world—the simplicity of bread still warm on the table, the aroma of coffee wafting around us, the postman chatting at our door as he leaves a letter, our neighbor sweeping the path—all of this is foreign to war. War, that nightmare whose scale is impossible to grasp until it turns our lives upside down with a bombing. How could we not understand the Irish and all the oppressed peoples of the world? It is so easy to feel a kinship with those invaded nations deprived of their freedom. Imposed borders disappear when the outstretched hands of different peoples form a circle of solidarity for peace.

Every so often, the friends would meet at the train station. Under the eaves of the big warehouses, smoking in secret, they would delight in the adventures Liam read about in his books. When they were by the sea, they would watch the sunset, the immense red disk disappearing, dyeing everything bloodred, burning above the houses and people. They liked to spot the boats' different flags and guess where they came from. They imagined themselves adventuring out in the world. When the sun shone brightly, the park sheltered them under its leafy old trees, welcoming them with a sweet, warm air. If it was drizzling, the best refuge was a decaying carriage abandoned to the passage of time. Anywhere the sun warmed their bodies was an ideal place to read. Liam would take out the book he had hidden among his clothes and share his latest literary discoveries with his friends. When he was a child, his parents did not allow him to lend books or remove them from their home, so this ritual gave rise to a clandestine pleasure that soon became a habit. In those days, books were expensive and difficult to procure. Liam would share with his friends captivating tales of some distant adventure, tales of castaways lost on paradise islands or headless horsemen roaming the streets of London on a dark night. But what he most loved to share was his enthusiasm for all that came from the New World: the Americas!

The American continents revealed themselves to Liam as a mysterious and fantastic world. He had read chronicles of the settlers in the United States, about the fierce resistance of the natives to the whites, and about the bravery and love of the settlers who wished to bring civilization and the Christian faith to the Indigenous people. His mother always prayed for the priests and nuns who abandoned the warmth and comforts of home to live among barbaric Indians in the hope of converting them to Christ and wresting those souls destined for hell away from the devil.

One day, he heard his father speaking with other men about Patagonia, a vast land in the south of the world, inhabited by giants: cannibal giants who ate the hearts of their enemies, and lustful women who wore only animal skins to cover their nudity. His friends were especially interested in the details of these naked and lusty women. These were details that Liam made up with a comic edge, since he had never seen a naked woman before.

Sean was the quietest of the four and seemed always withdrawn. He showed little enthusiasm for anything, but he always accompanied his friends. He had a beautiful sister, Christine, who was the object of the first stirrings of love for both Liam and John. Each time he visited his friend, Liam saw her. He loved to watch her play the piano. She was sweet, quiet, and shy. He was captivated by her chestnut curls. Her beautiful face, those big blue eyes, and her freckled cheeks gave her an angelic air. Sometimes, Christine joined them on the walk to school, talking and showing her perfect teeth when she laughed. John also felt a strong attraction to her. The two friends grew jealous, competing for her attention and approval. Sometimes their games became a grotesque boxing or wrestling match. Without meaning to, Christine had such an effect on them that they both grew up vying for her love.

On rainy days, Liam recalled that as a child, he was not allowed outside. From his bedroom window, he saw how the other children ran and jumped in puddles, frolicking in the rain. When he tired of watching them, he would lie on his bed and read. Thanks to his imagination and the power of books, his room became a dense jungle, humid, tropical, and full of danger. At other times, his room was a train fleeing at high speed from the villainous Indians who called for his death. And without exception, Liam always rescued his beloved, who was of course the beautiful Christine.

But while Liam daydreamed and allowed himself, in his innocent mind, to take her hand, walk with her, and even give her a kiss, John was moving gradually toward making those dreams a reality.

Childhood lay behind them, and youth blossomed in their bodies, bursting with vitality and desires. They had been rivals for Christine's love for four years when John finally managed to seduce the young woman's innocent heart. She felt irresistibly drawn to this boy who carried himself with such confidence. John was attentive and gallant. He would always bring her flowers or some other kind of surprise. Christine would blush, shy and coquettish.

For his part, Liam would write her letters and poetry, but she hardly read them. Her innocent, youthful heart belonged to one owner, and this was John. While Liam realized that the girl's glances and her captivating smile were meant for his friend, he still did everything in his power to gain her attention. The two boys knew they were rivals in love, yet this had little effect on their friendship. The tension was only apparent in her presence.

Each afternoon, Christine waited for John when she came out of her piano lesson. They would walk together along Dublin's cobbled streets to Phoenix Park. She felt safe by his side. She would glance at him secretly, engrossed in his neck, his back, his shoulders, his face. She felt captivated by his charming smile, the expression of his lips, the way he raised an eyebrow when he asked a question. She was attracted to his jet-black hair, his pale skin, and his rosy cheeks. But what she liked most of all—so much, in fact, that it unsettled her—was the way he gazed at her with his big blue eyes. It was a very particular gaze, reflecting admiration and desire. The boldness of this free and dreamy young man had caused her to fall hopelessly in love. She dreamed of marrying him, though she was aware of his reputation as a womanizer. Sean said that all the girls who knew him were rivals for John's heart. But Christine felt that she had already won it.

When he turned fifteen, John Walton began to collaborate with his uncle on small jobs for the Irish Citizen Army, an armed group that had arisen to defend the workers. One of John's older sisters, Ciara, had become involved with Cumann na mBan, the Irish women's army, an independent organization of the Irish Republican Movement. That year, her main job was to sew uniforms with other women. Ciara was dark haired with large emerald-green eyes. She was extremely bad tempered, and though John had long left his childhood behind, she continued to treat him like a little boy. This infuriated him.

One afternoon in the summer of 1915, Ciara brought her friend Deidre home. As soon as John saw her, he felt he would never stop loving her. He thought she was beautiful. She was a mature young woman, perhaps ten years older than he was, and full of determination. Her eyes shone with bravery and enthusiasm.

My grandmother taught me that the twinkle in someone's eye is the pupil of their soul. What must it look like in the eyes of a woman willing to wrest her dreams from fate? I imagine that Irish women must be like Mapuche women when their eyes light up with so much passion for life.

Deidre's presence made John tingle all over, erasing Christine's image in a single stroke.

At that time, John and Christine had been courting in secret. Christine was afraid that her parents would find out. She knew all too well that her mother did not like John. Their romantic relationship had begun during Liam's absence the previous summer. Every summer, Sarah and Niall went on vacation to the country to see Sarah's family, and they made Liam stay with them for part of the vacation. As a child, Liam had enjoyed this, but as he grew older, he missed the city, his friends, and Christine.

Liam, oblivious to his friends' romance, patiently awaited the right moment to declare his love to Christine. Meanwhile, also patiently awaiting the right moment was John, who now wished to end his relationship with Christine without hurting her feelings.

So when Christine embroidered John a handkerchief with their initials as a token of love, John gently rejected the gesture, saying that he had decided to be alone to concentrate more on important tasks to help his people's struggle. He told her he didn't wish to hurt her, but that his heart and mind were now focused on other things. She asked for more of an explanation but did not receive it. She begged, cried, and finally fled, sprinkling the streets of Dublin with tears.

Christine locked herself in her room for a week. Her parents believed she was sick. She neither ate nor spoke, and if anyone tried to approach her, she burst into tears.

They took her to the doctor. She allowed herself to be led, wishing that she could die then and there or for the doctor to diagnose her with a terrible illness that would fill John with guilt and remorse and make him return to her. But none of this was to be. The doctor examined her and asked for them to be left alone. Then he questioned her. He discovered that all her ills were caused by a common affliction known as lovesickness.

No one ever learned what had happened in the doctor's office, but Christine emerged strong and determined, as if the episode had been a minor mishap. When she reached home, she ate, drank tea, spoke, and took up her embroidery.

From then on, Christine was cold and aloof toward John. When he was with her brother in the sitting room, she pretended not to notice him. She also decided to change her routine, and now it was Liam who waited with his bicycle when she came out of her piano lessons. John remained blind to all these changes: his interests lay elsewhere and were not amorous but political.

The Irish also had their great longkos. Many of them had to leave their lands due to the persecution they suffered at the hands of the English. One of these was Jeremiah O'Donovan Rossa, who died on June 29, 1915, in New York. He had been a member and leader of the Irish Republican Brotherhood, which fought for independence and for the creation of a republic. His widow asked her dead husband's brethren to hold a public funeral in Ireland. This event was a prelude to what was to happen later, at Easter 1916. Occasionally, those who give their lives for the unity and freedom of their people achieve by their death what they could not when they walked the world. A funeral can give rise to a birth.

Just like his friends, Liam became involved in small logistic tasks to help with the funeral's organization. Thousands and thousands of Irish people came from all over the country to bid farewell to their leader. In those July days, a feeling of pride and duty burst forth. The solemn farewell to their leader imbued them with love and solidarity, uniting and galvanizing them and giving them hope. The funeral finally took place on August 1 of that year. The streets were painted three colors, the cobblestones rang out to the steps of the military march accompanying the coffin, and thousands of Irish men and women sang and cheered for their leader. For the first time their faces seemed lit with hope.

Though it may seem strange, freedom fighters do not fully leave when they die; rather, they are multiplied. Not even death can get the better of them. They are transformed into a rainbow of unity and rebellion, a bridge between the people and their dreams. In those days, the cloud of war hung over life in a Europe racked with poverty and drained of color. Yet Ireland, accustomed to pain and suffering, displayed other hues, and was recovering the strength of its history, its roots, and the winds of freedom blowing close to its heart.

After the funeral, John and his friends were reaffirmed in their desire to join the struggle. They were ready to devote themselves to it fully, come what may.

Chapter 15

LEARNING TO SPEAK FROM THE HEART

That year, Liam had finally decided to confess his feelings to Christine. He felt as if he'd explode inside if he didn't. Many times he had imagined how he'd do it, even rehearsing the words he would say. In the end, nothing went as he had planned.

One hot day in July, Sean, Ernest, and Liam went for a ride on their bikes, skirting the edge of the River Liffey. They raced each other to the water, enjoying the coolness of the liquid and playing and laughing more than they had in a long time. They collapsed happily on the grassy riverbank and reminisced about their childhood. Liam let out a sigh of pleasure.

"Now I understand why they call it a bed of strawberries . . . ," he said to his friends, closing his eyes and surrendering to the sun, which lulled his senses with its warmth.

The friends gazed at the clouds, absorbed in the contemplation of their gradual drifting. Suddenly, Liam confessed to his friends, "I'm in love with Christine, and I want to marry her. What do you think? Will she accept?" He turned to see the expression worn by Sean, who was lying next to him, with his eyes closed.

"I don't think so. She likes John," Sean answered calmly.

Liam sat up to better question his friend. "How do you know? Did she tell you?"

"No," Sean replied calmly, oblivious to Liam's desperation.

"Then why are you telling me that?" Liam asked, annoyed.

Sean looked surprised. "I know because she gets so silly when she's anywhere near him. She's away with the fairies, my mother says. She seems like she's in love," he replied categorically.

"It's not fair," said Liam angrily. "John has so many girlfriends." He stood, determined to leave. "I've had enough of being here."

"Why are you angry with me?" Sean asked. "What have I done to you?"

"Leave it, he'll get over it." Ernest tried to calm him down.

Liam climbed onto his bike in fury and pedaled all the way home without stopping. He was blinded by jealousy. He wanted to punch John so hard that it would disfigure his handsome face. Then it occurred to him that his tragedy was his parents' fault for sending him far away from Christine. He felt miserable. His emotions roiled like volcanic lava. He was at an age where his feelings could not be rationalized; everything in him took on an excessive intensity. He wondered how he could win her love.

Meanwhile, on the other side of the city, John stood in front of Deidre, the girl who made his heart skip a beat and who would be responsible for recruiting him into the independence struggle. John listened, enraptured by the way she spoke, the way she expressed her ideas, the intonation with which she pronounced her words. He felt drawn to a seductive, irresistible, and unfamiliar force: the passion for ideas. To Deidre, John was just a boy playing at being a man. He was undoubtedly charismatic, but he was still a boy beginning to open himself up to life, one she would have to give both human and political shape to.

John went to visit Deidre at his sister's request; he had to deliver an urgent message to her. When he arrived at the specified place, Deidre was giving a rousing, passionate speech to hundreds of working women, inviting them to join the fight for a free and egalitarian Ireland. She spoke from the heart. She was also a worker; she understood their exhaustion and sorrow, the exploitation of their bodies. She despised the suffragette women, accusing them of being bourgeois oppressors.

"We must fight for our rights! No one else will give them to us!" she urged.

The women cheered wildly. The atmosphere was steeped in joy and hope. This was how the members of Cumann na mBan recruited women, managing to convene hundreds of delegations throughout Ireland. Deidre was an admirer of Helena Molony, the lady of Irish syndicalism. Molony had introduced her to feminism and appointed her as one of her main collaborators. Deidre listened to her closely, trying to absorb all her ideas, just as Pirenrayen was doing with her grandmother on the other side of the world. Women with dreams listen with all their senses and learn to speak from the heart. There will always be another woman eager to share her knowledge and strength, guiding us toward our goals.

When the women began to disperse, John approached her.

"Hello, Deidre. It was lovely to hear you," he said, blushing slightly.

"Thank you, John. What brings you here?" Deidre responded flirtatiously.

"This is from my sister." He held out his hand and passed her an envelope.

She read it, thanked him, and placed it in her skirt pocket.

"I have something very important for you. I need you to deliver it to a comrade," Deidre said with a hint of mystery. "Can you come with me to my house?"

"Of course. You know you can always count on me whenever you need me," John answered excitedly.

Deidre gave John a smile that looked like heaven. She came so close he could feel her breath on his face.

"You're very sweet, John," she whispered, looking into his eyes. "But you should be less chivalrous. It's better to be sharper and more discreet."

He blushed in befuddlement. Then they took to the cobbled streets of Dublin under a broad blue sky, the air filled with the scent of flowers.

They arrived at a modest building and went inside. Deidre lived on the top floor. Her home was a small, strikingly cluttered room stuffed full of flags and books. A cat with gray and black patches watched them arrive. Deidre hurried to open the window to let in the sun. The room seemed like an abandoned place, cold and forgotten. Deidre offered him tea, and John accepted. While she was making it, his eyes fell on a gun amid the disarray. It was a small revolver. John knew nothing about guns, but he was excited by the idea of learning to handle them.

"I'm going to join the Irish Citizen Army," John confessed to Deidre, breaking the silence.

She gave him a cheerful look as she served the tea.

"Why do you want to join?" she asked, curious and amused.

John didn't like the expression on her face one bit. "For the same reasons you yourself fight, Miss Deidre," he replied in irritation.

She sat next to him on the bed with a maternal gesture; it was the only available seat in the tiny room. She stroked his face and said, "You're a child. You shouldn't charge into hell when you can still enjoy a piece of heaven."

John looked into her eyes with great seriousness and replied, "I stopped being a child a long time ago. I know more about pain and loneliness than many men. Believe me, Miss Deidre. I know more about hell than heaven."

"Tell me," she said, and he unburdened himself of his sorrows.

His voice was undergoing a transformation. At times it sounded like that of a lugubrious, melancholy, distant man, but suddenly it became that of the usual unwavering, daring youngster again. Deidre was touched. She took his hand impulsively and began kissing his fingers with such sensuality and ease that John was perplexed and paralyzed. She detected his fear and began to laugh. She was amused by the situation: the young man who made advances toward her and looked defiant in public was trembling with fear and shame behind closed doors.

"I don't invite children into my heart," she said playfully. "I will open the door only to the best of men. We're in an unequal war. We women are our own weapons, and I know how to take care of myself."

John was silent. That woman hypnotized him, emptying him of words, lustfully stripping bare his soul. He did not have the strength to respond to her captivating and sensual determination. Until she broke the glassy silence with an order.

"Lie down," she said.

John, nervous and aroused, obeyed.

Deidre lay down beside him and began kissing his cheeks. Then she paused gently at his trembling, restless lips. She climbed on top of him and slowly peeled off his shirt. His strong and youthful torso allowed her a glimpse of the handsome man he would become. Panting and aroused, she kissed his trembling body. She undressed slowly, eager to be caressed. She unbuttoned her blouse and freed her breasts. She took the young man's hand and guided him to them. In an ecstasy of pleasure, unable to control his words, John murmured between moans and whispers, "Deidre, you're beautiful! I think I love you."

And that confession broke the spell.

Deidre awakened her conscience, which had, perhaps, been lulled by desire. Repentant, fearful, and full of shame, she sat bolt upright and sprang out of bed as she buttoned her blouse.

"Get dressed and get out of my bed," she ordered.

John didn't understand what was happening. Why was she rejecting him? He tried to embrace her, but she resisted.

"It was a mistake, let's forget about it," Deidre said, and went on as if nothing had happened. "Take this package to this address." She handed him a scrap of paper with some directions scrawled on it.

John said nothing. Mute and bewildered, he left the apartment. He carried out the errand and headed home, still despondent at what had happened. He had wanted that moment so much, yet that bitter taste, that feeling of abandonment and shame, tormented him.

Back in his neighborhood, lost in thought, he spotted Liam barreling toward him at full speed. When he was near, Liam jumped off his bike and left it lying on its side. Without a word, he pounced on John and punched him with clenched fists. John was caught off guard and fell to the ground, blindsided.

"Defend yourself, you coward!" Liam shouted.

"Why are you attacking me?" John asked.

"For lying, stealing, and having no shame!" Liam yelled in response.

John still had no idea what was going on. "What do you mean, my friend?" he answered, still in disbelief.

"I'm not your friend anymore," Liam said angrily.

"Why not?" John asked, completely baffled.

"If you were my friend, you wouldn't have stolen my girl," Liam declared.

John was even more perplexed.

"What girl?" he responded angrily, still hurt by his friend's assault.

"Christine!" Liam cried. "You took advantage of my being gone to seduce her," he added with resentment. Liam attacked him again. This time, John responded with a right hook that gave Liam a nosebleed. This only enraged Liam even more, and he attacked his rival with kicks and punches. As they fought, John confessed.

"I don't love Christine! She's not my girlfriend! I'm interested in another woman. Her name is Deidre."

Liam stopped. "You're not lying to me?" he asked in a pleading tone.

"Never," John replied.

"Forgive me, my friend," Liam said, ashamed. "I don't know why I reacted like that. I should have asked before punching you."

The two friends embraced. Both were injured. Liam's nose was swollen and still bleeding, and John had a black eye. They felt ridiculous and laughed at themselves. They wouldn't speak of the matter again for many years, until life, in an inescapable circle, returned them to the same accusations, enveloping them in the same questions.

Days later, Liam went to visit Christine; he wanted to confess his feelings to her. He brought her a beautiful bone hairpin he had carved himself. She welcomed him unmoved and listened with a stoic gaze. Liam was terribly nervous. He clumsily offered her his gift and then, almost stuttering, and with unusually formal language, declared his affection.

"Miss Christine, would you do me the honor of being my girlfriend? I can't stop thinking about you, dreaming about you. I want to marry you and make you happy."

The young girl couldn't answer. Suddenly, she felt her cheeks burning with embarrassment, and tears opened the floodgates of her heart. She fled from her suitor and locked herself in her room, where she could cry without holding back.

Liam, hovering awkwardly next to the piano, said nothing. Christine's parents, who were in the dining room and had overheard the young couple's conversation, immediately intervened. They loved Liam very much, and they calmed him, advising him to give Christine time. Her whims would pass soon enough, and she would meditate seriously on his proposal.

"Both of you are still such children . . . ," said Christine's mother.

After that failure, Liam decided to take things slowly, attempting to win Christine's affection with small, daily gestures of kindness. In the weeks following his declaration, he avoided her and took time to muster his courage. When he was ready, he appeared at the school Christine attended to walk her home. She accepted.

From that day on, they went everywhere together. They enjoyed cycling to her piano lessons and racing along the seafront or across the city. Liam gradually became part of Christine's daily life and routine, while John, increasingly distant from her, cleared the way for their marriage.

Chapter 16

Everyone Has a Right to Freedom

Liam and his gang had met James Connolly one day when they'd slipped into the shipyards at the port and stumbled upon a workers' rally. The boys were captivated by Connolly's charisma and oratory skills.

The period known in Ireland as An Gorta Mór, the Great Famine, resembles what we Mapuches suffered soon after the so-called Desert Campaign, when we were subjugated by the Argentine state. In the Irish case, the famine spread discontent among the people. In those days, many still placed their hope in Charles Stewart Parnell, though his glory days had already passed. The violence unleashed against the Irish people had caused more radical and independent expressions of unrest to brew, which drew greater enthusiasm and amassed many followers. At that time, Irish workers were setting the pace for events in the independence movement.

As Connolly left the gathering and stepped down from his improvised stage, he came upon the group of friends, who were gazing at him with joyful and excited faces.

"Eh, come over here!" he called out to them affectionately. "Where are you from?"

"From the west side," John answered.

"We're friends," Liam added.

"I thought as much," said James Connolly. "What are your names?"

One by one, the four friends introduced themselves.

"Do your parents know you're here?" Connolly asked. "Do they want to help us?"

"Yes!" the boys said all at once.

"There will be an important meeting at the Donovans' house this Wednesday. We need strong and clever lads, and I think you fit the bill," Connolly said.

"Of course, Mr. Connolly, don't doubt it. Besides, my family wants our people to be free, just like you," John answered gravely.

James Connolly smiled, pleased.

"Well then, lads, I hope to see you there," he said.

Over dinner, Niall listened to his son with little enthusiasm. When Liam finished his story, he asked his father, "Will you go?"

"It's la-la-late, I'll be go-go-going to bed" was his father's terse response.

That night, Liam's mind was flooded with questions that kept him from sleeping. He could not understand why his people were so riven with conflict and hatred. If, as his father often said, the only trouble afflicting the Irish were the English, why then were Catholics and Protestants tearing each other apart? Connolly had said that everyone had a right to freedom, and he had also spoken of unity.

Liam had no desire to fight. He didn't want to be on the defensive, his fists always clenched. He wanted to go to the south of the city, but he couldn't. The people there were too vicious. The last time the gang had tried to cross that line, they'd been met with a beating.

By the time he turned sixteen, John had become an essential assistant to his uncle in his work for the Irish Citizen Army. His uncle assigned him different tasks and missions. John had also plunged into an ardent romance with his sister Ciara's friend Deidre, who by now had overcome any shame and introduced him simultaneously to the pleasures of sex and politics.

During Easter of 1916, John invited his friends to go to the train station. He and Liam had always shared a love of railways. They paid attention to every mechanical detail that made possible the miracle of their operation. They could identify the type of engine and the year it was made by the locomotive's whistle. Their senses seemed to sharpen by the day, and they even made bets with each other. So when John invited them to join the uprising that would lead to the establishment of an Irish republic, it seemed to the friends a magnificent idea. It wasn't too risky a task: they'd simply go to the train station and await the train bringing the militiamen who would join the insurgent forces. There, the rebels would give them posters that were printed with the declaration of the republic, which the friends would paste on the walls of the city center.

When the train pulled in, hundreds of working men and women spilled out of its crowded cars. All of them were armed. John told his friends to follow them. As they walked, they were handed the posters they were to quickly stick to the walls.

The clouds began to weave a grayish tulle across the sky, gradually shrouding the city. The air was frigid and damp, but they didn't feel the cold. They ran around smoking and chatting as they hurriedly stuck up the posters. The streets took on a peculiar look as Dublin was plastered with posters. The city came alive with the racket and the astonishing sight of the rebel columns marching resolutely to the central post office building. John met his beloved in the street. Deidre gave a hint of a smile when she saw him. They were secret lovers. She had made him promise never to tell anyone about their romance, but of course, John had confessed his love for Deidre to Liam. So when John saw her alongside all the women of Cumann na mBan, excited and happy, he stifled his desire to speak to her, to tell her how beautiful she looked and how her enthusiasm for her ideals had made him fall deeper and deeper in love with her.

Liam and his friends walked hurriedly. John asked Sean for a cigarette. He pulled out a few and handed them to his friends. Passersby sensed something unusual in the streets but couldn't yet tell what was going on.

Everything happened quickly. The marchers took the post office, and from there took control of the means of communication, announcing to the country the declaration of the republic. A group of militiamen began to advance toward the castle where the invading government was stationed. The English were completely unprepared.

Everything moved slowly around the boys, almost imperceptibly.

Ernest and Liam had fallen in line behind the men and women with their rifles, heading toward the castle. Liam sensed the danger but had faith in their victory. That day, he and his friends felt important, capable of anything. They had set out on a mission, and they had accomplished it.

John and Sean were surrounding the post office with the women enlisted in Helena Molony's movement and the armed men guarding the strategic takeover of the building as Liam and Ernest were drawing closer and closer to the castle. When they arrived, they heard gunshots, and the smoke of gunpowder started clouding the air. Everything was hazy. There were screams. People were running. The two friends hid behind a column. They watched in horror as the English police and soldiers took control of the streets. The repression was brutal, and the wounded and dead lay around them.

"Ernest, we've got to get away right now," Liam said, watching the swirl of movement surrounding him.

But Ernest did not answer. Liam looked back and saw his friend lying in the street in a pool of blood. A bullet had struck him in the back of the neck. Liam began to cry and call out his name. For a few minutes, he held his friend in his arms, blinded by his despair. Then he picked him up and ran wildly, not knowing where he was going. An old man saw him and, believing that he was carrying a wounded boy, called to him and took him into his home.

For several hours, they hid in a basement. When the day was almost over, Liam went in search of his other friends. Together, they carried Ernest's body and took him home. His mother fainted at the sight of him. She could not accept his death. Neither could his friends.

The night of the funeral, Liam came down with a fever. In one of his dreams, his numb body once again walked through a distant land full of mountains that touched the sky. A strange landscape emerged before him. He was lost in a gloomy forest with sharp, thorny bushes that scratched his skin. He was a child again and called out to his friends.

"Ernest! John! Sean! Where are you?"

He did not know if he should go on or stay where he was. Finally, he decided to wait for his friends. He felt terribly alone again. Then he saw something strange leaping between the treetops and dropping down to the bushes. He couldn't make out what it was. He stiffened, as if petrified. He sat down on a rock under a large tree. He hugged his knees and hid his face between his legs. He needed to cry.

Then a warm breath blew on the back of his neck. He lifted his head and opened his eyes wide in surprise. A beautiful girl stood before him. He thought he recognized her. It was as if they had crossed paths somewhere. The girl was dressed strangely. She spoke to him in an unknown language, but Liam understood her.

"Do not suffer. Soon you will be healed. It won't be long until we can ride the mountains together," said the girl, who instantly turned into a bird and flew away.

Liam awoke remembering his dream. The girl was the same one he had dreamed of as a child. "Who is she?" he wondered. "What language does she speak? Why do I understand her?"

That Easter of 1916 remained seared into the memory of the Irish as one of the bloodiest events of the resistance. The civil war would break out shortly after the end of the First World War. For two years, there was no truce. Poverty and hunger took hold in the homes of all the Irish. Liam had to leave school to work. His house had been bombed, and his parents were forced to close the bakery. Without a doubt, those events made him more sensitive and, at the same time, more prudent.

John's uncertain whereabouts, and the fate that seemed to separate them further with each new event, made Christine accept Liam's proposal of marriage. Time helped lessen the pain of absence and the bitter longing for what she had experienced only in her fanciful, romantic, girlish head. Liam was now a handsome, strong, and affectionate young man, and he had begun to work on the railway. Christine slowly resigned herself to her fate. Life was gradually falling into place. But it was only a brief respite. Rough waves would soon return to moisten her eyes with tears.

My grandmother spoke to me of the intricate stories that Liam O'Sullivan drew from his memory and revealed only to her. I treasure Liam's diary and a notebook of his as precious gifts from the past. I have always thought that perhaps one day his descendants will seek me out and ask me for them. So far, this hasn't happened.

Telling you who this man was and how he came into our lives helps me to recover scraps that, after so many years of silence, have begun to unravel in my memory. The yellowed pages and blurry words of that diary and notebook are all that Liam left as an inheritance to my grandmother.

But excuse me, I seem to have gotten distracted again. Would you like me to go on with my story? When I stray along the branches of my memories, just ask me, "Grandmother Llankaray, what happened next?" That way, I'll know I've veered off course and I need to come back.

For now, I'll simply tell you that just as Liam was beginning his life with Christine, on the other side of the world, Pirenrayen and Linkoyan were overcome by a new kind of feeling.

PART THREE

PART THREE

Chapter 17

Amid Passionate Kisses and Caresses

Autumn was a time to store away medicine for winter. There were many tasks: preparing firewood; drying meat; picking fruit, plants, and mushrooms. The work began in summertime and lasted into the fall. Linkoyan had become a strong and sinewy youth. He was often at Fresia's house, helping her with her work. His mother, Chekeken, had married her brother-in-law Huentemilla, the youngest of her deceased husband's brothers. She had captivated him since the moment he'd met her, when he was reunited with his brother. When his brother died, Huentemilla was determined to care for and protect her, and they'd become close friends. To Chekeken, he was at first almost a child, a little brother to laugh with and order around. Only with him could she break her glassy silences and tell him her dreams, her troubles, her sorrows, and her joys. He loved her and understood the fragility of her body, which had somehow grown taller and taller, beyond her control. In their own way, they were very happy. Like his brother Pichiliempe, Huentemilla was a strong and hardworking man. He decided to acquire lots of animals so he could ask Chekeken to be his wife. And that is just what he did. Four children were born from that marriage. Linkoyan preferred to be closer to Pirenrayen and her grandmother, rather than living with his little siblings.

Pirenrayen didn't know exactly when she first began to have a bodily sensation that set her nerves on edge. But Linkoyan's absences felt like an eternity and drove her to despair. Each time he went away, the girl asked the sacred tree to bring news of him. Sometimes, when she went galloping out to hunt, and saw the peuco, she sang to it, asking it about her beloved. When Linkoyan was by her side, she was overcome with an unyielding sense of well-being; and Linkoyan, for his part, could not stop thinking about Pirenrayen. At times, he could hardly bear the desire to take her in his arms and become one with her. He brought her gifts, and Fresia Coliman's granddaughter's face would light up.

One day when he spotted her alone on horseback, trying to hunt a guanaco with an old handgun, he noticed that she was heading straight toward a recently installed barbed-wire fence. Pirenrayen was riding at a gallop, unaware of those scarcely visible threads rising between free creatures like a deadly trap. Linkoyan tried desperately to warn her, but it was too late. The animal got tangled up in the wire and collapsed. When she fell from the horse, Pirenrayen split open her forehead on the edge of a rock and dislocated her ankle. As she fell, the weapon fired, wounding her beloved horse, which lay bleeding to death. Linkoyan arrived in a panic, fearing the worst. Pirenrayen, whose eyes were closed in pain and fear, heard him speak urgently.

"How do you feel? Where does it hurt?" Linkoyan asked, taking her hand in alarm.

"My foot hurts. Aye, my foot," Pirenrayen whimpered as tears rolled down her face.

Linkoyan lifted her in his arms with great care and seated her in front of him on his horse. Before setting off, he had to put the wounded horse out of its pain. Pirenrayen cried for the fate of her friend, the bay stud pony that had been with her all through her childhood.

Fresia and Linkoyan went to great lengths to nurse Pirenrayen quickly back to health. On one occasion, Linkoyan arrived at the ruka and found her alone. Taking advantage of Fresia's absence, he kissed her for the first time, though not on the lips. Their cheekbones scarcely grazed each other, slowly and softly. This is a way of kissing among the Mapuches that the Wingka world has not discovered, on the most sensitive parts of the face, in the tracks of our tears. For Pirenrayen and Linkoyan, it was as if each were discovering the other's existence for the first time. They looked at each other in a new way, sought closeness, touched and recognized one another. They gave themselves over to their bodies' bewilderment, eager, but were concerned about being found out.

Linkoyan decided to speak to Fresia and lay out his love for Pirenrayen: he wanted to marry her. First, he told Chekeken of his intentions, and she helped him prepare. One day at noon, they arrived at Fresia's house in a procession, bearing many gifts. Fresia and Pirenrayen agreed and were overjoyed. The union had been greatly desired and was approved by both families, who had been friends for a long time.

Beyond the animals Linkoyan already had, Huentemilla offered him a flock of sheep and a herd of cows for the mafün, the ceremony that would unite them as husband and wife. The husband-to-be spent those weeks preparing everything with great delight. No detail was overlooked in the celebration of the wedding. But on the wedding night, the groom had stuffed himself with food and had so much to drink that he collapsed onto the makeshift bed. He awoke at dusk the next day. When he opened his eyes, he found himself alone in the little house. Summer was steeping the days in its languor, and he went to the stream to bathe. Then he waited for his wife and Fresia to return. For the first time, he cast his eyes over the things that made up his treasured home, sighed with satisfaction, and went out to the patio to chop wood for the fire.

That night they embraced, huddled beneath the heavy woven blankets. Pirenrayen was so tiny that she got lost in the arms of that hefty man who held her passionately to his chest. Pirenrayen stroked his body with her small, plump hands, pausing at his strong, muscular arms. Her fingers played with every inch of that generous, sinewy hunter's flesh. She touched his sex, brushing it with her hand. Linkoyan seized the hand fiercely and kept it there.

"Milk me," he whispered into her ear.

She laughed and replied, "How can I milk a bull?"

But she obeyed. She felt the game turn their breath to panting, and moans and words of love blossomed on their lips like spring flowers. Amid passionate kisses and caresses, the young Linkoyan and his beloved entered the realm of pleasure with their wild bodies and untamed spirits.

In time, Linkoyan built a house to live in with his wife. There, they frolicked and played. They made love so much that the nights were not long enough, and they had to interrupt their daily tasks to obey the urgency of their bodies and souls in their desire to merge with one another.

Linkoyan had inherited great height from his Tehuelche stock and a broad back and solid muscles from his Mapuche father. Sometimes he tied back his long hair, but mostly he wore it loose. Pirenrayen had woven him a trailongko, a band that he wore around his head. Two things shone through when you saw him: his independence and his physical strength. These were two qualities that would determine his fate.

In the year 1916, during the government of Hipólito Yrigoyen, the Honorary Commission for the Indigenous Settlements was created. With this policy, the president aimed to do away with the "savage" characteristics of the recently annexed territories. He imposed assimilation measures to turn the rebellious Indigenous people into mere rural laborers. The Patagonian landowners applauded these measures since they solved a significant problem for them: the lack of labor for rural work. Free labor, of course, was supplied through the enslavement of Mapuche men. The criollo population was still in its infancy, with only a few clusters of houses and families scattered across Patagonia. Our strong and vigorous men refused to work their lands without any pay. The workdays were grueling, from the early hours of dawn until after darkness had fallen. There was no rest to be had, only the exploitation of those bodies marked by history and humiliation.

For a while, though, Linkoyan managed to escape those forced obligations. He used his days to work diligently on the land, sowing, raising animals, and shearing them. He accompanied his wife and Fresia to the high peaks of the mountains in search of medicine. The young couple was happy and still played as they had when they were children. On one of those outings, they came upon some men herding cows. Their leader was a white man struggling to make himself understood in broken Spanish. Another man translated what he wanted to say to them, offering Linkoyan a job on the ranch the white man managed. Linkoyan had no interest in the proposal and politely took his leave to go on his way.

"Arrogant Indian. You'll come begging for work eventually, when you need something to eat," the interpreter said contemptuously.

Linkoyan dreamed of expanding his small herd and worked hard alongside Pirenrayen. They plowed and sowed the land, went hunting together, and cared for their animals. Pirenrayen wove with her grandmother and sold her crafts to Galensho.

Pirenrayen fell pregnant almost a year after they married. Linkoyan was overjoyed to become a father. Each night as they held each other before they fell asleep, they would talk about the baby, make plans, reminisce about their childhood, and imagine what their child would be like. He would hold her tight, kissing her passionately, tenderly. A lifetime together. Linkoyan couldn't imagine his world without her, and now he would have a child with the woman he so adored. The wonder of love could hardly be greater. His ancestors had given him health, strength, and a heart to experience these moments of wholeness.

Pirenrayen was heavily pregnant when she dreamed of her child. She awoke as her husband was coming in with freshly chopped wood to light the fire.

"I dreamed of our child," she said.

Linkoyan kept at his work. "What happened in the dream?"

Then she sat up, still wrapped in blankets because the morning cold was swirling about the ruka, and began to tell him her dream as she watched the first flames emerge from the hearth. Linkoyan took a blackened kettle, filled it with the water he had collected in ceramic pots the previous evening, and placed it over the fire. He sat on a small wooden bench that had a colorful handwoven blanket made by Pirenrayen on the seat. She had made it especially for that bench, one of the few pieces of furniture in that modest house her husband had built. Linkoyan gazed at her with a seductive smile.

"Tell me," he said.

"The pewma went like this," Pirenrayen said excitedly, and went on with her story.

"I was walking across a plain of reeds and coiron grass. The ground I stepped on was flat. I could tell there was water nearby; I could smell its salty moisture. It was like a giant lake or a river that went on forever. Its waves were high and roaring, and they shook so much that the serpents, Kay Kay and Treng Treng, seemed to be fighting in the water's depths. The wind kept blowing. I walked heavily, with difficulty. I felt hurried, as if I needed to get somewhere quickly, but I didn't know where. I began to climb a sand dune. The sand became heavy and slippery, but I managed to reach the top. From there, I saw Lake Futalaufquen, sonorous and raging, its waves getting bigger and bigger. The waves drew closer, and grew to enormous heights, covering everything. I felt as if I would die there, dragged away by the waters. In my anguish, I begged my mother for help. 'Kalfurayen, I do not know you, but you are my mother. Tell me, why have I come here? This is a dangerous place! Help me get home!' Then the sky filled with light. The waters were calmed as if they belonged to a great lagoon. Bright colors tinted the waters, and many horses sprang from the sea, of all breeds and sizes. They galloped, beautiful and strong, from the depths of Futalaufquen up to the surface, and on to the water's edge, where there was nothing but sand. I lifted a fistful, touched it, and clasped my hand around a bay-colored kawel. It looked very old. It came close to me and said, 'Your seed will be prolific, like the sand you hold in your hand.' And then I awoke."

When the tale was over, a sweet silence enveloped them. Pirenrayen's husband drew closer and kissed her. Both were happy; they felt as if the night had brought a good omen through Pirenrayen's dream.

In the days that came afterward, Pirenrayen shared her dream with her grandmother, seizing the chance to walk with her toward the stream to wash wool. Fresia listened, then spoke.

"The life in your womb is a man. His spirit has come to speak to you in a dream. Call him Kawel. This child will be free and strong. And from him will come a great lineage, numerous and steadfast, like the wild horses."

Four moons had passed since that dream, when Pirenrayen began feeling contractions as the life inside her announced its desire to emerge from the warm, comforting embrace of its mother's body. It was a mild and clear summer night. A serene, bright moon hung sharply over the mountains. Gently radiant, flickering silver lights dotted the fabric of darkness, painting a singular night—the night Kawel chose to be born.

Pirenrayen awoke to faint pains in her belly and realized immediately that she was wet. She spoke to Linkoyan.

"Wake up, my love. The baby is coming," she said.

Linkoyan had gone to bed exhausted from the hard work of the previous day. He was in such a deep sleep that it was difficult to rouse him. It took him a while to activate all his senses, and only when Pirenrayen shook him and scolded his laziness did he finally understand what was going on. His child was on its way; there was no time to waste. He dressed quickly and went looking for Fresia. He dashed across the courtyard and knocked urgently on the small and rickety door to Fresia's house.

"Who is it? What do you want?" she called from inside.

"It's me, Linkoyan, Doña Fresia. Pirenrayen is about to give birth!"

The old woman quickly sat up, dressed, and headed straight to the stream. There, she washed her hands and face before making her way to her granddaughter's house.

Linkoyan was already there, tending the fire. He had put the kettle on. Seeing the fire lit, Doña Fresia ordered him, "Put on the black pot, my son. I'll need plenty of hot water."

Linkoyan, clumsy and nervous, moved to obey.

"My little one, how are you feeling?" Fresia asked Pirenrayen sweetly.

"It hurts a little, Grandmother."

"That's how it always is," the old woman said. "Stay strong, for the baby will soon be here. He'll be beautiful, tough like his father. Spoiled like his mother," she added tenderly, with a chuckle, trying to coax a little laughter from her granddaughter.

"Grandmother, is there anything else you need from me? If not, I'll go and chop wood to heat the water," interrupted Linkoyan.

The old woman looked at him sternly. "Why didn't you chop enough firewood yesterday, boy? Off you go!" she replied curtly.

Lying on a blanket, Pirenrayen felt her grandmother's warm hands gently massaging her belly.

"Does it hurt?" Fresia asked.

"Not much," Pirenrayen replied.

The grandmother recounted how, soon after Pirenrayen was born, she had rubbed her hips with wind eggs. This explained why the pain was bearable.

"The baby is coming," the grandmother said. "Come, sit on the wooden tub."

The young woman squatted and began to push. She emptied her bowels inadvertently and felt ashamed. The old woman reassured her.

"Don't worry, my dear. This always happens. The body lets everything out first, cleansing itself from within, and then the child comes."

Pirenrayen's legs trembled, but her grandmother encouraged her. She cleaned and sanitized her, and after four pushes, Kawel emerged, squawking vigorously.

"This one will be fierce," Fresia said, laughing with overwhelming joy.

Linkoyan heard his son's cries from outside. He dropped his axe and ran toward the house, arriving just as the grandmother cut the umbilical cord.

"This is your son. A strong little boy," Fresia said.

She washed him and handed him to his father as she waited for Pirenrayen to expel the placenta. It came out whole. Fresia placed the placenta in the wooden tub.

"I'll bury it in the morning," she announced.

She washed her granddaughter, laid her on her cot, and gave her a warm honeyed concoction to drink.

"This will do you good, my dear. Drink it all up, every last drop," she said.

While the mother drank the healing infusion, the father proudly held the baby in his arms. The newborn wouldn't stop crying. Pirenrayen placed him on her chest. She felt the pain of the first suckling, and then the flow of her abundant milk. At times, there was so much that the baby seemed to be choking. He turned out to be voracious, drinking a great deal of milk.

When dawn broke, mother and son were sleeping. Fresia asked Linkoyan to accompany her to the aliwen, carrying the trutruka, a long trumpetlike instrument that makes a piercing sound. Together, they took the wooden tub containing the placenta.

They arrived at the sacred tree. Linkoyan played his trutruka while Fresia prayed and sang, burying the placenta. Then the proud father butchered and roasted a lamb. Fresia made bread and roasted potatoes over the embers and prepared muday and chicha to celebrate her great-grandson's birth.

That day coincided with the arrival of Nawelpangui. He was Pirenrayen's only uncle who still lived in the lof, working seasonally on the English estate and occasionally sheepshearing farther south. It had been a long time since he had last visited his niece and his mother. He was surprised and delighted by the news, which he helped spread among relatives and acquaintances. And so, the first month of Kawel's life became a social occasion, attracting even distant relatives who came to meet and greet the lof's newest member.

Nawelpangui and Linkoyan spent lively days celebrating Kawel's birth. The uncle gifted the child a promising young colt, piebald and small in stature. He told Pirenrayen that he would tame it himself so it would be a good horse. She smiled with delight.

During those days, Chekeken also came to visit, bringing clothes she had woven for her grandson. She stayed through the spring and part of the summer to keep them company. When it was time for her to leave, Fresia bid her farewell and felt a pang in her chest. She embraced Chekeken tightly, and a few tears rolled down her cheeks. Chekeken smiled tenderly.

"But what's the matter, ñaña? How can you make me cry like this? Has my grandson made you this tearful?" she said, embracing her once more.

Then Chekeken climbed into her cart and disappeared over the crest of a nearby hill.

Chapter 18

LOVE TENDS TO ELUDE CONFORMISTS

On the day Kawel was born, on the other side of the world, Liam O'Sullivan became officially engaged to Christine. Liam had been working on the railway for a year by now. Many men toiled on the railways, underpaid and exploited, enduring exhausting workdays. It was 1918, and the war made it necessary for the British to transport troops and weapons by rail. The war had swept away hope and was claiming hundreds of lives every day. Each new dawn was a miracle. Liam's father, who had closed his bakery, sat down to await the end of the conflict. As time passed, his life trickled away. Sarah continued teaching.

Niall O'Sullivan had a brother who lived in the Americas. He was the youngest and had left a few years before the war broke out. Niall received the occasional letter from him, recounting his adventures. The most recent missive had revealed his current location, the place he had chosen to settle for good: the city of Buenos Aires, Argentina. In those days, thousands upon thousands of Irish people left their homes in search of a future in the Americas. For many decades, the fantasy of growing rich in the New World and returning home wealthy and powerful had fueled their aspirations. Despite the insistence of his brother, Patrick, that he leave everything behind and settle in Buenos Aires, Niall had never considered the idea. He patiently awaited the end of the war, dreaming of reopening his bombed-out bakery.

Liam failed to notice that his father had been gradually sinking into a melancholic apathy, a gray detachment that slowly and stealthily overwhelmed his heart. Liam focused excitedly on his new job, devoting himself each day to absorbing as much information and technical knowledge about the functioning of the trains as possible, with the goal of driving them one day. His task was to place wood in the fire that ran the engine. The firebox was constructed with refractory bricks and sand, guaranteeing high temperatures. Inside the box was the tube plate, the first part of the boiler, composed of tubes approximately two and a half yards in diameter. The heat passed through these tubes, heating the water in the boiler barrel. It was there that steam was produced to set the entire machine in motion. Liam took his responsibility seriously, observing the gauges and thermometers. The boiler had a safety valve calibrated to twenty-six pounds; if the pressure exceeded that limit, the steam was released as a safety measure. Railway accidents were all too common and often resulted from human error, so Liam paid close attention and showed himself to be responsible. The Englishmen viewed him favorably, even though he worked as a simple stoker. He carefully observed the changes, the functions of the various levers, and the needles that showed the temperature of the machine. He delighted in sounding the whistle as they approached the stations where they were to stop. Sometimes they transported passengers, and on certain journeys, they carried cargo, mostly soldiers, food, and artillery.

After two years of courtship, Liam and Christine were engaged. Love tends to elude conformists, those weak-spirited people who allow themselves to be pulled along by circumstances and don't fight with the conviction of their dreams and affections. They lead mediocre lives, and time flows for them through a narrow corridor of fears. Safety is a rocky ground that cuts into the soles of their feet. Only those who stop walking and dare to fly can achieve freedom and fulfill their dreams. Christine was far from being so bold, especially with her heart, but a luminous flame fed her soul whenever she sat down to play the piano. That sublime, ineffable music spoke to her heart with a velvety voice.

At the end of each workday, just before dinner, Liam would appear at his fiancée's house, freshly bathed, clean-shaven, and dressed in his finest clothes. There, his future in-laws received him more warmly than his beloved. Christine would stay silent during dinner. The men discussed politics, the war, and their work. Liam would often glance at her, fascinated by her beauty, and she would politely lower her gaze, always distant and lost in thought, as if she were somewhere else. In her mind, she and John walked hand in hand through a green meadow filled with flowers and kissed beneath a blushing coral sunset.

Then the men would retire to the sitting room to smoke and drink brandy. Sometimes, Sean invited Liam to have a few beers. Then Liam would take his leave from his future in-laws and his fiancée and set out to enjoy the chilly nights of Dublin with his friend and future brother-in-law.

Liam was aware that Christine did not love him, but he trusted that with time and care, he would win her heart. They set a date for the wedding and set about organizing it. In the days leading up to their marriage, Christine began to show more affection and kindness toward Liam and even seemed more than content with her fate. For the first time, Liam felt assured in his decision. She was everything he desired.

Finally, the summer of 1919 arrived, and with it, the wedding. The ceremony was simple and warm. Niall and Sarah provided music for the nuptials, with Sarah on the piano and Niall playing the tin whistle. The guests and the couple delighted in Liam's parents' harmonious and well-arranged melodies. The bride and groom were elegantly, albeit modestly, dressed. Christine wore her mother's dress with some minor alterations, along with some accessories from her mother-in-law's wedding. Liam had rented a nice suit for the occasion. The celebration was joyous, and though the postwar years were times of scarcity, there was an abundance of food and drink. Liam's uncle, Patrick O'Sullivan, had sent a significant sum of money from Argentina as a wedding gift for his nephew, which helped cover the expenses. He himself could not attend. Though they all knew the real reasons he could not return, they chose not to mention them out of decorum.

While the guests danced and enjoyed the festivities, Liam longed to be alone with his wife. His youthful and inexperienced body yearned desperately to taste the pleasures of marriage. They spent their wedding night on the rails since they were to honeymoon in Belfast. Though they were in a comfortable compartment, Christine had a terrible time, vomiting throughout the journey.

When they arrived at the hotel, she asked her husband to leave her alone in the room to rest, so Liam went out for a walk, eager to explore the city. Though he felt uneasy about leaving his wife alone, he respected her request and left her sleeping. The Belfast air had a refreshing maritime chill that swelled his lungs and left his heart invigorated. Seagulls squawked noisily in the bright-blue midday sky. His veins throbbed with desires, longings, and life. He noticed some women smiling at him approvingly. It pleased him, but he had no interest in gazing deeper into the eyes that watched him. He ambled along the harbor, observing the enormous ships and bustling shipyards filled with noisy crowds. Each person performed their role as if in a metallic opera made up of iron, wood, and wind. He was wandering with a combination of curiosity and distraction when he heard someone cry his name. He turned in the direction of the voice, and it was John. They embraced, thrilled to meet again.

"My friend, it's been so long since I've heard anything from you!" said Liam.

"Well, here I am. I've been in this area, moving around a lot. And you, old pal, what are you doing here?" asked John.

"I'm on my honeymoon."

"You got married! Congratulations! And who's the lucky woman?"

"Christine Campbell."

John gave him a startled look. "You're a lucky man, Liam!" he said finally, overcoming his shock. He smiled and embraced him.

"And what have you been up to all this time?"

"Let's have a drink, and I'll tell you all about it," suggested John.

At dusk, Liam and John arrived drunkenly at the hotel where the newlyweds were staying. In the lobby stood Christine, who was anxious and had come downstairs to await her husband's return. When she caught sight of John, she was alarmed and flustered. She felt as if her heart might leap out of her chest; she did not know how to act. She was upset and bewildered to see them both so intoxicated. John, who was less drunk than his friend, helped Christine drag Liam to their room. She took off his boots, and together they laid him down on the bed.

John stood silent in front of her. He approached, and caressed her hair.

"Forgive me," he said, gazing into her eyes.

"It doesn't matter," Christine replied. "I know you men like to drink when you're together."

"I'm not asking you to forgive me for that, but for not being able to stay by your side," he interrupted.

Christine hardened her gaze. "That, I can never forgive you for," she said. "Now, please leave. I must look after my husband."

That was the last time they saw each other in Ireland. The next day, John, along with his girlfriend Deidre and some other militiamen, would set out on a special mission to Scotland. As he closed the hotel room door, Christine burst into tears. She cried so much that she fell asleep on the couch, defeated by sadness.

During their honeymoon, Liam tried to seek intimacy with his wife, but she resisted with various excuses. Since he loved her, he decided to be patient. But on their return to Dublin, she continued to reject his advances. Liam asked his father's advice.

"Ta-ta-take her," said Niall. "She's your wi-wife, she should p-please you, she be-belongs to you."

That night, Liam could no longer hold back. He began to force himself on her, and she resisted. Liam gripped her by the waist and pulled her toward him. Christine struggled. Liam tried to kiss her. She slapped him and burst into tears. Liam took his coat and left in a fury. That night, he paid for sex in a brothel. The women fought over taking him as a client, and some even offered their services free of charge. Liam got drunk and lost his virginity to a middle-aged woman.

Christine went to mass and prayed three times a day; she confessed daily. She asked the priest for advice.

"Father, I am troubled. My husband comes to me every night to sin. I have refused, but I won't be able to prevent him for much longer. What can I do?"

"My child, it is no sin to submit to your husband's desires. Tell me, were you a virgin when you married?"

"Of course, Father! How can you ask such a thing?"

"What are you afraid of, my child? Don't you want to have children?"

"Yes, Father, I would like to have a child."

"Then you must submit. Pray to the Almighty Lord to grant you the grace of life, to give you strength to face your responsibilities and duties as a wife."

That night, Christine allowed her husband to make love to her for the first time. She wore a long white nightgown with a slit at the level of her vulva so that her husband could enter without undressing her completely. She prayed before she surrendered, then laid herself on the bed in the shape of a cross. Liam stared at her, shocked and terrified. He had no idea what to do. If he went ahead, she might cry as she did every night. He approached her tenderly and caressed and kissed her. Christine didn't react; she simply lay still and let him do as he pleased. That was how all their nights went during their first year of marriage.

Liam was frustrated by his wife's lack of passion and desire, and as time passed, he became less insistent. Since Christine did not become pregnant and was indifferent to her husband, she sought support from her mother and friends. She wanted to overcome the hurdles in her marriage and become the wife Liam deserved. She listened to their advice, put some into practice, and gradually embraced and began to trust the sensations of her body. Time, and the experience of living together, built trust between them.

They moved to the city center, where they found a bright and spacious apartment. Henrietta Street was in a bustling neighborhood with a market, grocery stores, and some pubs. There was a Catholic church only two streets away from their new home. Christine filled the balcony with flowers and plants. She immersed herself in cooking, making the recipes passed down by her mother and her close friends. Many of them attended the same church, and after mass, they would gather for tea.

Their second year found them more united, their marriage a peaceful haven disrupted only when Christine was gripped by the anxiety to become a mother, especially in the mornings, when Liam left for the railway station to work. This was when she felt the loneliness of the house, the emptiness that swallowed her dreams. To remedy this, she began to teach piano lessons to children at Father Patrick Wilde's church.

This old priest, with a strong build and a kind smile, welcomed Christine's offer warmly. During Sunday mass, he announced the free piano lessons and invited Christine to help with the choir, too. At first, she dedicated two days a week to this endeavor, but Father Patrick always added small tasks that she happily accepted and performed with joy. But as her absences from home became more frequent, Liam began to feel uneasy.

One afternoon, when he returned from work, he found himself alone. As he ate dinner, he stared fixedly at the door, as if wanting to pierce through it. At the slightest noise in the building, he expected to see his wife walk in. When she finally arrived, his anger had spread from his heart to his mind, and he was consumed by rage.

"Where have you been, woman?" he asked furiously.

"At church, of course. Where else would I be?" she answered in anger.

"What is that priest up to, keeping you there so long?" he said, raising his voice and standing up.

She felt so humiliated by her husband's insinuation that, blinded by anger, she slapped him.

"How dare you suspect me and Father Patrick? What kind of vile sinner are you?" And she burst into tears.

Ashamed of himself, Liam embraced her, knelt before her, and begged.

"Christine, forgive me. I've been blinded by jealousy. I don't want to share you with anyone else."

He clung to her legs, still kneeling. Christine was overwhelmed with tenderness and stroked his hair.

"Get up," she said sweetly.

Liam obeyed, and as he stood up, he saw that her face was still wet with tears. He began to kiss her, took her in his arms, and led her to the bedroom, where they made love with neither haste nor fear.

To celebrate their second anniversary, Liam gave her a piano. He told her that she no longer needed to give classes at the church; now the children could come to their home. Christine accepted happily, believing that her husband's gesture reflected all the love he felt for her. But she missed her walks along the tree-lined paths that led to the church, and she also felt the absence of her friend Father Patrick, whom she now saw only at mass on Sundays. The priest missed her, too.

For a while, there was peace and harmony in the young couple's life.

Chapter 19

THE BEGINNING OF THE END

In the spring of 1920, injustice knocked on the door of Pirenrayen's home. It was the hour of the siesta. That day, Linkoyan refused to rest; he was in a rush to get all the spring chores done. Without warning, a group of armed thugs arrived at their house, recruiting labor for the English-owned estates. The couple was out sowing crops when they saw them approaching. They sensed from the way the men galloped in on their horses that something grim was about to happen. Their fears were confirmed when the men started firing shots into the sky. Pirenrayen was frightened and swiftly picked up the baby and carried him back to the house. She asked her grandmother to look after him and returned to stand by her husband.

"What do you want?" Linkoyan asked once they were near.

The white man he had met in the mountains, the one who had offered him work, was among the villainous riders. He dismounted, feigning friendliness.

"We come in peace. We just want to add some laborers to our estate, and since you are so strong and skilled, it would help us greatly to have you as a worker."

"I already told you I'm not interested," Linkoyan answered curtly.

"How little disposed you are to work!" the man said ironically. He mounted his horse and rode away.

But that night, the thugs returned and set fire to the shed where Linkoyan stored wool, grain, and animal hides. He also kept food there to survive the winter. The three of them worked tirelessly to put out the fire. Fresia carried water with Kawel in her arms, while she and Pirenrayen cried in anger and sorrow. The shed was consumed by flames, but the stream that separated it from the houses acted as a barrier, preventing the fire from spreading.

The following day, the police arrived, claiming to have found hides belonging to the ranch and cattle that had been missing for some time and had been reported as lost. Pirenrayen and Fresia, neither of whom spoke a word of Spanish, begged and pleaded in Mapudungun. Linkoyan explained that it was impossible for those hides to have appeared on his land since he had never laid eyes on them, but they detained him on charges of cattle rustling. When Fresia and Pirenrayen tried to hold on to the prisoner, the authorities pushed and beat them. Kawel cried from hunger while Pirenrayen kept talking, pleading for her husband.

It was all part of a scheme orchestrated by the English estate and the police to break the will of the communities and the men, reducing them to full-time servitude, enslaving them. Linkoyan spent two months imprisoned for a crime he did not commit. After his release, he was given a few days to gather his belongings and immediately join the estate as a laborer.

"From your home, straight to the ranch headquarters," the police commissioner warned him. "We don't want thieving Indians or vagrants roaming around."

Linkoyan lowered his head. There was no escape. What could he do? But he couldn't leave his women alone in the middle of the planting season, and the animals would soon be giving birth. It was too much work for an elderly woman and a young mother.

He returned home, and Pirenrayen spotted him walking toward her from a distance. He was ragged, filthy, starving, and humiliated; he had lost all hope, and his spirit was crushed. She was tilling the soil when she saw him. She threw down her tools and ran to meet him, embracing him tightly and kissing him tenderly, urgently. He gently pushed her away. His body was covered in bruises. He had received a terrible beating, and they had broken one of his ribs. Pirenrayen wept silently and helped him back to the house.

Fresia was spinning yarn. The spindle danced on its axis, growing heavier with each fine strand of wool winding around it. Just like life itself, growing heavier and heavier with pain. Fresia left her work and examined him. She carefully adjusted his rib, bandaged his waist, and tended to his wounds. Pirenrayen prepared a special soup, a chicken broth with cilantro and spices. She helped him drink it as if he were a child. She lay down beside him until he fell asleep. Tears streamed down Pirenrayen's cheeks; she could not hold them back.

Some of the sorrow from that time was passed on to Kawel, who grew up quiet and melancholic, with a sweet sadness about him.

Pirenrayen wept as she breastfed her son and wept as she did her work. She began to grow thin and gaunt from lack of appetite. Fresia was anguished by her granddaughter's state and spoke to her from the depths of her heart.

"My child, you must not let yourself be defeated by sorrow. Our ancestors have lived through injustices like this, and worse. We must be strong; your son, Kawel, needs you. How much longer will I be here to help you, dear child? Please eat. You must feed yourself."

Fresia embraced her granddaughter, allowing Pirenrayen's tears to moisten her shoulder. Then she served her a delicious soup with some freshly baked bread, knowing that there are aromas and flavors that can nourish our spirit and restore our soul.

After an intense month of care, Linkoyan fully recovered. He knew he must present himself at the ranch; otherwise, the police would come looking for him. The potatoes were already planted, and the quinoa was starting to sprout. Life was conspiring to return, full of newen. "Rain *kushe*, rain *futchá*, rain *Ülcha*, rain *weche*." In this way, standing at the foot of the rewe, the mountains, Doña Fresia named all the renewing forces of spring.

One hot midday with a turquoise sky, when the mountain range was showing its silvery crown with proud white peaks fading slowly into the distance, Galensho arrived. He was always joyfully welcomed. He had a warm and kindly spirit and a comical way of delivering news. He knew it amused people. He used to say that the Mapuches had given him back his joy. Among his fellow Welshmen—on the rare occasions he saw them—Roig Evans adopted a cold, almost hostile attitude. He worked as a guide and interpreter for officials and traders. He was measured in his speech, distrustful of all the white people who came to trade with the Mapuches. He had witnessed the Wingkas' constant abuse of Mapuche hospitality. His children were multilingual, speaking both their ñuke's Mapudungun and their father's Welsh perfectly, in addition to speaking the colonizing languages, Spanish and English, quite well. His wife did not want their children to speak Mapudungun for fear of punishment, but he insisted that his children not forget their mother tongue.

"This is the language of the land, the language of love, the sound of your ñuke. You must never lose it," he would tell them.

He arrived laden with goods as he always did. He brought a good wine as a gift, and Fresia used it to make *chupilka*, a drink we still make with wine, and *ñaco*, flour ground from wheat. Roig bought all Pirenrayen's weavings, and she took the chance to give Linkoyan some chocolate. They roasted meat, and they ate and drank. They laughed uproariously at Galensho's tales. My grandmother used to say that he never laughed at them; he always laughed at himself when telling his stories. Our people never thought he was clumsy or foolish; they knew he exaggerated his own mistakes in his tales to make people laugh. That afternoon, after lunch, there was music. Roig Evans took out the accordion from his cart, and they danced and celebrated their joyful reunion well into the night. Summer was approaching boldly, stealing days away from the spring.

Roig Evans departed in the early hours of the next day. Before he set out on the dusty, tortuous mountain roads, he asked his friend Linkoyan to fulfill his promise and present himself to work at the estate.

"Son, please don't break your promise. I know these people; their cruelty and wickedness have no bounds. Go and work for them, and I will come later and ask them to pay you. They won't be able to keep punishing you for long; they know you haven't done anything wrong. I'm sure they'll recognize your skills and pay for your work."

A few days later, Linkoyan left for the estate. For Pirenrayen, his departure marked the beginning of the end. She missed her husband sorely. But Kawel was almost two and had begun to walk. Pirenrayen delighted so much in her son's progress that at times, the joy of having him there eased the pain of Linkoyan's absence.

Meanwhile, all Linkoyan could think about was completing the period of his punishment and returning to his family. Life at the estate began before dawn. Each morning, the men and women who worked as servants and laborers had to gather in the courtyard of the English estate and sing the anthem while raising the British flag. Linkoyan had been placed there to serve his sentence for cattle rustling and laziness. The judge and the commissioner explained to him that for one year, he must work without receiving a penny as payment.

"The estate owner, Mr. Brown, was too lenient," said the judge. "He had the right to ask us to keep you in jail, you sneaky, thieving Indian, so you'd do well to try and be a good worker on the estate."

His first job there was as a builder of barbed-wire fences. He quickly learned the trade, although he found the Wingkas' obsession with enclosing the mapu absurd. He learned how to select wood for the posts, how to cut and prepare the rods, and the appropriate number of wire strands—skills he never would have dreamed necessary in his world.

A drunken and quarrelsome foreman named Gutiérrez had been working for the English for several years. Extremely accommodating to the bosses, he had gained Mr. Brown's trust. His task was to monitor and report any irregularities. The workers were extremely poor; their food, meat, and liquor were deducted from their wages. Every four months, the senior workers were allowed to visit their families. The newcomers, on the other hand, had to work twice as hard to make up for their absence. Gutiérrez was strict and mocking. He worked alongside everyone else and gave himself Sundays off to drink and chase women. The female servants at the ranch suffered through these Sundays; avoiding the bosses and Gutiérrez became a survival strategy. The English bosses would get drunk on brandy or whiskey while the workers settled for the cheapest spirits. The women had to stay on the alert, never letting down their guard. Any heedless moment might become an opportunity for their assailants. Some of the women had been raped on their way to the henhouse for eggs, others while working in the garden, and even inside the house while cleaning.

The only place no man dared enter was the kitchen, where the cook made the rules. She was a strong-willed Basque woman who had been widowed in Patagonia. In Europe, she had married a Scottish fisherman, who later became a foreman to the English for many years, until he died in an accident on the ranch one winter. Mr. Brown offered the widow the chance to continue as a cook with better pay, and she accepted. Her culinary skills were highly valued by the owners when they visited the estate.

The Basque woman's name was Amaya Irigoyen. She was sturdy, strong, and industrious. The kitchen was her kingdom, and she was its undisputed monarch. She was an older woman, and she despised Gutiérrez. Whenever she had the chance, she would compare his work to that of her late husband in front of the bosses. She accused him of being lazy and making trouble. One day, she asked the boss to appoint a strong young man to assist her in the kitchen, since she considered the tasks of butchering animals and gathering firewood men's work. Brown agreed and brought Linkoyan to the kitchen.

"What do you think of this specimen?" the boss asked Amaya, who stared in amazement at the young man's height and muscular build. "He's muscular and hardworking, and he doesn't drink as much as the rest," he added.

She nodded without a word, and immediately put him to work. They soon understood each other well. Linkoyan had arrived in Amaya's kitchen after two years at the ranch without seeing his family, without receiving a penny in payment, and without permission to leave. Gutiérrez belittled him and treated him mockingly, and Linkoyan's resentment toward him had grown. Each time he tried to leave the estate, Gutiérrez would threaten to go to his house with the police and take his wife as well.

"When the judge tells me you've served your time, I'll let you go," he would say.

And so, two years passed, despite his sentence being one year. Amaya pitied the young Mapuche and persuaded Mr. Brown to allow Linkoyan to visit his family. After several days of persistent requests, he agreed. The cook prepared a bag full of food, sweet and savory bread, preserved meats, delicious sausages—flavors Linkoyan had never tasted before. With his pack loaded, he set off for home.

When she saw him arrive, Pirenrayen's surprise and joy were immense. She clung to his neck, just as she had when she was a child and hadn't wanted to let him go. She held on to his body for a long while, feeling him, breathing in his smell. Linkoyan also prolonged their reunion embrace. In that moment, life became a cocoon shielded from oblivion, reviving the happy days of their past in the sensations of their skin and the scent of their bodies.

Linkoyan's return to his home nourished him with a natural strength that can come only from dignity and love. He decided not to go back to the ranch. Instead, he stayed home to work hard on his land

and support his family. During his absence, Pirenrayen had tried to take over all his tasks, but motherhood, caring for her grandmother, and her sorrows had diminished her strength and concentration. Together, they repaired the house, expanded the garden, extended the cornfield, and acquired a flock of sheep and a new pair of oxen.

Pirenrayen became pregnant after Linkoyan's return, and fertility and prosperity embraced them once again. Even though all signs pointed toward better times, the harassment and threats did not cease. Furthermore, Linkoyan had picked up the habit of drinking the alcohol the Wingkas had brought to our land. Whenever he went to town to buy "vices," the food they did not produce themselves, he would meet his friends and get drunk, reminiscing about old times. It was a habit that Pirenrayen couldn't make him give up, and one day she opened her heart to her grandmother.

"My husband has changed; he isn't the same anymore. He drinks so much, and it's like he doesn't know me. He shouts, and it scares me. Grandmother, what can I do?"

Doña Fresia answered with an expression full of sorrow.

"Pirenrayen, my dear granddaughter, it's very difficult to weaken the powers hidden in the bottle. The transparent liquid the Wingka brought is stronger than our chicha and our muday. Men lose the path to good sense under its influence. I cannot speak to the spirit of that bottle; there is no ngen, no life, in it, no pewma, no speech. Your husband, Linkoyan, has been harmed on that estate. They poison the souls of men with that drink. Don Cornejo Flores, the Chilean man, told me that they never paid him for his work. All they did on their days off was drink, and all they drink is gin. That's what the gringos gave them as payment, never money. That's why he left. Soon after, they came to find Linkoyan to replace him," she said, sighing sadly. "I don't know what will become of him if he keeps drinking like this."

During those days, Doña Amaya, the cook at the ranch, sent for him with the consent of the boss. Linkoyan did not want to go, but he remembered well that he had promised the cook to return, and so he did. He brought with him a cousin, a young girl, who, harassed by her mother's husband, had asked for his help finding work at the estate. In her own home, she was continually mistreated and beaten along with her mother by a drunken criollo laborer who, with the help of the judge and the police, had taken away her mother's land. Each time he got drunk, he tried to rape her, but she had managed to escape his clutches. When she told Linkoyan her sorrows, he didn't hesitate to help her.

His return to the ranch was difficult. He had encountered Gutiérrez on several occasions, and there was always tension between them, but he had formed close friendships with some of the other workers. Two of them came from distant places: Ramón Sosa was from Santa Fe, and Gregorio Méndez from Córdoba. Fausto Kalfual was from Río Negro, and Venancio Antiman was from nearby, a neighbor of the estate. They were all were good men, hardworking and humble, who had ended up there for different reasons, but due to the insufficient or sometimes nonexistent wages, they were unable to make their way home. They generously shared their knowledge of rural life and supported one another. Sosa and Méndez were barbed-wire fence builders and skilled at their work, and Linkoyan had learned the trade from them before being assigned to the kitchen. Doña Amaya was fond of them and saved them the best portions of food. Kalfual was responsible for the horses, feeding and taking care of their needs, especially the breeding studs, which required extra attention since they were imported, expensive animals. Antiman was a general laborer; he was sent to do all sorts of work. He was a young man who looked old before his time, worn down by the years and the vicissitudes of life. He was small and agile, an orphan with no wife or children, deaf but not mute. Despite his difficulties, he made himself understood through signs. He was highly intelligent, though most people mocked him. Both Linkoyan and Doña Amaya looked after him, and he always preferred to be by Linkoyan's side.

One day, when all the workers sat down to have lunch together, the friends moved to the far end of the barn that served as a dining room, near an improvised fire, and as they chewed on the meat from a spicy stew, they began to daydream about their future. Sosa was the first to share his plans.

"I'll be leaving this shit soon. I already talked to the foreman of a ranch in La Pampa. He came here to buy animals with his boss, and he liked my fencing work. He offered me a job for the summer."

"Damned if my brother didn't get lucky!" Méndez quickly interjected.

Everyone laughed. Méndez looked at Sosa intently.

"Are you the only wire fence builder around here?" he asked sarcastically.

"No, my friend," Sosa replied. "You know full well that we work together, but when that man came from La Pampa, you were working with your team on the upper paddocks. If you want, I can talk to him and see if he'll take you, too. What do you think?"

Méndez thought for a moment.

"Perhaps, my friend, perhaps . . . ," he finally answered.

Kalfual also chimed in. "I want to leave, too. I was thinking of heading farther south. I have relatives in those parts." He looked at Linkoyan and asked, "What about you, my friend? Could you come with me? What do you think?"

Linkoyan smiled and replied, "I just want to finish my sentence here. My plan is to work my land and take care of my animals. My son is still just a pup. I want to be with my family."

The conversation was interrupted by Gutiérrez, who ordered them with arrogance, "Hey, stop loafing around and look lively. You're paid for work, not for idle chatter."

Sosa, fed up with Gutiérrez's constant abuses, leaped up in anger.

"You know what, gaucho? Nobody pays us here. We work from dawn to dusk and never see a penny. So the one in the wrong here is you, still thinking that you're all so clever and we're the fools. And I'll tell you what else, if we don't get paid by the end of the month, I'm leaving this shit behind!"

Gutiérrez was taken aback at first, but he soon reacted, drawing his knife and approaching Sosa to threaten him while hurling insults.

"Since when do you lowlife paupers dare tell me what to do? What the hell has made you so frisky all of a sudden?"

Gutiérrez reached out to stab Sosa with his knife, and a hand twisted his arm. It was Linkoyan, stepping in to defend his friend. He was the tallest and strongest of them all. Nobody ever crossed him, and perhaps that was why Gutiérrez despised him so much. On that day, Gutiérrez backed down, but he swore to get his revenge. As soon as he had the chance, he would even the score with Linkoyan and Sosa.

One fateful Sunday, Gutiérrez emerged from his lair in an alcoholic haze and with a thirst for violence and brutality, determined to have his way with Linkoyan's cousin. It wasn't so much that he desired her, but that he was in the habit of claiming any woman for himself, and the idea that the young girl was related to the man he most loathed took his fancy. Brandishing the hatred he had long been sharpening, he left the bar and headed toward the estate, half-drunk and half-lucid, greedy for adrenaline and blood.

It was noon, and autumn was in the air. The young woman was chopping and hurriedly carrying firewood to the cook, and her bare feet made the dry leaves rustle. The short, sharp utterance of her axe could be heard not far from the house. Monosyllables in the language of the mountain. Axe, blade, and firewood; strong arms that moved with determination; the blow of metal on wood; and the chopping into many pieces what was once a single tree, standing tall and wise.

Linkoyan, still groggy from alcohol, heard the sound of the axe. He had been drinking with his friends until the wee hours of the morning. He thought about getting up and starting to chop wood, but then remembered that it was Sunday, and he didn't have to work.

While the young woman, absorbed in her task, continued chopping, Gutiérrez approached the woodpile. Strangely, the dogs did not bark. Perhaps he had called them by name. We will never know. Suddenly, he took the girl by surprise from behind. She tried to scream, but Gutiérrez covered her mouth. She fought back furiously, but he was much stronger than she was. Gradually, she began to surrender, letting her body fall limp as he took out his member. But then, with the strength of an untamed filly, she jabbed him powerfully in the ribs with an elbow, the pain forcing him to release her. She screamed desperately for help, fleeing toward the house and straight into the kitchen.

Doña Amaya saw her stumble in, shaken and pale, her eyes filled with terror. Moments later, Gutiérrez burst into the kitchen. Amaya cursed him and tried to chase him away, but he was furious and responded with a slap. The elderly cook stumbled and fell, her ample body meeting the floor with a thud. She tried to stand up, but the pain in her left ankle made it impossible. Gutiérrez cursed her and grabbed her by the hair, just as Linkoyan entered the kitchen.

Both men drew their knives and began to fight. Linkoyan struck Gutiérrez, causing him to fall to the ground, but he sprang back up swiftly. Gutiérrez seized an iron poker from the fireplace and delivered a violent blow to Linkoyan's head, causing him to collapse. Once Linkoyan was on the ground, Gutiérrez took the chance to stab him. Yet he had no time to celebrate his victory. A sharp, cold, damp pain pierced him in the back. Antiman had killed him. Doña Amaya had seen him come into the kitchen but had remained silent.

Amaya was taken to the nearest town to treat her broken ankle, but she never returned to the ranch. She left without saying goodbye, and none of the workers ever heard from her again. Gutiérrez was buried on the estate. Linkoyan's body was carried back to the lof by his friends.

Linkoyan's cousin led the procession. Alongside her were Sosa, Méndez, Kalfual, and Antiman, who bore Linkoyan's body to Pirenrayen's house.

Dreams had spoken in previous moons, and the spirits had foretold what would happen. Chekeken had dreamed of her son. That morning, she had awoken feverish and drenched in sweat, and a sharp pain had pierced her chest. She asked Huentemilla to take her to her son's house. Just as they had decided upon the journey and were preparing to leave, a relative arrived with the news. Chekeken listened in disbelief, refusing to accept the truth. *It can't be him, they might be mistaken,* she thought. But they set out hurriedly for her son's house. By the time they arrived, many people had gathered, awaiting the arrival of the body. Chekeken fainted.

On the day Linkoyan was going to die, Pirenrayen also knew. It was a cold and windy autumnal dawn. Pirenrayen opened the door of her ruka, and suddenly a peuco appeared, almost touching her face. The bird screeched, flapped clumsily into the air, and flew away wounded. She caught a glimpse of the bleeding peuco and called out to it. She sang to it in anguish, and in the end, she ran after it, weeping and crying out, feeling a tightness in her chest and throat. "My man, my love, my brother, the father of my children," she cried as she ran toward nothingness. She stopped in exhaustion. She was five months pregnant. She did not have to wait long until she knew what the peuco bird was announcing.

Linkoyan's cousin and companions arrived in a horse-drawn cart with his shrouded body, by now fetid, since he had been dead several days.

The funeral was held according to our customs. My grandmother told me how hard it was for her to say farewell and let him go. She remembered the women scolding her harshly.

"Let the dead go! Don't be stubborn!" said some of them.

"Don't you know that we must die well? We must depart in harmony and strength. Linkoyan feels his heart, he knows his thoughts. He will do whatever you wish, but we who remain here do not know the needs of those who leave. His spirit must ride along the path of the stars to the wenu mapu. His voice is now crystal, his words will be his pewmas. His caresses will be the spring breezes, and he will see how the pain of his soul passes like the wind caressing the river's water," others reproached her.

Two weeks after the funeral, Pirenrayen lost the baby she had been carrying.

All this happened to my grandmother. That is how she told me the story, and that is how I stored it away in my heart.

Chapter 20

He Almost Swerved from His Destiny

In the winter of 1926, Liam was driving a train from Dublin to Belfast. He rarely stopped at the stations along the way but would be advised in advance when there were passengers to collect. Three stations before arriving at Belfast, the train slowed down, since an important British official, apparently a member of the royal family and the Supreme Court, was going to board.

Just as the train was about to pull in, almost fifty-five yards from the station, armed men with their faces covered took control of the driver's cab. Liam, who had just taken over as engine driver, immediately recognized the voice of the man giving orders: it was John, there could be no doubt. Once the official had boarded the train and they set out, the hooded men demanded that he divert its course. Liam swerved to the right and took another track, a track that was still unfinished. It was clear that they were planning to derail the train. Liam came to blows with one of them. They were locked in a brawl when the train was derailed.

One of the assailants died after hitting the boiler's feed pipe. The stoker was trapped under an iron bar that fell on his leg. Liam was catapulted through the air but came out unscathed. The other rebel had dislocated his shoulder. Throughout the carriages, screams and groans of pain could be heard. A commando group from the Irish Republican Army had managed to kidnap the judge, with the intention of exchanging him for one of their important imprisoned leaders. The police arrived promptly. Shots were fired, the crossfire steeped in hatred.

Liam lunged at the wounded man, who tried to defend himself despite his pain. It was John. Liam uncovered his face and confirmed his suspicion, but before he had a chance to ask anything, he felt the whistle of a bullet grazing his ear: an English police officer was firing at John at point-blank range. His militia uniform had given him away. Liam took John's gun and gave the officer a well-aimed shot in the leg.

"Kill him," John ordered, but Liam could not bring himself to do it.

Liam crouched down to help his friend stand up and escape. Just then, another police officer began to shoot. Liam, sensing the danger, acted on impulse and planted a bullet in his head. The man collapsed. The other injured police officer, whom Liam had spared, witnessed everything. Pale and with pleading eyes, he gazed at the armed men, determined to beg for his life. It was not necessary, since Liam had decided to escape immediately with his friend. Was it a mistake to spare his life and leave him as a witness? Perhaps. But it may also have been an act of fate.

The government wasted no time in publishing the names of the official's kidnappers, offering a handsome reward for the heads of each of the conspirators and masterminds of the Belfast train's derailment. On the night of the kidnapping, Liam sent a messenger to his house. Christine was informed of what had happened and took refuge at the house of some relatives. The police raided their home, destroying the furniture and turning the whole house upside down. They found nothing that would confirm Liam's involvement in the kidnapping, so they did not include his name among those of the fugitives.

Liam remained in hiding for a week, unsure what to do. John tried to persuade him to join the ranks of the IRA, but after a meeting with Christine, Liam knew that the best course of action would be to escape and return to her. His mother reminded him that his uncle, his father's younger brother, had been living in Argentina for several years. The news and gifts he sent seemed to come from a land blessed with peace and abundance.

Liam's parents engaged in a heated argument. Niall O'Sullivan did not want his son to flee.

"Wh-wh-what k-k-kind of c-c-coward d-do I ha-have f-f-for a s-s-son?" he asked his wife, stuttering more than ever.

"You have the bravest and worthiest son a father could have, one who managed to save his friend from the jaws of a certain death and was forced to kill to do so. Do you want to know whose idea it was for him to go to Argentina? Well, it was mine. I'm not going to make a sacrificial offering of the only son God gave me. I'm not going to give him up to a certain death in the hands of the British. I don't care whether it helps the republic. Other mothers can offer their sons. I'd rather die than see my son dead. This time, I'm not letting you decide for him."

Niall stared at her in fright. Never had he witnessed such bitterness or desperation in his wife. He approached and embraced her. With neither words nor tears, they agreed on their son's flight.

The last night Liam saw his wife, he found her more beautiful than ever. Christine wept silently. He promised to send for her soon. Before, Christine had idealized John. In her romantic and childish head, John was a hero and Liam a dunce. John was the handsome, seductive one; Liam was dull and cold. Yet now, in her heart and mind, all this had changed. John was responsible for her misfortune. Once again, he was mocking her distress and her solitude. She felt rage and contempt for this man who had disdained her love and who was now taking away the only man who loved her and could offer her the security she longed for.

For many people, the Americas represented pure savagery, total uncertainty. Christine was plagued with anxiety and fears, yet she stayed calm and showed strength to her husband and tried to inspire confidence in his parents. They dined together for the last time in a gloomy basement, lit by a flickering candle that cast a golden glow. During this farewell dinner, Liam's parents hardly spoke. Niall still believed that his son was acting like a coward, that he ought to stay and fight for the freedom of the Irish instead of fleeing to the ends of the earth. But he said nothing. He was convinced that they would never see each other again, and that was how it was. Niall died just a few years later.

During Liam's trip to Buenos Aires, he spent the time writing about his journey and his life. He took notes for the letters he planned to send Christine as soon as he reached his destination. All the adventure stories he had read as a child paled in comparison to what his eyes were seeing.

The boat he sailed on dropped anchor twice before reaching its final destination. Panama and Venezuela, and the turquoise Caribbean Sea with its reefs, looked like paradise to Liam. He almost swerved from his destiny, but his desire to see the end of the earth, Patagonia, guided him to our mapu.

Here begins the story that determined my grandmother's fate and that of my family.

Chapter 21

All Will Be Well

This ancient and yellowing diary I have in my hands belonged to Liam O'Sullivan. My grandmother used to ask me to read it, and I loved to do so. It began like this:

Today, February 12, 1926, I am on board the Irish Mist, *which measures 136 yards from prow to stern. According to the captain's calculations, we should be about thirty days or more away from our first port of call. After many days of discomfort and seasickness, today I awoke feeling better. Before, I couldn't stay on deck; the nausea immediately overcame me.*

I have been assigned a small room on the starboard side of the ship. The only spacious accommodation on the vessel is that of the captain. It is a ship with three bridges. The first is at the stern on the quarterdeck, and the second is on the tween deck. It includes a cabin and a stateroom. The crew members sleep in multiple cabins toward the rear of the first deck. Immediately ahead of these compartments, scarcely separated by some canvas curtains, are the deck and hold boatswains' berths. The ship's crew and garrison, composed of seventy men on three decks, sleep in bunks or hammocks hung from the bulkheads. The officers have their own cabins. The tables are bolted down.

My job is to keep the bow clean and help with the requests of the first officer, the boatswain of the deck. Luckily, this man is very approachable and understanding, unlike the captain, who always seems crabby and downcast. I think of Christine constantly, but I do my best not to, since every thought causes a tremor in my spirit that leaves me weak and dejected. I imagine how hard my departure must be for her, and it worries me to think that she won't have me by her side to run the household. I have caused my saintly mother an unforgivable amount of pain.

But when I manage to escape these bleak reflections, I fully enjoy the sea. I amuse myself by watching the white brushstrokes that paint the wake in the blue water. The seagulls' squawking tells us of a nearby port. The ocean is a fertile maritime land that we, the intrepid sailors, plow through to sow our dreams. The sea air floods my lungs with life. Despite the intense and sometimes unbearable cold, I never stop contemplating the sea. Its waves, sometimes gentle, remind me of meadows caressed by the wind. At other times, it shakes the ship so vigorously that it seems like the end is nigh. Yet I notice that I am the only one startled. The many crew members remain focused on their routine, calm, undisturbed by the provocative waves. They say there are only two great masters of sailing: the sea and the ship. Both are unknown to me; all I know is railways and trains.

I have run into two old classmates here with whom I barely used to speak. Now, we have been brought together by our exile and this adventure that will take us to distant, mysterious lands.

February 15, 1926, somewhere in the Atlantic Ocean, on board the Irish Mist

Finally, I have time to write. We have been busy repairing the boat. Two days of rough waves dislodged the cargo and caused some damage on the starboard side.

Yesterday, I had a strange dream. I was at the train station in Dublin with Christine. She took my hand, and I could feel its warmth. The train arrived, and only I boarded it. She remained standing on the platform, bidding me goodbye with her beautiful smile. I felt no distress at leaving. Inside the train, the sun shone brightly. I settled into the last seat, gazing out the window at the landscape. I saw fields of wheat swaying in the breeze. Then they turned watery, and the train traveled on rails through the sea. Fish of all colors and sizes swam around us. I watched them in astonishment and fascination. Suddenly, the train was jolted and derailed. An immense whale emerged from the depths and lifted the train on its back. The train rose to the surface. The waters were jade colored, and the sky was ablaze with reds and oranges. The whale gently placed us on placid waters and swam away. I climbed onto the train's roof to get a better view, and the whale leaped, as if trying to touch the sky, then plunged back into the depths of the sea. During one of those leaps, the waves seethed and splashed my face with frigid water.

When I opened my eyes, I was drenched. The ill-humored captain had thrown water on me to wake me up. According to him, I should have been awake and moving

*for over an hour. I didn't argue with him; I simply got up
and dressed swiftly and worked very hard that day.*

It took Liam O'Sullivan five months to reach Buenos Aires. The
fishing vessel he had boarded suffered serious damage and had to remain
in a shipyard in Panama for two months undergoing repairs. Alongside
his friends, Pat O'Donnell and the Scotsman Ryan Mackwell, who
had been his schoolmates in childhood, he had some unforgettable
experiences there. Despite his initial regrets that the lack of money and
sudden departure prevented him from traveling in better conditions,
Liam later felt grateful for his fate. During those months, he witnessed
the harshness of life on board a ship, the danger the crew faced every day
for meager rewards. He saw two men die in different circumstances, but
the cause was the same: the fierceness of the sea that defied those who
sought to tame it. Yet he also encountered the humanity and solidarity
that emerged from the depths of the souls in those lonely and rugged
men, simultaneously brave and resigned, who knew that the wind and
the sea dictated their destinies. In his diary, he writes about his new
friends as follows:

April 24, 1926, approaching the shores of Panama
   *The breeze is warm. Pat and Ryan have told me
everything they have read about this place. Today we
caught a glimpse of Coral Island and are heading toward
San Blas Bay. Pat is a little younger than me. He is short
and sturdy, with a cheerful and youthful expression. He
has a booming laugh, and his good humor is infectious.
He is always cracking jokes, at which he is very clever,
and finds something amusing in everything to make us
laugh. Ryan is shy. We call him the Scot, just as we did at
school. He is very tall and thin. His voice doesn't match
his appearance. Sometimes a high-pitched note escapes
from his mouth, and then he clears his throat and repeats*

himself. It's as if his vocal cords are slowly wearing out. We still don't know how long we will be staying here. I am very curious to explore this country and anxious to reach my destination soon.

April 29, 1926, Panama City

We have been in Panama for several days now, but only yesterday were we able to go out and explore the city. The scent of the trees and flowers is intoxicating. The streets are crowded with people, many of them foreigners who came during the building of the Panama Canal and ended up staying to seek their fortunes. The beauty and grace of the women here leave me mesmerized. They walk through the city's narrow streets, swaying their bodies as if dancing to the sun. Most of the population is of mixed race. The African slaves brought during the colonial period mixed with the native populations. In their faces you can see a past of pain and nostalgia, but also the Indigenous features that convey strength and determination. The people show such beauty and vibrancy that I believe it will be difficult for me to leave.

We wandered through the streets of the city center, hungry, and along Balboa Avenue, we found a small tavern where some unusual local dishes were served that smelled delicious. As soon as we went in, a sullen-faced criollo man of medium height asked us where we came from in broken English. Pat is the one who speaks Spanish the best, so he acted as our translator. We ate and drank until we were stuffed. Pat kept telling of our misadventures at sea with great humor, and I laughed until my stomach ached. One by one, the other patrons left, and finally, the owner approached and asked us to pay, since it was closing time. My friend asked him if it was possible to meet the person who prepared such delicious dishes. The man kindly agreed and called out to the cook in a booming voice. An Indigenous girl came shyly to the door. Her beauty was exotic and captivating but, at the same time, simple. Her hair was gathered in a long braid. She was a young Buglé Indian, no older than fifteen or sixteen. The owner ordered her to come closer to our table. The girl resisted, but he took her by the arm and spoke to her in their language. She kept her head lowered, never looking at us, until Pat stood and approached her as if bewitched and said in Spanish, "Thank you, miss. Good food." Realizing that we were entranced by the young girl's allure, the man said, "She is my wife. We are married." We were left perplexed. The man was twenty years older than her. On our way back to the ship, we could hardly talk of anything but that beautiful girl.

April 30, 1926, Panama City
We went back to the tavern. We learned that the young Buglé girl works alone at lunchtime, so starting today, we will only go there for lunch. One of the women who helps her told us that from morning until afternoon, the owner works for the Americans at the canal, then later takes charge at the tavern. The girl is not alone in the kitchen; two women assist her. One is a robust middle-aged woman of African descent, quick to laugh, and the other is an elderly woman with gray hair and a hunched back.

May 5, 1926, Panama City

Something happened yesterday. We were at the tavern, having a lively conversation. We watched the young cook coming and going from the street, never stopping for a minute. On one of her trips, she came in weighed down with vegetables and bananas. She made her way toward the kitchen, trying to keep her balance. We were sitting, as usual, at the tables arranged on the sidewalk, beneath a reed canopy to shield us from the scorching sun, and we watched her go along with the grace of a tightrope walker. But the spectacle didn't last long, since the pyramid she carried in her arms collapsed. Pat rushed to help her pick up the bananas and vegetables, offering to carry everything to the kitchen. When he returned to the table, his expression had changed. He looked at us and said, "She has the most beautiful smile I have ever seen in my life." To our surprise, our cheerful and chatty friend remained silent for the rest of the meal.

Liam's diary is full of little anecdotes and descriptions of places, animals, and plants, but the story of his friend Pat is the one my grandmother most loved to hear. And that is the one I'll keep telling as I read a few sections of the diary.

June 15, 1926, Panama City

This morning, the captain told us that we will set sail in fifteen days. The suffocating heat and mosquitoes have left me feeling wilted and irritable, so this news has lifted my spirits. Although at first, I thought it would be very hard for me to leave this beautiful country, the news has brought us joy, especially to Ryan and me. Pat has shown no interest in leaving. Since the day he helped the young Buglé girl with her vegetables, something has happened inside him, and we have noticed his transfor-mation. He only eats what she makes, so each day when we go for lunch, he requests a meal to take with him for dinner. This has offended our on-board cook. At night, we hear him slip out of his hammock and leave. He returns almost at dawn. He sleeps peacefully, but every morning, he looks exhausted. We haven't dared to ask what's going on with him.

June 20, 1926, Panama City

Today we sailed on a small boat through San Blas Bay, visiting the islands where the Kuna people live. We brought many coconuts to the ship, which we traded with the Kuna. Pat admitted that he won't be going on with us; he has decided to stay. Ryan is furious with him; they argued, and I had to intervene to prevent them from fighting. They have been friends since childhood. Ryan feels betrayed; they had agreed to go to Buenos Aires together. Furthermore, it was Pat who convinced him to make the journey, and now he wants to stay here. We don't understand his reasons.

June 22, 1926, Panama City

We have heard nothing from Pat. Yesterday, he slipped out of his hammock like every other night, but this time he didn't come back. We decided to go down to the city and have lunch at the tavern, hoping to find him there. Then we were shaken by some news. It hit us like a hurricane, leaving us stunned. The tavern has been burned down by its owner, who, armed and accompanied by other men, has set out in search of his wife and our friend Pat, who seems to have run away with her. They had been seeing each other in secret. Now we know why he was stealthily slipping away at night.

When we arrived, the robust black woman stood frozen in front of the charred remains of what used to be the tavern. She saw us coming and burst into tears. We could hardly make out what she was telling us; we grasped only a few words. Until a North American missionary who speaks perfect Spanish, whom we often see on the streets, passed by and acted as translator. We were able to question the woman, who, of course, doesn't know much, but she told us enough to understand that our friend had put his life at risk by falling madly in love with the girl. We are worried that her husband might catch them, but the woman reassured us, saying that the girl knows her land better than anyone and that they have probably already nearly reached her tribe. It will be difficult for anyone pursuing them to catch them.

We still don't know the name of the young cook, whom everyone calls Taina. I will miss Pat; the journey won't be as much fun without him.

June 30, 1926, Atlantic Ocean

We have set out from Panama and are venturing into the farthest reaches of the ocean. The sun is still scorching, and although much of our time is taken up by the tasks on board, I find moments of solitude where I can gaze at the horizon and imagine my new life. We have once again had the company of whales. I even thought I saw the one that appeared in my dream.

July 2, 1926, Sailing near Colombia

The captain has decided not to make a stop in Colombia, though we are sailing through its waters. He would rather go on to Venezuela, where cargo is to be delivered.

July 15, 1926, City of Maracaibo, Venezuela

We have dropped anchor on the Venezuelan coast for ten days. This afternoon, Ryan and I will take a walk around the city. The heat and mosquitoes make their presence felt here as well, but the air is less stifling.

July 16, 1926, City of Maracaibo, Venezuela

Yesterday, we walked a lot. We explored the city center and ventured up the narrow dirt lanes to the hills dotted with modest, hand-built dwellings made of mud, reeds, and cane. The people here are very friendly, and my Spanish has improved a great deal. I surprise myself when I can speak fluently with the locals. The food here is delicious and fresh. I tried a kind of cornbread they call an arepa and liked it very much.

Ryan is not as lively as he was at the beginning of the journey; he misses Pat. They used to work together at a printing press, and they were planning to start one in Buenos Aires. Now he is unsure what he wants to do. We have decided to visit the railway station here and have a look at the trains. Tomorrow, a railway worker we met on our excursion will take us to the engine houses. I miss trains a lot—the smell of petrol, the steam forced angrily out from the engine, the whistle. Even the rails seem to me symmetrical lines of steely beauty, inviting us to get

179

lost on paths to the unknown. I am excited to climb back onto a train again.

Yesterday, I sent letters to Christine and my mother. I know my father does not want to hear from me. I don't know if exile is a worse sentence than prison, but at times, I think it must be. I may never be able to return to Ireland. I must concentrate all my efforts on making a new life possible in Buenos Aires. Christine and I deserve to have peace and happiness.

July 20, 1926, City of Maracaibo, Venezuela
These days, as soon as I finish my tasks on the ship, I get ready to meet my new railway friend Fortunato Sánchez. He is a highly intelligent, modest, and practical man. His knowledge as an engineer has surprised me. He knows a great deal about the mechanics as well as the history of trains. Each train evokes a story about its origin and how it got here. Everywhere, the Americans and British have left their wicked, plundering mark. Venezuela is no exception. I am not remotely surprised by the stories people tell me of unjust wars, of the newcomers' lying and swindling ways. Corrupt governments colluding with the usual thieves. I can see people's suffering and frustrations in their faces.

I have felt very much at ease with Fortunato's family. Ryan has begun to smile again and has offered to help Mr. Fortunato build an engine house. I have also offered to help, but I am not as eager as my friend. The heat and the mosquitoes are not good hosts, and the extra tasks, in addition to my arduous work on the ship, inspire no enthusiasm in me.

July 24, 1926, City of Maracaibo, Venezuela
    The captain gathered us and told us that we will have to stay longer than we were first told, since they are expecting an important cargo that we will transport to the port of Santos in Brazil. While we are waiting, we have been ordered to leave the ship until we hear news. It seems that with the whole crew on board, they lose money. Only the boatswain and some officers will stay with the captain.
    Ryan and I have decided to visit Caracas. But first, we will finish Mr. Fortunato Sánchez's engine house.

July 30, 1926, Caracas, Venezuela
    We have only been in Caracas for a day. I arrived here with a fever and am feeling weak. I decided not to go out today. I asked Ryan not to stay with me. I want him to enjoy himself and tell me later what he has seen. As soon as I feel better, I will join him on his outings.

August 5, 1926, Caracas, Venezuela
    These past few days, I have had a high fever. Today, I was able to get up and take a few steps around the room, still feeling dizzy, and with a terrible headache. Poor Ryan has had to look after me and has not left my side. I have ended up here in this modest hospital. I seem to have taken ill with a strange fever caused by mosquitoes, but fortunately, I will recover. The doctor told us that these bites can be lethal.
    For two feverish nights, I dreamed of the girl again, the one who appears in my dreams whenever something serious happens to me. This time, I could see her face

very clearly. When I close my eyes and recall that dream, her gaze becomes vivid again. Her brown skin, her Indigenous features. Her eyes are intensely green. As in the previous dreams, she continues to speak to me in an unknown language, but I understand what she says. After dreaming of her, I began to heal.

I tried to share this experience with Ryan, but he started mocking me. He assured me that it was all part of the nightmares caused by the illness, that the girl in my dreams had nothing to do with my recovery.

August 8, 1926, Caracas, Venezuela

Tomorrow I will be discharged. I am keen to go out into the streets. I have been locked up here for a week, and since I was ill on my arrival, I haven't been able to see anything. I must take it slow and steady; I am still very weak. Today it is raining hard, like a biblical deluge. The sky growls with thunder, and lightning briefly lights up the beautiful city. The crowds have taken shelter in their homes. From the corridor of this modest hospital, I gaze at the inner courtyard, and from my window, I see the comings and goings in the street. I think of Christine. I long to have her with me, to love her, to hold her. Oh, what I would give to see her at the piano, to approach slowly and silently and caress her neck, her long and beautiful neck! I wonder what time it is there, in Dublin. What is Christine doing? Not a day has gone by that I don't think of her, through all these months of travel. I regret holding all the passion inside me and not having overpowered her unyielding coldness with tenderness. Perhaps I was too clumsy, too full of pride.

August 11, 1926, Caracas, Venezuela

This morning Ryan and I bid each other farewell; he has decided to try his luck in Caracas. He met an enthusiastic young Basque man who suggested that they go into business and set up a small printing press. I will miss him.

I am at the train station, about to set out for Maracaibo. My heart is pounding; I believe it's nerves about the journey, this journey, which has been prolonged and has helped me understand this continent. But the fears that once plagued me have gradually vanished. I try to find hope every day. I have written to my uncle, and he seems excited to welcome me. All will be well. I can sense it.

PART FOUR

PART FOUR

Chapter 22

Taking on the Identity of the Enemy

Liam O'Sullivan reached Buenos Aires in the early spring of 1927. He was met by a beautiful city in a young country, where everything had yet to be built. He did not know his paternal uncle in person; it had been a long time since he had left Ireland. Liam had seen the odd picture of him along with the brief letters he sent to his older brother, Niall. As soon as Liam set foot in his house, where he was to stay for a while, Liam learned that his uncle Patrick O'Sullivan went by the name of Lord George Husprum here and had married a wealthy criolla woman of high birth, a woman whose youth was fading but who had been courted by almost every eligible bachelor of the Buenos Aires oligarchy in her day. Yet none of them succeeded in winning her heart. It used to amuse my grandmother to tell me this story, so unusual for the time and place.

The day they met, María Isabel Alvear Rosas realized immediately that Lord Husprum was a fraud and that his fame as a bearer of blue blood, much like his adventure stories, was an invention and nothing but a sham. He was undoubtedly a seducer, but also a liar, a fortune hunter who would have married even a doddering old lady to secure her wealth. María Isabel sought ways to reject his advances, but the cunning Lord Husprum would appear at moments when she least expected, with tempting proposals that compelled her to leave her seclusion to enjoy the invitation. They went on horseback rides through dreamlike places, bathing in pools in the countryside. He even managed to arrange an airplane for them to fly over the sea. He always came up with brilliant ideas, and María Isabel accepted them gladly.

The young ladies of Buenos Aires society sighed at the very thought of him. His perfect smile, with a gentle curl of the lips, revealed a manly and resolute mouth. Tall and elegant, with broad shoulders and strong arms, light-blond hair, and deep-blue eyes, he captivated all the women, but set out to seduce and marry only one: the wealthiest of them all, Miss María Isabel Alvear Rosas. She, of course, became an object of envy and jealousy.

No one could imagine the real person hidden behind the amiable and alluring appearance of Patrick O'Sullivan, who enjoyed only the fleeting love found in brothels and viewed women as a necessary evil in life. He was driven by an inescapable need lodged deep in his core. He unleashed the desperation of his fears and the alienation of his soul on female bodies, convinced that he could exorcise them through sex; for these brief moments, at least, he managed to feel free and at peace.

María Isabel, too, was hiding a secret, one that concealed the nature of her true love: Marie Le Duvont, a young French orphan girl. The war had stripped Marie of everything: her mother, her father, and her younger brother had perished beneath the rubble during a bombing on the outskirts of Paris. When she was still a child, she had had to fend for herself. After many trials and a great deal of desperation, she decided to set out for the Americas. At first, she intended to reach French Guiana, but fate wove her a different future and led her to other territories. Marie boarded the wrong ship and ended up in the Río de la Plata. She spent a few months on an estate in Uruguay as a governess for three capricious girls, daughters of a cousin of María Isabel.

María Isabel Alvear Rosas visited the estate for a few days, enough to fall head over heels in love with Marie. When the time came to leave, María Isabel promised to give her cousin the gift of a luxurious automobile in exchange for permission to take young Marie as a house-keeper. In those days, only wealthy men owned cars; women did not, so this was a tempting offer. The cousin gladly accepted.

They never parted again. But under the watchful gaze of María Isabel's mother, living together was not easy for them. This was why María Isabel decided to investigate Lord Husprum; she had a feeling that this man could hold the key to her freedom. As soon as she had irrefutable proof in her hands that he was a fraud, without hesitation or delay, she decided to propose a deal.

One afternoon, when Lord Husprum arrived at the Alvear Rosas house with gifts for María Isabel, she greeted him with excitement instead of her usual scorn, much to her suitor's surprise. Husprum was delighted and thought absurdly that her change of tune was due to the new fragrance he was wearing.

"Miss María Isabel," Husprum said, "how happy and radiant you look today."

"Perhaps it's love," she responded suggestively, setting his ego alight. "Would you like to go for a walk in the garden? There are some beautiful African flowers I'd like to show you."

Leaving their still-full teacups on the drawing room table, they walked out of the house to stroll through the garden.

"Miss María Isabel, have you considered my previous proposal of marriage?" Husprum asked determinedly.

"Lord Husprum, not only have I considered it, but I have also adjusted it," María Isabel said with a mischievous glint in her eye, smiling at his bewildered expression.

"I don't understand what you mean . . ."

"If I am going to get married, I must know very well whom I will be marrying. Don't you believe, Mr. Patrick O'Sullivan, that in a marriage there can be no lies?"

The false Husprum paled upon hearing his name.

"How did you know?" he ventured to ask once he regained his composure.

189

"That is of no importance, Mr. O'Sullivan," she said. "I know all about you. For instance, I know that you come from a humble Irish family on the outskirts of Belfast and regularly exchange letters with your older brother, who lives in Dublin. But don't worry, I am discreet. I am the sort of woman who knows how to keep secrets. I am, you might say, as mysterious as a fathomless ocean."

"What proposal do you have for me?" Patrick asked, by now grave and nervous.

"I am in love with someone whom I can never marry. We will never be able to live our love freely. This person also loves me and will accept any strategy to keep us from being parted. I will agree to marry you in exchange for my freedom. I will reveal nothing of your true identity as long as you say nothing of my secret relationship."

Containing his vexation, the false Husprum let out a long sigh before he replied. "I still fail to understand, Miss María Isabel. Are you planning to bring another man into the house once we are married? How will you prevent your parents from objecting?"

"But I do not love a man. My love already lives with me; she and I have been living together for some time now."

Husprum froze upon hearing her confession. "You love a woman!" he exclaimed. "Does anyone else know?"

"No" was her sharp reply. She added firmly and curtly, "Mr. Patrick O'Sullivan, let's not make a drama out of this. You do not love me, and I do not love you, either. You want my fortune, and I want my freedom. If we both commit to respecting our agreement, each of us will get what we are seeking. Besides, you have no choice: you are bankrupt and penniless, with creditors on your trail."

There was a long silence, during which he seemed to be staring into space. Suddenly, he regained his strength and looked her straight in the eye. "Very well, I accept your conditions, but you will have to sign a prenuptial agreement ensuring me half of your fortune if you leave me."

María Isabel burst into peals of laughter, shaking her head. "You are even more of a shameless swindler than I thought. I have proof of several of your scams in Ireland, England, and Belgium. I can imagine how delighted your victims, all prominent merchants, would be to find out where the swindler is. Believe me, you won't be able to defeat me. I will establish the clauses. You will simply sign."

They agreed on a date for the wedding, the social event of the year. María Isabel was radiant and happy, while Patrick felt relieved and secure. The ceremony took place in the Buenos Aires cathedral, and the wedding was long remembered; though for Mademoiselle Marie, it was a sorrowful day. But she had placed all her trust in María Isabel; she knew that María Isabel would never betray her and that everything she did was to make sure they could stay together.

Marie decided to send María Isabel a powerful message to remind her how much she loved her: she rose unexpectedly amid the guests and began to sing with a voice full of strength, passion, sweetness, and devotion. Her love song brought tears to the eyes of those present and almost caused a scandal. The bride, dressed in white before the altar, turned her back to the priest, walked as if in a trance toward Marie, and embraced her fervently.

"I will never stop loving you, never," she whispered into her ear. Then she returned to the altar to say, "I do."

For Liam, the fact that his uncle had changed his name and called himself Lord Husprum was an indicator either of mental disturbance or a perverse kind of cunning. Lord Husprum had stopped frequenting brothels, but he had a lover whom he visited often. The Buenos Aires bourgeoisie knew all about it. Lord Husprum's improper behavior troubled his nephew. But despite his eccentricities and the rumors that flew about him, Liam viewed him as sensitive and attentive to his wife, kind to his workers, and generous to his friends. He would hear the couple laughing and talking until late at night in María Isabel's room; then the door would slowly open and close again. Liam would hear his uncle's soft and hesitant steps going down the stairs and out into the street. It was a nightly routine.

One night, his uncle came to his bedroom and invited him for a drink. Buenos Aires was more beautiful at night, he explained, especially as summer drew near. In the street, the air smelled of jasmine and magnolia. The heady aroma caused both men's worries to fade, and suddenly they felt free and happy.

They entered a bar in the city center. A tango quartet was playing improvised, fashionable melodies. The bandonion player closed his eyes to caress his instrument, making it weep with a long note of nostalgia for the city's outskirts. They drank whiskey, smoked cigars, and talked about their homeland, their family, and the future. Well into the night, feeling an easy intimacy, Liam took the chance to ask about the new identity his uncle had made for himself. He wanted to know why.

"Uncle, why did you come to Argentina?"

"I had to get away. Some of my business ventures didn't work out as planned, and my life was in danger. I wanted to reach the end of the world, to have a fresh start. I couldn't bring my past here, that would have ruined everything. Do you understand? Everything had to be new. The Argentines are quite amusing: they love Europe and want to be like it in every way. What saddens me about them is their fondness for the scourge of the English. It's inconceivable to me that despite feeling contempt from the English, they are so accommodating. I thought that perhaps by pretending to be one of them, a lord, extravagant and adventurous, the doors of this wealthy country would open for me. And you know what, my boy? That is exactly what's happened," he said, bursting into laughter.

"I don't find it funny," Liam said, staring at him, disillusioned. "It's sad, and I'm disappointed that you deny being Irish. I understand having to change your name, but your whole identity? Taking on the identity of the enemy?"

"Who is the enemy, my boy? The English? You haven't understood a thing. Our enemy is victimization. We love being poor, being the ones to suffer. We think, God will reward us with a supposed paradise. If it weren't the English, others would take advantage of our stupid Christian innocence. We resign ourselves to everything, believing that this is the fate God has chosen for us. My god is money, my boy, and I seize every opportunity that comes my way to get it. I am not like your father. I shall never resign myself to poverty."

"And what about your wife, Uncle? Does she know the truth?" Liam inquired.

"Of course she knows," his uncle answered with a hint of sadness. "I could never hide anything from her. First, because she is the cleverest person I have ever known, and second, because I am madly in love with her." He confessed this with his eyes welling up.

"I'm glad, Uncle, that you love your wife so much. She must love you, too," said Liam, wishing to confirm their happiness.

Patrick O'Sullivan looked up and replied with his sad revelation. "No, my boy, she doesn't love me. I think perhaps she is fond of me, since I have seen her face light up when she sees me, but it is merely a friendly feeling I have managed to cultivate in her heart. She does not want me as I want her; she will never love me as I love her. Her heart belongs to someone else, and I've seen the look on her face when that person is nearby. I sense the desire taking hold of her body and her skin. She will never be able to love me as long as that person is by her side. I am merely the entertaining brother she would have liked to have."

A bitter silence took hold of both men. Liam remembered Christine and John and thought that perhaps his uncle was forecasting the married life that awaited him. Suddenly, the whiskey, smoke, voices, and music all unsettled his thoughts, and everything began to spin before his eyes.

"I'm going for a walk," he said to his uncle, feeling terribly dizzy.

He rose clumsily from his chair and looked around for the exit. He gulped the pure breeze from the river, which filled his lungs, making him dizzier still. He felt as if the Buenos Aires air was returning to him the painful homesickness he had been determined to overcome. He drunkenly called out Christine's name. Lights came on in some of the houses. Their inhabitants had surely woken up, startled by his cries. His stomach churned, forcing him to lean against the wall of a shop while he vomited. Feeling relieved, he kept walking through the deserted cobbled streets, until his body could no longer go on, and he stopped again.

His uncle went out to look for him and found him sitting on the edge of a sidewalk. He convinced him to return home. In his uncle's comfortable car, Liam slowly recovered. He felt lighter now, and his head was clearer. He felt protected, like when he was a child and his father was by his side.

The grand mansion stood proudly in a leafy neighborhood, near the city center and not far from the Río de la Plata. His uncle's in-laws had given it to him as a gift when he married María Isabel, so delighted were they that their eldest daughter would not be confined to spinsterhood after all.

Liam slept until past noon in the plush bed. When he woke up, his uncle was no longer there. He had left for the coast to oversee one of his estates. Liam went out into the garden and found María Isabel and Marie, who were picking flowers and pruning trees. When they saw him, María Isabel raised a hand to greet him, beckoning him closer.

"Good morning, Liam. Did you sleep well?" she asked.

"Yes, thank you," he replied politely.

"Have you had something to eat?" María Isabel inquired.

"Yes, Aunt, thank you for asking. You are too kind."

"I'm glad," she said with a wide smile. She was the only person in the house who spoke perfect English, so she was the only one with whom Liam could have long conversations. He practiced his Spanish with the servants, but he noticed that they would often laugh, probably at his poor pronunciation. He spent a good while with the women, then decided to go for a walk.

He strolled through the city and got lost. Feeling sorrowful and reflective, he came upon the riverbank. There he paused, gazing at the river for a long while. All alone, facing that vast, wide river that looked like a sea, he felt tiny and insignificant. He recognized once again his immense loneliness and felt adrift. *Yes, I am lost,* he told himself. Deep in a daydream, he saw the moon appear while the sun still hung in the sky, hiding itself lazily, and he was overcome with regret. *I have been imprudent,* he thought. *It was disrespectful to question my uncle as I did. He is a gracious host. After all, who am I to judge him? How dare I reproach his behavior?* He thought of his father, the disappointment he must feel toward such an ungrateful son, his only son, who instead of adding his strength to the fight had fled like a coward. Yes, undoubtedly, he was a coward. He felt deeply remorseful and ashamed, but there was nothing he could do now. He was so far from home and from those he loved. Now he must focus on starting a new life there and bringing Christine and his parents to join him soon.

He arrived back at the mansion just in time for dinner. It was a cheerful meal, and his aunt offered him work at one of her father's estates. As it turned out, María Isabel was a highly cultured and curious woman. There was a certain magic about her that injected good humor into the mood of the family. She was generous with her loved ones. She detested flattery and obsequiousness. She was private about her own life and distrustful of new people who approached her. But she saw Liam for the man he was—honorable, straightforward, and sincere. A young man who was simply asking life for another chance.

Chapter 23

The Fertility of a Generous Land

A few weeks after the beginning of 1927, Liam found himself managing the La Herradura estate, about sixty miles from the city of Buenos Aires, in the south of the province. La Herradura spanned sixty thousand fertile, well-irrigated acres of pampa, with plentiful grazing for animals. It was a bountiful, generous land, bubbling with freshwater springs.

Liam carried out his duties responsibly for a year, yet he did not come into his own in his work, and he did not feel comfortable at the helm. At first, his limited command of Spanish made it difficult for him to communicate with the workers. His closest subordinate was a Scottish foreman who had been working at the estate for about ten years. He was bilingual and called himself the Scot, downplaying the importance of his name. The laborers referred to him as Señor Scot, but Liam opted to call him by his name, Gregory Mackern. Gregory guided him through all the tasks he needed to oversee. The ranch employed around fifty-seven people engaged in a range of jobs. Their primary output was livestock, though they also grew wheat.

Liam's uncle rarely visited the place, preferring to stay at the larger estate near the sea, where he spent most of his days. Sometimes, he would bring María Isabel along; only then was she not accompanied by Mademoiselle Marie. For some time now, María Isabel had wanted to become a mother, but so far, she had been unable to conceive. Mademoiselle Marie could not bear those trips to the estate without her. Before each departure, the young woman would lock herself in her room to cry, which both distressed and annoyed María Isabel, who would try to console her.

"Marie, I want a child for us to care for together. A baby will bring us complete happiness. We shall be whole." And she would embrace her, showering her tear-stained face with kisses.

"I cannot imagine you with him. It pains me to think of you in his arms. I think he enjoys it . . . ," Mademoiselle Marie would confess.

María Isabel would laugh and gently reproach her for being so jealous. She tried to calm her, reminding her that she was the only person she lived for and that she would rather die than be without her love. Once Marie seemed more serene, María Isabel would finally set off to be with her husband.

At times, María Isabel felt confused, thinking that perhaps she loved them both. In his wife's presence, Patrick O'Sullivan took off the mask of Lord Husprum and could be his authentic self. When he was with her, all that mattered to him was making her happy. They would sometimes reminisce about their wedding night and burst into laughter. That night, he had clumsily attempted to deflower her, only to receive a slap. Defiant, she looked him in the eyes with pure determination.

"I do not love you. I am not attracted to you. I despise your skin, your body, and the way you smell. I married you because I couldn't stand to be imprisoned under my parents' watchful gaze. I have told you before: I have simply bought my freedom. I ask nothing of you. You are free to enjoy all that you have gained from this false union. Whatever you do with your time, your body, or your feelings is of no interest to me. I assure you that I will be ruthless in demanding my freedom. That is my only requirement. I want nothing but my freedom. From now on, let us pretend to be happy. We must be discreet, we must keep up appearances to keep protecting ourselves," she said in perfect English.

Her new husband stared at her in astonishment. That night, a deep admiration was born in him, for her character, her determination, and her intelligence. Those were the qualities that made him fall in love with her.

In time, her feelings also changed, but she preferred not to analyze or put a name to them; she simply enjoyed them just as she enjoyed her beloved Marie. Lord Husprum, for his part, tried to conceal the jealousy and disdain he felt for Mademoiselle Marie. He almost never spoke to her when he arrived home, and she hid away in her bedchamber to avoid him, though for dinner, María Isabel required both to be at her side. Only María Isabel could puncture the awkward and hostile atmosphere with her good humor and witty stories. This awakened in Lord Husprum the deft and amusing storyteller he really was, able to make up ludicrous tales with a veneer of plausibility. Mademoiselle Marie could not help but laugh, and this, for María Isabel, was the greatest gift.

Spurred on by the sorrowful stories Marie had told of her life, María Isabel felt drawn to helping the victims of war, especially little girls. In those days, there was a sizable wave of migration. But her desire to become a mother overcame her with such force that the frustration of her inability to become pregnant made her troubled and short tempered. Yet she did not lose hope, and she enjoyed her intimate encounters with her husband.

Before the first rays of light of the new day softened the night, Liam was already among the workers, assigning tasks to the day laborers as well as to the employees. Every evening, he spent a few hours learning Spanish. He wrote often to his wife and parents. Just as he was feeling ready to bring Christine, he received a telegram from her telling him that Niall O'Sullivan had died, and that Sarah was gravely ill and in the hospital. She would take care of her mother-in-law; as soon as she recovered, she would advise him so they could organize both women's journey to Argentina.

The news grieved and anguished him greatly. Liam sent all the money he had saved for his wife to use for his father's funeral and his mother's hospital care. From then on, their arrival was inexplicably postponed, and seemed to become increasingly distant. Thanks to Liam's support, both women lived well and were even able to restore the house. Defying the myth of enmity between mother- and daughter-in-law, they lived together and seemed to love each other very much; it was a relationship of mutual respect and care.

After two years with his uncle, Liam decided to leave the estate and apply to work on the railway. He had heard that the British were hiring men to extend the railway into Patagonia. It was the place he had longed to visit since he was a boy, and his railway spirit returned to inhabit him, giving him hope and enthusiasm. His uncle understood and accepted his decision, using his contacts to obtain an immediate position for his nephew.

Liam set out on February 20, 1929, eager and happy, for Patagonia. Finally, he would reach the land he'd dreamed of for so long.

Chapter 24

The Best Man for the Job

The day Liam O'Sullivan set foot in the province of Chubut, the end of summer was fast approaching. Pirenrayen had no inkling that her life would soon be changed forever. Almost eight years had gone by since she had become a widow. Her son, Kawel, had become an independent, confident, and curious little boy. In those days, my father, *ñi chaw*, must have been about ten.

Fresia Coliman was an old woman and was beginning to lose her sight. A whitish gauze like a thin curtain slowly lowered over one of her pupils and was darkening her world. That was why she had decided to stop attending to the sick and spent her days spinning and weaving. With Kawel's help, she had set up a big loom on which she had begun to weave a blanket for her granddaughter. She had been making it for years, and always found a reason to unravel and weave it again, as if her days were going to end when the weaving was finished. Perhaps that labor truly was a spell to lengthen her life.

Fresia enjoyed her great-grandson's wit very much; he was affectionate toward the old woman and obeyed all her orders, unlike with his ñuke, to whom he answered back and whom he occasionally disobeyed.

Liam O'Sullivan was unloading his luggage from the Ford Model T that had brought him to the center of the estate where he would stay until the first railway accommodations were ready. Meanwhile a few miles away, Fresia was playing with Kawel while Pirenrayen toasted wheat in a cast-iron pan that hung above the fire. Every so often, she shook the pan, and the rusty old chains clanked as they swayed. Fresia drew near the fire and gazed fixedly into the flames.

"I had a pewma last night, my dear, and it has me worried."

"What happened, Grandmother? Was it a bad dream?"

Deep in the night, a blue butterfly had visited Fresia.

"I took a caterpillar inside its cocoon in my hands and placed it near the fire," Fresia began. "It looked like it was going to die, and I felt sorry for it. I cried and bathed the caterpillar with my tears, and it began to emerge from its cocoon. Little by little, it shed its covering, until it was completely naked, and I saw its blue, sparkling wings grow. It was so pretty! It gave me joy to see it flap its wings. And off it flew. But as it flew, it grew and grew, until it was too big for the house. Each beat of its wings hit me, and I felt the pain all through my body, and I ran away from my ruka into the dark."

"What a strange dream, Grandmother. It scares me. What does it mean?"

"A time of pain will come here, and those days will come like a caterpillar. We have not noticed its presence, but it is already here. Those who will suffer most will need our care. Then evil will beat its wings vigorously, but it will not conquer us."

"*Chuchu*, how shall we defend ourselves?"

"My dear, the spirits of our ancestors speak to us through our dreams; they tell us what is coming so that we will be strong, but only when the time comes will they tell us what to do. This is why we must know how to listen."

"My Linkoyan will surely protect us. Every day, I ask him to care for us. See, Grandmother? There he is again, just like every day, taking care of us," said Pirenrayen, pointing to the enormous peuco that came there at dusk and perched on the lone cypress that grew in front of the house. It left each day at dawn and always returned at twilight.

Fresia stowed her dream away in her memory chest. She never forgot her dreams.

Liam O'Sullivan's restless feet stepped onto our Puelmapu in the fall of 1929. His first destination was Patagones, and there he took up the position of superintendent. His task was to oversee the mechanical workshops where the train engines were housed. He felt absorbed by such a vast expanse, emptied of people and mechanical noises. An immense ocher plain opened before his eyes, an infinite plateau. Despite the invasion of cattle, certain grasslands remained, with tall and abundant vegetation. Undulating mountains rose occasionally over the plain. The wind whipped the tussocks of golden coiron grass and swept over the earth, dragging with it the fallen leaves.

His large green eyes scanned the horizon. He felt like the protagonist of something historic: progress, advancing along the rails with a whistle. This was Patagonia, the mythical Patagonia he had heard about since childhood through travelers' stories and read about in his adventure books. But where were the natives? Were they really giants, as the books said? It wouldn't take him long to learn the truth and the fate of those native nations, who no longer ruled proudly over their ancestral territories but had been reduced to servitude on the estates and in the homes of the emerging Patagonian bourgeoisie. Many immigrants with Ottoman passports settled in those remote corners and became traders, selling everything they could and buying land and animals for next to nothing. They arrived poor and quickly got rich. This economic and social phenomenon was called "making it in Patagonia," just as it had been "making it in the Americas" before.

Liam set out to explore the region. He enjoyed the climate, and although the Patagonian wind seemed to blow fiercely, sweeping away the good spirits of the few locals, he felt very comfortable there. Sometimes, the cold gnawed at his eyes and made them water; his hands grew rough, and his cheeks reddened. His wavy, fire-colored hair was often disheveled. He made trips in his Ford Model T to nearby places, following the roads marked by the oxcarts' tracks. And he set about organizing the work crews he oversaw to lay the tracks. The train was to reach the town of Ingeniero Jacobacci, in the province of Río Negro. Despite many difficulties, Liam intended to be part of the group of intrepid men who would succeed in bringing the railway to the far south of the country.

His early days in Patagones were calm. There, he met some Mapuches for the first time. Back then, our people were quiet and reserved. They did not like to speak to the Wingkas. They knew that, sooner or later, this would bring them many troubles. History and time had filled our fate with mistrust. His first Patagonian winter was a benevolent one and went by with ease, but although he lived in an enormous house with two kind and polite English engineers, Liam felt terribly lonely. He longed for spring to come so he could throw himself into the most important elements of the railway work. Sometimes, he saw Mapuche families pass through the streets of the town on horseback, coming to buy provisions and sell animal hides and wool. He was struck by their faces: their coppery skin, their hardened features, their blank gazes. Their dignified poise, their distant manner. He watched them and asked himself many questions.

When spring came, he felt renewed, in good health and full of vitality. He received a telegram instructing him to form a crew of fifty men to start work on the southern line. He contacted Buenos Aires to ask for details of the order and was told to speak with the estate manager and the police commissioner. Liam considered the order absurd. How could the estate manager and the police commissioner help? He disregarded it and asked for the help of Carlos Cabrera, his assistant and the only administrative member of staff the company had in that place. Cabrera agreed to spread the news that the company would take on laborers for a daily wage. He hung a notice on his office door that read, WORKERS NEEDED. REPORT TOMORROW MORNING, 9:00 A.M. TO 1:00 P.M.

The following day, and the day after that, Liam spoke to his assistant.

"What's going on? Don't they like to work?"

"What they don't like, boss, is to work and not be paid."

Liam smiled. "But that's ridiculous. The work will of course be paid."

Cabrera cleared his throat and replied with a certain amount of reticence.

"Pardon me for interfering, boss, but the company never pays."

Liam stared at him, stupefied. "I don't understand. What do you mean it never pays? The people who work for us work for free?"

"I suggest you speak to the police commissioner. He will explain it all."

Liam rose decisively, put on his coat, and went out to walk the streets, which were covered in mud and the remnants of snow, of a damp and still-frozen spring.

The police station was a modest building. There was an office that the police commissioner shared with the corporal, and a cell; in one corner, a log fire flickered, while in another, across the room, a kettle was whistling on a small woodstove with water for yerba maté.

Liam stepped cautiously inside.

"Good day," he said in his halting Spanish. "Is the commissioner here?"

The corporal reached for the kettle, lifted the lid, tested the water with a fingertip, and answered casually, "No."

"Is he coming back?" asked Liam.

The corporal nodded and poured the water for his first maté. "Would you like to wait?" he asked. "Come in and have a seat, he should be on his way. Would you like a maté?" he added.

Liam accepted and burned his mouth as soon as he sucked. The corporal laughed but soon apologized.

"Forgive me, I didn't tell you the water was boiling."

When the police commissioner arrived, he saw Liam sitting and drinking maté and chatting with the corporal.

"You must be Sullivan," he said, offering his hand in greeting.

Liam returned the greeting and corrected him. "O'Sullivan is my surname."

"Yes, of course. So tell me, Sullivan, what took you so long to come?"

Liam was baffled. "You were waiting for me?" he asked.

"Of course, the company told me you needed some fifty men for your crew."

"That's right," said Liam.

"Very well. This is how things work here: you give me all the money meant for the fifty men's wages, and I will make sure you get them."

"But if I give you my budget, I won't be able to pay the fifty workers!"

The police commissioner laughed, and the corporal let out a guffaw along with him.

"I see your employers haven't explained. You pay me, and I round up the men. I am the contractor. You needn't worry. Tell me, have you spoken to the estate manager?"

Liam shook his head.

The police commissioner went on. "Don't worry, I'll talk to him. When do you need the fifty men?"

Liam looked at him, dubious. "As soon as possible."

And that was where the conversation ended.

Liam left the police station with more questions than when he had arrived. He decided to await the results of the agreement, even though he could sense that something wasn't right.

The next day, just as he had promised, the police commissioner appeared at the company office along with the corporal and fifty men. The recruits looked ragged and some looked as if they'd been beaten. Lank hair, coppery skin, large and calloused hands. They were poorly clothed. Very few spoke Spanish. Liam was taken aback. He turned to the police commissioner, who had lined the men up in a row before him like a general before his platoon, and asked him where the men came from.

"Who cares where they came from! You asked me for fifty men, and here they are!"

"They've been mistreated and beaten. Have they come from the jail?"

"You're not like other foreigners who've come here. I don't like to be questioned."

Liam stared at him in rage and called Cabrera.

"Cabrera, I need you to translate. Can you speak the Indians' language?"

Cabrera kept an eye on the police commissioner and hesitated, but finally nodded.

"I will hire you by the day. You'll work from eight in the morning to five in the afternoon, and I'll pay you at the end of each day. Those interested, come to my office."

Upon hearing this, the police commissioner was enraged.

"I want my pay," he said.

"I won't give it to you; you don't deserve it. They are the ones who will work. I can well imagine how you rounded them up and brought them here."

"Don't give me that crap. We had an agreement, and you must comply."

Liam drew near the police commissioner, who was about five inches shorter than Liam, and, towering above him, gave him a warning.

"Do not tell me what to do. I am not your employee."

The police commissioner and the corporal withdrew, but most of the men remained.

Liam O'Sullivan, imagining that the commissioner would seek a way to reduce their numbers, prohibited drinking, set up a barn with pallets and several stoves, and, along with Cabrera, organized four daily meals. He slept with the workers so he could oversee all that went on.

The work progressed rapidly. The railway tracks emerged shining in the arid landscape. Everyone was in good spirits except at the police station and among the landowners, who, on learning of the quarrel, did not accept Liam's reasons for disregarding orders. When summer began, they sent another man to replace Liam and transferred him to Chubut.

He had heard about this place. It was said to be a region where many Indigenous people lived, and where there was also an extensive Welsh colony. The Englishmen with whom he had lived in the early days after his arrival described it to him as an earthly paradise. Tall, snow-capped peaks, from which waterfalls and steep slopes dropped down; a lush, pristine forest, full of abundant food; succulent unknown fruits; many animals; enormous lakes that looked like wide rivers; but also a sparsely populated area with rebellious Indians who would occasionally skirmish. Liam's curiosity was piqued, and he wanted to visit that far-flung place.

The English transferred him in part to punish him for not obeying their orders and in part because they considered him the best man for the job of extending the railway into that territory. He had gained the company's approval to bring Cabrera, who moved there with his wife and two children.

The extension of those stretches of railway was undertaken by the Argentine state, so the English, at no cost to themselves, could make a reality their idea of transporting by train the products that they would export to Europe. The task of supervising the work in the area was Liam O'Sullivan's. He was given an enormous house, which he shared with two superintendents, both of them English. On cold and silent nights, when nature seemed to fall mute, these outsiders took to drinking brandy and gazing into the fire. They shared their impressions of daily life there, and politics and economics were recurring themes in their conversations.

"This country is our best colony. It doesn't cost us a penny to maintain, and it offers us everything. It's surprising how willing and compliant the Argentines are when it comes to doing business. I think if we offered them the status of British colony, they would gladly accept it."

The men laughed, but Liam was pensive and serious. From the beginning, his attitude had been different. The company did not fully trust the Argentine officials, thinking them inept; but it needed to organize the layout of the railway corridor, the hiring of staff, and the camp for the workers who would be extending the tracks, so it had requested more workers from the Argentine government and decided to put Liam O'Sullivan in charge of the project.

The English engineers would stay only a short time in one place; they traveled throughout the country, visiting the projects and their supervisors, so Liam's time living with them was brief. They also had to travel regularly to their own country to report their commercial progress here to the Crown, as well as reporting anything that might be considered strategic information.

Summer slid away quickly, and a cold and rainy autumn arrived. Loneliness flattened Liam's spirits again. There was anxiety in his heart, and he was homesick. He set about finding a house he could soon bring his wife to. He wrote to her excitedly, telling her about his new job, and tried to convey his impressions of Patagonia. A month later, he heard news from home: his mother-in-law was seriously ill, and Christine was absorbed in her care and distressed by her poor health. On the other hand, she told him that his own mother, Sarah, was very well. In the same envelope, Liam found a letter from his mother.

For the moment, both women suggested delaying their voyage to Argentina. Liam was a little disheartened.

Chapter 25

Nothing Good Is Born of Fear

Winter dragged on and was boring for Liam. His work, more tedious still, consisted of filling out forms and reviewing numbers, since the real checks fell to the technical staff. The cold was intense, but his house remained warm. The company provided firewood, meat, and other provisions. He was in a privileged position, and although he had sensed this, he had not been able to confirm it until a workers' strike in the spring, the season when the work was to recommence, showed him the bitter reality of the workers' lives.

The English were disappointed with the Argentine state for having acquired narrow-gauge trains. They claimed that the railway would not work for transporting livestock or other products. They refused to cooperate with the government and progress with the work, arguing that their agreement had been broken. The government, in turn, could not decide what to do and stopped sending supplies and money, which of course were already scarce. Meanwhile, hundreds of workers in extremely precarious conditions, without food, without shelter, and poorly clothed, decided to rebel against this inhuman treatment and went on strike. Most of those workers were Puelches from Argentina and Nguleches from Chile. In other words, they were all Mapuches who had been forced to work in slave conditions and were subject to vagrancy laws if they refused. The *wentru*, our men, spoke little Spanish—just a few words, the bare minimum for making themselves understood. The workers rallied at the center of the main estate, where the railway was meant to pass through, and took control of the house. Among them were some anarchists of Spanish and Italian origin who sympathized with our people, although the wentru were cautious in their association with them.

We used to believe that evil and ambition dwelled beneath white skin. We feared and mistrusted all Wingkas. With time and coexistence, we discovered that evil is not a matter of skin color. That in life, nothing is black and white; that there are nuances, and that people's hearts are multicolored and contain the essence of humanity, but that humanity is sometimes lost in extreme situations. My grandmother used to say that the piwke mapu, the heart of the land, is one that beats with life in all its forms. That was the kind of heart that Liam carried inside him.

He reached his place of work in the midst of the revolt and witnessed how the army shattered the workers' demands with gunfire. A few days later, he saw the strikers return to their labor with no improvement to their working conditions. Liam felt ashamed to be part of the company's management, because his peers had abused and enslaved those men, especially the Mapuches who had ended up there.

The European anarchists I mentioned fled to Patagonia from persecution by the Argentine government in the young country's major cities. They saw in the Mapuches the necessary strength and temperament to rebel, but the main obstacle to coordinating a collaborative action was our people's limited knowledge of Spanish. This was what stood in the way of a successful insurrection. One of them, whom they called Tano, a fervent anarchist, wondered how to lead a revolt if the vast majority of the Mapuches understood none of his teachings. Yet he did not give up. He seized every opportunity to instill in his fellow workers any kind of initiative that might conspire toward a coordinated rebellion.

Several factors contributed to a second uprising, one of which was the arrival of Liam O'Sullivan as supervisor, who brought with him

Cabrera, a speaker of Mapudungun as well as Spanish. Each night, Tano gathered the men in the same barn where they slept. Around the fire, they shared a little liquor to make the cold easier to bear. They always managed to hide a flask or two from Liam's watchful gaze, and they laughed and talked as the drink was passed around. That was when Tano, with Cabrera's help, explained his anarchist ideas.

Cabrera would slip away from his house soon before midnight. His wife endured his sneaking around and said nothing about it. She thought that perhaps on those suspicious outings, some other woman was welcoming him to her bed. She was highly submissive and timid and would never have dared to scold her husband. Elena Lauro, or Tita, as everyone called her, was a woman from the country, the fifth of eight children from a family in the south of Tucumán, who had met Cabrera through one of her brothers. Tita was a quiet, industrious young woman with fair skin and brown eyes. They had two children, and Cabrera had never let her want for anything. She loved him wholeheartedly, without question; she kept her doubts and fears hidden away in her heart.

The other factor in the rebellion was hunger. Their food supplies had run out. The superintendent could see the fury an empty stomach can arouse, that beast that growls inside hungry bodies, awakening the urge to devour anything at all. He decided to designate three men, providing them with weapons to go out hunting so they could feed the crew. Cabrera and Liam were about to return to the office, which lay six miles away, when something unexpected happened.

The hunters had departed in the wee hours, and the rest of the laborers toiled with what remained of their dwindling energy. Summer was breathing its last gasp, and they worked under a searing sun. They were laying the tracks and had had to build a tunnel, which was blown open with dynamite. Suddenly, a rare landslide was unleashed above them. Gigantic rocks broke furiously from the slopes and rolled down, crushing some of the workers. On hearing the mountain's rumble, the hunters returned to the camp, where they found two relatives and another worker dead. One of the foremen, in his indifference and disdain, ordered the men to keep working; the bodies could be retrieved the following day. He snatched the freshly caught prey from their hands and ordered the cook to prepare a meal. One of the hunters told his people in Mapudungun to help him retrieve the bodies, and everyone, including Cabrera, set about removing the rocks. Liam helped the men with the heaviest rocks, and while they exerted themselves, the foreman, feeling ignored, confronted the hunter and tried to strike him.

"What did I say, God damn it? Didn't you hear me?" he cried.

The hunter, full of range and indignation, threw himself upon the foreman and began punching him mercilessly. The watchmen opened fire on him. Liam cried at them not to shoot, but the guards disobeyed, and one of them fired with such precise aim that he killed the hunter. The other Mapuches who had gone hunting were still armed in that very spot and shot back at the guards. This sparked a conflict that lasted from the early evening well into the night. As the workers felled the guards, they retrieved their weapons to defend themselves. My people remember that there were many dead and wounded.

Liam decided to help the workers. He dispatched Cabrera to the town for help while he stayed behind to try and save lives. When he saw that one of the Mapuches who had most courageously defended his workmates lay gravely wounded and groaning a few yards away, he rushed to his aid. The cruelest foreman noticed this and approached the wounded man, determined to finish him off. He lunged at him, knife in hand, just as Liam was tending to him. Liam saw him coming, sprang up swiftly, and, in the ensuing brawl, managed to snatch the foreman's knife and sink it into his stomach. The foreman died instantly. The superintendent had witnessed Liam's crime and, amid the gunfire, raised his weapon and fired at Liam just as he was fleeing with one of the wounded in his arms. He felt the impact of the bullet piercing his leg, while a second grazed his shoulder and a third entered his right arm. Liam crumpled onto the ground, and his attacker fled.

Liam O'Sullivan felt the blood flow from his body. He believed he had met his end, that life was ebbing away from him in that distant land.

Several days later, he awoke in a modest ruka, where the sweet voice of a woman was humming a tune he had never heard before.

The survivors, including the European anarchists, fled on horse-back into the mountains, carrying the wounded with them on their mounts. Cabrera could recruit no one to help transport the injured. The police commissioner, who had only a corporal and an assistant, did not dare go. He contacted his superiors to request reinforcements, and they called in the army. When he returned to the scene of the conflict, Cabrera searched for his boss among the dead and wounded, but most of the scattered bodies belonged to the guards. Cabrera realized that Liam must be in serious trouble, perhaps kidnapped by the workers or severely wounded.

The next day, they organized a search operation. Meanwhile, the wounded were carried on horseback by a few Mapuches; others walked, and several managed to reach the nearest Mapuche lof in the mountains. They went straight to Pirenrayen's ruka and begged Fresia Coliman and her granddaughter to tend to the wounded. The women agreed to try and save those lives, and after several sleepless nights, they succeeded. One of those men was Liam O'Sullivan, who had lost a significant amount of blood. An infection had spread through one of his legs. Pirenrayen argued with one of the men who had brought him.

"Brother, why have you brought me this Wingka? Don't you know how much I have suffered at the hands of the Wingkas? Men like him took my husband away, and now you want me to heal him. Why are you punishing me like this?"

The man whom Liam had helped then spoke.

"Lamngen, your sorrow is mine and your pain is my pain, but this man has nothing to do with the Wingkas who took away our brother *peñi* Linkoyan. This man came to my rescue and saved my life. We must help him in return. I cannot force you to do it, but are we going to be like our enemies? They do not understand reciprocity, nor respect for life. You do, lamngen; you have *kimun*, you have wisdom."

Pirenrayen did not answer. She undressed Liam and cleaned his wounds, removed the bullets, and studied his infected leg. She feared that if the infection could not be controlled, she would have to amputate it. She went out to forage for medicinal plants and some special clay from the hillside. She ground them together and made a lawen, which she gave the patient to drink. She cleaned his wounds again, disinfecting them with brandy, and applied a poultice made with healing plants and an ointment made from beeswax and dried, ground lizard skin.

There were moments when he recovered awareness of his body, but soon the pain and fever plunged him into the world of dreams. He dreamed again of being a child, and the dream was like the one he'd had as a boy, but this time he was running naked through Patagonia, calling to his mother and father in fright, and receiving no answer. Lost and alone in the overwhelming vastness, he began to cry. At that moment, an Indigenous girl with beautiful almond eyes appeared and gazed fondly at him. It was the girl he had dreamed about many times before. She took his hand and lifted him through the air toward the sky. When he looked at her, she was no longer a girl but an immense bird. When he saw the bird, he identified it as a condor. The girl's fingers had turned into talons. Desperate, he tried to let go, but she held on to him firmly and took him to a beautiful lake. There, she laid him down in a meadow of soft grass and flowers of many colors. A bright rainbow hung in the sky. She turned back into a girl. She took a pot and filled it with water, then moistened his brow and gave him fresh, cool water to drink, which flowed through his body like a shaft of light.

The girl stroked his hair, and Liam felt better. A deep peace inhabited him, and he fell asleep to the beautiful song of a mermaid who emerged from the lake and was greeted by the girl with a smile. When he awoke, the fever had gone, and his pain had lessened. He opened his eyes and discovered that the song came not from a dream, but from a woman in front of him, singing and freshening his brow with compresses soaked in cool water. When she saw him open his eyes, she called to Fresia.

The old woman examined him and said to her granddaughter, "The fever has gone down. He will survive. He has the light of the living around his body."

For several days, Liam lay semiconscious, slipping between reality and the world of dreams. His recovery was long, and he would have a slight limp in his left leg for the rest of his life. Like him, all the workers who came looking for help were healed and soon set off in different directions in search of their destiny.

Fresia did not take kindly to Liam. When the patient's spirits improved, she put her granddaughter in charge of his care and recommended that she ask him to leave as soon as he was strong enough.

Fresia read the stranger's urine and pronounced, "He has a cowardly heart. Nothing good is born of fear. Fear is a Wingka illness."

Pirenrayen saw in Liam the face of the enemy, the skin and color of those who had snatched from her what she most loved in life: Linkoyan. Kawel, her son, was oblivious to prejudices and speculations; he opened himself lovingly to the world, wanting to learn and to have fun at the same time. He was wrapped in love as a little boy, always joyful and full of questions. Liam was a curious character who made him laugh and expanded his horizons.

In those years, the Argentine state had established Indian schools in many Mapuche communities and was now colonizing from within the territories. The only good thing about this was that it freed the young from the boarding schools, even though the new schools were few and small. Kawel went to one in the afternoons that had been built in the middle of the lof, on a communal plot of land. The teacher was a northerner from Santa Fe, a gruff man of few words and harsh silences. Kawel learned to read and write at the school and had a strong command of Spanish.

Liam's wounded leg was still very weak, and he couldn't walk quickly. Pirenrayen cleaned the wound and changed the bandage every day. It was a morning chore she carried out automatically, along with her daily household tasks. She said nothing, and she barely looked at him. If he asked or said something in his broken Spanish, she ignored him; she didn't even glance at him when she heard him speak. This worried Liam greatly, since he felt like a burden to this unknown woman who had saved his life. He longed to recover soon, before autumn gave way to winter.

What he most loved during the day was to play with Kawel. The boy got up early in the morning and had to wait until the patient had been treated before going to greet him. When he saw his mother come back from the shed where they'd set up a simple, warm, makeshift room for their guest, Kawel ran happily to Liam's abode. They would meet there to tell each other about their dreams. Kawel had made a cane from a cypress branch for Liam to steady himself as he walked. In exchange, Liam had made him a train with several carriages. It was difficult to gather enough tins, which were always so easy to find in Ireland and so difficult to obtain in the Puelmapu. Kawel, who had never even seen a train, didn't understand the gift he was given; he was disappointed but accepted it gratefully. He showed it to his mother and his great-grandmother Fresia, who were also unfamiliar with the strange toy, then stowed it away and went off to play with his orphan goat.

In the mornings, Kawel took short walks with the patient. He gave him his hand and went with him to the ruka, where Pirenrayen waited for them with breakfast. She listened to them speak in Spanish. Liam asked the boy to tell him words in Mapudungun. Each time he made a mistake or mispronounced a word, Kawel roared with laughter. His mother would listen to them, and she'd laugh, too. Liam had learned to drink yerba maté and prepare it well, pouring the water and passing it to Pirenrayen while she cooked or wove. When he came home from school, Kawel would seek out his friend so they could play.

One morning, like many others, Pirenrayen went to treat her patient. She found him ready and waiting for her.

"Mari mari küme fachiuntü, señora," he greeted his nurse in Mapudungun, finishing the sentence in Spanish.

Pirenrayen smiled in surprise and answered, *"Mari mari küme fachiuntü, Wingka."*

He smiled happily, as if he'd discovered the secret key to an ancient papyrus that from now on he would be able to decipher. That day, he wrote in his journal:

> *May 1930*
> *I have been recovering from my injuries for two months. My arm and shoulder were slightly hurt, but my leg was shot by a lethal bullet that would have crippled me if it weren't for a Mapuche medicine woman who is helping me to recover with her knowledge of medicinal herbs. Her name is Pirenrayen. Today I made her smile for the first time.*

That young woman with the sorrowful face was not physically attractive to Liam, but he found her enigmatic. There was something about her that made her different from the other Mapuche women he had seen in Patagones, and of course, she was nothing like the criolla women he'd met in Buenos Aires. She belonged to a world that was utterly strange to him. Pirenrayen was silent and nimble. She sang in a sweet voice, and her songs moved him despite being foreign and guttural. Her sad songs seemed to evoke a better time, a time torn from her along with her freedom. She was short and round, with wide hips and strong, firm, stocky legs for roaming across the mapu. Her hair was as black as night and as long as a bridal veil that reached beneath her hips, straight and soft. She gathered it into two colored braids. She wore a long, flowery tunic that she placed her black *küpan* over. The küpan is a fine rectangular wool blanket. It is usually black and cinched with a *trariwe*, a long multicolored belt.

Pirenrayen smelled of wildflowers and medicinal plants. Liam loved to sense her aroma and sought to be near her. There was something beyond her wild perfume that attracted him like a spell: it was the warmth of her silence, which seemed to rock everything around her in peace, and the way her eyes lit up when she held and caressed her son. He saw in her a young, loving mother who was attentive yet firm. Kawel was a pure little boy, free and imaginative. Liam felt part of a circle of affection, where love was a simple, daily poetry.

Liam was captivated by the curiosity my grandmother awakened in him. At dusk, he would watch her walk away toward an enormous old cypress that stood a hundred yards from the house. A large bird would come to the tree, a hawk that perched near her, on the lowest branches. Pirenrayen would spend long hours talking to the hawk. She spoke more to the plants and animals than to other humans. Far from thinking it madness, Liam found this curious and fascinating. When night crept in and its cool fingers secretly grazed the landscape, she would return. It was the same every day. "A woman who speaks to a bird, what must she tell him?" he asked himself of this mystery. On his continent, she would have been viewed as a witch. He wasn't afraid of my grandmother, because in his country he had grown up with stories about shaman women, fortune-tellers, and healers who were burned by the Inquisition. All the Gaelic priestesses were persecuted and murdered by the colonial church of the era, so he felt fortunate to know one of those women in this part of the world.

Liam felt committed to lightening that woman's load however he could, and helping her with her chores. He carried water from the stream, chopped wood, and taught Pirenrayen to bake bread in an oven he built himself out of mud and rocks. Before then, my grandmother had only known how to cook over a fire.

One Saturday morning, Galensho arrived. He had acquired a noisy little truck, in which he now drove from town to town, selling food and other items with the help of one of his sons. He did not arrive alone. Liam was pleasantly surprised to see his own assistant, Carlos Cabrera, with him. Galensho usually brought a small gift for Fresia, and when the old woman thanked him, Galensho remembered how she had saved his life. Roig Evans had heard about the wounded gringo who had come to stay with Pirenrayen and was curious to meet him. On one of those days, Carlos Cabrera went to his general store to ask if he could go with him. Evans accepted immediately, and they set out on their journey.

Roig greeted Liam kindly in English. Liam was happy to be able to speak his own language. It was the beginning of a friendship that lasted until the end of Liam's days. Cabrera told Liam that the guard who'd been a witness had accused Liam of the crime, but for some strange reason, the company had decided to doubt the man's truthfulness. However, they had already replaced Liam with a young man recently arrived from Buenos Aires. The news of his replacement upset Liam, but in his situation, there was nothing he could do: he could barely walk steadily on his injured leg. For now, he was confined to that isolated little patch of the mountains, gradually recovering from his wounds—wounds afflicting not only his body but also his soul.

Liam had written several letters to his wife. He asked Evans if he could send them, and Galensho agreed. This way, he could communicate slowly but fluently with his family. He decided not to worry his wife and mother with news of recent events. Through Roig Evans, he was able to understand the curious world in which he had arrived; he found in him a confidant, and a friend who would never judge him, though Galensho might often disagree with Liam's decisions.

Galensho loved Pirenrayen dearly. She was like a daughter to him. He had watched her grow up and believed that she was destined to radiate wisdom. Ever since she was a girl, she had shown great curiosity for the world around her; she listened carefully and humbly to her elders. She was generous and willing to work and enjoyed helping other people.

Roig Evans had witnessed Pirenrayen's days of happiness with Linkoyan and had even attended their mafün. He watched sadly as fine lines of bitterness furrowed her youthful face. The sorrow of Linkoyan's death had taken hold of her spirit.

Galensho spoke to his wife about the uncertain future of Pirenrayen and the Mapuche people. He knew it wouldn't be long before the authorities came for what was left of their territory. *What will happen then? Where will all these people go?* he wondered. He experienced the contradiction of guilt and tranquility. He knew that the privilege of being white and European would allow him to stay; even though his wife was Mapuche, they would be left in peace. But what was the point of staying? He wouldn't be able to bear the displacement of those he now considered his brothers and sisters.

Liam's Mapudungun was gradually improving, and he could have brief conversations with Pirenrayen. His leg was healing more and more by the day, and he could now wander independently through the house and its surroundings with the help of a cane.

One morning, Pirenrayen awoke with a fever that sapped her strength. Her whole body felt like a river of pain. She tried to sit up but couldn't. Kawel called Fresia, and she touched her brow, palpated her thighs and stomach. Fresia was worried and asked Kawel to fetch the Wingka; she would ask him to stay with her granddaughter while they went in search of the medicine she needed.

Liam dressed hurriedly and limped over to the little house. He sat by Pirenrayen's side, pressing cloths soaked in cool water onto her brow. Around midafternoon, she asked him to help her climb up to the *wingkul*, the nearest hill to her house. She wrapped her naked body in an ulkilla, a long women's poncho that covered her from head to toe, and they set out uphill.

She seemed to have aged. She moved slowly, and at every step let out a whimper; she was a prisoner of her pain. Liam offered his arm for her to lean on, and she accepted. They walked at a lethargic pace, as if Pirenrayen were dragging her whole being along. Liam encouraged her, feeling the anguish of her pain as well. It reminded him of his own body, his own injuries. He felt powerless. His heart was brimming with gratitude toward this woman, and now that she needed him, he didn't know what to do.

It was the lowest hill, yet it took them just over an hour to reach the summit, when she would usually ascend in a few minutes as she herded the goats. A warm winter sun welcomed them at the top. Pirenrayen began to speak in the ancient language of the land. She sang, and as she did so, a new strength took root inside her, as if she were exorcising from her throat the *wesha* newen, the dark forces that burrow into the spirits of those who are healing. She trembled and felt needles piercing her heart, her knees, her arms.

A breeze gathered strength, swelling into great gusts summoned forth by her song. Standing on the hilltop, she embraced the wind. Stretching her whole body, her arms open wide and her ulkilla flapping open, she offered herself to be buffeted by the gale. Only the kurruf, the wind, would sweep away the malignant forces, cleansing her, ridding her of all illness. Woman and wind in an intimate, eternal embrace. Her naked body healing before Liam's eyes. She blew in the wind, and her spirit, too, was blown. She closed her eyes and felt like she was shedding a thin, invisible skin. She breathed deeply, as if swallowing the wind in eager gulps.

He had never seen anything like this ritual. The kurruf and the lawentuchefe. The wind massaged her skin, drawing out her pain in invisible shrouds; it caressed her hair, shook her thighs, refreshed her cheeks. The wind blew through her entire body, cleansing even the recesses of her soul. Liam watched, transfixed. A metamorphosis was occurring before his eyes in the body of that medicine woman: she stood erect, her strengthened bones restoring the confident posture of someone determined to live, gazing at the horizon with pride and dignity. Liam wanted to understand, to possess that mysterious knowledge: a small woman speaking to the wind. *In Ireland, no one would believe me if I told them the wind can be an effective medicine,* he thought to himself.

He was astonished and entranced. The woman was wise, mysterious, enigmatic. He longed to know more about her, and that day, he resolved to win her trust.

When Fresia returned with Kawel, they found Pirenrayen healthy and happy. While the women spoke of what had happened, Liam once more felt excluded from the conversation since he did not fully understand Mapudungun. He asked his little friend to tell him what his great-grandmother and mother had said.

"My ñuke said that the last person she cared for had a powerful sickness that was gradually killing him. When the sickness was removed from his body, the person was healed, but the wesha newen took hold of my ñuke's whole body. Those are dark and powerful spirits looking for somewhere to perch. My ñuke asked for help from the peuco—"

"Who is the peuco?" Liam interrupted.

"The bird my mama talks to."

Liam remembered having seen it arrive that morning. It had caught his attention because it came there every day at dusk. But that day, it had arrived in the early hours to tap on the window facing the corner where Pirenrayen lay. He had thought he'd heard her speak to the bird, but then thought perhaps it was only her involuntary whimpers of pain. Now, through the little boy's story, it all made sense.

"The peuco told my ñuke what to do, and she did it. That's why she's better."

Chapter 26

A FLICKERING PORTAL TO DESIRE

Before the rooster crowed, the women of the house would begin their day. Their first act was to connect with the spirits and the forces of nature. In a small and intimate ceremony, they performed a *ngellipun* in which they greeted the new day and asked for wisdom. Although the winter had come, Liam still slept in the shed; when he heard them, he would get up quickly. He greeted them and went straight to the woodpile to chop plenty of logs, as if it were part of an exercise routine. Then he joined the yerba maté circle around the fire, ate some warm fried biscuits, and talked animatedly with his half knowledge of the language and many gestures. The women laughed heartily with him. Kawel thought highly of Liam; together they went hunting and riding and shared adventures. The Irishman no longer needed his cane, though he sometimes complained of the pain in his leg. Then Pirenrayen would apply a poultice made of clay and giant rhubarb.

Winter prevented Liam from leaving. The snowstorms came one after the other, falling heavily and muting the earth, silencing the voices of the mapu with their cold dampness. The sun shone starkly, crowning the snow with its brilliance. The skies turned a shade of coral, and twilight clouded memory with melancholy. Gazing up at the sky, Liam felt as if he could weep. He knew that sooner or later he must leave, but something prevented him from making a decision. A similar struggle afflicted Pirenrayen, who refused to ask him to leave as Fresia had commanded her to do.

Pirenrayen and Fresia decided that it was best to invite him to sleep with them inside the ruka; they suggested this, and Liam accepted gladly. They made up a bed for him beside Kawel. When food was scarce, Liam and Kawel went out hunting. The days they spent indoors allowed them to get to know one another, to talk, and the women could hear tales of his far-off homeland. That winter, Fresia's eyes turned as white as snow. Kawel asked his mother if, when spring came, the snow would melt away from them.

"I don't think Grandmother will ever see again. This is an eternal snow, like the snows that stay forever in the elderly and in the high mountains."

"Ñuke, why does Liam have the forest in his eyes?" Kawel went on to ask, watching Liam all the while.

"And you, little boy, why do you have the mapu in yours?" Pirenrayen answered, and they all laughed. Then she added affectionately, "Because that's how life is, because that's how the land is, full of colors and variety."

Fresia nodded.

Liam gazed into Pirenrayen's eyes and saw in her a luminous color radiating from the depths of her being. He found her beautiful. Around the fire, Liam told stories of the sea, of his people, of his life. But he spoke little to nothing of his family.

After the winter, spring arrived, and the forces of nature were renewed. The animals were giving birth, and this multiplied everyone's tasks because they had to keep watch and tend to the lambing and calving.

One morning, Roig Evans came to deliver a letter for Liam. It was from Christine, and he read it eagerly. She told him that she was well, though times were hard and the war had led to a great deal of hunger.

She asked if he was settled enough for her to come and live with him. The letter left him overwhelmed with anxiety. But he had agreed to remain there until it was time to round up the livestock and drive them to their summer pastures; only then he would depart. He felt that in this way he could return some of that family's kindness and hospitality.

Roig invited them all to the mafün for his youngest son, which would be held in late spring. Everyone accepted.

After a long time apart, Pirenrayen saw Chekeken, and they embraced lovingly. It was a special time: scattered families were reunited. There was joy in the air, filling them with laughter, hugs, stories. They heard news of the fates of brothers and sisters, nieces and nephews, and even children.

At that mafün, Pirenrayen learned of the government's plan to displace her people from the crowded pastoral reservations to which they had been granted access after being removed from their ancestral lands. Metal wires were tightening around their territories by the day. One of the longkos at the mafün relayed how some officials from Buenos Aires had told them they must sign an agreement ceding their land to the railway. Pirenrayen was alarmed and agreed with the longko that they must urgently call the *pu lof*, the communities, together, to convene a futa trawun, a great council.

Summer came earlier than usual, warm and full of color, and Liam helped drive the animals to their summer pastures, that beautiful place Pirenrayen had loved so much as a girl. It was a lush forest, up above in the mountains. A communal space, where all the families of the lof came with their herds, and they shared many great times together. Summer meant not only work, but also celebration.

The days there were arduous. The sun melted the snow, which rushed down, swelling the streams, lakes, and rivers. The improvised little house was built near an immense lake, home to pink flamingos and to the great grebe, a small, dark, duck-like bird that today has been driven almost to extinction by hunting and corporate pollution.

One hot afternoon, they all went to cool off in the *lafken*, the lake. There, they met with other families who were laughing and playing. Children, grownups, the elderly—all were naked. At first, Liam was shocked: his Catholic prejudices were still lodged within his civilizing mindset, and nudity was disturbing to him. Everyone called him to join them, but he resisted, until the *pichikeches*, the children, who were playing at the shore, came out of the water and pushed him toward the lake. They threw him into the water amid cries and laughter.

Liam was delighted. He shed his soaked clothing, discarding the garments along with his shame, and began to swim. He remembered his summers in Dublin, swimming in the river with his friends. He felt free and weightless, as if the burden of his whole life had sunk into the depths of that immense lake. Lost in this sublime moment, he didn't notice that Pirenrayen had emerged from the water. Not seeing her bathing, he looked for her on the shore; he longed to be near her. He did not spot her and decided to leave the water himself. He wrung out his clothes, put on his damp long underwear, and laid the rest of his garments on some large, sun-warmed rocks to dry.

Liam walked west along the lakeshore. Prickly grasses mercilessly pierced the soles of his feet. He cursed them under his breath, keeping an eye on the path, until he lifted his gaze and suddenly saw Pirenrayen naked, sunbathing on a large rock. Her skin glistened, her eyes were closed, and her long black hair cascaded gently over the stone. He was bewitched and completely disarmed. He seemed to be petrified.

Oblivious to his presence, not sensing the gaze resting on her body, Pirenrayen abandoned herself to the caresses of the sun, which embraced her, laying the tips of its golden fingers upon her skin. Pirenrayen felt the sun burning her breasts with unusual power, and the strange heat made her feel aroused. An irresistible urge led her to place her hand on her breast, and she began to stroke herself, as if she had taken the sun's hands and guided them to the most sensitive terrain on the androgynous map of her body and was savoring the intimacy between herself and *Antü*. She ran her hand all over her body, feeling her hot, moist skin. She lowered it to her pelvis and paused there awhile, touching herself shyly at first. But then she ventured inside, into her womanly depths, until she shivered with moans of pleasure. The sun shone with rare brightness on the milky liquid that trickled between her thighs. She felt as if the sun had made love to her; she felt caressed, held, and grateful.

She rose and bathed beneath a thunderous waterfall crashing down from the snow-capped peaks. Liam watched her walk away. He felt ashamed to have secretly intruded on a moment that ought to belong to her alone.

From then on, he was gripped by an overwhelming desire. The mere proximity of Pirenrayen made him feel flustered. Liam found her smile enchanting, and when she stared out at the horizon, her gaze was led by inscrutable thoughts. He wanted to know every recess of those thoughts; he would have liked to know if he was present in them. He loved to listen to her sing, and by now, he could understand her songs.

On several occasions their eyes met as they drank maté around the fire. Liam couldn't help but stare deep into her eyes, but Pirenrayen would avert her gaze, pretending not to realize what he was feeling. More than once, his hand had brushed against hers when she passed him the maté gourd or a plate of food.

At the end of summer, they took the animals back to their winter camp. When the first gusts of autumn wind returned to the land, Fresia told Pirenrayen that it was time for the outsider to depart. As they were speaking, they heard the cries of Liam, who came running toward them with Kawel in his arms. The little boy was convulsing. The distraught women laid him on an improvised bed on the floor. He was foaming at the mouth and shaking incessantly. Liam could remember a similar episode with a man who had been poisoned, and he had seen how he was made to vomit. The man was given milk and made to purge the poison from his stomach, and he was saved.

Liam lifted Kawel and inserted a finger into his mouth, forcing him to vomit. He asked Pirenrayen to bring some milk and gave it to him to drink. As soon as he swallowed, Liam made him vomit again. He did this several times, until the boy had purged all the poison from his body. Pirenrayen prepared a lawen for him. Meanwhile, Liam held Kawel in his arms. He looked close to death, but gradually he grew calmer, until his trembling ceased. His breathing became regular, and he fell asleep peacefully. They had fought death, and they had conquered it.

Fresia and Pirenrayen wondered in their anguish what kind of poison this was, and who had brought it into their midst and why. Kawel was too feeble to speak. They would wait until he recovered and could tell them what had happened; then they would be able to take precautions. A long silence enveloped the little house. Liam held the boy in his arms across his knee, willing him to wake soon, safe and sound. He felt the pounding in the child's heart begin to slow. Pirenrayen brought a cup of medicine and asked Liam to feed it to him, drop by drop. The mixture was bitter and hot, and Kawel sipped it with difficulty. When they had coaxed him into swallowing the lawen, he fell asleep again.

Pirenrayen settled her son onto the cot and tucked him in, then stayed by his side stroking his brow. Tears rolled down her cheeks while Liam silently stoked the fire.

Fresia began to voice her thoughts. "It was the Wingkas. They have poisoned our well. I sent him to the well to fetch water. I didn't want him to go to the stream since it's farther away. He always dawdles and takes his time to come back. The Wingkas want to drive us away from here, from our mapu. How far will their evil go? Where will their ambition end? They understand nothing. How can they poison the water, which is sacred? The ñengko, the water guardians, will punish them! Is this how they will finish us off? Will they take everything they want? Will they tear the life out of us?"

Liam felt ashamed and full of sorrow for being part of that cruel and merciless civilization, one that spread death and dispossession. He prayed silently, begging God for the boy's health.

Kawel awoke exhausted the next morning. His ñuke gave him more lawen to drink, and the boy took the medicine and fell asleep again. Liam kept him by his side, stroking his hair. Pirenrayen observed his tenderness; she could feel the love that bound him to Kawel, her little boy. In that moment, she felt less alone in this new onslaught of anguish that life, challenging and sometimes cruel, had brought her. Her eyes grew tinged with love.

On one of those nights, when they were both up late tending to Kawel, Pirenrayen came to understand the depths that Liam's eyes harbored. At times, he spoke to her in a whisper, careful not to wake the boy. The fire illuminated them with glimmers of flame. Pirenrayen was distraught and defenseless, faced with the possibility of losing her beloved son. As her eyes filled with tears, Liam looked at her lovingly and embraced her. She allowed herself to be wrapped in his strong arms, and she cried as she had never cried in front of anyone before. Pirenrayen and Liam gazed at one another. They were both yearning to be caressed, kissed, and embraced. They gave themselves over without inhibition.

Fresia was asleep on the other side of the courtyard, in her room made of thatched adobe. Kawel was sailing through the world of dreams. The only witness to that burgeoning passion was the fire, a flickering portal to desire. So many thoughts and longings were liberated by the light of its warm presence. On that cold and starry autumn night, Pirenrayen spread a thick woven rug out on the dirt floor. They lay on it naked, covering themselves with a blanket made of guanaco hides, the very one that on so many nights had covered her and Linkoyan, to make love and then sleep in each other's arms.

Chapter 27

LAST NIGHTS OF FURTIVE LOVE

My grandmother used to say that the Irish carry the sea in their blood, that the oceans dwell in their hearts, and this is why their feelings are stormy but punctuated by moments of calm. We Mapuches, on the other hand, harbor the spirit of the land, the mapu; it speaks through us with its earthly force, awakening our dormant senses like an erupting volcano. Sea and land can love one another, but there is no fertility in that love. The sea kisses the land with its lips, turning it to gray and lifeless sand. That was how they met, and that was what the love between the Irish railwayman and the Mapuche medicine woman was like.

Liam found all kinds of excuses not to leave. Pirenrayen would wait for night to fall stealthily. While everyone was asleep, passion awakened; they made love and invented caresses. He discovered how much she liked him to stroke her from shoulder to neck with his beard: it gave her an erotic tingle that made her shiver with a mixture of pleasure and laughter. She knew which kisses and caresses Liam would lose himself in, opening all his senses, given over to exploring his body through the lips of her passion.

When Fresia was downcast or in pain, Pirenrayen would invite her to sleep in her ruka. The old woman would lie down by the hearth, and her granddaughter would tend to her. On those nights, Pirenrayen missed Liam's company. She would think of him and laugh silently, remembering his kisses, his caresses, his body. Liam would toss and turn, unable to sleep, because he needed her warmth. Before dawn, Pirenrayen would leave her house, not making a sound, and run to the barn. The barking of the dogs always betrayed her. Pirenrayen would try to hush them with whispers, but they barked indiscreetly all the same. When Liam heard her, his heart leaped with eagerness. She would climb into his bed, and he would embrace her, covering her in kisses, grateful for her daily devotion. Liam would caress and squeeze Pirenrayen's small and fleshy hands.

Sometimes, they went out to collect medicine together. Riding bareback on her chestnut horse, she galloped swiftly across land not yet fenced in with barbed wire. He tried to keep up with her, but it was always she who allowed herself to be caught. They played like children. Liam drew beside her at a gallop. She gazed at him and smiled with joy. She stretched out a hand, and he tried to touch it; just when it seemed he could reach it, she spurred her horse vigorously and flew along like the wind. Then she paused to wait for him on the shore of the lagoon, and there they made love with a mixture of urgency and tenderness.

When the *wiñoy tripantü*, the return of the sun, arrived once more, Pirenrayen said to Liam, "I have been thinking that we should live together. I don't want to sneak into your bed at night or wait for you to come to mine anymore. I don't understand why we must love each other in secret."

"In my culture, when two people love each other and they are free to do so, they marry. That way, they can live their love openly, without having to hide. But I will never be able to marry you, because I am already married," Liam answered.

"What is married? What does it mean? Is it something bad?"

"You're so beautiful when you ask questions," Liam responded with a giggle.

"Don't laugh at me, I know nothing of your customs."

"I could never laugh at you. I can only admire you and love you the way I love you," he said, putting his arms around her and kissing her passionately.

"Then let's live together," she said brightly.

"It isn't that easy for me," he said, still holding her. "There is another woman, her name is Christine. She is my wife. I am bound to her before God. We lived together in Ireland, before I came to this country. She is waiting for me to bring her here."

Pirenrayen heard this confession cheerfully.

"Then bring her! She'll be happy here with us. She'll be your first wife, and I'll be your second wife. We'll be sisters."

"No, Pirenrayen. In my country, men can have only one wife."

"I don't understand the Wingkas' customs. Why do they insist on being unhappy?" she said, and she left. Liam bowed his head in thought.

For several nights, Pirenrayen refused to welcome him to her bed, nor did she visit his. She barely spoke to him, which was torture for Liam. On the day of the wiñoy tripantü ceremony, she set off with Kawel and her grandmother, leaving him alone. Liam did not blame her. He thought that if he wasn't invited, he should not go. He felt like an intruder in her world, even though by now he felt as close to it as to his own. He assumed that for them, he would always be a mere outsider. While Liam was feeding the cows in the corral, Kawel went to bid him goodbye.

"Liam, you should come with us . . . You'll like it! We must all go and greet the sun."

"I will greet it, my friend. I'll make my own fire here. I have the *pifilka* you gave me."

"You should come and play it with us at the ceremony. Have you heard how good it sounds?" he asked, as if in affirmation.

Liam would have liked to admit that he was dying to go, but that Kawel's mother did not want him to, because he wouldn't agree to live with her. He loved her, but he was confused. It was impossible for him to renounce his past and stay there forever.

Those days were unending for Liam. The landscape seemed vast and empty, and he was bitterly lonely. The night before Pirenrayen returned, Liam dreamed about her. They were together on horseback, crossing a crystalline river full of fish that glittered with different colors. She was on the same horse, seated in front. He embraced her as he held the reins firmly. He smelled her loose hair, felt the warmth of her back against his chest. A warm breeze tickled his skin. When they had almost crossed the river, he saw Christine on the shore, calling to him. Her voice stirred the current, and the river turned rough and murky. The horse grew agitated and neighed in fear. Liam wanted to hold on to Pirenrayen, but the horse reared on its hind legs, then bucked so furiously that she was thrown into the water. He leaped into the river and swam in search of her, but he could not find her, and when he grew weak and believed he was going to drown, a hand rescued him from the water. It was Christine. When he emerged, he was no longer in Patagonia but in Dublin. "Where is Pirenrayen?" he asked Christine. She answered in bafflement, "I don't know who you are talking about." He insisted, "The woman I came with, where is she?" She answered him, "You never came with anyone, because you never left." At that point in the dream, he awoke.

That day, when he saw them arrive, his heart leaped with joy and relief. Kawel galloped over to him.

"Liam, Liam!" the boy cried as he approached, raising a hand in greeting.

"I'm glad you're home, my friend," Liam said as the boy unsaddled his horse.

Kawel reached out his little hand, and Liam took it. Then they embraced like two old friends reunited.

"I brought you some colt meat, and a surprise!"

"What kind of surprise? Can you tell me now?"

Kawel removed from his saddlebag a pipe made of larch wood that he had seen in Roig Evans's store. The boy had done a job for Galensho, and he had paid him back with the pipe. Liam was touched by the boy's gesture. He gave him a long embrace. Then they went together into the kitchen, where the kettle was boiling over the fire. He served the boy some tea. As they were talking, Fresia and her granddaughter arrived. Liam had to restrain himself when he saw her come into the kitchen; he wanted to fling his arms around her and tell her how much he had missed her, that he could not be happy without her.

By now, the anger in her passionate heart had dissolved. Pirenrayen had missed and longed for him, too. She had even regretted making him stay behind to look after the house and tend to the animals. She knew very well that it wasn't necessary, but the frenzy of anger had blinded her.

That night, they made love with all the tenderness and passion they were capable of feeling. He had made a decision: he was saying farewell. She wept as they became one beneath the cover and complicity of the fur blanket. Although Liam had not told her, Pirenrayen knew. Those were their last nights of furtive love. She wanted to remember his beard, his eyes, his mouth, his nose, his chin, his gaze. She studied him in the firelight, as if stowing her beloved's face away in her memory.

One week later, Liam left for the town. From there, he would arrange his travel to Buenos Aires to reclaim his position.

The day he left, Pirenrayen followed him on her old horse and challenged him to a gallop again. He drew near, as he always did when she reached out her hand; he thought that as soon as he touched her, she would spur on her horse like before and run off like the wind. But this time, she let him reach her, and their fingers caressed. Liam ached as he gazed at her; he did not want to leave her, but he could find neither the strength nor the courage to stay. She paused for a moment, and he went on.

My grandmother told me that it began to snow that day, that it was bitterly cold, but that she remained there unable to move, rooted to the spot, watching his silhouette vanish into the hills. She cried, and her tears seemed to crystallize. There was no lawen for her sorrow, no magic potion that could bring peace to her heart. Soon after Liam's departure, Pirenrayen confirmed that she was pregnant.

Liam reached the town and went straight to Carlos Cabrera's house. He needed to know the latest company news and was determined to reclaim his job.

Cabrera was thrilled to see him. Liam went into the house, which was cozy and warm. Tita was visibly pregnant, seven months along with her third child. She asked after Pirenrayen and Kawel and inquired about Fresia's health. Liam answered in a straightforward manner, though the mere thought of them caused him a mute, stabbing pain in his chest. He drank some maté, caught up on the news, and said goodbye courteously. That night, he planned to stay with his friend Roig Evans. He would leave his horse there, the one given to him by the Mapuche he had saved from the guard during the rebellion. He cherished that horse.

When he left Cabrera's house, Tita remarked to her husband, "Don Liam doesn't look well. He seems troubled. What can be wrong with him?"

"He must be worried about the death he caused, and about his work. When he comes back from Buenos Aires, I'm sure he'll bring good news."

Cabrera held Liam in high regard, considering him a fine man and a good leader. The young man who was now in O'Sullivan's post was arrogant and cruel, an urbanite who loathed Patagonia and was hoping to soon be transferred to some important city.

When Roig Evans saw his friend walk into his store, he was behind the counter, attending to customers; his children were working alongside him. He was surprised to see him alone, since on the two occasions Liam had gone there, Pirenrayen had been with him. Galensho was pleased that they were a couple, noting the deep love and respect they had for one another. The two men greeted each other with joy.

Liam stayed at Roig's house for several days. In private, they always spoke English. This allowed Liam to be more precise with his words and to share with Evans many things that he would never tell anyone else. They spoke of different subjects, and Liam was able to unburden himself, confessing his feelings for Pirenrayen and the impossibility of living with her. On one of those nights, after dinner, they stayed up talking, smoking, and drinking wine.

"My friend, I think Pirenrayen has already endured enough pain with the loss of her husband. I've known her since she was small, and Linkoyan, too. They were inseparable. It was so hard for her to be widowed, and Kawel was so little. And now her grandmother is blind. It pains me that you'll be yet another source of sorrow in her life. My poor Pirenrayen . . . she deserves to be happy, and is given nothing but trials."

"I never wanted to hurt her, and I don't want to be another source of pain in her life. Things simply happened that way, and believe me, I'm suffering, too. You have no idea how much I love that woman. That whole family. I will miss Kawel dearly, and even Doña Fresia, whom I know has never cared for me."

"Well, that old woman sees beyond what you and I see. Perhaps she foresaw what's happening now."

"I have to go back to Buenos Aires and accept my fate. If I'm prosecuted for the guard's death, I'll face my guilt. That death weighs on me like an ox on my back, but I know the death of an innocent man would have been a greater burden. I defended that innocent man from the guard's wickedness. The man was lying there wounded, his life lay in God's hands. No one has the right to snatch the life away from a defenseless, dying man, and that callous guard tried to stab him. I know I've sinned. I took the life of one man to defend the life of another."

"My friend, the worst of all sins isn't listed in the Ten Commandments, and believe me, you will never commit it."

"Which sin is that?" asked Liam, staring at him in puzzlement.
"Indifference. The mother of all crimes."

Pirenrayen did not know how to tell her grandmother that she was pregnant, and that she was in love with the foreigner whom they had criticized and even mocked together so many times. One afternoon, while both women were spinning yarn, she watched how her grandmother relied on her sense of touch to spin, twirling the spindle that transformed raw wool into fine threads. Absorbed in her silent task, she thought it was the right moment to share the news.

"Grandmother, I am pregnant," she confessed plainly.

"I know, my child. I was waiting for you to tell me. And I have heard you crying at night ever since he left. That is what men do . . . they give a woman a child and as soon as they find out, they run off without a care."

"But he doesn't know. I didn't want to tell him."

"And why didn't you tell him, my dear? You did wrong. You should have told him."

"Because he'd already decided to leave, and he doesn't want to live with me. If I'd told him I was expecting a child, he might have stayed, but out of obligation rather than love. And I don't need a man by my side who stays out of pity. I can raise this child myself—"

"Girl," interrupted Fresia. "She's a girl. She has already announced herself. She came to me in a dream. She'll be a beautiful girl."

Pirenrayen listened in silence and wept, embracing her grandmother.

"I don't know why I'm crying so much, Grandmother."

Fresia took her hand and answered her, stroking it. "My child, you're crying because the spirit of this new being is enveloping your heart. Two wombs cradle our children: one in the belly, for them to grow, and another in the heart, for them to feel."

Pirenrayen's belly grew. As soon as word spread in the region that she was pregnant, nobody doubted the identity of the father.

Chapter 28

That We Might Live Well

The winter of 1933 brought many developments. One of these was the arrival of Christine, Sarah, and John Walton. After Niall O'Sullivan's death, Sarah decided that she did not wish to stay in Dublin; the latest letters from her son had been encouraging—he seemed happy in his new job. Liam had never confessed to his mother or wife any of what had happened to him in the revolt. He was afraid of causing them unwarranted anguish.

They had saved money to make the trip. John had unexpectedly blown back into their lives and, seeing them so alone, began to assist them in any way he could. He told them several times of his desire to visit Liam in Argentina and perhaps try his luck in that young country. His presence swayed them in their final decision to leave, but all three waited until the spring to make their plans firm.

Sarah had a difficult voyage, enduring almost constant bouts of seasickness and discomfort. She spent much of the time in her cabin. Christine and John would meet on deck to breathe in the sea air and talk. John watched Christine and was drawn to her beauty. He liked watching the wind tousle the golden ringlets that fell on her brow. On cold days, the tip of her nose turned pink and her eyes glistened with moisture, giving her blue irises an angelic beauty. He still held a seductive power over her that frightened her. Although there was trust between them, she had not managed to dissolve the fine veil of tension that kept them apart. When, as they exchanged looks, silence crept over them, they feared falling into the urgent temptation of kissing each other.

During one of those many silences, John confessed.

"How fortunate my friend Liam is! The most beautiful woman in the world crossing the ocean to be by his side. I don't have that kind of luck."

"You shouldn't speak that way. Liam is your friend, and he is my husband. I don't want to go back to the past, but you know well that it isn't about luck. You could have been in Liam's place, but you chose a different path."

"Yes, that's true. I'll never forgive myself for that awful mistake, and I can't undo it now."

"Please, John, don't talk like this anymore. It pains me."

"I'm sorry, Christine. It's hard to be near you and have to restrain my desire to embrace you, to kiss you."

John took Christine's trembling hands and kissed them passionately.

"Please, don't do that ever again," she said, withdrawing her hands.

She went off to her cabin in fright, leaving him alone on the deck.

From that moment on, Christine tried to distance herself from John. But it was difficult, for she still loved him.

While he was staying at Roig's house, Liam learned through a letter from his uncle of his wife and mother's voyage to Argentina. He tried to imagine himself welcoming his mother to the Patagonian mountains alongside Pirenrayen, but he could not reconcile himself to the idea. The two worlds were so different, impossible to bring together. He did not belong to that land or to that people. And though that love had been happy and wonderful while it lasted, he was certain that it was only a dream. Waking up to reality reminded him of his responsibilities as a husband and son. His father was no longer in this world. He had loved his father dearly, and it saddened him that he wasn't by his side to say goodbye, to tell him how much he loved him, how much he admired him. His real life was with his wife and mother. That was why he swiftly took his leave of Roig and set out to meet Christine and Sarah.

Liam reached his destination almost a month after leaving the mountains, after a journey full of unforeseen challenges. Once in the city, he went to his uncle's mansion. When he walked into the house and saw Christine in the drawing room, he was overjoyed. He embraced her urgently and felt as if he could cry in her arms. She embodied the warmth and scent of his old life.

Christine had trouble recognizing him, with his thick beard and long hair gathered into a braid. It gave her a strange impression, but when he embraced her, she was filled with affection. His mother cried as she put her arms around him. His friend John was also there, and Liam was astonished to see him. They were thrilled to be reunited, though each saw the change in the other. After the initial surprise, they, too, gave each other a hug.

Meanwhile, in the Puelwillimapu, Doña Severina Acuipil, Galensho's wife, asked her husband to take her to Pirenrayen's house; Cabrera's wife, Tita, would accompany her. They had gathered up some baby clothes and some fruit jams they had made. Pirenrayen and Fresia were happy to welcome them, and they talked and laughed a great deal. But there remained a glint of sorrow in Pirenrayen's eyes. Severina, who had known her since she was a girl, could tell.

"Are you getting enough rest, Pirenrayen? You look exhausted," she asked affectionately.

"Yes, I get enough, Doña Severina. Every so often, I have a sleepless night. I think it's my belly. The baby is always moving."

"And Don Liam? Has he written? What does he say?"

Pirenrayen did not appreciate the question, but she saw great interest in Severina's eyes. Since Liam was a close friend of her husband's, she held him in high regard.

"I haven't heard anything from him."

Tita noticed Pirenrayen's sadness and changed the subject.

"Carlos and I want to give you a bed. It won't be big, but it won't be too small, either. So that you'll be more comfortable feeding the baby."

"*Mañun*, Doña Tita, but I don't think it's necessary. I have never needed one. I've always slept like that, on the cot. Do you know? It's a little girl I'm carrying. My grandmother dreamed it. Tell her about your dream, Grandmother," she said, almost shouting, since Fresia had been going deaf for some time, and this was the only way they could communicate.

Then the grandmother recounted her dream, and when she finished her tale, she said, "I am worried about that baby; my granddaughter carries so much sorrow. She is passing all that heartache on to the little girl. It would be good if you would help me to gather some *ayelawen*. It's a flower that grows in the grasslands at the edge of the lake. A little yellow flower it is, and so good for healing heartache. Pirenrayen cannot go, it isn't safe for a pregnant woman to go near the lakes."

Severina and Tita agreed gladly, and they arranged to harvest the flower the same Sunday they were to bring the bed. Fresia would work out by smell and touch whether it was the flower she was searching for. It had been a long time since she had gone looking for medicine, and she missed those outings very much. She waited keenly for Sunday to come.

Liam was nervous and anxious. Roig's telegram had left him startled and disoriented. He was going to be a father. He would have a child with the woman he loved so much, but he could not imagine how he would tell Christine. His worrying affected his mood and made him ill tempered. Suddenly, he no longer knew what was right. He had never felt so lost. After a few days, he resolved to speak to his uncle about it.

The morning he approached him to tell him about his woes, he found his uncle in his office stuffed with papers. He was in a hurry because in the afternoon he had to set out for one of the estates and wanted to leave everything in order before his absence.

"What a surprise to see you here, my boy," his uncle said with a smile, knowing that Liam wasn't keen on the office atmosphere, or on the din of the city center.

"I need your advice, Uncle."

"If you're worried about the matter of the guard in the southern revolt, María Isabel has already solved it," he went on. "She is very friendly with the judge who heard the case, and explained to him that it was self-defense. What's more, the case has already been filed. The English had to give too many explanations, there were lots of irregularities. Some socialists are asking awkward questions. So you can relax. Just focus on getting your job back. We'll help you with that as well."

"That isn't what I came to talk about, though I'm grateful to you and my aunt for everything you've done for me. It's another, very private matter."

Lord Husprum grew concerned when he heard this. "Very well, I'm listening."

"The whole time I was away, I was living with the Mapuches."

"Yes, I know."

"I met a woman there who healed and took care of me. We fell in love, and now she is pregnant. I don't know what to do . . ."

Lord Husprum burst out laughing. "Young man, I thought you were going to confess something serious. An Indian woman? What man cares about the fate of an Indian woman? That's no cause for worry, my boy. Just forget about her."

"But I can't live with this lie. This is a child! How can I forget about it?"

"My boy, a truth irresponsibly told can ruin a harmonious life built on necessary lies. Truth and lies are conjoined twins. They coexist, and both are necessary in this life. Don't disdain the generosity of the hand of God. Tread carefully. Your wife is here and has spent what little she had to be by your side. Who's going to take care of her and give her a decent life, if not you? She's a beautiful woman. Any man would feel lucky to have a wife like Christine. My boy, if it makes you feel better, send that woman some money to cover your child's needs. She'll surely appreciate it."

Liam said nothing more. He thanked his uncle and left the building, dejected. He wondered what he had expected from his uncle, and instantly knew the answer: nothing. He simply needed someone to share his woes with.

It was several days until his interview with the railway company manager. Liam's hands shook with nerves, and he couldn't sleep. He and Christine slept in separate rooms, but one thunderous, stormy night, Christine knocked on his door and asked if she could sleep with him. She was afraid of thunder; she wanted to rest, but she couldn't sleep, either. Liam welcomed her into his bed. They embraced shyly, like lovers sleeping together for the first time. She kissed him and clung to his body; he kissed her in return. Liam drew comfort from her warmth, caresses, and kisses. Then she went further, placing her hand on his sex, but he removed it.

"Go to sleep, it's very late. I have a lot to do tomorrow."

Christine thought that perhaps it had been a long time, too long, since he'd had sex. It was several years since they had been forced to part; perhaps that was why her husband was unwilling. Was he simply out of the habit? The situation was repeated twice, and each time, he rejected her. Sometimes, she cried alone, not knowing that Liam was suffering the same sorrow.

Pirenrayen had seeped into his skin, his way of loving, his flights of ecstasy; with her, he had learned a whole world of caresses and sounds that filled his soul. Without her, he felt empty, but he also knew himself to be a coward. He needed to forget her; he had to go back to his old life. Christine was part of his real life, and Pirenrayen was part of his adventure. Liam was certain of the pain this inflicted on Pirenrayen, but he was unwilling to leave Christine, who would suffer terribly if he did. It would not have been fair on her. Pirenrayen was strong. He had no doubt that she would overcome it. The beautiful Christine, on the other hand, was fragile, insecure, and living in a foreign country without her loved ones or family. She had traveled across the world for him, and he was all she had.

Finally, the day of his interview with the railway authorities came. The company manager would be present at the meeting. Liam got ready a few days early: he had his hair cut, shaved his long beard, and went back to wearing his European suits. Nothing was left of the Liam that had been free and wild. He introduced himself to the English officials, who greeted him courteously. They listened, questioned him, and not only accepted him back into the company but rewarded him with a promotion, making him supervisor of the branch lines. He spoke rousingly in the workers' favor, but of course, none of this mattered to his superiors. The promotion was simply meant to ensure his silence. Liam knew too much. The circumstances were not favorable for the company; it was more convenient to have him on the inside than on the outside.

Liam set aside part of his salary for Pirenrayen. He wrote to her often, promising to visit her. Roig Evans served as his postman, since he visited her quite regularly. Pirenrayen would keep the letters, but she rejected the money. She would try to hide her excitement while Galensho read her the letters. She wished she knew how to read, so that she could study over and over what Liam really felt through his writing.

She did not lose hope that someday he might arrive at the moment she least expected.

The bed that Cabrera and Tita gave Pirenrayen took up a large part of the small house. They tried to give her a mattress as well, but she would not accept, setting herself to the task of making one instead. Her mood grew lighter as the due date approached. She bathed with the flowers of happiness and drank them first thing in the morning so that her spirit would strengthen and flourish. She and Kawel often spoke to the baby girl.

"When my little sister is born, she'll know it's me when she hears me. That's why I always talk to her," Kawel would say.

One day, before she had finished the mattress, Pirenrayen went to the cypress tree. Dusk was falling, and as always, the peuco arrived. She sang to him, then spoke to him for a long time. She knelt before him and begged him to understand, and not to be jealous or sad or angry, because he would always be in her heart.

"Linkoyan, I ask for my daughter to have a good birth, for her to help us be happy, for there to be no sorrows or trials, and that we might live well."

As she spoke, streams of tears cascaded down her face, as if in a waterfall. She made offerings of everything the departed Linkoyan liked to eat and drink. When she had finished, she left the empty vessel under the tree. She rose feeling renewed, feeling that she had been heard and that something good was going to happen.

Chapter 29

A Tiny Dark Speck in the Distance

Finally, Liam had returned. That spring of 1931, the work on extending the tracks had started up again, and the mechanical workshops where all the trains in the southern zone would be checked and repaired were about to be built. Liam was to stay for a month, supervising and monitoring the operations.

He reached the town in a company truck and went straight to greet his assistant, Carlos Cabrera. Tita had had her new baby, and they were happy to see Liam. The men drank maté. Tita prepared it in silence while serving them bread and fruit jams. The men spoke a great deal, about work, weather, and people. Tita was dying to tell him about Pirenrayen, but Liam neither asked nor remarked about her. Over an hour had gone by when Liam announced that he was going to see his friend Roig and that he was sure he would be staying there. He said goodbye and went out into the street.

Flowers festooned the town with color, the sky was turquoise blue, and the wind was cool but gentle, eased by summer's approach. Snow was still visible on the mountains' peaks, like an old woman's silver mane. As he walked, a welter of passions and sensations fluttered in Liam's heart. The joy of once again feeling the air and aromas of Patagonia, the proximity of the woman he loved so much, the hope that he could somehow make up for how he had wronged her. Perhaps she would forgive him and welcome him lovingly. He wondered what she would look like pregnant, and tried to imagine it.

Liam went into Evans's store. Only his children were there, serving customers. They greeted him amiably.

"And your father?" Liam asked with a smile.

"He's gone out with Mama," one of them answered. "They won't be long."

And so it was. When they came home, there was great surprise and merriment. They roasted meat to celebrate his arrival. Roig placed a bottle of his best wine on the table. They filled the surface with cured meats and bread and cheese while they roasted the meat. Then they ate, drank, and rejoiced.

By the time midnight had passed, they were quite inebriated, since a demijohn of sangria had followed the initial bottle. Severina Acuipil disliked it when the men gathered to drink. When he was drunk, her husband started speaking in English; she did not understand and felt as if he was mocking her, and this made her angry. She left them in the kitchen and went to bed. At first, Liam didn't want to ask about Pirenrayen, but the drinking had softened his heart.

"Tell me, my friend," Liam said to Galensho. "How is she?"

"Very pregnant," he said, laughing, then added, "It was wrong of you to leave her like that. She's a great woman."

"I had no choice. She didn't tell me she was pregnant."

"But it's never too late to set things right, my friend."

"I want to see her," Liam said in a tone of distress.

"Let's go, then, my friend," Evans invited him.

"Tomorrow, tomorrow. Right now my head is spinning. I need to sleep."

In the distance, dogs barked in the street, cats fought on the rooftops, and a sleepy rooster crowed in the melancholy air. Both men went to sleep with the intention of setting out early the next morning.

Inside the house, they heard the clatter of Roig Evans's little truck. Kawel went out to look.

"Here comes Galensho, Mama," said the boy.

"Very well, child, just wait for him," answered Pirenrayen.

"How strange of him to come so early," remarked Fresia.

The two women had just started their day. Pirenrayen was combing her long hair. She heard the dogs barking and her son talking to Roig Evans. Kawel came in with Galensho. The recent arrival greeted them and then said to Pirenrayen, "There's someone in the truck asking after you. He has a question for you."

Pirenrayen thought it must be someone who was ill. In fact, that was how patients often came to her house. Roig had brought seriously sick men and women there on countless occasions, whom Pirenrayen managed to save. She stepped out of the house with her hair still loose.

It was a bright morning, and a fragrant breeze made the leaves shake. Pirenrayen walked toward the truck. Liam saw her approach like a magical vision. Her belly was swollen, and her long, loose hair fluttered like silk. As she came closer, she recognized him. A pang of joy left her speechless, and she quickened her step. They looked at one another, embraced, and kissed with all the passion and love they could muster to show their feelings. He tried to explain why he had left, he tried to say sorry, but she would not let him go on. She stroked his face and gazed sweetly into his eyes.

"I don't need all those words. I know who you are, I know who I am, but above all, I know how we feel."

He smiled and looked at her belly, big and round. He caressed it, then embraced her again.

"I've never loved any woman the way I love you," he whispered into her ear. "Believe me, my heart will live in yours, even if I can't live with you."

From that day on, he stayed at Pirenrayen's house. Kawel was delighted by his return. Only Fresia was uncomfortable with his presence, but she did not want to oppose her granddaughter. After so many months of sorrow, she could tell Pirenrayen was happy, and Fresia enjoyed seeing her that way.

Liam decided to build a bigger house out of stone and adobe, with two rooms and several windows, something uncommon in the area, so he interspersed his work hours with building. He hired two men to help him, and the house was finished before he returned to Buenos Aires. Pirenrayen accepted that he would be in her life that way, in scraps of time. For her, love was like a blanket covering her from the cold of loneliness; a blanket woven from scraps, with each moment lived intensely, each memory an unbreakable thread in the whole.

Liam was happy. For the first time, he felt like part of a family, a community. His sense of his own being expanded with the one on its way, and he felt that the woman he loved truly loved him in return. Yet he did not forget Christine. As soon as he could, he went back to the city. He had prolonged his visit, and been there for two months.

The morning he was to leave, he spent a long while in bed, hugging and stroking Pirenrayen's belly. He could feel his daughter moving inside her.

Liam looked into her eyes and said with a sigh, "How I will miss you! When I come back, I'll make you an adobe oven for bread."

"I'll wait for you with our daughter in my arms."

He embraced her more tightly still, and kissed her brow. Then he dressed and went out to the patio for firewood. Pirenrayen stayed a little longer in bed. She felt heavy. Kawel came in. Since Liam's arrival, he had slept on the other side of the patio, in Fresia's room. Pirenrayen had asked him to move there to look after her grandmother, who got up several times a night to satisfy the needs of her kidneys. Her blindness had caused her more than one fall.

The boy made a fire and put the kettle on. Pirenrayen, feeling lethargic, sat on the bed and began to dress in the same unhurried manner as when she was a girl. She washed her face and combed her hair, and when Liam came in with the chopped firewood, she was preparing some bread with cheese and fruit jams to serve as they passed the yerba maté between the three of them. Doña Fresia had been awake for a while, but she did not like to share with Liam. Since his arrival, she came up with endless excuses to stay in her room.

Not long before noon, Liam set out for the town on his horse. He had to go to the nearest station and travel from there to Buenos Aires by different modes of transport. Pirenrayen stood still on the patio, watching him disappear and reappear in the undulating landscape, until he was no longer anything but a tiny dark speck in the distance. This time, there were no tears: she was certain that he would return.

Chapter 30

MEN ARE ALLOWED TO FORGET

While all this was happening in the life of my family, in Buenos Aires, Christine had found friends in María Isabel and Marie. They took her to social gatherings, dinners, and on outings to the countryside—a bourgeois life she would never have had in Ireland. Christine enjoyed it, but Sarah found it disagreeable and sometimes preferred not to accompany her. This was awkward for Christine, who on more than one occasion ended up refraining from going out, instead staying at home with her mother-in-law to please her. This duty began to envelop her like a shroud she longed to escape from, but she seldom managed to do so.

Liam was oblivious to his wife's sorrow and loneliness and took advantage of every trip into the country to distance himself from his dull home and what he thought of as his marital prison. His friend John accompanied him several times. Christine noticed how her husband had changed, but she felt lost. She could not understand what was happening to him; she felt as if she had married a stranger. María Isabel and Mademoiselle Marie tried to cheer her. They taught her Spanish and to make traditional dishes, enjoying themselves together in the kitchen.

Liam had managed to move out of his uncle's mansion and into a large and beautiful house that the railway company had built for its senior employees, but Christine was unhappy with the idea of living in a house that did not belong to them. For this reason, she made no effort to decorate it and spent nearly all her afternoons at María Isabel's house. Christine had no suspicions about her friends' relationship; she assumed the women were very close, almost like sisters. She was unaware of the rumors that flew around about such an odd and intimate relationship between a married woman and a young lady of marriageable age who showed no interest whatsoever in her suitors.

But Sarah was not fond of María Isabel. She had no personal motive or any firm reason to dislike her, but she was dismayed by her anticlerical attitude. She had heard her tease Christine for never missing mass, and it seemed to her in very poor taste to make fun of a person's faith. María Isabel claimed to be Catholic, but never set foot in a church. She never learned of Sarah's disapproval; and she scarcely had time to distract Christine from her worries, since she was busy setting up a foundation for orphaned children.

María Isabel tried to give Liam and Christine a house, which Liam refused.

"Why won't you accept this gift from your aunt when we need it so much? Do you really think you can offer me anything better than this beautiful house?" Christine complained.

Liam was irritated and gave her a mocking look.

"Then you should have married her, since she can offer you better things than I can," he replied.

He went out into the street, slamming the door, and wandered in the foggy night of a cold and lonely Buenos Aires. Almost every night, Liam had a reason to slam the door and come home in the wee hours, when Christine was already asleep. On one of these nights, Liam was so drunk that John had to carry him home. Christine decided not to bother the sleeping staff and asked John to help her take her husband up to his room. They put him to bed without undressing him, John removing only his shoes. Christine offered John some tea, and he accepted. They went down to the kitchen, and as the water was boiling, they sat down to talk.

"You've seemed tired and downcast in the last few days. Can I be of any help?"

Christine smiled with embarrassment. "You're imagining it," she answered, adding, "I am fine, don't worry."

"I will always worry about you, don't ask me not to. It's impossible for me not to think of you every day."

The kettle whistled its announcement. An awkward silence thickened the air as they drank their tea. She was feeling fragile and longing for affection; he was burning with passion. Christine placed her hands on the table, and John stretched his own out to touch her. He caressed her fingertips, then explored the backs of her hands. She watched him, entranced. John rose and knelt before her while she remained seated, dumbstruck. She was paralyzed, somewhere between surprise and fright, and simply allowed her hands to be kissed. He sat on her lap, and she stroked his hair tenderly. John lifted his face, and his eyes met Christine's, which gleamed with tears and desires. He kissed her gently, restraining his fervent desire. A sudden sound in the drawing room disturbed them. Composing himself after their amorous reverie, John stood hurriedly and went to the other room to find Sarah in her dressing gown and carrying a lantern, believing that there were burglars in the house. That was the only time John and Christine gave themselves to their budding desire; their fears and their moral scruples were more powerful, even though they both knew that they were in love.

With no major changes in the life of the country, a new year began. Pirenrayen's due date was near. She kept continual watch on the moon, that luminous midwife that lights the way for all births, for all lives.

Galensho came to visit. Several weeks had passed since he had last come. Severina came with him and was surprised by the size of Pirenrayen's belly.

"She's going to be a huge baby, your belly is very low today," she said in a worried tone. She reached out and measured with her palm how many inches the baby had dropped.

They went to see the new house, just a few yards away.

"It's big and light," said Galensho. "I have the stove Liam sent in the truck."

"When Kawel comes home from school, he can help you unload it, it must be heavy."

"Yes, it's very heavy."

They went back to the ruka. Galensho sat down on the wood bench for visitors, for which Pirenrayen had woven a small, brightly colored blanket. He watched her hurry to put the blackened kettle on the stove. His wife sat across from him; out of the corner of her eye, she saw Fresia, who was spinning deftly. Her sense of touch had replaced her eyes.

It was a hot day in February. As she prepared the maté, Pirenrayen felt a warm liquid trickle down her legs and knew that the time had come to give birth. She approached Severina discreetly.

"Doña Severina, the baby is coming, I'm soaked," she said.

The women asked Roig Evans to leave them alone. Fresia no longer attended births due to her blindness, but she decided to stay so that she could give her advice. Doña Severina offered to help and acted as midwife, under strict instruction. She cut the umbilical cord, washed the baby, and removed the placenta once the mother had painfully expelled it.

When Kawel arrived home from school, Galensho gave him the news: his mother was trying to push his sister out of her belly. Kawel was a teen by now, and he was becoming a strong and tall young man. He often visited Chekeken, his grandmother, who always spoiled him. Chekeken could no longer get out of bed; she was dying slowly, becoming more and more giant and more and more loving, too. Kawel had been thinking of visiting her that day, but when he learned his sister was about to be born, he stayed.

He helped Evans install the new cast-iron range, which ran on wood, in the new house. He was fascinated by this novelty. They put the pipes in place, and once it was installed, they tested it. Roig and Kawel were absorbed in this task when they heard the little girl's cries. Pirenrayen suffered greatly to bring her to life, but when the baby emerged, her cries were as loud as a *trankal*, a clap of thunder.

"This little girl has a hearty cry," said Fresia Coliman, and they laughed.

"She'll be very strong," predicted Pirenrayen, between sobs of pain and joy, and she kissed the baby's tiny, still-bloody head.

Pirenrayen was exhausted. She had been in labor for many hours, from midafternoon until late at night. They named the girl Wanguelen, star, because she was born on a starry night—Wang, affectionately, for short. She was chubby, long, and she was very hungry. Pirenrayen asked her grandmother to bury the placenta under the sacred tree so that the little girl would be cared for. And the tiny old woman did so immediately, with Kawel's help. Finally, Wang lay in her mother's arms, feeding desperately. She suckled vigorously, and Pirenrayen's breasts grew full of milk.

"My little girl, you are my star," Pirenrayen whispered to her. "From my womb, you lit up the saddest and darkest nights. You are my light, so there will be no darkness in me. *Iñce poyeimi ñi puñen moyo.* I love you, my child."

Sarah answered to the postman, who had brought a telegram for Liam O'Sullivan. She opened and read it, though she knew it was not right to do so. It was written in English and said, "Your daughter has been born. Mother and baby are well. Roig Evans." Sarah paled when she read the news. Her son soon came into the dining room, and she went to him.

"This came for you," she said, handing him the telegram.

"It's open. Have you read it?"

"Yes, unfortunately, I have read it. I would like you to explain . . ."

Liam felt uneasy in front of his mother all over again, like when he was a boy and had done something wrong.

"I met a woman in Patagonia, we fell in love, and I have a daughter with her."

"And does Christine know this?"

"Of course not, I would never tell her. And I would rather you forgot about it."

"Ah, of course. That is the way of the world. Forgetting is a healthy custom, isn't it?" she said dryly, before going on. "Men are allowed to forget. Sometimes they forget in pieces, fragments of the past shatter in the fragile memories of the present. The civilized man's way is to forget what has been done wrong, to forget the uncomfortable past and erase it from his mind, his heart, as if that life had never been, as if it was all part of the blurry stuff of a dream or a nightmare. We women do not have that privilege. Our mistakes are remembered to teach others a lesson. We must be chaste and immaculate. Women 'with a past' are condemned in perpetuity to society's gossiping tongues. Of course, my son, you can forget, but I cannot. I will not forget this news. I ask myself, where is my Liam, the one I raised, the one I taught to tell the truth and to be respectful? Where is my son? Because the man in front of me is a stranger. It's just as well that Niall is no longer with us. I would not like for him to see what his son has become," she said, and withdrew from the dining room in tears.

Liam remained there, unflinching, watching the summer rain begin to fall.

Chapter 31

His Home Was There, in Puelmapu

The day Wanguelen was born, Chekeken was found dead. She had died in her sleep. Pirenrayen cried abundantly when she heard the news, not just because of her love for Chekeken, but because she hadn't been able to say goodbye. The last time they had seen each other was at the celebration of wiñoy tripantü, and at the time, Pirenrayen was absorbed in sorrow and contemplation of her uncertain relationship with Liam. She felt Chekeken's departure was a bad omen. She couldn't attend the funeral, and this saddened her even more. My people believe that babies are carriers of fragile spirits, and that at a funeral, they can be affected by the spirits that come down to guide the deceased toward the wenu mapu. For this reason, pregnant women and babies should not be present at burials.

Though Fresia cheered them up, those days were hard and full of grief for Kawel and Pirenrayen. The boy felt the loss of his grandmother keenly. The baby cried disconsolately from hunger, adding to the atmosphere of tension and sorrow that prevailed in the house. They say that mothers' breast milk can dry up due to fright or sadness; that is what happened to my grandmother, who called on Tita for advice.

This time, Tita came with her niece, a girl around thirteen or fourteen years old. Her name was Ambrosia. She had arrived in the town recently; she had come looking for work, for a chance at a better life. She was the fourth daughter of eight children; her parents, a country couple from Tucumán, worked from dawn to dusk on the sugar plantations. Ambrosia's mother was Tita's older sister and had asked Tita to bring the girl to Patagonia; she knew that if she did not send her away, the landowners would rape her, just as they had already done to Ambrosia's older sister.

Tita had some milk left in her breasts; she was still feeding her youngest son, who had just turned two. She placed Wang at her chest. At first, the baby cried so desperately that she could not find the nipple to suck, but finally, she latched on to it and began to calm down until she had drunk her fill and fell asleep.

"I've brought my niece to help you," Tita said to her friend. "You needn't pay her. Food and a roof over her head will be enough. She's hardworking and a quick learner. She'll be a good help to you. I'd rather she was in the country than in the town. She's growing up, and the men in the town are so bold, and she's an innocent girl."

That was how Ambrosia came into Pirenrayen's life, and they grew very fond of each other.

The girl was always full of joy. She was a nimble worker and quick to laugh, but Fresia complained that she liked to sleep a lot. Ambrosia lightened the load of Pirenrayen's daily chores, especially her care of Fresia, freeing Pirenrayen to better care for Wang. The milk returned to her body and the peace to her soul.

It was Kawel who felt afflicted by a sweet and wonderful whirl of feelings. He grew clumsy and shy whenever Ambrosia was near. Since her arrival, Kawel almost never left the house. Pirenrayen chided him for neglecting his farming tasks; he was responsible for grazing the animals and helping with the planting. He grumbled as he went out to complete his chores. Sometimes, when Ambrosia had nothing to do, he would ask, "Ñuke, can Ambrosia come with me?"

"Well, if Ambrosia wants to . . ."

"Yes, Aunt, I want to," Ambrosia would answer. She called my grandmother Aunt out of affection, a custom still seen among my people.

Kawel and Ambrosia played and were always talking. He taught her everything he knew about his homeland and customs. She shared stories with him about where she was from, the names of animals that weren't seen in this region. Sometimes, Ambrosia shed a tear when she remembered her mother, and Kawel cheered her up by telling a joke or inviting her to play. They especially loved to gallop on horseback across the lof, which in those days had no barbed wire. The English estate pressed forward with its metallic strands of power, but still had not managed to fulfill its aim. My people were always able to hinder its greed.

Summer vanished without Liam's presence. Only his letters arrived, and the money he sent regularly, though Pirenrayen returned it. What she did not know was that, at Liam's request, Roig Evans was depositing it in a bank, so that if she should ever need anything, that money would be available.

It was a difficult summer for Liam. He wanted to reestablish his home, strengthen his ties with Christine, but Sarah would hardly speak to him. He was afflicted with tedium and exhaustion, so he suggested to the women that they go to the beach for a few days. They set out for María Isabel's estate, the one his uncle loved so much. It was near the small seaside town of Mar del Plata, and the main house had a sea view. Liam delegated his pending tasks in the north to his friend John Walton. Their friendship had changed; it was one of mutual appreciation, but they were far from the kind of friends who share their deepest secrets and their most private fears. They spent pleasant moments together, perhaps the only ones in which Liam relaxed and laughed like he used to. But the friendship rested more on nostalgia than on any connection in the present.

During his travels, sometimes joining Liam as his assistant and other times alone, John got to know the injustices of the government and the impoverished conditions in which the workers and their families lived. In the country, as in the city, there was hunger, poverty, and exploitation. He wondered why the people didn't rise and rebel against so much oppression. Liam, on the other hand, had stopped wondering after he witnessed the massacre. He knew that sowing death meant a harvest of fear.

Liam, Christine, and Sarah settled in at the estate, which was occupied only by servants. Lord Husprum, María Isabel, and Mademoiselle Marie had traveled to the United States in pursuit of business and pleasure.

Outside, the heat was suffocating; inside, the house was an oasis of cool. They settled into the bedrooms, and Liam asked Christine to share a bed for the days they were there. She smiled in satisfaction. She wanted a child and imagined that this might be her chance to try to get pregnant.

They went out to walk on the beach. The surroundings were enveloped in absolute calm; every so often, a seagull's squawk could be heard, along with the song of the gently rolling waves. Sarah couldn't stand the heat and stayed at home. Perhaps this was just an excuse to leave the couple alone. Her son's behavior pained her and made her feel ashamed. She told herself over and over that Christine did not deserve to be treated that way.

Liam took off his shoes.

"The sand is scorching," he complained with a laugh. "My feet will get cooked. Come, let's get in the water." He smiled at his wife.

She hesitated, but took off some of her clothes, leaving just her petticoat and bra. She stepped into the sea and felt the chill of its embrace.

"It's lovely!" she said to her husband.

They swam a little, emerging from the water refreshed, and lying down on the sand. Liam moved close to her, pressing against her body. He contemplated her all over, as if discovering her for the first time, and he found her beautiful. He stroked her hands and her hair and kissed her. Her kisses were salty, and her skin covered in sand. He felt overwhelmed with desire, but when he tried to take off the wet clothes that clung to her skin, she stopped him.

"No, Liam," she said. "Please, I'm your wife. Not like that. Let's wait until tonight. Someone might see us here."

They went back to the house, talking and laughing. Christine would remember those summer days as the happiest of her life. They both applied themselves to the task of conceiving a child. Between pleasure and duty, they each used up all their strength in every attempt. But nature denied them the seed they longed for. Their days of rest ended along with the summer, and they returned to their routine, their hearts steeped in doubt and fear.

Sarah made a decision and accepted María Isabel's invitation to help with the foundation she had started. The foundation had an orphanage, and María Isabel decided to set up an art school as well. Knowing that Sarah was a teacher, she asked her to help run the school, and Christine taught piano lessons there.

Before the first May snowstorms, the company sent Liam back to the south. When he learned of his impending trip, he went to a toy shop for the first time in many years. It was the first of its kind in the country. He bought a porcelain doll with a camisole and a tulle skirt. He bought something for Kawel, too, though he was no longer a little boy. He went to another store and bought chocolates for Pirenrayen. He felt excited and happy. A strange thought crossed his mind, and he realized that in the south, he was free; that there, he was the true Liam, untroubled and open, while in Buenos Aires, he became only a vague representation of himself. Without a doubt, his home was there in Puelmapu, with Pirenrayen, Kawel, Fresia, and now with his daughter, too.

The next day, on the train, in the isolation of his cabin, he remembered his friend Pat O'Donnell, who had run off with a young

Indigenous girl in Panama. He envied his freedom. At the time, he had thought the decision madness, but now he understood it. Pat O'Donnell had found love and freedom in those exotic lands, just like Liam.

One autumn day at noon, Liam set foot in Pirenrayen's house again. He had not ridden his horse there this time, nor had Roig Evans brought him. Now, he was driving a new company truck. Pirenrayen was making fried biscuits. She peered out to see who was coming and saw him arrive. She was thrilled, but she masked her feelings. Feigning indifference, she did not go out to welcome him. Kawel was not home, Wang was asleep on the bed, and Fresia was in the garden with Ambrosia, who had become her guide.

"Mari mari poyen," Liam said in greeting as soon as he came into the kitchen, in his accented Mapudungun.

Pirenrayen approached him, put her arms around him, and whispered into his ear, chiding him.

"You took too long; I had nearly forgotten about you." She pointed at the baby. "There's our daughter," she said affectionately.

He moved closer and stroked her face with his fingers.

"She's the most beautiful little girl I've ever seen," he said, and his gaze was captivated by her.

Liam stayed there, taking a tiny hand while he watched Pirenrayen fish the still-sizzling fried biscuits out of a hot pan of fat. When she finished, she put a full plate on the small table that Liam had built with Kawel's help. She prepared some yerba maté, and they sat by the baby and talked of their news. Liam felt that now he had really come home.

When lunch was ready, all those who'd been absent came in, as if they had sniffed out the food. Liam gave his gifts and laid the doll on the bed beside Wang.

Over the next few days, they moved into the new house. Wanguelen filled their lives with joy and grew strong and happy. Her father would spend the spring and fall with them, and the summer and winter with his other family. He carved her a little wooden horse.

Liam tracked the progress of the railway. The train was getting closer and closer to the town. He strove to increase the efficiency of the work, which was sometimes poorly done, and this forced them to double back. During the months he spent in the south, he optimized his time responsibly, striving to meet the goals he set for himself. Cabrera was by his side constantly, helping him even in tasks that didn't correspond to him. At the end of every day, they went to their respective homes. When he arrived, Liam allowed himself to be overcome with love and affection for his little girl. He used to hold her in his arms as he walked with Pirenrayen, searching for medicinal plants. They saw little of Fresia since they had moved to the new house. She was increasingly elderly; her blindness dampened her spirits, and her strength was slipping away.

Pirenrayen did not want her to leave them. She felt that she still needed her.

PART FIVE

Chapter 32

We Take Nothing with Us from This Place

The years went by at the same speed at which pages are torn off the cal-endar. Christine and Liam had almost fallen out of the habit of sharing a bed. Occasionally, they met there to make love and try to conceive a child. They saw the best doctors, but it was impossible. After exhaustive testing, Christine was told that she would never be able to be a mother. The news plunged her into depression.

One sleepless night in August 1935, Sarah and her son ran into each other in the kitchen. She made them both some tea, and as they sat face to face, they spoke of their worries and concerns.

"I want to meet her," Sarah said.

Liam was lost for words.

"How old is she?" Sarah asked.

"Three."

"What is her name?"

"Wanguelen."

"What? I didn't catch that."

"Wanguelen," Liam said again, growing more and more uneasy and downcast.

"What an odd name!"

"It's Mapuche. It means star."

"I want to meet her, my son."

"Mother, please . . . It's complicated. I don't think it's possible."

"I am her grandmother. I have a right to know her and be known to her. My son, how much longer do you think I'll be here? It wouldn't be fair for me to leave this world knowing that I have a granddaughter I could not meet."

"I'll see what I can do for you to meet her."

"Thank you, my son," she said, taking his hand and adding, "Do you want some chocolate biscuits to go with your tea?" Sarah winked and placed the biscuits on the table without waiting for an answer. That night, mother and son went to sleep late and in peace, comforted by the sweetness of an infinite and eternal love.

The very night Liam stayed up talking to his mother, Pirenrayen couldn't sleep. She had received a visit from Longko Mankiñ, who had come seeking lawen and to invite her to a trawun to decide how to respond to the government's threat to remove them from their lands.

"The railway will soon cut through our land," he told her. "They say we must leave."

But the trawun had to be postponed due to a blizzard. The storm was so harsh that many animals died.

That winter, Ambrosia and Kawel decided to live together. Kawel asked his ñuke's permission to move with Ambrosia to the ruka, the same one he had grown up in, made by his dead father's hands. It was crumbling and battered, but he loved its every wall. That ruka was the museum of his childhood, the sanctuary of his memory. They decided to repair it and make it their home.

Fresia refused to move to the new house Liam had built. She was content in her little one-room house. Her granddaughter visited several times a day, along with Wanguelen. Fresia adored the little girl, who reminded her of Pirenrayen when she was small. She was three years old, but she spoke clearly and was bilingual.

Wanguelen arrived at her great-grandmother's house wrapped up warm. It was a short distance, but the snow was deep. The sun was shining after days of incessant snow. It was the end of August. September would come, renewing the forces of life in a season of births and growth. That day, Fresia was feeling unusually vigorous. I cannot calculate her exact age, but based on what my grandmother told me, I imagine she must have been over ninety.

"Help me, my dear, I want to butcher a hen to make myself a stew," Fresia said to Pirenrayen.

"Of course, Chuchu," she answered willingly.

Quickly, Pirenrayen looked among the hens roaming freely in the narrow henhouse, sheltered from the snowstorm, absorbed in the only task that mattered to them: eating corn. One of them, the tenderest, had reached its inevitable fate. She picked it up and wrung its neck, and within minutes was conversing with her grandmother as she plucked it. That final summer, Fresia and Wang were very close.

Wang was full of mischief and joy, and loved to run after the chicks until she caught one. She would hold it gently in her hands, stroke it awhile, and then let it go. Her great-grandmother Fresia had given her an orphaned baby goat she had called Pichi, which means "little" in Mapudungun. She was a tiny, spindly goat, abandoned by her mother. Wang paid close attention to Pichi, preparing her food and helping Fresia to bottle-feed her.

Every day without fail, the same fuss occurred when Pirenrayen wanted to comb Wang's hair. Wang would cry and wail and sometimes would even scamper away, and her mother would run after her, grumbling and pleading. But when her father was visiting, the little girl let herself be caught. Liam would bribe her with pieces of chocolate he had hidden for the occasion. Wang was tall for her age. Her skin was earthy, and her eyes were penetrating and green like her father's. Her hair was jet black, long, straight, and shone like the day. Pirenrayen combed her hair and tied it in two braids. "Mapuche blood is very strong," Liam used to say when he observed that all his daughter had inherited from him was his green eyes and small nose.

On that winter's day, they ate stew until they were completely full. Wang played with Fresia, making the old woman laugh heartily. In the evening, as dusk was about to fall, they left her to rest and went back home.

Fresia was fast asleep when someone knocked on her door. Her surprise was great when she saw Kalfurayen on the other side.

"My daughter, how did you get here?" she asked the young woman, taken aback.

"You called me," Kalfurayen answered sweetly. "Don't you remember? The walk here was difficult . . . the snow made this place hard to recognize. Everything has changed so much."

"Yes, my daughter, everything has changed a great deal since you lived here," Fresia answered with sorrow.

"Don't be sad, ñuke. I've come to get you. It's time for you to rest. And there is a lot to do on the other side, too," Kalfurayen said, taking Fresia's hand.

Fresia took a few steps and felt the freezing cold of winter. The snow was still deep, but she seemed to glide along with ease. She walked hand in hand with her daughter, who guided her, helping her pass through the night. Suddenly, they spied a tethering post where two strong and beautiful horses were tied. One was white and luminous. On the other, dark and glossy, her first husband, Ñankuray, was seated. Fresia felt a shiver of joy when she saw him. He looked youthful. He helped her to climb up with him, and she wrapped her arms tightly around his waist.

They began to ride. Fresia felt weightless and free of pain. Suddenly, they began to rise. Then she saw how she was drifting away from her tiny ruka, her garden, the corral, her life. Everything emitted a brilliant light that seemed like it would blind her all over again. And that was how the three of them galloped toward the stars, Fresia, her beloved husband, and their horse. And that was how Doña Fresia Coliman, my great-great-grandmother, went to the wenu mapu.

After Kawel found Fresia's body buried in the snow, Wang asked her mother if their great-grandmother was going to wake up and play with her. The little girl had been a great companion for Fresia, and her seeing-eye guide. Pirenrayen could not answer. She cried for her departure, but as she prepared her body for the funeral, she chose to remember their most special moments together, so that her spirit would not rise in sorrow, soaked with tears.

For a long time, Pirenrayen had been anticipating her absence. Her grandmother's eyes had been covered by a thick white cloud. Wanguelen's huge, green, almond eyes stared at her in great curiosity. Pirenrayen recalled an autumn afternoon when the three of them sat by the edge of the stream, warming their bodies in the sun. As Pirenrayen washed the clothes, Wanguelen peppered Fresia with questions.

"Grandmother, why are your eyes so white?"

"It seems, my dear, that my ancestors think I have seen too much, that it is enough already," answered Fresia. "And they sent me two white clouds so that I can take a rest from looking. First a little white cloud came along, and it started growing, and then it called for the other. And the two of them stayed in my eyes to live."

"And does it hurt, Grandmother?" asked Wang.

"No, my dear. The things my eyes used to see caused me more pain. Now my eyes see only the past; memories of my people, my children, and of Longko Ñankuray. I see them all the time, but everything has turned yellow and old-looking."

During those days, Fresia saw Ñankuray near the sacred tree. She saw him come on his dark horse, dismount, and lean against the trunk, holding the horse's reins. He smiled at her happily, and she knew that the time had come for her to go with him. She prepared the few things she had and shared them out among her people. Even Liam was given a knife with a carved silver handle that Fresia had inherited from her first husband. She shared with her granddaughter all the advice she had stored in her heart, and with her great-grandchildren, all the memories that the few nights by the fire before her departure allowed.

The day Fresia died, a fine rain shrouded the land, and the snow began to melt. Ambrosia had made a great quantity of fried biscuits to serve to the funeral guests. Kawel was the messenger, carrying the news to all their people, at the speed of wind. Roig Evans sent Liam a telegram, and he did not delay his southward departure for a moment. He wanted to say goodbye to that old woman from whom he had learned so much. He knew she didn't hold him in high regard, but in her final days, Fresia had ended up accepting the relationship Liam had with Pirenrayen. Above all, Liam wanted to be with the woman he loved so much. Anticipating her pain, he wished he could be there already, holding her, taking her hands in his, caressing them. He thought of his little girl, who was also sure to be sad. Meditating on all this, he was overcome with anxiety and desperation.

The extension of the railway had progressed through the territory, but it was still far from reaching the town where the lof was located. The winter had made its path difficult, and each obstacle postponed its arrival. The train stopped before reaching its destination, and the snow impeded its progress. A crew of workers had been sent ahead to clear the way, but the handcar they were traveling in had capsized and was blocking the tracks.

The passengers got off the train complaining. Liam went up to the engine and spoke to the engine driver.

"Tell me, what's going on?"

At first, the man paid no attention, but when Liam identified himself, he began to explain what had happened. The conductor said that upon braking, they had collided with the maintenance handcar, also known as a jigger, which had been abandoned by the workers for several days. He also learned that the train would be delayed for a considerable amount of time until the locomotive could be replaced. The broken-down engine needed to be taken into the workshop. Liam grew restless and implored them to fetch him a handcar that was available. With surprising swiftness, it was brought to him. He mounted it and set off.

He covered countless miles in the handcar, his arms aching with exhaustion. Just as he thought he might fade away from the strain, a fierce white wind whipped down from the mountain. He couldn't see a single thing. He shivered from the cold, despite the constant motion of his arms propelling the handcar along the tracks. Liam thought he might perish then and there in his desperate attempt to reach the funeral. Then an idea crossed his mind: this white blindness produced by the wind sweeping the snow was none other than Fresia's damning gaze. "It's her!" he exclaimed with conviction, and he began to speak to her in Mapudungun, imploring her to help him reach his destination and begging her for forgiveness.

"Grandmother Fresia, forgive me for all the pain I've caused your granddaughter. Forgive me for my cowardly heart. My heart is full of fears, I know, but it is also full of so much love, so much love that here I am, struggling to reach your funeral. Help me. Pirenrayen needs me by her side, and so does my little girl."

After he said this, he wept bitter tears. When he finished speaking and crying, the wind abated until it had vanished, the sky cleared, and in the distance, he saw a black shape approaching. As it drew closer, he realized it was two men on horseback. Seeing his predicament, they offered to help him. Liam was able to ride with them to a nearby town, where he arranged for a truck to take him to his destination. He never forgot that episode, and from that moment on, he believed that the white wind comes when the blind are watching over us.

Finally, Liam found himself in Pirenrayen's arms. It was a long, tight embrace, and she wept, her tears moistening the lapel of his coat. Pirenrayen handed him the knife her grandmother had left him as a gift. Liam put on the makun, the woven poncho that Pirenrayen had given him, and a trailongko, a headband, crafted by Fresia especially for him. He placed it on his head and joined the funeral party.

The funeral was well attended: about three hundred people came during the four days of eluwün. They came to express their gratitude to this elder who had healed bodies and spirits while she was in this world.

She had saved as many lives as she could from death's grasp. Thankful that their lives had been lengthened, these people sang and offered their gratitude. There was music, dances around the fire, and divinatory chants that knocked on the doors of the cosmos, so that Fresia might enter strengthened by the love of her kin. My people know that when we depart from this mapu, we take nothing with us from this place; only the spiritual forces with which we have sown our path, and our affections, which give further energy for us to ride through the stars and reach the sun and beyond.

Pirenrayen grieved, but she drew solace from her grandmother's peaceful passing: her journey to the wenu mapu had been harmonious.

Liam did not leave her side and showed her affection and under-standing. He thought that if life were to tear Pirenrayen or their daughter away from him, he would not be able to bear it; he loved them deeply, and Kawel, too. Yet he could not abandon everything to stay there permanently. After the funeral, Liam remained with them for only a while, until spring arrived.

Chapter 33

He Could Not Find Peace

Kawel was preparing for his mafün with Ambrosia, which would take place in the summer of 1937. He was seventeen now, and he was a strong, intelligent, hardworking young man. Wang would soon be turning four, and her father decided that it was time for them to meet Sarah. So he returned to Buenos Aires full of enthusiasm, to propose to his mother that she go with him on his next visit.

In Buenos Aires, Sarah and Christine were busy with their responsibilities at the foundation. Spring 1935 was in bloom, fragrant and fertile, but the vitality in the air contrasted with Christine's anguished mood. She had considered the possibility of adopting a child, but she didn't know how to broach the matter with her husband; she yearned so much to be a mother and was suffering greatly. Each afternoon, the boys and girls she taught music to brought back her joy and good humor, and she showed them sweetness and dedication. When Liam came home, Christine took pains to welcome him warmly, preparing a special dinner and dressing up for her husband.

Sarah set the table. Christine had cooked with the help of the servants, who were excited about their master's arrival. Liam quietly savored the delicacies his wife had prepared. She told him that there had been protests in Buenos Aires over the results of the Roca-Runciman

Treaty, signed two years earlier, and that his uncle Patrick had said sarcastically that the British had managed to drive the country into agreements so humiliating that they wouldn't have inflicted them even on their own colonies. Lord Husprum never spoke of politics with women; it was in fact María Isabel who had told her what her husband thought.

Each time Liam returned from his trips to the north or south of the country, it took him a few days to acclimate to his home and his life. In his mind, he traced the spiraling, undulating, ocher route that led him to his other home in Puelmapu. He treated the servants kindly and was affectionate with his wife and mother, yet he could not find peace, and when telegrams arrived, assigning him tasks in other provinces, he breathed a sigh of relief.

After Liam's return, Christine mustered the courage to propose to him that they adopt a child. Her husband showed only bewilderment, and her anger and indignation drove her to unleash all the silent reproaches she had accumulated over time.

"I feel so alone here. You pay no attention to me. You hardly look at me anymore, and we never talk. You wander around the house absently. Sometimes at night I hear you talking in the language of the Indians. I want to come to you, be with you, and support you, but I don't know how to do that anymore. Look at me, Liam," she said, fixing him with a gaze as sharp as a dagger piercing the tunnels of his soul. "Tell me, do you still love me?"

"Of course I do! How could you dare to doubt it? I'm under a lot of pressure at work—"

"We both know that isn't true. You don't love me," Christine interrupted, and lowering her voice, she confessed, "I don't think I know how I feel anymore. I'm so tired."

Tears rolled silently down Christine's cheeks. Liam couldn't bear to see her break down. He put his arms around her and covered her face in kisses and caresses.

"You're right. I have been selfish."

An awkward silence came between them. Liam would have liked to tell her the truth. He believed she could sense it, but he didn't want to confirm it. And anyway, what was the real truth? He loved her, too, and wanted a life with her.

Liam and Christine embraced for a long while. She felt relief in her spirit and let out a sigh. He kissed her brow again.

"Come to the north with me, and when we get back, we can talk. I will have an answer to your request."

She accepted gladly; they would leave the next week. Liam knew that he could no longer neglect his relationship with Christine, and that this meant leaving Pirenrayen; but his daughter was also part of his life. Furthermore, he remembered the promise he had made to his mother, that he would do what he could to make it possible for them to meet.

He was dispatched to the north; the work there had to be finished so that the cotton and sugar harvests could be transported. Most of the mills were owned by the governors of Salta, Tucumán, and Jujuy, who were impatient and indignant at the delay. Liam took Christine to the finest hotel in San Miguel de Tucumán, and they stayed there. It was the last time he asked John to look after her during his absence. He had no idea how long the commission he had been assigned would take.

It took him a month to return. They had to endure several transfers in the stifling heat. Liam documented the progress of the construction during the journey, curiously observing the landscapes they passed through amid whistles and steam. The small stations in picturesque towns were filled with aromas and sounds that painted a smile on his face, restoring the sparkle to his melancholic green eyes. Occasionally, a copper-skinned woman with long black braids reminded him of his beloved Pirenrayen; then the pain, sorrow, and shame would cloud his vision and torment his thoughts. Yet he always managed to escape that torture. He clung to the present with Christine, to that earthly world teeming with details. He managed to guide his thoughts toward his duties and the tasks that lay ahead. At night, the scrolls of his memory would unfurl like long papyri, and his mind would fill with images. Little Wang would appear with her broad smile, saying, "Papa, Papa, let's play." He would picture himself with her, rolling around and laughing on the green grass on a sunny spring day. These sharp memories pierced his heart like stakes. The only way to survive those melancholic dark nights of his soul was by imagining his return. No, he couldn't abandon them. But neither could he leave Christine.

Chapter 34

The Ritual of Return

The summer winds of that year brought terrible news: María Isabel had died in a plane crash abroad. The fatal accident was too much for her elderly parents to bear. She was their only daughter. They entrusted the arrangements for the funeral to their son-in-law. Lord Husprum felt lost, wandering through a narrow corridor of solitude and uncertainty; a solitude as empty and deep as a sandy desert, where walking itself becomes a great challenge. María Isabel Alvear Rosas was the only woman he had ever loved. He agreed to be second in her heart, never questioned her decisions, and never took a step without first asking her advice. María Isabel had been the recipient of his confessions, the guardian of the most private truths of his being, his friend, his accomplice, and his companion.

Mademoiselle Marie had witnessed the tragedy. They were in Brazil, enjoying a few days of vacation. María Isabel had decided to learn how to pilot an airplane; she had been taking lessons for almost a week and was becoming quite adept at flying. On the day of the accident, Marie waved enthusiastically from the beach. Suddenly, something caused one of the wings to catch fire; María Isabel lost control, and the plane crashed into the sea.

When they managed to retrieve her body from the wreckage, they saw that her lower limbs were charred. Mademoiselle Marie arrived on the same flight as the coffin. Her gaze was vacant, gray; her pallor contributed to the ghostly look that Lord Husprum had often seen in her. For the first time, their rivalry melted away and they embraced, drowning in tears; for the first time, they needed each other. Without María Isabel, they both felt utterly defenseless. The two set about arranging the funeral, attended by ambassadors, high officials, intellectuals, and the wealthiest society families. Those very same women who had criticized and condemned María Isabel for her impropriety now mourned and bid her farewell with heavy hearts. There was also no shortage of opportunistic women who took an interest in the widower, rushing to offer him comfort.

The floral tributes were abundant. An emotional priest read from the Bible; Lord Husprum and Mademoiselle Marie exchanged knowing glances, almost stifling a giggle as they imagined María Isabel in that setting. She, who despised the church. Liam and Christine felt heavy with grief. Christine stayed by Mademoiselle Marie's side throughout. Before they lowered the casket, Marie sang a song. Her voice and melody plunged all those present into a pure and celestial atmosphere of love. "That voice isn't human, it's the voice of an angel," someone remarked. The moment helped Lord Husprum to understand, finally, why María Isabel had loved that young woman so much. He told himself that someone who sang like that was not of this world.

The week following the burial, the gardener found Mademoiselle Marie's body hanging from the weeping willow tree. She departed as she had lived: silent and discreet.

That summer, Liam did not dare leave his uncle alone, since he was deeply depressed and drowning his sorrow in whiskey. He had to supervise the railway's progress and decided to take his uncle with him to the south, so that Pirenrayen could care for him. He also sent Christine to spend a few months with her family. Sarah stayed behind to join her son and brother-in-law. The trip proved to be restorative for all three of them. Liam missed Pirenrayen and his daughter terribly; they exchanged letters, but he knew little of how things were going there.

In the autumn of 1936, the first signs were seen of what was to come. The railway administrators were under pressure to finish the construction quickly, with only one obstacle before them: the Mapuches. The tracks had to cross through the territories of our people, which were organized into settlements known as "rural-Indigenous reservations." On the day Liam, his mother, and his uncle arrived in the town, some landowners and managers from the largest estates in the area had gathered in the offices of the Rural Society to assess the situation. They were willing to do anything to seize the fertile lands that were still in our hands. Liam was obliged to attend the meeting. He was dismayed by the racist, contemptuous expressions they used to refer to our people, but he knew it was unwise to show any sensitivity, since he wanted to gauge how far they were willing to go.

The pu lof were also organizing; they knew it wouldn't be long before the authorities tried to take their lands. The Argentine Southern Land Company would provide the perfect excuse, demanding that the government confiscate the Mapuche communities' territory so that the train could pass through freely and safely.

Sarah and her brother-in-law stayed in a simple hotel, the only one in the small town. Liam wanted to visit his friend Roig Evans. He invited his mother and uncle to walk through the town, greeting some friends along the way. Among the houses they visited was Carlos Cabrera's. Tita was thrilled about Sarah's arrival, even though their communication was limited since Sarah had only a basic command of Spanish and was at times incomprehensible. Tita found her beautiful and kind.

Roig Evans arranged a special lunch in their honor. The encounter was memorable for Sarah: she was struck by the host's charismatic personality and the hostess's reserved and cold demeanor. Severina Acuipil did not appreciate her husband's boundless warmth toward these strangers. She remained quiet until the guests left the house.

The day that Sarah, Lord Husprum, and Liam set out for Pirenrayen's lof, frost began to coat the ground with a glassy shimmer. Sarah felt the cold buffet her face, turning her nose and cheeks bright pink. Far from bothering her, the climate reminded her of her Ireland. The entire landscape took on a beautiful green hue. Liam drove silently while his mother gazed out the window at the lush nature unfolding before them as they traveled along. Lord Husprum wept silently, his tears resembling frozen, crystalline droplets.

"This is all so beautiful, my son! Now I understand why you love Patagonia."

"When you meet Wang, you'll see that you can hardly ask life for more."

Their arrival was heralded by the barking dogs, signaling the presence of visitors. Wang heard her father's truck and rushed out of the house to greet him. When he parked and got out, the little girl flung herself into his arms, holding on to him with all her might.

"I see you missed me a lot, sweetie," Liam said, smiling. "I missed you, too, very much."

They embraced in silence. He enjoyed feeling her, smelling her; it was the ritual of his return, one he repeated every time. Sarah and Lord Husprum observed them quietly. Suddenly, the girl noticed their gaze and grew timid. She hid her face in her father's chest, and he held her up, finding great amusement in his daughter's shyness.

"I'm going to introduce you," Liam said. "This man is my uncle Patrick."

Lord Husprum took the little girl's hand and kissed it, making her giggle.

"And this is my mother. Her name is Sarah, and she is your grandmother," Liam continued.

Wang shook her head and said, "She's not my grandmother. My grandma is Fresia, and she's dead, don't you remember?"

"Yes, sweetie, I remember, but Sarah is your grandmother, too, and she came from far away to meet you."

He then set her down gently and guided her toward her grandmother. The girl watched her closely. Tentatively, she reached out her chubby little hand to greet her. Being close to her, Sarah stroked her small head. Then they went into Pirenrayen's house. Liam embraced her for a long while and kissed her forehead exuberantly. Sarah was surprised by her son's behavior; she had never seen him like this with Christine.

Pirenrayen welcomed them with a long pentukun, which Liam translated. The pentukun is a speech full of beautiful, deep, and heartfelt words; it's the ceremonial Mapuche greeting. Sarah and Lord Husprum introduced themselves and expressed gratitude for the welcome. Sarah was astonished by Liam's command of Mapudungun. It was strange for her to hear her son speak the language of our people so fluently. And his behavior was so different here. He seemed happy and spontaneous.

At dawn the next day, Pirenrayen ministered to Lord Husprum, who recounted his suffering in great detail. Liam served as translator. He dwelled especially on the tragic love story of María Isabel and Mademoiselle Marie. His account left a profound impact on my grandmother. She told me that story several times, perhaps because she did not want me to forget where passion can lead.

Sarah gradually won Wanguelen's trust and affection, and stayed two months. During that time, there wasn't a day when she didn't spend time with her granddaughter. She taught her to paint with watercolors, to write English words, and to sing songs. Wanguelen taught her grandmother many things as well—how to identify fruits and nests, and words in Mapudungun and Spanish, too. The girl played with the animals constantly and loved to climb trees. Sarah feared the girl's daring nature might lead to an accident. Wang learned to love her, and showed Sarah how a child's embrace can heal the soul.

When winter came, Liam, Sarah, and Patrick returned to Buenos Aires. Sarah felt fulfilled by what had until then been an unfamiliar feeling—the love of a grandmother—and she was also captivated by Pirenrayen's strength and wisdom. During those days, she had witnessed the healing effects Pirenrayen's medicine had on people. Miraculous processes were set in motion with plants and ground stones.

An idea began to take shape in her mind and heart: perhaps Pirenrayen could heal Christine's barren womb.

At the end of winter, Christine had returned from Ireland rejuvenated and happy. Lord Husprum asked her to lead the foundation, and this task filled her with excitement. It was a challenge that would allow her to do what she had always wanted: to teach and use all her ideas in the service of children's education. But despite the renewed strength she found in running the foundation and the joy she drew from educational projects with orphaned children, there was still a lingering bitterness in Christine's heart that would not allow her to find peace. Liam refused to discuss adoption again. She decided to seek support from her mother-in-law, confident that she would never deny her help.

One rainy spring afternoon, Christine sat at the piano, playing alone, submerged in her grief and her loneliness. It was a Sunday of absences and silence. Lost in her bitter thoughts, she did not hear her mother-in-law come in. Her tears fell heavily onto the keys. Sarah watched the heartrending scene in silence, filled with compassion. Christine rested her head on the piano. Sarah drew close and gently stroked her hair.

"Christine, Christine," she said maternally. "Don't cry. Your tears cloud my life with sorrow. I feel responsible for your misfortune, my dear. Tell me what would make you happy, please."

Christine lifted her head and looked into her eyes.

"A child, Mother. I want a child," she answered, clinging to Sarah's waist and sobbing like a disconsolate little girl.

Sarah drew up a chair and sat opposite her.

"Have you prayed to the Virgin Mary for help?" she asked sweetly.

"Yes, Mother, and to all the saints. I pray constantly. I've tried everything, but I can't get pregnant. After so many attempts, I have had medical tests, and the doctors say there is nothing they can do for me. I have asked Liam to be tested, but he refuses. He says he is fertile and doesn't need any doctor to examine him. Liam assures me that I am the problem. He may never be able to give me a child, and that is what I most want in life."

Sarah would have loved to tell Christine her son's secret, to admit that Liam was sure of his fertility because he had fathered a little girl, but she had given him her word: in exchange for meeting her grand-daughter, she would never reveal the truth. There, in Patagonia, every-one knew Liam and Pirenrayen's story. She could hardly believe that shy, sweet Liam had become a man of mystery, adventures, secrets, and inscrutable character.

"Christine, I beg you not to despair. God is just and watches over us. He knows your burden, and believe me, my dear, he will answer your prayers very soon. Moreover, I believe I can help you" was all she managed to say.

Christine, still crying, gazed at her in astonishment. "How do you think you can help me, Mother?" she asked, almost in desperation.

"When I was in Patagonia, I learned of an Indigenous woman who can cure all ailments, even the barren wombs of white women. Mapuche women tend to have many children and don't need that medi-cine. I saw the long line of patients waiting to see her. I even spoke with some of them, and they told me her knowledge is miraculous. I think you should try it. I'll take you there if you allow me."

"I should tell my husband about this, Mother, and ask for his bless-ing to make the journey. I know how much he respects the Mapuches and believes in their medicine."

"I don't think it's wise to tell him. Liam knows that woman well, and for some reason, he hasn't mentioned her. Perhaps he doesn't think it's a good idea."

"Why would he consider it bad? You would never suggest something dangerous to me, would you?"

"Of course not. I would never put you at risk. Do this, and you won't regret it. I'll be by your side the whole time, and this way, your dream will come true. You'll see. My only wish in this life is to see you both happy. I will find the right time for us to make this journey."

Christine looked at her with eyes full of love, gratitude, and hope. But Sarah averted her gaze; she feared that Christine might discover the truth in her eyes, her son's secret hidden away in her heart. She held on to the reins of her conscience. She loved Christine like a daughter and had no desire to hurt her, but she would not break the promise she had made to Liam. Sarah had decided to return to Chubut, but she would wait until Christine was strong enough before departing.

This time, she didn't need Liam to go with her. She organized her trip with the help of her brother-in-law, who had decided to buy land in the south and settle there to start a new life. Sarah was the kind of woman who was attentive and caring toward her loved ones, always seeking to support and help them in any way she could. After her brother-in-law's painful widowhood, she had been the one to take care of him—feeding him, giving him his medicine, taking him for walks, hiding whatever bottles of whiskey she found, and, above all, encouraging him to keep moving forward in life. In return, he felt deeply grateful. He had found in her an older sister, one of those who step in to replace mothers when orphanhood robs us of care and, most importantly, of tenderness.

Chapter 35

ON THE VERGE OF TELLING THE TRUTH

It was the height of spring. In the mountains, the verdure was intense; the flowers emerged from a carpet of green and perfumed the air in a captivating riot of shimmering colors. Lord Husprum felt his sorrows diminish in the face of this dazzling sight, and Sarah planned delightful little activities for Wang. Her eagerness to embrace her granddaughter, see her laugh, and play with her painted a smile on her soft face, scarcely marked with faint wrinkles, which gave her an air of youth despite her years.

Meanwhile, Liam was in Buenos Aires, where he would celebrate Christmas with his wife and friends. He would return to the south a few weeks later, since he had promised to take Christine to the beach. Then they would travel to Uruguay, where Christine would stay for a visit with the late María Isabel's cousin.

Lord Husprum wasted no time in making favorable deals: he bought an extensive plot of land in the valley of the cordillera. Sarah, for her part, arrived in the company of Tita. In the morning, Wang had collected flowers with Ambrosia's help, sorted them by size, and put them in a pitcher that her mother used to wash her hands. The little girl was overjoyed to see her grandmother arrive laden with gifts. An array of dresses, blouses, shoes, and coats for the little girl had been transported in a wooden chest. There were also gifts for Pirenrayen, consisting of carefully transported dishes and a high-quality coat that Pirenrayen would never wear. Wang also received a large doll, books with colorful drawings, canvases, and watercolors. For Kawel and Ambrosia, there were presents in advance of their wedding, and for Tita, a pair of patent-leather shoes, impractical for the place, but which she donned as soon as Sarah gave them to her.

Several days earlier, Tita had told her friend Pirenrayen of Sarah's desire to stay there for a while. Liam's mother settled into the modest house that her son had built; it was the best house in the lof and had all the comforts the place could offer. Pirenrayen had prepared the room for her with Kawel and Ambrosia's help.

Sarah savored every second she spent there; her greatest joy was listening to her granddaughter and being entertained by her antics. She awoke at the first crow of the rooster every day, immediately rose, and joined in the daily tasks: she fed corn to the chickens, fetched water from the well, and brought in the firewood that Pirenrayen chopped, always assisted by Wang, who offered up her little world with joy. The child taught her grandmother Mapudungun, and Sarah wrote the words in a notebook that Wang found very beautiful; its cover featured a reproduction of a painting by Georges Seurat, one of Sarah's favorite artists.

For Kawel and Ambrosia's mafün, which was to be held in the summer, cattle, horses, and sheep would be slaughtered. Sarah was excited and curious to witness a Mapuche wedding. She was learning a great deal from Pirenrayen and Wanguelen, but not as quickly as her granddaughter absorbed all that she taught her.

The harvest had been a good one that year. Pirenrayen was busy with the preparations for her son's ceremony of union; furthermore, each day many people came to her hoping to be healed. Sarah's presence eased Pirenrayen's workload, but they communicated little, though they respected each other and had a friendly relationship. Sarah held a certain heightened respect for Pirenrayen that could easily be mistaken for fear. Liam's mother was looking for the right moment to speak to her about Christine.

One warm evening strewn with stars, the two women and the little girl were in the courtyard, sitting around a bonfire where Pirenrayen was toasting wheat. A beautiful peace and joy filled the air. Next to the large tray where the wheat turned golden as Pirenrayen swayed it rhythmically, Sarah was cooking a stew over a small fire. She was practicing her Mapudungun, and mother and daughter burst into laughter. Sarah found this amusing. She thought to ask her granddaughter to translate what she needed to discuss with Pirenrayen.

"Wang, can you translate what I'm about to say to your mother?" Sarah asked.

"Yes, Grandmother," the girl replied eagerly.

"Very well, thank you very much. Pirenrayen," Sarah said, pronouncing the medicine woman's name perfectly, "I've seen that you have miraculous powers, that you heal anyone in need, asking for nothing in return, and give yourself to your patients with love and humility. I need your medicine, not for myself, but for a young friend of whom I am very fond. Her greatest desire is to have a child, and she suffers because she cannot get pregnant. She is all alone in this country. Her family stayed behind in Europe. Her husband travels a great deal, leaving her alone for long periods of time. Can you help her? Please . . ."

Pirenrayen understood that woman's anguish; she was well acquainted with the loneliness, the feeling of waiting for the man you love and of letting him go, over and over again. She pictured her as she herself had often been, gazing at the horizon, longing to see him appear. Luckily, in her case, she had Wang, the fruit of that love, a small piece of the man she loved passionately. But the stranger that Sarah spoke of had no one; she could only overcome such loneliness with a child. All this passed through Lawentuchefe Pirenrayen's mind, and she agreed to Sarah's request.

Wang translated between both women until she grew exhausted and fell asleep without having any dinner. Pirenrayen lifted her into her arms and carried her to bed. There, she paused to watch her, gently stroking her cheek with her fingers, feeling truly fortunate. Soon, Liam would come, and she would feel whole again.

In Buenos Aires, rumors began to circulate about a significant operation planned for the fall in Patagonia. Liam was not officially informed, but there were hints that something sinister was afoot. Neither the English businessmen nor the Argentine officials considered him trustworthy, so they were careful about the information that reached him. A doubt settled into his mind, and the doubt became a worry, which eventually transformed into a distressing intuition.

He was ordered to keep his vacation short since he would soon be needed in Chubut. The company intended to complete all the railway workshops so that it could finish laying the tracks. There was, however, an unspoken obstacle of which Liam O'Sullivan was well aware: the Mapuche communities were unwilling to give up significant portions of their already diminished land to the English company, which was using the pretext of railway advancement to claim those lands from the government.

Liam took his vacation amid these rumors: it was highly likely that the pu lofs in the region would be displaced. He tried to detach himself from his frightening thoughts and give himself over to fully relaxing with his wife, to enjoying the seaside as he had when he managed to rekindle his desire on a deserted beach, but it was impossible. He missed Pirenrayen and Wang almost desperately, and something inside him warned him that they were in danger. That week they spent alone, Liam felt suffocated, and Christine was confused and hurt by his cold and distant demeanor. They thought that visiting María Isabel's cousin would make them feel better, but it was not so. Both felt relieved when Liam received a telegram urgently summoning him back to Buenos Aires. Christine stayed with María Isabel's cousin for much of the summer.

When he returned to the company's offices, he was called to a very important meeting with the company's manager, which he attended with a certain amount of distrust. Once there, he discovered that a council of officials and high-ranking military personnel was also present, all sitting around a long table, on which lay several enormous, slightly battered maps of the mountainous region of Chubut.

After the initial formalities, the manager addressed the attendees in English, and the meeting proceeded entirely in that language. The Argentine officials didn't complain; on the contrary, they showed off their English-speaking skills. The manager stood up and began the meeting.

"I will give the floor to the architect of our dreams: Engineer Smith."

The attendees nodded in agreement, smiling with approval. Smith began his explanatory presentation, detailing every aspect of the railway lines that would be opened in Patagonia as well as those already functioning. On one of the maps, each aboriginal pastoral reservation was outlined. In one of the largest, the tracks that were intended to connect the Atlantic and Pacific Oceans were traced. One obstacle stood in the way of this project: a people who had lived there for millennia, who seemed not to understand that they could no longer make any demands. A people whom they would surely annihilate. But to accomplish this, they needed precise information—the locations of those they called "rebellious chiefs"—and they also needed details about their internal organization. That was why they had summoned Liam O'Sullivan.

Leaning back in his comfortable chair, the manager addressed Liam.

"Mr. O'Sullivan, you could be of great assistance to us. We are aware of your excellent relationship with the Indians."

Liam felt his temper rise, but he tried to stay calm and composed. "Tell me," he replied, "what exactly do you need from me? Perhaps I can help."

"There is no *perhaps* about it, Mr. O'Sullivan. You will help us. Gather all the rebellious chiefs and tell them that it would be in their interest to leave before midspring, since by then we will be starting the serious work. I hope you will be deft at persuading them, since otherwise, we shall be forced to take action," said one of the generals present.

The manager thanked Liam for attending and invited him to leave, as they needed to continue the meeting to discuss other matters. He left the room full of rage and indignation.

The next day, Liam O'Sullivan set out for Chubut. He had decided to seek advice from the person he considered the wisest: his beloved lawentuchefe. He reached the town in the rosy twilight of a windy evening. There, he found his friend Roig conversing with Cabrera in the deserted store. They were always glad to see one another. Liam joined them for some yerba maté. After some anecdotes, gossip, laughter, and news, Roig invited him into the house. Severina Acuipil welcomed him warmly.

Roig Evans and Severina Acuipil's sons and daughters had all left home, some to study, but most had already married. By then, Roig and Severina had seven grandchildren. Severina prepared the room where Liam usually stayed. Liam learned from his friend that Pirenrayen was to visit them the next day, and his face lit up when he learned he would see her so soon. Severina told him of the excitement about Kawel and Ambrosia's impending mafün and how everyone was preparing for a great celebration. Liam was delighted to hear that Kawel was happy. He loved him like a son.

Around midmorning, Pirenrayen arrived; she had patients to see that day. When she smelled the coffee in Roig's house, she knew that Liam was there. The scent of coffee always evoked her beloved and would stir her skin's memory until her dying day. Their bodies making love, and a manly voice whispering sweet Mapudungun words in a foreign accent into her ear. Their lips seeking each other, and the coffee made lovingly by this man who would invite her to take sips from his cup, exploring the secrets and mysteries of her mouth. She could almost see him with his cup, gazing into the flames; after each sip, they sought each other's gaze among the shadows of a kitchen lit by the flicker of a complicit fire, inviting them to make love until dawn. In public, they never displayed their affection; they greeted each other with the same politeness as if they had seen each other the day before, but everyone noticed how their eyes sparkled differently, how their laughter was effortless, how a certain fullness relaxed their foreheads and brought serenity to their faces.

That day, Pirenrayen ministered to many people. In the afternoon, Liam invited her for a walk. They talked and frolicked, hidden from the world, bathing naked in the river. They made love with no witness but the warm sun, and the turquoise blue expanse of the wenu mapu enveloped them, capturing the sounds of their pleasure and desire.

That night, as they lay in bed at Roig's house, Liam was able to tell Pirenrayen about the lurking danger.

"I will speak with my people," she said. "Don't say anything for now. They won't take our land from us; they won't stand a chance against us."

Back at the house with Pirenrayen, Liam was glad to see his mother and daughter so attached to one another. Sarah was different around her. He could see again in his mother that tender and sweet young woman she had once been. In those days, she seemed to have no anxieties or sorrows.

The time came for Kawel and Ambrosia's mafün. The bride wore white, and the elders complained because it saddened them to see how customs were being eroded and everything was changing.

"This could never have happened in our time," one wrinkled old woman said to another, "but these days, everyone wants to be like the Wingkas."

The machi initiated the ceremony, and the offerings were meticulously prepared. After the ngellipun came the celebration and dancing. There was abundant food and drink. The afafan, loud cries of joy, for the groom and the bride echoed through the air. "Yayayayayaeeuuu," the guests shouted exuberantly.

The wedding lasted three days. Liam's mother was alarmed and scandalized by how drunk he got at the party. Pirenrayen, on the other hand, laughed at his antics. She had to carry him home with the help of Roig Evans and Carlos Cabrera; they put him to bed, and the three of them returned to the festivities. When everyone left, the newlyweds shut themselves inside to rest and enjoy their union.

A few days after the wedding, Liam and Sarah departed for Buenos Aires. Liam wanted to be there to welcome Christine. Pirenrayen never asked about his other life. She knew he had a wife; he never lied to her. She tried to understand his complex world, though she didn't fully succeed.

They arrived in Buenos Aires on a scorching day. The heat dampened everyone's mood; the sun was suffocating and relentless, and they could find no relief. But the house was clean and cool, and the servants awaited their master with lunch prepared. The heat didn't bother Liam; he could only think of confronting his superiors with the truth. He felt strong and determined. What he didn't know was that his bosses would not be surprised by his lack of commitment; they already knew, and it was even part of their plan.

Liam contacted the manager and requested a meeting. The manager directed him to speak with Engineer Smith. When Smith and Liam met, they got straight to the point. Smith preemptively told Liam that he was there only to listen to the results of his efforts.

"How did it go with the Indians? Do you know when they will leave?"

"No, I don't know yet because I haven't given them any warning. I believe it won't be necessary. Here, I have a map that my collaborator and some settlers have put together. We can divert the railway extension by a few miles, and not only will the terrain be flatter and more favorable, but we'll also avoid any conflict. Many families live in the area. President Roca granted them that land permanently."

The engineer did not let him continue.

"I'm not here to listen to what you think. Give me that map, and we'll assess the situation."

Liam handed him the map, hoping that his suggestions would be accepted.

"Will you inform me of your decision, sir?"

"Of course not. This is no concern of yours."

A few days later, Christine arrived. Sarah felt happy to be reunited and to be together again in the house. She felt great love and loyalty to her son, and great anxiety and tension about breaching her principles, but she needed to help Christine.

"I missed you so much, Mother. Believe me, I felt your absence deeply. María Isabel's memory was so present in that great big house; her cousin never stopped talking about her. And of Marie, too. I think I know them both a little better now. Well, Sarah, please tell me about Patagonia. I'm sure I'll join you next summer," she said with a broad smile.

"We'll be delighted to have you, dear," Sarah replied. "The land-scape is welcoming and stirs your soul with its beauty. Everything there is pure. When I breathe there, I feel like it's the air itself that's breathing me in and out. I stayed with the Mapuche people this time."

"What are they like, Mother?"

"They're reserved with outsiders and distrustful, but when they warm to you, they're incredibly kind and affectionate. They speak little Spanish. I stayed the whole time in the home of a young medicine woman. They call her a lawentuchefe. I've spoken to you of her before."

"Yes, of course, I remember. What's her name?"

"Pirenrayen. It means snow flower. She's a very free-spirited and determined woman."

"And her husband? What is he like?"

"Well, she's actually a widow."

"Poor woman. It must be hard for her."

"It has been. That happened a long time ago when her son, Kawel, was still very small. Now he's a grown man, and she is strong."

"Mother, why did you stay with her? Was it because of me?"

"Yes, but also because she has a beautiful little girl."

"She has a little girl, too? Did she remarry?"

"No, she is alone. She loves a man who is not right for her, and she had that lovely little girl with him."

"Why isn't he the right man? Doesn't he love her?"

"Yes, he loves her, I have no doubt of that. I've seen them together, and their love moved me deeply, but he is white and does not belong to her world. Besides, he is married. He should never have deceived his wife or that poor woman. I imagine she's unaware of his situation."

"Some men are disgusting, dishonorable. What will become of our society, with so much immorality?"

"Perhaps that man is also a victim of his love. He may not want to hurt anyone, but he also hasn't had the spiritual strength of our Lord Jesus Christ to overcome temptation. I'm sure he's suffering his own kind of torment."

"Mother, I don't understand how you can try to consider a sinner and make excuses for him."

"Jesus taught us that God hates sin but loves sinners and gives them the chance to repent. We shan't be the ones to judge him. That is out of our hands. Only a divine force can do that."

"You're right, Mother. I feel relieved to be married to Liam and not to be that poor woman."

Sarah fell silent and felt her conscience attacking her fiercely. She was on the verge of telling the truth but once again held back. The right moment to reveal a harsh truth never comes.

Christine lowered her voice in case Liam approached unexpectedly. "Did you ask her for help on my behalf?"

Sarah nodded.

"She told me she'll help you. I know everything will turn out fine. We must have faith and pray," she said.

"Thank you, Mother. Your news makes me so happy."

"Pirenrayen is very wise and knows the world of plants perfectly. You'll have a child, I know you will," Sarah said, and they embraced emotionally.

As they watched the sun disappear behind the elegant houses in that Buenos Aires neighborhood that was slowly beginning to change, both women became absorbed in their hopes and reflections. They kept silently weaving the muzzles that train us to be quiet, not to ask, and, above all, to endure.

Chapter 36

A Different Kind of Sorrow

In early autumn, Liam returned to Chubut. The train repair and maintenance workshops were nearly ready to be used, and there would also be new railway facilities—ticket counters, offices, and other spaces and a small neighborhood made up of rows of railway houses built of wood and brick. When the construction was all finished, he decided it was time to rest with his daughter and Pirenrayen. There was a colorful ceremony with a ribbon-cutting and some randomly recruited police musicians playing the national anthem. Liam did not stay for the festivities; he knew perfectly well how it would continue—there would be roasted meat, dancing, and drinking. He headed to Pirenrayen's house and stayed there with her until the first signs of winter.

Kawel had begun to work on the railway as a laborer in a crew supervised by Carlos Cabrera, who valued him greatly and assured Liam that he was a reliable, hardworking young man. Ambrosia was three months pregnant, and Wang was eager for her little nephew or niece to be born so they could play together. Liam didn't want to return to Buenos Aires; he felt so comfortable there, overflowing with love for his women.

Pirenrayen, on the other hand, was suffering through many sleepless nights due to terrible nightmares that seemed like premonitions;

she would wake up agitated and weeping. Then Liam would hold and comfort her with caresses and kisses until he managed to immerse her again in the sweet drowsiness of happy dreams.

The day Liam left for the city seemed like any other, but they were gripped by an inexplicable sense of unease. Both Pirenrayen and Liam felt overcome with a different kind of sorrow. Liam held his little daughter for a long time in silence; then, as he bid Pirenrayen farewell, their bodies melded together in an interminable embrace, and she shed a few tears that to him seemed superfluous.

Winter was drawing to a close, and Liam would soon return to the south. He was in his office when he saw trucks and military units outside the window. Following behind them was a squadron of young soldiers marching rhythmically through the cobblestone streets. Liam's staff crowded around the window, watching the unusual spectacle, and making comments.

"Where can they be going?" one of them asked.

"They're heading south, to Patagonia," said another.

At that moment, Liam understood what was happening. With no time to waste, he rushed out into the street and ran to catch up with the soldiers.

"Do you know where you're going?" he asked one of them.

"We've been told we're going south, to Patagonia," replied the young soldier.

"To which part of Patagonia?" Liam pressed him.

"I don't know, sir," the young man replied, and kept marching.

Liam was stunned. How could he find out for sure what was happening? He crossed the avenue and headed to Smith's office. Once there, he announced himself and waited a few minutes that felt an eternity.

It was a mild September morning. When Smith finally received him, Liam wasted no time in asking if they had considered his proposal.

"No," Smith answered indifferently, adding, "We will take action. They must be removed from the tracks."

"The tracks aren't even there yet. But those people's lives are!" Liam protested.

Smith stared at him in annoyance. "Have you finished? I have lots of work to do, Mr. O'Sullivan, and I assume you do as well. So if you'd let me get on, I'd appreciate it."

Liam left the office, crushed. He contacted some people in the military whom he had met in the days when he used to attend María Isabel's parties. Through them, he learned that those soldiers had been sent to Chubut, to the Mountain Infantry Regiment in the city of Esquel. It was there that the invasion and removal of the communities would be organized.

In the cold early morning of a late spring day in 1937, Pirenrayen was still in bed with her little girl. The night before, she had stayed up late preparing medicine for a woman in the town who wanted to have another child but whose womb was unable to sustain her pregnancies. Suddenly, they heard the barking of dogs and a burst of gunfire. They both leaped out of bed and, half-dressed, went outside to see what was happening. They were met with the sight of hundreds of soldiers setting houses and fields on fire. Pirenrayen rushed into her ruka, dressed hurriedly, and got Wanguelen ready.

The soldiers arrived in no time. Pirenrayen, with her daughter in her arms, mounted her horse and fled. Bullets whistled past their ears, and the ravenous fire roared and crackled. Wanguelen rode behind her mother, clinging to her waist. They headed up the trail that led to the high summer pastures. Pirenrayen saw that many had already escaped and that she was lagging behind. She quickened her pace.

On the path, she encountered all her relatives, including her son, Kawel, who had risen early because his flock was giving birth. Ambrosia wept in desperation. They comforted one another. The ascent was dangerous, and it was impossible to gallop. The army pursued them with dogs that tore into my people's flesh fiercely. There were gunshot wounds, but many from dog bites, too.

On that fateful day, the army killed little Wanguelen with a bullet that pierced her lungs. Pirenrayen heard a gasp and felt the small hands entwined around her waist slacken as the girl collapsed to the ground and rolled down the steep path. She dismounted in terror and ran to her, lifting the child in her arms, shedding tears on her beloved daughter's tiny, lifeless frame. She mounted her horse, carrying her daughter's body, and began to ascend the trail. She thought that perhaps she could heal her, bring her back to life.

The others were up ahead, unaware of what had happened. When they reached a clearing, they paused to rest, hidden from the soldiers. They dismounted and waited for their loved ones who were gradually arriving with news of those bringing up the rear. They saw Pirenrayen coming at a trot. Something was not right. She began to shout, flooded with the direst anguish. She dismounted with her daughter in her arms and laid her on the ground, but she was already dead. A piercing, heart-wrenching scream emerged from her throat. Kawel leaped from his horse and ran to his mother. He reached out his arms to hold his little sister and cried out in agony. All who were there embraced and cried along with them, not only from the pain that tormented Pirenrayen and her son, but from the despair, the sorrow ingrained in their hearts, weary of so many injustices that seemed to go on without end.

That day, Pirenrayen held her daughter in her arms until nightfall. She fell asleep, defeated by sadness and tears. A few campfires had been lit to ward off the cold. In an instant, they had lost everything. Once again, the state had torn from them their peace and hope, the chance to exist and live on their land, to continue their traditional lives as Mapuches. It seemed a right impossible to attain.

For many days, they continued their ascent to the high summer pastures with neither food nor water in the freezing cold. They lost all their animals. But none of this was as harsh as the desolation of their spirits, which slowed their steps. They felt their bodies stiffen, and every step forward required the utmost energy. Those footprints, trodden by feet walking into the future, conquering pain and despair, are deep and enduring. They are not merely human tracks. They are marks of territories with memory, they are the indelible footprints of peoples refusing to die. My grandmother knew this, and over the years, she turned those footprints into pathways of affirmation, into intangible memorials that would justify the return to our mapu.

They reached the high summer pastures and settled there. My grandmother and my father buried my aunt. Everyone had a family member to whom they were forced to bid farewell from the *wente mapu*, the land above. There were no funerals, only digging and burying, as if it were inevitable. My grandmother, amid tears and tahiel, sang a farewell to her little daughter; her voice fractured into mournful cries, and the air fled her lungs, suffocating her in her grief. The whole community stood by her side, not saying a word, shedding silent tears.

Where can we go? How long must we keep fleeing? my grandmother wondered. They raised a chenke, a grave. That's what Pirenrayen dreamed and that's what she told Kawel to do. That stone mound, like a tomb, would forever protect the remains of her beloved child. Her only daughter.

Within a few days, it was known that the brutal eviction had been carried out in the name of progress; that's how the newspapers of the time justified the atrocity. The English railway was expanding, just as British dominion over the land that had once belonged to my Mapuche people was expanding.

Some Mapuches remarked that Liam must have known and said nothing. "He's a traitor," they said. Gradually, the rumor solidified into truth, and soon no one from the lof had any doubt: it was a betrayal, he had deceived them. A trawun was called for Pirenrayen and Kawel, at which they were asked to admit the truth of whether Liam had participated in the Wingkas' scheme. Everyone wore an accusing expression; no one trusted him anymore. Pirenrayen refused to go, but she spoke to her son and asked him to be her messenger: all suspicions and accusations should be directed not to Liam but to her.

"I knew vaguely what they were plotting," she explained, "because Liam received orders from his superiors to gather the lofs together and ask us to leave the mapu. I decided that we wouldn't go, that we should not succumb to fear. I consulted the *puju*, spirit, and had a vision where we were elders, celebrating kamarikun on our land. I thought then that they would never drive us away, that these were only threats like so many times before, to make us leave quietly, like cowards." She cried bitter tears.

Her son embraced her, promising to tell everything.

"I was wrong," she said over and over.

Kawel attended the trawun, the assembly convened for the people. Everyone was there, not only the people from his own lof but also from others that had been displaced. He recounted exactly what his mother had told him. Additionally, he offered to go before the Wingka authorities to warn them that if they returned, this time the Mapuche would defend themselves. Perhaps that would help facilitate the immediate return of the pu lofs to the place where they wintered. Everyone agreed. He also proposed forming a delegation composed of longkos and werken, messengers. They would go after the summer; for now, they needed to recover their animals and rebuild their homes.

Kawel prepared to go down to the town. He needed to talk to Cabrera, since he would no longer be able to perform his railway work. Now he would have to throw himself into building a house for himself and Ambrosia and improving the one his mother had there.

Carlos Cabrera was a good man and was deeply afflicted by what had happened. Many in the town were outraged by the evictions and helped the victims in any way they could. Cabrera decided to grant

Kawel leave, and once he was settled on his new land, he would have his job waiting for him.

My father and Cabrera became good friends. As the years went by, Cabrera felt proud of my father. Cabrera claimed that thanks to him, my father had become a great railway unionist. There was some truth to that statement.

The days following the displacement felt endless for my grandmother, Pirenrayen. She felt like the veil of her love had been torn in her spirit and the winter cold had a grip on her bones and heart. That man she loved so much, the man to whom she had given so much, had become the source of so much misery and loss. She wished she had never known him, wished she could tell him and all the Wingkas to leave, expel them just as our people were now being expelled. She felt that she had no strength left to start again, that not even together could they overcome so much pain, but she could not speak; silence had bound up and driven a stake into all her words. After she buried her daughter, she had fallen mute. The day Liam had left, she knew deep in her heart that it was not her man who was leaving but her life, that nothing would ever be the same as before. She recalled her late grandmother's pewma, the caterpillar that had transformed into a butterfly; she thought their time together had been like the butterfly's time, beautiful but fleeting. She handed him her rokiñ, with the freshly baked bread that Liam had taught her to knead, and the dried meat that Liam said no one prepared better than she did. He had tried to kiss her, but she chose to hold him for a long, interminable moment, as if that embrace could stop time itself.

How ironic and cruel life can be when it gives us everything and then strips it away, showing us the transitory nature of our existence. My grandmother and Liam felt as if they had everything; they needed nothing more to enjoy the fullness, prosperity, and harmony of their lives. But that other world, the world of power, which seeks not the prosperity of the many but the wealth of the few, imposed its will, devouring the plans and dreams of those who toiled with sweat and sacrifice to create a good life for themselves and the generations to come.

The triumphant company organized its return, to continue with the extension of the railway. Now, almost all the lands of the Indigenous reservation that the tracks would pass through were under their control and, in some cases, under their ownership.

Chapter 37

In the Shade of the Great Coihué

Liam's friend Roig informed him of the death of his daughter, Wanguelen, via telegram. Liam O'Sullivan turned white as a sheet as he read the tragic news. He swiftly left his office and, in a state of shock, oblivious to the present moment, was drawn by an invisible force to the riverbank. There he sat, his gaze lost in the vastness of the Río de la Plata. Memories of moments with his daughter flooded his mind—her laughter, the chubby little hands Liam cherished so much. He wept in solitude, and the floodgates of his heart burst open, releasing all the pent-up, bitter tears we so often hold in. He had no idea how many hours he had spent there, but suddenly, two young cyclists skirting the river chatting and laughing jolted him out of his grief-stricken daze.

When he reached home, he sought out his mother, who was in the garden. Without a word, he handed her the telegram discreetly. Christine observed them from her room upstairs. Sarah raised a hand to her mouth in horror. She embraced her son, and both broke down in tears. Then Sarah withdrew to her room and neither ate nor spoke for three days; she wanted only to be alone.

Liam left the day after hearing the news. He was returning to Puelmapu with a shattered heart. Roig and Tita asked for his help with Pirenrayen, who was in a terrible state.

When he was reunited with her, Liam O'Sullivan could hardly fathom the extent of my grandmother's suffering and transformation. No sooner than she had buried her daughter and stopped speaking, my grandmother also stopped eating. Her vacant gaze shielded her from the words she did not want to speak; her voice fell silent, and her spirit was deadened. She brimmed with a searing sorrow that was eating away at her. When she brushed her hair, it fell out; she stopped grooming or washing herself. She wished only to depart from this world. She did not want any visitors, though her son came daily, despairing at her condition.

"Ñuke, please come back, don't let yourself die. I need you," Kawel pleaded, his voice breaking into silent weeping that would not let him go on.

He sat by her side, watching his mother slowly fade away, crushed by his powerlessness. Severina stayed with her for a few days, taking turns with Tita to care for her. Friends and relatives visited, pained to see her this way. My grandmother's skin dried out, dehydrated from so many tears. When she slept, her little girl would come to her in her dreams; she would stroke Wanguelen's hair and whisper sweet words in her ear. When she awoke, the memory of what had happened returned, bringing the pain and tears all over again.

The little house in the summer pastures, where they had been so happy, was filled with memories. When Pirenrayen summoned the strength to force her body to rise, even if only to satisfy her physical needs, memories awaited her outside the house. She seemed to hear her daughter's laughter in the yard, playing with her father, saying, "Mama, Mama, look at me," as she swayed in the hammock her father had made her. There it was now, the empty hammock, gray and forlorn. The wind carried the voice of her daughter, of Liam, and even her own, playing, laughing, and singing. Then her weakened legs would give way, and she would collapse onto the ground to the crunch of dry leaves. Several times Ambrosia, Kawel, or someone else would come to her aid as she lay unconscious on a ground of icy solitude.

Roig Evans accompanied Liam to the summer pastures where the survivors of the displacement had settled. Pirenrayen lived in the little house where she and Liam had fallen in love. It had been weathered by the gray brushstrokes of time. Every summer, they had brought their animals up there to graze. Liam had been happy in the lush forest, playing with his daughter, teaching her to climb trees, searching for nests, gazing at clouds as they lay in the soft grass. When he returned, those memories painfully swirled together, driving into his spirit like thorns.

The dogs barked and rushed to meet him. As they drew closer and recognized him, they wagged their tails in celebration of his arrival. Severina Acuipil was tending to Pirenrayen. She came out to see who was coming and spotted her husband, who, mounted on his old tobiano horse, was approaching with Liam. It took several years for the roads to be made accessible for vehicles; at the time, the only way to get there was on horseback.

As he entered the dwelling, the gloom struck Liam with even more darkness, in contrast to the brightness outside. His eyes grew accustomed to the space, and he could see Pirenrayen lying there, curled up like a child. He approached her cot and lifted the part of the blanket that covered her face. She was sleeping deeply. He saw how she had aged and grown thin; she had been fasting for more than thirty days. Her friends bathed her and combed her hair, but they could not persuade her to eat; she scarcely allowed them to offer her water. Liam cried when he saw her like this. He told Roig and Severina that he would take care of Pirenrayen, that if they wished, they could return home. They agreed. They embraced him and left in sorrow.

Liam was determined to save her. He cleaned and organized the small house, chopped enough firewood to keep the fire constantly burning, and heated water. In a large wooden barrel, he placed warm water infused with flowers, just as he had seen Pirenrayen do before. He wished he had known more of his lawentuchefe's medicinal secrets so he could save her. He added perfumes and the soap his mother had left in a small wooden trunk brought the previous summer. He drew back the blanket Pirenrayen was using to cover herself, and she opened her eyes, but closed them again. He undressed her, and she did not resist; he lifted her in his arms and placed her gently into the water. At that moment, she showed a glimmer of recognition, but thought he was a vision.

"Why have you come to disturb my death? Spirit of the wenu mapu, bring me the vision of my daughter, not the vision of the man who abandoned me," she said.

"My love, it's me, Liam," he answered with great tenderness. "I don't want to leave you ever again. I'll be here, I won't go away."

Despite her drowsiness and dwindling strength, Pirenrayen persisted. "You are not Liam. He is far away from here. He always leaves us, always goes away."

He fell silent. He washed her body, her hair. He lifted her out of the makeshift tub, wrapped her up, and carried her back to the cot. There he dried her, bundled her up, and covered her again with the blanket. As he prepared some broth, he spoke to her; he promised to stay by her side and told her about all the things they would do together in that place.

"Have a little of my soup, my beautiful lawentuchefe. Just a little, please," Liam pleaded.

She pressed her lips even tighter together to prevent the spoon from slipping in.

The days went by in this way, and Pirenrayen's health deteriorated. Liam prayed over his daughter's chenke; he prayed for Pirenrayen's recovery and for his little girl's forgiveness. "I should have been here," he said to himself over and over.

Many moons would pass before time eased Pirenrayen's sorrow. The wait felt like an eternity.

One morning, while Liam was building a chicken coop, the peuco came to the house. It tapped hard on the window insistently until it managed to wake Pirenrayen. She strained to lift her eyelids and, upon opening her eyes, met the fixed gaze of the bird watching her through the glass. With great effort, she scolded it.

"Linkoyan, what are you doing here? Let me die in peace so we can finally be together. It's the only way for me to be with my daughter, my grandmother, and you, and finally be happy . . . Leave me alone, Linkoyan. Go away!" she ordered the bird.

But the peuco kept tapping on the small window. Angry at this troublesome noise that shattered the sacred silence, Pirenrayen rose in a fury and, with her limited strength, went out half-naked into the yard. She'd lost a great deal of weight; she seemed so small and slight that from a distance, anyone might have thought she was an old woman, with her graying and disheveled hair.

Pirenrayen looked up and saw an immense, sturdy, graceful coihué tree in her yard. *When did this sprout?* she wondered. Just as curiosity filled her, she stared intently at its dense canopy and then lowered her gaze until she met the eyes of her grandmother Fresia. There, in the shade of the great coihué, stood all the loved ones she had lost to death: her grandmother, her daughter, Linkoyan. Pirenrayen flung herself at the coihué to embrace them and felt the warmth of their bodies. Her skin tingled with joy as Wang hugged her and took her hand. What immense and healing happiness overcame her when she felt her daughter's warm little hand again! Tears welled in Pirenrayen's eyes.

"Have you come to get me?" she asked with a gentle and delicate smile.

"No," they answered.

Her grandmother Fresia caressed her cheek and then spoke.

"It isn't your time yet, my child. You must stay and overcome. You will have a granddaughter. She must receive all that I have taught you. She will finish what we have started. She will tell our story. Here, my child," said Fresia, reaching out her arms. She opened her hands, which were full of amancay flowers. "Their petals will help heal your wounded heart. Make a potion and bathe with it."

Absorbed in his work, Liam had not seen Pirenrayen leave the house. He found her on his way back, standing in the yard, talking to herself, holding a bouquet of amancay flowers. She had covered her nakedness with a blanket. He lifted her in his arms and carried her back inside.

After that apparition, my grandmother came back to life. At first, she had to eat gradually to regain her strength. She never stopped bathing with amancay flowers. Liam was so grateful; he didn't know if it was Wanguelen who had heard his pleas, or God. It didn't matter. Every day, he left flowers on the chenke and prayed as well.

Several weeks had passed since her son's last visit. Kawel and Ambrosia returned and found Pirenrayen clean, her hair neatly combed, having lunch by the hearth. They were astonished by the improvement. She told them what had happened and showed them the tree. The coihué, a silent witness to the event, stood there like a miraculous apparition. Pirenrayen announced to them that Ambrosia, my mother, was carrying the life of a little girl.

"You will name her Llankaray," she commanded.

And so, before I was born, my name was chosen. I was born in the summer of 1938. After my birth, my grandmother regained the vitality and energy she had always possessed, but now, her medicine held even more power. Almost every day, she had visions, often anticipating both small and significant events. For instance, a few seconds before a plate fell off the shelf, she would say, "Be careful with the white plate; it's going to fall." When those present looked at the shelf, it would happen just as she had said. Or she would say, "Put the blanket on the seat. Galensho will be here soon," and sure enough, within an hour, Roig Evans would appear. I grew up following her advice and believing in her predictions.

Liam wanted to stay and live with her forever, but my grandmother did not allow it. Something had happened in her heart, like when glass falls and shatters with the slightest movement. That was how Pirenrayen felt: she now had a heart made of glass, and she no longer wanted to keep on loving a cowardly heart.

He understood. Liam decided to return to Buenos Aires. Embittered, he mounted his horse without saying a word and left. My grandmother mounted her horse and galloped after him. She didn't take long to reach him. Like in those playful and affectionate races of their early days, she reached out her hand for him to take. Liam was moved by the gesture and gently brushed it. They gazed lovingly at each other, and my grandmother rode away until she disappeared.

Liam felt his throat burn as if pierced with a knife. It was impossible for him to hold back the tears that streamed silently down his cheeks, wetting his face. That was their farewell. Both of them sensed that they would never be together again, despite their deep love for one another. Beyond their skin, beyond even the sensations of their bodies, there existed a world of feelings and certainties, beneath which lay truths that became presages. Other times, other paths were unfurling for both of them. Pirenrayen wept, too. She had just said goodbye to the man she had loved so deeply, the man with whom she'd believed she would share her life.

Chapter 38

LIKE THE LAND, WHICH ALWAYS SPROUTS ANEW

The railway company's manager punished Liam: he was demoted in rank and became an administrative employee. His days were dull and tedious. The few outings with his uncle were the only moments his face would relax and he could laugh. The rest of the time, his afflicted gaze and hermitlike air made those around him uneasy. His uncle scarcely recognized him anymore; he assured Christine that frequent contact with the Mapuches had negatively affected his nephew's character.

During that time when Liam O'Sullivan was lost among monotonous, yellowing papers, I was growing up with my grandmother Pirenrayen. She was there with me as I took my first steps, as my milk teeth grew in, and when I spoke my first words. I know that my presence filled her days with joy. My mother was glad to see her mother-in-law in such good spirits; it was a relief for her to have Pirenrayen there to help with my care. Being a grandmother was a soothing balm of honey for her bitter heart. Unbeknownst to me, I was the most powerful medicine to heal her wounds.

Sarah kept traveling to the south, where she settled permanently in 1939. She no longer had any desire to return to the city. She decided to create a Mapudungun-English dictionary, and she loved to visit Pirenrayen and talk to her granddaughter at the chenke. Pirenrayen never asked her about Liam, and Sarah respected her silence. Both of them spoke more now, perhaps because Sarah knew many more words in Mapudungun, or perhaps because my grandmother had also learned Spanish, which she called "castilla," from castellano. Sarah would stay in the town throughout the spring and summer. Her brother-in-law had bought her a small farm, where he built her a large house with fruit trees, rosebushes, and a vegetable garden. She loved this place, the little town nestled at the foot of the mountains, between the pallid steppe and the green cordillera, with the Chubut River rushing thunderously through. She felt that Patagonia was truly her home.

The townspeople loved her; she was always surrounded by children and attentive to the needs of the poorest. Her days in the south were divided between her farm and the lof where Pirenrayen lived. She loved to join her in the search for medicinal plants. It was invigorating to breathe the fresh Patagonian air, feeling the coolness of gentle gusts buffeting her cheeks, the graceful dance of the coiron grasses swaying with the wind, the spiny pepper trees reaching toward the sky. What tranquility flowed through her body, enveloping her soul in the sun's warmth and in heady aromas. She had learned as she walked alongside Pirenrayen that words were troublesome and silence necessary. My grandmother didn't always invite her to explore the mapu for lawen. Sarah believed that perhaps the plants, flowers, and trees spoke to Pirenrayen in solitude, that maybe that was the true power of a lawentuchefe.

Pirenrayen and Longko Mankiñ had become close friends; they often visited one another and shared the latest news. The longko had been widowed in the days of the 1937 eviction and missed his companion sorely. He was a wise and generous man. He was already very old. Knowing that he would soon be reunited with his wife, he was now preparing his son to be the future longko. That son's name was Victoriano Mankiñ. He led the resistance against the railway's encroachment on our lands.

One sunny Sunday in the last days of winter in 1939, a parliament was held where all the lofs were represented. Rumors were flying that the rewe was to be fenced off by the company, and that they would no longer allow our ceremonies to be held. Summer was approaching, along with the time for offerings and for renewing our vows of harmony with the mapu.

This is what Longko Mankiñ said:

"The Wingka refuses to understand that the land has its own order. The mapu has its ngen, its guardians, who do not dwell just anywhere. Those forces reside where they can be at peace, and it is there we must go to speak to them. They listen to us because they know we make sacrifices to be there, singing to them, speaking to them, feeding the fire and the word. The cosmos has its rules. In these sacred spaces, the spirits of our ancestors descend. That is why we must not surrender that place, where we perform our ceremonies to speak with the mapu. Because the only law that matters is the one established by nature, for she is the mother of all life. Can a child impose its will on its parents? We are insignificant beings in the face of the cosmic order, yet the Wingka believes he can get his way. The rivers will always return to their course. The mountains have been here forever; from them spring forth life, water, forest, snow. The volcanoes are the *pillañ*, the spirits who watch over everything. We must do things right and not fear the Wingka. We must respect what we have been taught, even if it costs us our lives. The territories hold our voice. The mountains and hills recognize our spirits; they rejoice when we return, mourn when we depart. They grow angry if we scorn them, and they defend themselves if we attack them. Let us not fear, for we will fare well. The ancients will guide us; we must defend the rewe. We will prevail! *Marici weu!*" He concluded his speech with the historic cry of our Mapuche people, which means, "Ten times we shall overcome."

Since the times of Longko Naweltripay, our lof had held its ceremonies in that place. It was a fertile valley surrounded by ocher-colored hills, an immense wetland meadow, and a vast plain, protected by all the families. Nobody let their animals graze there. When they were evicted from the fertile valleys where the Welsh later settled, my great-great-grandfather obtained permission to go down to that place every summer to perform his ceremony. The government knew that the resistance would be harsh: my people would not give up that *leufün,* our ceremonial space.

But the train had already reached the town. Its journey had paused there, and they had to build more tracks. After the station was inaugurated, everything changed for that small mountain town. The railway brought workers from all over the country. Poor women crowded the station, offering homemade bread and fried biscuits to passengers. Many of them married railway workers from other parts. There was joy. The train connected towns and revitalized the economy. In that small forgotten town in Patagonia, nothing was more important than the train's arrival; it was the social event of those days. La Trochita, the old Patagonian train, announced its departures and arrivals with a high-pitched screech. Its whistle echoed and woke up the town, interrupting the siesta.

When I, Ambrosia's firstborn, had just turned a year and three months old, my mother, who was still breastfeeding me, received the sign of another pregnancy. Pirenrayen dreamed that she was walking along a steep path that opened like a long, narrow passageway between huge, tall, reddish cliffs. She heard a clap of thunder, and upon reaching the top of the hill, marked by the path, she found two precious stones: one shone like the sun, somewhere between golden and whitish; the other was bright blue, smaller but strong and radiant. She bent down to pick them up, but a gust of wind forced her to close her eyes. When she opened them, the stones were no longer there. She searched desperately, digging in the earth until she found them, side by side. She picked up the blue one, then the golden one, and kept them.

My grandmother woke up happy and went to tell her dream to my parents, Kawel and Ambrosia. When she finished recounting it, she said to her daughter-in-law, "There are two lives in your womb, my child. You will suffer some difficult times during the pregnancy, but they will be born well. A girl and a boy," she predicted. Then she looked at my father and added, "Kawel, my son, just as your birth was announced in the pewma, through you a long and numerous lineage will develop. Our seed will perpetuate itself on the *wallmapu*, our ancestral territory. Our lineage will be like the land, which always sprouts anew."

Kawel and Ambrosia moved to the town, occupying a railway sleeper cottage that Cabrera assigned to my father, built entirely with quebracho wood. Kawel had started to take an interest in train driving. He was captivated by that machine that seemed like an iron horse neighing and exhaling smoke. Pirenrayen would often come down to visit them.

The summer of 1940 brought droughts and unusual heat. Longko Mankiñ asked Pirenrayen for help performing the *kamaruko* ceremony to ask for rain and well-being for all. My grandmother agreed to organize the ceremony and, together with her lof, prepared everything that was needed to make sure the kamaruko was performed correctly so that the *wenu chaw* and ngen mawun, the forces of the sky and rain, would moisten the land, turning it green again and making it flourish with life.

During those days of preparation for the ceremony, Christine arrived. She had come to stay with her mother-in-law for a while, for they were missing each other. Liam did not wish to join her, knowing that his mother would return with Christine to Buenos Aires to visit him for a few weeks. Christine's first few days there were surprising and pleasant, but the monotony and stillness soon bored her. She could not believe that the only interesting thing the town had to offer was a train.

Every Thursday, Pirenrayen would come down to the town to tend to her patients. At Roig Evans's house, a long line of people would be waiting for her in the early morning. She would arrive, smiling warmly, offering her medicine to everyone without exception. She asked for nothing in return, though many brought her gifts to express their gratitude. Christine was strolling through the narrow streets when she noticed the crowd gathered in Roig Evans's yard.

"Mother, I have just seen a throng of people crowded in Mr. Evans's yard . . . Has something happened to him?" she asked her mother-in-law when she returned home.

"Every Thursday, the Mapuche medicine woman comes down from the high mountains to tend to the sick. She's the one I had told you about, the one I thought would be able to help you."

"Yes, of course, I remember. Do you think she would still see me, Mother?"

"I don't know. So many things have happened here with the English, she's wary of us."

"But that's absurd! We aren't English!"

"Christine, don't we confuse all the peoples here? We call them all Indians. We don't even take the chance to learn the names of each group. Why should they distinguish an Irishman from a Scotsman or an Englishman? We are the Wingkas who came to their beautiful lands to live, while they are condemned to dispossession and death. All of us have harmed them in one way or another," Sarah said, and she once again remembered her granddaughter, the violent way in which she had died. Tears welled in her eyes.

"I am so sorry, Mother," Christine said, ashamed. "I didn't think this would upset you so much. You're right, forgive me."

Sarah hugged her daughter-in-law. "Don't worry, you're the most innocent and good-hearted person I've ever met," she said, and she was not mistaken. Christine was like a child in the guise of an adult, incapable of conceiving of evil and lies. Christine immediately asked Sarah to go with her the following Thursday to visit the lawentuchefe. Sarah agreed reluctantly, but it was the least she could do for her daughter-in-law, who had longed so much to become a mother.

When the next Thursday arrived, Christine rose in the early hours and, without eating breakfast, set off with Sarah to Roig Evans's house. Galensho invited them in as soon as he saw them and offered them tea, and they chatted until Pirenrayen arrived. Evans opened the waiting room, a small room furnished with only two long rustic wood benches placed facing each other. Between the benches, a wood-burning stove heated the space. This was where the patients sat; since the place was small, once it was full, they'd have to wait outside in a line.

Christine waited patiently for her turn. When it came, her heartbeat quickened, and she felt paralyzed. But Sarah held her hand and urged her to go in. Pirenrayen welcomed Sarah, embracing her. Christine greeted her in Spanish, and my grandmother replied in Mapudungun. Pirenrayen asked if Christine had brought some urine, as she usually did in such cases. Sarah had explained to her daughter-in-law beforehand that she needed to bring a sample for Pirenrayen to observe. Christine shyly removed a small, tightly closed glass bottle from her elegant purse and handed it over. Pirenrayen invited them to sit in front of her. The silence was tense and expectant.

The lawentuchefe observed the glass bottle with such concentration that it seemed her eyes were trying to shatter it with their gaze. Immediately, her expression became troubled, and her eyes filled with tears. Without a word, my grandmother left the room. Sarah thought she knew what was happening, and she understood the reason for her tears.

A noise broke the silence, and Roig went out to the yard to see what had happened. He saw the shattered bottle on the ground, and the patch of urine absorbed by the dry earth. He embraced Pirenrayen and spoke to her tenderly.

"Now I know who that woman is. She must not know that you have both loved the same man. I am sure she has come with good intentions. But, lamngen, do you want me to ask her to leave?"

Pirenrayen looked at him gratefully. "No, tell her to wait for me. Give me a moment," she said as she wiped her tears and added, "She's suffering great pain, too. I will help her. She's not responsible for anything that has happened to me."

Roig obeyed and asked the women to wait. Feeling more composed, Pirenrayen took a deep breath, adjusted her headscarf and braids, and went back into the room, proud and earnest. Still seated, Christine and Sarah exchanged glances and said nothing. Both were dispirited and confused.

Pirenrayen addressed Christine. "I will give you lawen for your womb, señora. You will be healed, and will have a child. You and your husband must drink it for three nights. He must take it without fail. Tell him that you have come to see me and that I ask him to join you in your treatment, to trust, and that both of you will be very good parents."

Christine was touched and embraced her tearfully. She thanked her and tried to pay her, but Pirenrayen would not accept the money. She dismissed them brusquely and invited in the next patient.

The days that week had been long and hot. The two women decided to walk along the banks of the Chubut River. As they listened to a raucous chorus of lapwings joyfully bidding farewell to the sun, Christine held the bottle of medicine close to her chest, as if guarding a great treasure. She felt a renewed happiness, nourished by blind faith in that enigmatic woman. She had felt her most private self exposed, and the idea embarrassed her. *Perhaps she saw something within me, but she assured me that I will be a mother, and a good one,* she thought. Yes, her happiness lay in that bottle. She gazed at the sky and saw the last shimmering rays of an enormous orange sun, tinting the water with flashes of purple and light.

On that day in Buenos Aires, oblivious to everything, Liam watched the slow shamble of a white cat stepping delicately along a railway sleeper. Sitting at the station, along with a crowd of people, he awaited the train's arrival. But he was not going anywhere, nor was he meeting anyone; he was there only to think. Train stations were his refuge. Sometimes, tired of the hustle and bustle, he would sit on a wooden bench by the tracks and doze in the sun. When he was half-asleep, he seemed to hear Pirenrayen's voice saying, "Wake up, my love! My wentru does not sleep unless he is in my arms." And he would awaken, only to realize that it had just been a dream bringing him memories of the most beautiful times in his life. When he lived with Pirenrayen, he loved to fall asleep in the wooden rocking chair he had carved for her when she was expecting Wanguelen. Pirenrayen used to catch him there, take his hand, and lead him away for a nap. They would make love and sleep for a while, their arms wrapped around each other. He missed her company, her scent, her skin, her voice, her body, so very much.

Chapter 39

THE SWEET TASTE OF COLLECTIVE VICTORIES

Liam welcomed his wife and mother with joy. He invited Christine to spend the last days of the summer by the sea. She was delighted with the idea, and they set off soon after her arrival.

The estate was perfumed with gardenias, lavender, and hyacinths. Their lungs swelled with pleasure in the cool sea air as they walked along the shore, listening to the sea crashing against the rocks.

On the first night, Christine told her husband about her visit to Pirenrayen. She repeated word for word what the lawentuchefe had said and placed the bottle of lawen on the table.

"We have to take it for three nights, and each night, we will try to conceive a child," she said.

He fell silent and looked nervous, but said he agreed. They raised their glasses to the child that would come and drank down the medicine my grandmother had given them. They gazed at one another with eyes full of hope, and before retiring to the bedroom, they carefully stored away the remaining potion. Liam found the new drink exquisite; it had been prepared by his beloved and contained not only the infertility cure for Christine, whom he loved as well, but also the remedy for his soul, which was plagued with guilt. Liam believed that if she had offered her healing power to give him the chance to become a father again, there could be no resentment in Pirenrayen's heart.

In April, they learned that Christine was pregnant. When she told him that he was going to be a father, Liam feared that he wouldn't love his child as deeply as he had loved Wang. He still spoke to her in his prayers, and she often visited him in his dreams.

That autumn, as Liam was absorbing the news of his impending fatherhood, Pirenrayen was locked in a battle with the English and Argentine authorities, who claimed that the ceremonial site no longer belonged to the Mapuche community, because the state had granted the land to the railway company for the train to pass through. Roig Evans offered to intervene with the manager. His name was Mr. Wilson, and he was from Birmingham, a city Roig Evans knew. Galensho went straight to see him.

"Mr. Wilson, how are you?"

"Hello, Mr. Evans. I'm well, if a little busy. Can I offer you something to drink?"

"No, thank you. I've come because I'm concerned about the situation with the Mapuche community . . . They have always performed their ceremony in that wetland meadow, near the spring. Longko Mankiñ tells me that you've fenced off those plots and won't let them in. Why? By what right have you fenced it off? You know full well that this land does not belong to you."

"Everything belongs to us, Mr. Evans. You ought to understand that. The savages know nothing about private property, but you are a cultured man, a European . . . there's no point in you worrying about them."

"This is unjust. I shall report it to the authorities!"

"Mr. Evans, we *are* the authorities. In Patagonia, in Wales, and in the world," he said firmly. Looking toward the central courtyard of the estate, he asked, "Tell me, Mr. Evans, what flag do you see flying there? It's our flag, the British flag. We are the authority here, and we have decided to fence in that land. It's a waste for them to use such fertile land only once a year for a pagan ritual. It's absurd to me that you don't understand this. Now, if you'll excuse me, I must get back to my business."

Roig Evans returned to the town in a fury and went straight to talk to the police commissioner and the justice of the peace, whom he knew well. He found the justice and the commissioner playing cards. The justice of the peace greeted him with a friendly smile.

"How are you, Evans, my friend? What brings you here?" Galensho shook hands with both men and spoke plainly of his concern, recounting the conversation he'd just had with the company's manager.

"There's nothing we can do, my dear friend," the commissioner replied. "Orders from above. If the company says that plot is theirs, that's because it's theirs! They'll surely have some paperwork to prove it."

Evans looked at the judge and asked, "Really? Do they own that plot? Did you sign any papers?"

The justice gave the commissioner a knowing look, as if seeking his help in concocting the story, and said, "That kind of documentation is handled in Buenos Aires. Everything is done there. It's the capital, don't forget. We only handle permits and minor business here."

Evans was worried. "I spoke with Pirenrayen and Longko Mankiñ, and they assured me that the date and location for kamarikun will be the same as always. They won't agree to give up the land. There will be resistance," he warned them.

The justice of the peace looked up from his cards, rose from his chair, and approached Galensho to give him a pat on the back, making light of the situation.

"Come on, don't blow this out of proportion! The Indians will back down when the time comes. Besides, it's the company's business, not yours. Leave it alone, my friend. Let the gringos and the Indians sort it out among themselves; it's nothing to do with us. By the way, have you received the brandy I ordered, Don Roig?"

The day came for the kamarikun, or kamaruko, as it is known these days. They say there were hundreds of people, nearly all of them related to my family; there were also many who, frightened by threats from the English, did not dare participate. My father told me that just as they were offering to the land the blood of the dark horse they were going to eat, the police arrived with henchmen from the English estate. They came on horseback and in trucks. They stormed into the leufün, the ceremonial land, firing shots. My grandmother stood in their way to keep them from the people; a policeman struck her with the butt of his rifle, and she fell unconscious. When she came around, she saw the wounded and the dead, all of them from only one side: ours.

The longko, my father, my grandmother, and even Roig Evans were detained. Galensho sent for one of his sons, who was a lawyer, though he worked as a journalist. He preferred writing to litigation; he had little experience, except for the few times he had defended himself for arrests during protests and for being drunk and disorderly in the street with his friends. His name was Nahuel Evans. He had gone to Buenos Aires to study a long time ago and had stayed there. He took charge of their defense.

Pirenrayen was very fond of Nahuel. She was ten years old when he was born. She had cradled him in her arms when he was a sturdy, chubby baby with big, dark eyes, and had even cared for him often. He had a beautiful smile that made dimples on his cheeks. As a child, Nahuel had adored Pirenrayen. He was very young when she married Linkoyan, and he could not conceal his jealousy. The boy's affection for my grandmother touched her deeply.

One afternoon, as they walked hand in hand from Galensho's store to the slaughterhouse, he looked at up her.

"When I grow up, I'm going to marry you, and that Linkoyan will be crying somewhere, because you'll always be with me," he said.

Pirenrayen laughed heartily, then paused for a moment. She crouched down to his level and gazed into his eyes.

"You will always be my *pichimotriley*. No man in the world is more beautiful than you," she replied in a voice full of tenderness. She liked to call him pichimotriley, which means chubby in Mapudungun. When Nahuel Evans left the town, Pirenrayen was a graceful young woman who had been widowed all too soon. She had a child in her care and a heart that was heavy with sorrow. Nahuel had just turned fourteen. He trusted that he would achieve his dream of returning as a graduate with a great deal of money, to marry her. But life had different plans for both, and fate led them through many separations before it finally brought them together again.

Nahuel did return as a graduate, but without a penny to his name. In the town, the prisoners' relatives and Severina Acuipil, his mother, gave him a hero's welcome, placing all their hopes in him. His mother embraced him tearfully, distressed about her husband; it was the first time Roig Evans had been arrested.

When he reached the police station, he was startled to learn from the commissioner that the English had taken custody of the detainees, housing them in the cells on their estate. Nahuel Evans confronted the commissioner sharply for allowing such an illegal maneuver.

"But, sir, what do you want me to do?" the commissioner asked him. "The inspector gives orders, and I obey."

Without hesitation, the young lawyer rallied the entire town to accompany him to the estate to free the detainees. Victoriano Mankiñ, the *inan* longko, led the procession.

"Patagonia is like a British colony. The English say what they want, and their Argentine lackeys take it as orders. What will become of this country?" Nahuel muttered along the way in anger and disillusionment.

Nahuel Evans managed to gather a considerable group of people, a little over a hundred. They traveled in Carlos Cabrera's pickup truck, in Galensho's truck, and in other vehicles that people offered; some chose to ride on horseback.

When they reached the estate, they saw that the foreman, with the support of a couple of laborers, was waiting at the gate. As Nahuel approached the spot, one of them dismounted and walked toward him. When they stood face to face, the lawyer held out his hand in greeting, but the man refused it.

"What do you want here?" he asked brusquely, fondling the revolver strapped to his waist.

"I am Nahuel Evans, defense attorney for the detainees, and I've come to request their immediate release. This arrest is illegal. They have committed no crimes, and I will prove it before an Argentine court, not before the English landowners."

"I don't understand a damn thing you're saying. If you keep making trouble here, I'll chase you all off with bullets."

Nahuel Evans was a very tall, stout, heavyset man with strong arms, who could flip a bull single-handedly. He was also passionate and quick tempered. Attempting to threaten him was a terrible idea.

The lawyer gave the clumsy foreman no time to react, knocking him out with a powerful punch. The frightened laborers fired a few shots into the air, but the people gathered there numbered over a hundred and were determined to go all the way, sick to death of the abuses committed by the English and the Argentine officials. They charged into the property as if in a raid and headed straight to the main house along with the lawyer. The estate manager was waiting there, alerted to the group's arrival by one of his laborers.

Mr. Wilson appeared on the porch of the house, looking astonished at the crowd. "Tell me, what do you need?" he asked.

Nahuel Evans took a few steps forward and introduced himself just as he had done to the foreman: "I've come for the detainees, including my father."

"Your father, Mr. Evans . . . ," began the manager in a falsetto voice. He only deigned to speak in English, though he spoke Spanish perfectly well, but the lawyer did not let him finish his sentence.

"Call me *sir*."

"Very well, as you wish. As I was saying, sir, your father is not detained. In fact, the laborers were mistaken in bringing him here. As soon as I saw him, I made my apologies and asked him to go home, but he refuses to leave unless we release all the others. As you will understand, that is not possible."

"No, I don't understand. As far as I can see, there is no arrest warrant issued by any judge."

"You are mistaken, sir. There is one," he said, and sent his secretary to retrieve the order from his office.

As soon as he had it in his hands, the lawyer read it.

"This is a farce, not a warrant!" Nahuel Evans exclaimed in fury. "It's just a letter sent by your friend the judge, authorizing you to repress and take action if necessary. This is inadmissible! They were all unarmed, performing a Mapuche ceremony that has been taking place there for centuries, and you attacked them."

While the two men argued in English, the rest grew impatient. They understood none of that conversation, so they asked Nahuel Evans to translate everything that was being said. First, he had to translate it into Mapudungun, and then into Spanish. They decided not to leave until their relatives were released. Among the detainees were not only Mapuches; many townspeople had been invited and had participated gladly in the ceremony since they, too, were affected by the drought.

It is curious how oppressors manage to instill in the memory of the oppressed only the battles they won; they turn these into epic narratives, promoting amnesia, stripping away the sweet taste of collective victories by the people. This was a glorious feat, a story worthy of being told and stored in a special chest of memories. Ambrosia, my mother, along with Tita and Severina, took the lead. Behind them, more than a hundred relatives entered and gained control of the main house on the estate. The manager admitted that this time the balance of power was against him, and in the end, agreed to release the prisoners. He ordered that the detainees be brought out.

The foreman was furious; his nose was still bleeding from the punch.

"Chickenshit gringo," he muttered under his breath, then shouted to a young man who was near one of the barns, "Hey, go to the cells and bring that rabble over here!"

The young man obeyed, and after a while, they all appeared in chains, with wounds to their ankles and wrists. Some could barely walk due to the beatings they had endured, and they smelled foul since they had been forced to relieve themselves in their clothes. Tears streamed down everyone's faces upon seeing them in such conditions. So much humiliation, so much suffering!

Nahuel Evans asked the little Englishman to remove their chains, and the man complied. Wilson saw himself through the others' horrified gazes, caught between disgust and shame. Consumed by an overwhelming desire to escape from the vile act he'd participated in, the manager set them free. He felt relieved that it was finally over, but at the same time, he was sure that if ordered to do it again, he would obey without hesitation.

The English wanted to treat us like animals, as did the Argentine state. But even animals have dignity that drives them to honor life by defending themselves; they are capable of killing or dying in their quest not to be caught. We Mapuches are like animals in some ways: they can never catch us all, there will always be one who escapes and multiplies by ten, just like in the marici weu.

That day, everyone returned home in sorrow, the taste of victory turned bitter with the suffering of their loved ones. The wet wind blew, and the procession dispersed along almost invisible paths unfurling over a wild, prickly carpet of dry and yellow land. They had only wanted to ask for rain, and instead were showered with injustice and anguish.

Pirenrayen took a deep breath of the humid air, gazed at the clouds, and assured her son and daughter-in-law that the next day, it would rain. And so it did.

Pirenrayen and Nahuel Evans saw each other that day, but they did not yet recognize each other.

The younger men from several lofs organized themselves, and removed the barbed-wire fences from the rewe land in the dead of night. This act of liberation bolstered the spirits of the communities, and especially Pirenrayen's spirit.

Chapter 40

Our Sacred Soil

The news of the English defeat didn't take long to reach the offices of Buenos Aires. Liam learned the details from his friend Roig Evans, who sent him a letter recounting all that had happened. The mission had failed; all that remained was to expedite the railway work as soon as possible.

One morning, he was summoned to an urgent meeting, where his superiors and some national officials were gathered. The consensus among all was clear: the construction must commence immediately. They would not allow a handful of Mapuches to halt progress. Liam was assigned to the delegation that would leave for Patagonia; his role was to act as translator and mediator.

It was early May when Liam O'Sullivan was finally dispatched to Puelwillimapu, Chubut. Argentine and English officials chose to position themselves at the heart of the conflict, seeking an agreement that would allow the railway work to resume. He agreed to go because he knew that, with his knowledge of Mapudungun, he could speak the whole truth to the Mapuches. He would translate what the English wished to convey but would also add what they were sure to conceal. He was resolved to conspire in the Mapuches' favor so they would not be stripped of their rewe. He owed it to the communities, but above all, he owed it to Pirenrayen. He could not bear to think of himself as a cog in that dreadful colonial machine, which, in the guise of a mission to bring modernity and progress, committed all kinds of injustices and abuse. Those flags betokening progress were soaked in blood.

The delegation, comprising officials from land, transportation, and security, alongside government advisers, accompanied the leaders of the construction project—all of them important officials from the British company. The Mapuche authorities were invited to a meeting.

All the longkos, werken, pillañ *cushe* (the older women who are bearers of spiritual knowledge), and other members of the pu lof gathered to listen and express their opinions. Among them were Nahuel Evans and Pirenrayen. After many long years apart, they embraced with joy at their reunion. He recognized her immediately: slightly graying, thinner, but still much the same as he remembered her. The years were beginning to trace faint lines of wrinkles across their eyelids and cheeks. She, on the other hand, did not recognize him until Ambrosia, my mother, pointed him out.

"There's Nahuel Evans!" she cried.

At that moment, as Pirenrayen turned her gaze, her eyes met the mischievous, boyish look she had once adored.

"Pichimotriley!" she called out, and opened her arms to welcome him. He embraced her with love and joy. Nahuel Evans had become a man, and a great man, too.

It was a windy and ocher afternoon when the government emissaries arrived. The trees were shedding their leaves, shaken by the merciless kurruf. The men from Buenos Aires looked on fearfully at the growing assembly. The school hall was filling up more and more. The people were hostile yet reserved.

Once every last space had been filled, the meeting commenced. The youngest of the officials stood haughtily and began to speak.

"We have summoned you to announce that we will be bringing the railway to these lands. The company needs workers, strong men who will contribute to completing the project swiftly. The railway will bring progress to these lands, to the benefit of everyone."

Those gathered observed quietly. No one spoke. After a few seconds of awkward silence, the young official asked Liam to come forward and translate. Pirenrayen, seated in the front row, felt her heart race when she saw Liam among those who sought to snatch away their sacred land. A bitter taste seeped into her mouth; she felt betrayed.

Liam O'Sullivan introduced himself and spoke only in Mapudungun. He explained that the only reason he had agreed to be there was to tell the truth.

"They come to you with false promises," he explained. "They want to take your land and its sacred leufu from you. I know what it means to you, and I want to help you."

When Liam finished speaking, one of the Englishmen stepped forward.

"I am Engineer Smith. I am here to assess the geography and terrain. Many men will be needed for the work. The company will pay those who volunteer to help handsomely. But we need you to collaborate for the future of this country, which will be the future of your children. We have learned what happened during the summer. You were informed that lot twelve no longer belongs to you; it is now the company's property. A railway station will be built there, exactly where you wish to perform your rites. We need the spring that is located there, do you understand?" he asked as if speaking to children.

After the engineer's speech, one of the longkos rose and, with a deep and raspy voice, introduced himself in Mapudungun. After speaking in our language, punctuated by a hoarse cough, he looked intently at those in attendance and questioned the visitors.

"Since when does the Wingka government come to our lands to inform us, to ask us, to listen to us? If you have called us here today, it's because you have something else in your thoughts. We are accustomed to deception. Will that iron kawel pass through our lands? There's always some reason to take our territory away from us. Now tell us the truth: Why have you come?"

That was when all the dormant voices awoke as if in a swarm. Everyone was asking the same question. Pirenrayen stood, approached the government officials, stared at them, and reminded them fiercely of the events that followed every government visit.

"You come here to lie and cheat. That's been your way ever since our people can remember. You came to take everything that our wallmapu, free and generous, provided us. You want it all for yourselves, you want to share nothing. When we remind you that you are intruders, you answer that you have brought us civilization. I wonder what civilization is. Your schools take away our wisdom, erode our memory, weaken our spirit, and you call that education. My mother was raped in your Wingka school. You killed my ñuke. The lands are fenced off, your animals watched over. If we eat one of your cows out of hunger, you imprison us and accuse us of theft. Now you want your train to pass through our lands, and you plan to snatch our sacred soil from us, the soil of our dreams. If we allow you to seize our leufu, our river, you will be snatching away our lives and the lives of my grandchildren. I do not believe in your promises, for your hearts are full of lies."

Then Pirenrayen turned to her people and exhorted them.

"*Pu longko ka pu lamngen*, do not be deceived again. *Weichan feulá, weichan!*"

"What did she say?" the young official asked Liam nervously.

"Longkos, brothers and sisters, do not be deceived. We must fight now, fight!" Liam translated, watching as Pirenrayen moved toward the exit, clearly intending to leave the premises.

Liam O'Sullivan and Nahuel Evans had the same impulse; they reached Pirenrayen together, as if with synchronized movements, urging her to stay. The lawyer saw in my grandmother's eyes the union of love and pain. He understood instantly that he was superfluous there;

he decided to turn and go back into the hall. Pirenrayen let Liam walk with her to the schoolyard, where they spoke briefly.

"Pirenrayen, don't be angry like this. I'll help you. They won't get what they want this time, you'll see. I'll stand by your side to defend your rewe."

"I don't want you by my side. I want you all to leave us alone!"

"I am not like them."

"They pay you to be here. You work for them. I don't think you're all that different."

"If you ask me, I will resign. I'll leave this job and go up to the mountain with you."

She took a deep breath, looked out at the landscape, then turned her gaze back to his eyes.

"Believe me, not a day goes by that I don't think of you, that I don't miss you. But even so, I would never let you come back. The time for what could have been is over, and now it's too late."

Just then, Smith came out to call him.

"Go, your people are calling you."

"You are my people. How can I prove it to you?"

Kawel, my father, approached them; he was late for the assembly. He embraced Liam, and they greeted each other joyfully.

"Aren't you coming in, ñuke?" Kawel asked his mother, my grandmother.

"No, I've heard too much already."

Pirenrayen climbed onto her horse and rode up the mountain; she needed to be at home to think. Liam watched her depart and then returned to the hall, alongside Kawel. He felt lost and defeated. They had experienced heaven together, he and that woman, and now they were left in hell.

The trawun dispersed as soon as Pirenrayen had left. The longkos and Mapuche authorities ordered their people not to sign, and most left with a bitter taste in their mouths. But the English decided to tempt the longkos one by one, visiting them at their homes, offering them money and cows in exchange for their signatures. There have always been *yanaconas*, traitors, among our people, and among all peoples everywhere. And so, a handful of Mapuches, including Inan Longko Victoriano Mankiñ, who had initiated the resistance, signed, legitimizing the English seizure of our leufu. That betrayal was like a stab in the heart for Pirenrayen and for Longko Mankiñ's father, but my grandmother and the communities would not learn of this truth until a few months later.

After the trawun, Nahuel Evans went to find Pirenrayen at her house. It was already late, and the May sun was setting quickly. When the dogs announced visitors, she came out to the courtyard, worried that only bad news could arrive at this hour. She was startled to see her beloved Pichimotriley.

"Pichimotriley, what brings you here so late?"

"It's you who brings me here; I haven't stopped thinking about you."

She smiled flirtatiously and invited him in. They talked for a long time. Night fell, and the darkness found them reminiscing, laughing about their childhood and the old times of peace and joy. She cooked a stew, and he uncorked a bottle of wine he had brought. Twilight spread a silken veil of stars across the sky and came hand in hand with *kuyen*, an enormous full moon. *Apoy* kuyen is what we call it. Its light merged with the day, its brightness confusing the creatures that come out at night.

Nahuel drew closer to Pirenrayen and kissed her impulsively. She tasted the sweet flavor of wine on his lips and responded with a kiss that was long, deep, and moist. Then came the embraces, the caresses, the words of love he had stored up inside him for many years. She spread her marital blanket, the same one, woven on an ancient loom, on which she had made love to Linkoyan, and later Liam. Now, these turbulent times were bringing her a new love.

That night, Liam O'Sullivan stayed up, unable to sleep. He was racked with worry about what was inevitably to come, and he couldn't stop thinking about how close he was to Pirenrayen, yet how far away she seemed from him.

The next morning, he went back to Buenos Aires. He did not return to Patagonia until after his son was born. Every month, without fail, he still sent a letter along with some money to Pirenrayen, via Roig Evans. As before, Galensho would hand her the envelope, and she would return it unopened. It was almost a ritual. A considerable amount had accumulated in the bank account Roig Evans had opened for Pirenrayen. My grandmother knew nothing about these savings until circumstances led her to need a large sum of money, and Galensho revealed to her that she held an account.

Liam spent the last days of his wife's pregnancy with her, feeling impatient and eager. Finally, the moment of the birth arrived. The hospital smelled of chlorine; a mortuary silence flooded the corridors, where white walls were adorned with signs forbidding speech. Liam and Sarah sat together on a long, polished wooden bench, watching the hospital staff come and go. They had been there for hours and would wait a little longer before hearing the newborn's cry. When the doctor approached to congratulate him and announce that all had gone well, his mother embraced him, filled with joy, just like when he was a child. They went in together to meet the baby, who was sleeping next to his mother. Liam found him beautiful, though somewhat purple; the little one had made a great effort to be born.

They named him Martin Niall O'Sullivan. In time, everyone would call him Martín, with the Spanish pronunciation. A month later, he was baptized in the cathedral, and they summoned John Walton from Santiago del Estero to be his godfather. There was a grand celebration in the criollo style, with roasted meats, plentiful food, and drinks. Liam was happy. John was moved to see him this way; it was like the old times in Dublin. And motherhood had made Christine even more beautiful.

John had brought his wife, a lovely mestiza woman from the countryside, with whom he already had two children. They stayed for a few weeks, then returned home. That was the last time John saw his friend. Liam bid him farewell at the station, content, but before he left, Christine said her goodbye to John at home. Their love continued intact, but neither said a word. It was enough for them to gaze into each other's eyes to rekindle the flame. They put their arms around each other, striving to pour their souls into that embrace.

Just as Christine had imagined, Liam soon resumed his long absences, traveling throughout the country, and especially to Patagonia. When he was at home, she felt relieved; he was attentive to the child and pampered Christine with small gestures of affection. But at times, he grew silent and lost in thought. Christine felt that there was a part of him that she was completely excluded from. But even if Liam had given her the key to his thoughts, she would not have dared to use it. She sensed he was hiding a truth and that it could shatter the life she was living, the life that had been so hard to create.

Christine would speak to Liam of society gossip, news of the baby's bodily functions, the furniture she wanted to buy, or the elegant shop windows that were now appearing, adding a touch of class to the city. Then Liam would fold the newspaper in his hands, finish his coffee, and gaze at her like a newcomer, observing and trying to understand what was happening. That vacant look of boredom and bafflement wounded her, made her feel miserable. So she devoted herself completely to her child, making motherhood the sole purpose of her existence. When solitude swelled inside her, despite the happiness her son brought, she resumed her work at the foundation started by María Isabel, who, despite her absence, continued to provide her with inspiration. María Isabel's memory remained vivid in her mind, just like that of Mademoiselle Marie.

Sarah decided to stay with her grandson for his early years, but she missed the south, the farm, her house, and Pirenrayen and her people. She was very sweet with the baby, and it touched her to watch him grow.

Chapter 41

The Language of Love

The beginning of the year 1942 brought Pirenrayen her definitive union with Nahuel Evans. They did not marry, nor did they celebrate. The lawyer's visits to my grandmother's house simply became so frequent that he decided to stay by her side. He did not ask her if he could stay, nor did he make any proposal. She did not ask him for anything. They loved each other, they enjoyed being together, and they needed each other.

Nahuel and Pirenrayen traveled through the communities together, getting to know their people's problems deeply and seeking solutions together. This meant that Nahuel would occasionally travel to the city of Buenos Aires, taking his articles with him. As I said before, he was a better journalist than a lawyer. He was always concerned about those condemned to suffer. He was an unwavering anarchist. When he went away, Pirenrayen dedicated her days to me, to her patients, and to her land. She never worried about Nahuel seeing other women. She never asked him. And she did not reproach him, even though rumors flew around that he was a ladies' man and that more than one woman was willing to take him secretly into her bed. He would come to her arms eager never to be far from that maternal and passionate woman.

Nahuel Evans loved my grandmother very much, despite knowing that he would never be her only love. He was fiercely jealous of Liam because he sensed that Pirenrayen loved him more than anyone else.

I was growing up, wrapped in the love of my parents and, above all, my grandmother. She used to take me walking with her in the mountains, searching for lawen; we would also go to a lake not far from our homes to spend the day bathing. Even in winter, she bathed in the lake's icy waters; she assured me that it made us stronger. If we saw a waterfall, we prayed to it: we spoke to it for a long time and then stood beneath it so we would get fully drenched. I used to laugh heartily at my grandmother's ways. Now I understand that they were not just ways but wisdom.

She liked to tell me stories, opening her heart to me and sharing her feelings, perhaps because she knew that such a young child would neither offer opinions nor judge her. I believe I was the only person to catch a glimpse of the deepest oceans of her heart. The peuco was always with her; she taught me to greet him, and would explain how this bird was my grandfather, always watching over us.

My grandmother Pirenrayen taught me how to cook. I was more of a hindrance than a skilled assistant, but she used to laugh a lot with me and was so patient. My ñuke had her hands full with the twins, so I spent more time with my chuchu, my grandmother, than with my parents. Nahuel Evans was very kind to me and would bring me chocolates and sweets from his father's store. He was always in a good mood and was playful with my grandmother and me. She cooked his favorite dishes with care, and he honored her cooking by eating enough for four men. Nahuel always seemed to me like a giant. When he lifted me in his arms, I felt like I was soaring through the sky, and it sent my heart into a flurry. I loved it so much when he lifted and spun me in circles that I begged him to do it often. Sometimes, I ended up vomiting; then my grandmother would get angry and scold him, warning him not to do it anymore. He would make excuses to her like a child and say that the blame was mine.

Nahuel earned little money. He wrote articles in English for foreign newspapers interested in bringing their readers closer to the fantastic Indigenous world of Patagonia. But his main journalistic work was unpaid; quite the opposite, he paid to help support the anarchist newspapers. He enjoyed discussing his ideas with Pirenrayen, even reading some of his articles to her. She understood Spanish perfectly by then, but she loathed speaking it and pronounced it poorly. She understood some English because Liam had made an effort to teach her. In their daily life, Nahuel spoke only Mapudungun with her. It was his mother's language; it was the language of love.

During the last years of the Infamous Decade, many evictions took place. Nahuel Evans and my grandmother scarcely had any rest; they traveled constantly to other communities because of the various abuses committed against our people. Nothing was changing here: the English were still lords and masters of our territories, and we were increasingly reduced and crowded. There was hunger. In the winter of 1942, it snowed so much that thousands of animals perished. We no longer had winter pastures; all the lowlands were in the hands of the company.

The Mapuche authorities, including Pirenrayen, resolved to travel to Buenos Aires to speak with the president or a close official and request the return of the communal pasture. Nahuel Evans thought the idea was absurd. He said he knew the civil and military officials linked to power very well and that they would in no way be interested in helping them; on the contrary, it was risky. They might even interpret it as a provocation. But he offered to go along; he believed that in any case he could be of some use to them.

My grandmother argued a lot with Nahuel Evans, but they were very close. She told me that she had never felt so cared for as she did with that man. She, who always took care of all of us, allowed herself to be cared for by Pichimotriley.

They organized themselves, raised money for the trip, drafted the petition, and left in the early days of October. That was a trip we would all remember forever. I remembered because I missed my grandmother. And I missed Pichimotriley, as my grandmother affectionately called Nahuel. No one but she was allowed to call him that. When I did so, he would chase me until he caught me and tickle me all over. He joked that he would cut out my tongue if I called him Pichimotriley, and I thought I would die of laughter. I grew to love him deeply, like a second father.

It took them a week to reach Buenos Aires. They left the town in a truck, traveled to Ingeniero Jacobacci, and from there took the train to Constitución. It was the first and only time my grandmother left her home region. She had only ever seen the railway in town, hearing the train arrive and depart, but she did not fully know what it was until she traveled on it. Her thoughts about the railway changed then; her emphatic rejection was transformed into admiration. She thought about what it meant for all the towns to know that they were connected by train. It was a gratifying trip, filled with laughter and anecdotes.

Nahuel Evans, despite his meager income, was very generous with his money; he enjoyed treating them to good food and fine wines. On the journey, they always ate in the dining car. My grandmother complained that she did not feel at ease there; the food tasted bland to her, it was missing cilantro and spice. Nahuel found her observations highly amusing, and she was irritated by how much he laughed.

"Why are you mocking me?" Pirenrayen would ask angrily.

"But, my love, I'm not laughing at you. On the contrary, it makes me happy that you're as unique as you are," he would answer, taking her by the hand. He would gaze at her with such adoration that all her anger melted away.

When they arrived in Buenos Aires, they stayed in a very modest guest house in the heart of the Monserrat neighborhood. Passersby stared at them in amazement: Pirenrayen wore all her Mapuche jewelry and her long black küpan. The rest of the people wore boots and hats, as well as their makun, a strange attire for the metropolis. The spring heat of the city was suffocating.

Nahuel Evans immediately started knocking on doors to make contacts, in the hope of securing an interview with some high-ranking officials close to the president. While they waited for some good news, Nahuel's friends showed them around the city. What impressed my grandmother the most was the Río de la Plata; she said it was a river with the spirit of the sea. It was immense, seemingly endless, with its gray waters and gigantic waves. My grandmother knew the ocean only from stories, and that river closely resembled the descriptions Liam would give whenever he recalled his memories at sea.

As she explored the city, my grandmother thought of Liam; so many times, she had tried to imagine him walking its streets, but she could not picture it, since that world was unknown to her. Now it was she who trod the same sidewalks where he might have walked. She wondered where he might live. There in the city, everything was paved, and people did not leave footprints. They crowded together like a caged flock of birds. *What a strange way to live!* she thought to herself. She could not understand why Liam had preferred that ugly gray and monochromatic world over the intense colors of her mountains.

The lawyer managed to secure a meeting with someone; he was not close to the president, but it was the first door to open, and they had to make the most of it. Although Argentina had remained neutral in the Second World War until then, the pressures from the British on one side and the Germans on the other created a delicate scenario; it was not the most opportune moment to present a demand like the one they wanted to make.

A colonel from the army received them in his office, accompanied by some of his advisers. He was kind and unassuming, listening to the concerns of the longkos and showing great interest in the details of the abuses and hostilities perpetrated by the English against their people. The encounter gave everyone hope, since this man had committed to meeting with the company's representatives to set up negotiations that would allow the Mapuche lofs to regain access to their communal pasture, now in the hands of the English. The colonel asked them to stay in the city for a few more days as he would try to arrange a meeting. They should wait. The only one who did not trust him was the lawyer Nahuel Evans.

Liam O'Sullivan used to take note of the events that moved him. This is how I know that on one of those days, in Recoleta, another part of the city, he sat leafing through the newspaper in a café. A headline in a small box caught his attention: "The Last Argentine Indians Visit Buenos Aires." He paused at a photo in which all the longkos he knew were gathered, and where he could even make out Pirenrayen and Kawel. His amazement was immense, and a strange sensation of anxiety and joy coursed through his body, stirring his soul.

The next day, he received a call from the company, asking him to attend a meeting in the colonel's office. He accepted, intrigued, sensing that this meeting had something to do with the Mapuches' visit to Buenos Aires. When he hung up the telephone, he saw Christine through the window overlooking the garden, carrying their son, Martin, in her arms. He smiled with tenderness. Once more, the memory of Wang, the morning he had held her close to his chest for the first time, assaulted his mind. He rid himself of the images paining his heart with the picture of here and now, seeing his healthy and happy son. He went into the garden, kissed his wife, and took the baby in his arms. This child was the only one who sweetened his bitter life. Sometimes, he grew frustrated with Christine for suffocating the child with too much control. But then he regretted reproaching her, understanding her feelings after her great effort to become a mother.

Although he detested visiting those establishments with her, he had promised to take her shopping that afternoon. His wife took all the time in the world to choose what she was looking for. She tried on dresses she did not buy; she asked about models and colors that were not yet available, since European fashions took a long time to reach here. She lived in a state of longing for her homeland. Liam stayed in the car, waiting for her to finish shopping. His son slept peacefully in an elegant Moses basket in the back seat.

The heat forced him to get out. He lit a cigarette and waited in the shade, leaning against his car, slowly exhaling. And suddenly, coming toward him on the sidewalk, he saw Pirenrayen, Kawel, that lawyer he disliked so much, and the longkos from the lof of Chubut, walking in a group. Everyone was greatly surprised. The men greeted him warmly, except for Nahuel Evans, who remained distant and cold. Pirenrayen was disconcerted at the coincidence, but it was inevitable that joy would seize her upon seeing him. He gazed at her with the eyes of a slaughtered calf.

They talked of the purpose of their visit to Buenos Aires and the meeting with the colonel. Liam told them that he had received a call that morning announcing the meeting they would have in the coming days.

"They will surely get in touch with you to confirm the exact day and time," Liam said. "I believe it will all be resolved. The company is not using the winter pasture, and the construction of the line that was supposed to cross that land has ended up being delayed. I don't think they will risk continuing the railway until the war is over. There will be no problem for you to go back there with your animals."

Pirenrayen, looking him in the eyes, replied, "Their thoughts and intentions can be deceptive, just like their words. We will go back to the pasture with or without an agreement. That land is ours, and we will reclaim it. Wingka thieves!" she exclaimed.

An uncomfortable silence followed until Kawel spoke up.

"My ñuke is right, Don Liam. We are struggling there. We have no place for our animals to graze; the winter has caught them already thin, and now they've scattered because of the snow."

Just then, Christine arrived. Liam was stunned and embarrassed and was forced to introduce his wife. She greeted everyone. The women recognized each other. Christine could not hide her surprise and excitement at seeing Pirenrayen.

"I'm so glad to see you," she said. "I've thought about you a lot, about how to thank you for what you've done for us. Our son has brought joy back into our lives. I want to show him to you."

Christine opened the car door and lifted the Moses basket where the baby was sleeping.

"I see I did not fail you; my medicine is powerful," Pirenrayen said, looking at Liam, then added, "You two have done your part."

"Yes," Christine said timidly. "Thank you."

Everyone felt tense, but they bid each other farewell politely. Liam hadn't known how to act; his wife had noticed his distress. What saddened her most was to recognize in his gaze the same sparks of light that his eyes had once directed at her. Now, seeing his reaction, she understood everything. She understood why, when she sought her help, the lawentuchefe had left the room in tears. Not only did they know each other; she concluded that they had, or had once had, a romance.

When they arrived home and sat in the living room, she could no longer hold back, and broke the silence.

"I know you love that woman."

Liam looked at her, stunned. "I don't understand what you're talking about," he said.

"The Mapuche woman, the healer. You're in love with her."

"Did she tell you that?"

"No, but the look in your eyes said it all. If it weren't for Martin, my life would be far more miserable than it is. I realized a long time ago that you don't love me. I deserve the truth from you. You need to tell me everything."

Liam wanted to get angry, but he couldn't. He, too, needed to put an end to so many hidden truths. She cried disconsolately as he told her the whole story.

"I understand what you and she have gone through. God knows I had no idea of this when I went to see her. She chose to help me, even knowing who I was. We are both indebted to that woman, God bless her. As for you, I'm not sure I can ever forgive you."

Liam slumped into an armchair and, for the first time, sobbed like a child in front of her. Christine approached shyly and stroked his head. She embraced him while letting tears of compassion roll down her face for this man who had caused the women he loved so much pain.

Nothing was ever the same between them after that confession. Yet there was a certainty that neither needed to lie or to hide from the other anymore; they were like friends who had survived the worst.

Pirenrayen was still awake. It wasn't her partner's thunderous snoring that had disturbed her sleep, but the memory of Liam, which once again returned to stir up her pain. She paced around the small hotel room, sighing, occasionally peering out of the window to gaze at fragments of the melancholy city. She climbed back into bed. The noises from the street kept her from resting. She gently shook her companion.

"Pichimotriley, Evans," she said as she shook him.

"What's the matter, woman?" he asked, still half-asleep.

"Do you love me?"

He sat up, now fully awake. "Why are you asking me this in the middle of the night?"

"And since when do we only ask questions during the day?"

"Oh, my dear woman," he said with a smile, "you always have an answer for everything. Of course, I love you. I've loved you for as long as I can remember . . ."

Pirenrayen rested her head on his chest. "Hold me tight," she said.

Nahuel Evans wrapped his arms around her and caressed her until she fell asleep.

The meeting was delayed by another week since the colonel had to travel inland. Upon his return, the appointment was scheduled, and representing the company were the lawyer, a railway manager, and Liam O'Sullivan. The meeting was difficult: our people demanded the return of the land, but the company offered a lease until they began to lay the tracks. This outraged Pirenrayen, who spoke, with Liam translating.

"What kind of a conversation is this? We come to claim what has been stolen from us, and the thief says he will only lend us what is ours for as long as he decides! Does the thief think we are children? Does he think we have no memory? I was born on that land, and my mother was before me. We have always lived there. Just as the stars have filled the sky, my people have lived in that territory and multiplied in it. The *weñefe* wants to lend us what he took away from us with bullets and blood."

She drew near the English official and, right up close to his face, cried, "Weñefe! Thief!"

The senior company official rose and reproached the colonel for his ill-judged decision to bring these savages to the meeting.

"It would have been sufficient for the company and the government to agree on how to resolve the issue," he said.

The colonel stood up and called for dialogue between the parties.

"But, sir, do not get angry so quickly. Have patience, for I still haven't spoken. And you, madam, trust me, we will do something to help solve this problem. First, I confirm that you will not return empty-handed; I have ordered a subsidy for the purchase of sheep and goats to make up for your losses."

The attending longkos nodded despite their dissatisfaction. Nahuel Evans wore an expression of indignation throughout the meeting.

"I am at Mr. Evans's disposal for any further requests," said the colonel. "For now, you must agree not to keep your animals in the estate's field. You are still using part of the lot for your rituals. The company is kind enough to allow you to use that area."

"Excuse me, Colonel," interrupted Liam. "The people here have used that place for their ceremonies forever. The company never claimed ownership of that space until last year. If a purchase was made by the company, they should have at least informed them, and that did not happen."

"Your role in this meeting is that of translator," the English engineer reminded Liam. "It was made clear that you should not express opinions."

Liam apologized but was still vexed. Nahuel Evans proposed ending the meeting. The longkos requested a written and signed document guaranteeing the delivery of the promised animals. Everyone was disappointed.

As they waited for the minutes to be written up, Liam and Pirenrayen sat face to face in a large hall. Some of the longkos present, like my grandmother, did not know how to write. The rest, along with the lawyer, were invited into the office of the colonel's adviser, where the minutes I have in my possession today were drafted.

Liam O'Sullivan watched my grandmother. He contemplated her with tenderness and gratitude. His eyes held the loving light of a river's still water at sunset. She sensed that something inside him had changed. She imagined that the truth had finally shed light on the shadows in his life, that now he could love his wife and child without guilt or remorse. Liam wanted to thank her for helping him become a father again, but it wasn't the time or place. Pirenrayen had always struck him as an extraordinary woman, but he had never imagined just how deeply she loved him. Now he saw it clearly. How base, cowardly, and insignificant he felt. He was even ashamed to acknowledge the jealousy that overcame him when the lawyer intentionally embraced her in front of him.

She returned his gaze with a sweet, understanding smile, as if she were reading his thoughts. Yes, that's how they were. They knew and understood each other so well and so deeply that even their thoughts were revealed to each other through their gazes.

"I love you," Liam told her, almost in a whisper. "I love you," he repeated.

She smiled faintly. They returned with the minutes, which Nahuel Evans translated into Mapudungun. Everyone seemed satisfied, and it was signed, but they left with the feeling of having failed.

Chapter 42

THE WINDS OF JUSTICE

The summer of 1943 found them very busy with late births and branding. In the past, the animals were all unbranded, but now the government was demanding distinct marks for families within the same lofche.

That summer was filled with joy and peace for my family. I had grown and was given chores to do; I had to help with the food for the animals, the hens, and the turkeys my mother was raising. So as soon as they gave me permission, I would go and see my grandmother; I would play there and learn many things from her. My mother already had four children: me, my two twin siblings, and a little boy who was only two months old, named Linkoyan in my grandfather's honor. I remember how happy my grandmother was that summer. We made apple chicha. Since there were many animals to be marked, there was plenty of food for the guests. Galensho came with his accordion, there were two guitarists, and we danced for three days straight.

Wingka dances were never to my grandmother's liking. She didn't know any rhythms or fancy steps, and she wasn't a party lover, but Nahuel Evans was a good dancer, cheerful, and always the first to liven up the festivities. He convinced her to join him in the dance. Animated by wine and joy, they laughed heartily. My grandmother stepped on his feet by accident many times, and he grumbled while she giggled. It was an unforgettable summer for me. Unlike other memories, this one has not yellowed in my mind; it is not a blurry, sepia image. I see the colors of her clothes, the almost turquoise blue dress with flowers that my grandmother wore, her long braids intertwined with ribbons of various colors that she had woven herself on her loom.

Throughout that year, they waited patiently for permission to enter the winter pastures. It never came. Pirenrayen called a trawun to address the issue. The previous winter had not been kind to them. The forest was thinning too much because the cows were eating the maiten trees and any new growth that emerged. Even my father grew impatient and, after a year of waiting, began to doubt. So many times, he had restrained his mother, telling her, "Let's wait, it's still too early to complain. All the paperwork takes time, it comes from far away. That's how things are here." But then we learned that they would not grant us permission, and that even the rewe belonged to them, because Victoriano Mankiñ had signed the papers in agreement.

My father continued to work on the railway. The days were very long: he left early in the morning and returned when night had swallowed everything up. On weekends, we would go to the countryside to visit my grandmother.

The war in Europe continued to drive away thousands of hungry and desperate people who arrived in Argentina, seeking an opportunity. We saw how our lands gradually filled with new arrivals. Some were respectful and kind; others were vile and opportunistic. But good and bad alike were unaware that the lands where they were now settling had, not so long before, been part of our territory.

Christmas brought joy to everyone's spirits for the first time. Liam had many plans for the coming year, and his son's presence filled them with happiness. Yet at times, he felt bewildered and unsatisfied. Sometimes, he thought he might lose his mind. He returned to his position as a supervisor, traveling to many train stations, checking the machines, the staff's performance, and the overall operation. Sometimes, sitting on the station bench, caressed by the sun, he would fall asleep and dream of the mountains of Puelmapu, of his daughter, and of Pirenrayen. Then the roar of the iron or the train whistle would jolt him awake from his nostalgic dreams.

As the train braked, Liam looked at his watch and confirmed the delay once again. He greeted the engineer and said, "Will we ever manage to make the trains run on time in this country?"

"We do what we can, boss," the engineer replied rudely, muttering under his breath as he walked away, "Damn gringo."

The engineer and stoker arrived for the next shift, and O'Sullivan climbed aboard. He observed the locomotive's good performance with satisfaction, asked some routine questions of the staff, and got off the train to go straight to the station office. It was the same routine every day. He felt the drudgery of obligations slowly chew away at his spirit, swallowing him whole. Patagonia, Puelmapu, with its powerful winds and vast geography, was far away. He, who had been so free and happy, was now imprisoned in a city life he never would have wished for. Occasionally, he felt that Pirenrayen was thinking of him from the south; he could sense her gaze on him again, as if it were hidden there, watching him.

April arrived, and autumn covered nature with a canvas of ocher, orange, and reddish hues. Some of the trees shed their leaves again, and some of the bushes became laden with fruits. The southern wind lashed furiously at the small houses. With a yerba maté in her hand, Pirenrayen went out to the yard to scold the dogs, who were bothering the hens. In the woodshed, Nahuel Evans was chopping wood, lost in thought. They had just woken up from their nap. She approached him.

"Motriley, let's have maté together. There are some freshly fried biscuits in the dish."

"I'm on my way, woman. I'm almost done," he replied with a smile.

Pirenrayen watched him for a moment, her gaze fixed on his arms, which lifted the axe high into the kalfu wenu, the blue sky, and then brought it down with precision onto the hard yaki wood. Nahuel stacked the logs onto a cart and headed with it to the kitchen. He washed his hands in a white enamel basin; the paint had chipped off from small, scattered blows, making it look as if ghostly faces were drawn on it.

Nahuel had given her a wood-burning stove. My grandmother made jams, and the little house smelled of sweet fruits and freshly fried biscuits. He breathed in those aromas deeply and felt full of joy. In that moment, he thought he could ask for nothing more from life. He felt complete; life had granted him these moments of happiness with the woman he had always loved and admired. He embraced her tightly, and she, so small, seemed to get lost in his great size. Nahuel was so tall and sturdy that everyone respected and admired him, yet for Pirenrayen, he was still the big, spoiled boy she affectionately called Pichimotriley.

Nahuel approached the pot with a cloth in hand and slowly lifted the lid; inside, the calafate berries mixed with apple were simmering. She liked to experiment, turning cooking into a delicious, serendipitous alchemy. He tried to dip his finger inside the pot and taste the flavor that smelled so good. She scolded him, gently tapping his hand.

"Don't spoil my sweets with your dirty hands. Why such a rush? Hold on, be patient, Pichimotriley," she said, feigning anger. "I wanted to talk to you about something," she went on. "I've run out of patience with the company and the military Wingka in Buenos Aires. They never sent us the paper for us to take the animals to our winter pasture. We're going to celebrate this wiñoy tripantü as we always have, in our shared winter quarters. We won't wait any longer for the thief to give us permission. Have you ever seen such nonsense?"

"You're right, dear," he answered. "I was waiting for you to make up your mind. What we need to do is convene a trawun and decide together. How will we get in?"

"My grandmother came to me in a dream and told me we must reclaim the winter pasture. She showed me how we should do it. Everything will be fine."

And so they did. On May 1, all the pu lof gathered for a trawun and deliberated until late, reaching an agreement to go in with all the animals on the first day of June.

In Buenos Aires, the high-ranking military officers and the British company officials were completely oblivious to what was happening in Puelwillimapu, the lands of the southeast. Their concerns were focused on the Second World War and its threat to their future.

The day came for the recovery of lot 12. The families from different lofs gathered, cut the padlocked chain, opened the gate, and let all the animals in. It was the dawn of June 1. Pirenrayen and Longko Mankiñ conducted the ceremony. The kultrun thundered its cosmic sound, awakening the ancestors' dormant forces. Night did not want to let go of the land; the nocturnal dew moistened people's bare feet as they made their offerings to the mapu, singing in our ancient language. They asked for permission from the pu newen, the forces of the mapu, the spirits that in her and from her sustain life.

While they prayed, Pirenrayen felt a force dwelling within her, coursing from her heart to her throat. Her voice exploded in pleas and songs; their voices expanded toward the wenu mapu. The sun sprouted like grass, slowly renewing the light. They finished the ceremony and set up camp, ready to resist, but nothing happened. Days went by, and no official, not even a police officer or the company's foreman, arrived at the site. They built shelters that gradually transformed into houses. Time passed.

"How odd that Mr. Smith hasn't come in all this time," Nahuel Evans remarked to Pirenrayen. After a pause, he added, as if thinking aloud, "Maybe it's not a good sign."

Pirenrayen nodded. "*Feley may*, that's how it will be," she said. "We must stay alert. We should never trust the Wingkas. They're like foxes lurking in the gloom, waiting to pounce on us when we least expect it."

A few days after reclaiming the land, Pirenrayen was the first to build a modest little house on lot 12 to spend the winter. Other families, inspired by her example, also set about building their rukas. Before the first snowfall began, with everyone's help, my father erected his own. They brought down a large quantity of firewood on several carts pulled by oxen. Up in the summer pastures, winter dressed in white; snow fell heavily for many days and nights. Down in the winter quarters, the snow was less abundant; the animals had good pasture, and the families had food and shelter. Pirenrayen sighed, gazing out of the window at the white sheet in which the land shrouded itself, where its dreams would hibernate.

"*Küme tufachi pukem*, this is a good winter," Pirenrayen said to her companion.

He kept on writing an article he would send to a European anarchist newspaper, expressing his views, from those distant southern lands, on Nazism and the war.

"Did you say something, dear?" Nahuel asked absentmindedly.

Pirenrayen stared at him curiously and asked, "What magic do you use to capture the sound of words? How do you make your words listen on the paper so quietly? You look at the paper and tell me, 'Here it talks about this or that,' but I don't hear anything. Only you can hear them, and I have to believe that those words only speak to you, just like the spirits speak to me, telling me how to heal the sick. I believe you, but I don't believe the paper."

He was bewildered and burst out laughing. She was offended. Then Nahuel laid his notebook on the table, got up from his chair, and embraced her tightly.

"My dear, I'm not laughing at you but at myself, at how foolish I am in the face of your wisdom." And he kissed her like a lovesick teenager.

Liam spent the whole winter with his family. As time went on, he enjoyed his son's antics more each day. He now ate baby food and crawled, and Liam could play with him. His relationship with Christine had improved, and above all, he spent a lot of time with his mother. He felt guilty for not having been present when his father died; he wanted somehow to ease the pain so much abandonment had caused her. His uncle, Patrick O'Sullivan, also received his care, and he responded with great affection to his nephew; he was also very fond of Martin.

Lord Husprum had inherited the assets of his wife and his in-laws; all three had now passed away. As the sole heir, he knew that upon his death, he would leave everything to Liam. He was troubled by his nephew's lack of ambition, fearing that all he had built under the persona of Lord Husprum would be squandered or simply neglected by him. He did not agree that Liam should continue to work on the railway; this was a subject of constant debate. His nephew argued that he would not leave something he'd been born for; he loved trains, knew perfectly how they worked, and was constantly training to be a good supervisor.

At the same time, many of the railway projects he supervised, both in the north and the south, were suspended due to the war in Europe. The expansion of the train tracks that would pass through the estate would allow them to transport wool from there. This would lower the cost of production and the shipping of raw material to England. But now, the British had other priorities. The new government was uncomfortable with the English because they were pressuring Argentina to take a firm position with the Allies. The United States used its advantageous position to do business here, which is why the Argentine government deepened its ties with the Americans. That neutrality allowed the circumstances to build a better scenario for us. Though it was fleeting, in the mid-1940s, our fate would change.

Liam received an order to travel urgently to the south. He was surprised, but he obeyed and bid his family goodbye. When he approached the baby to kiss him, he was overwhelmed by a sudden sorrow that wrung out his heart. His son slept, oblivious to it all, holding inside him all the peace that was missing from the world.

On September 19, Liam was on a train pulled by the steam engine PS11, which had been manufactured in 1930 and brought to Argentina at the end of the decade. Liam loved that locomotive; it was one of the best of its time. All the conditions were set for a pleasant journey, but he was troubled by the reason for his trip. It involved the transport of ten wagons loaded with soldiers heading to Puelmapu with strict orders to evict the communities from the land that they had reclaimed. Of course, he was unaware of this until he spoke to one of the lieutenants. That was how he learned about the occupation of lot 12. He understood why the government was deploying so many soldiers, determined to return to the English what they believed the Mapuches had taken from them. During the trip, he pondered how to delay the train's arrival. He sent a telegram to his friend Roig Evans, which read, "Lot 12 to be evicted. Train with soldiers coming."

When he received Liam's telegram, Roig Evans immediately traveled to the winter pastures in search of his son and Pirenrayen. When he arrived and saw the precariously built houses, he pictured how easy the eviction would be. Pirenrayen spotted him coming.

"Here comes your father," she said to Nahuel.

Pirenrayen smiled when she saw him, and Galensho, wasting no time, made his announcement.

"There's an eviction order!"

Upon hearing this, Nahuel emerged from inside the house. "How do you know, Father?"

Roig took the telegram from his pocket and showed it to him.

"That's just a telegram, not a judge's order," Nahuel said, dismissing Liam's message.

"Son, they're coming for lot twelve. Either we resist or they'll evict you without mercy. If you have any doubts, I suggest you call an assembly and discuss how to defend yourselves. I support you in everything," Roig replied as he put the telegram away.

Pirenrayen said goodbye to Roig, feeling alarmed, though Nahuel assured her that everything would be fine. The wet afternoon closed in. Pirenrayen listened to the rain while wrapped around Nahuel's body, feeling the drops falling through the holes in the roof.

"Pichimotriley, this summer we're going to put a new roof on the house so we'll be protected when winter comes."

"Yes, I'll do it," Nahuel said, half-asleep.

That night, she couldn't sleep; once more, she felt gripped by a dire premonition.

In the morning, the rain stopped. Nahuel Evans prepared his dark horse, had some yerba maté with his companion, and set off for the town at a leisurely pace, gazing at the landscape with pleasure, taking in the scent of the fresh green shoots and spring flowers.

Liam O'Sullivan could not sleep that night, either. A dreadful sense of anguish and fear engulfed him. He was awoken by a strong shudder of the train, which had ground to a halt. He went up to the engine to see what was happening.

"What's going on?" he asked the engineer.

"The brakes are failing," the engineer replied.

Liam gathered the men, and they began working on the repairs. The soldiers got off in the middle of the steppe, wandered around, and started playing soccer while waiting for the train to resume its journey.

At lot 12, Pirenrayen went alone to the rewe. There, she buried a stone she had received through an apparition from her grandmother Fresia a few days before the winter pastures were recovered. Once she had buried the powerful, brilliant stone, she made an offering of muday, tobacco, and quinoa and spoke to her ancestors. She asked for help from the forces of the mapu. She prayed that the soldiers would not come, and that justice would be served to those who spread death. She wept, remembering her daughter, and asked the little girl to watch over them. Doña Fresia appeared to her, sitting on a large rock. Pirenrayen approached.

"Grandmother, have you come to take me away?"

"No, my girl, I have come to help you. They won't be able to evict you. We have all come down; we are all here to protect you," she said, raising her hand and pointing to the river. "There are Longko Naweltripay; Kalfurayen; your daughter, Wanguelen; and hundreds on horseback, with spears and arrows."

Pirenrayen cried tears of joy and happiness, and peace flooded her heart.

"This time, no one from the community will die or be evicted," Fresia promised her granddaughter.

Pirenrayen felt confident and sighed with relief. She returned home.

Before the roosters scattered around the town could crow, Roig Evans was already up, having coffee and eating toast. Then he loaded his truck and trailer with food, warm clothing, and other useful items in case of removal. He was in the middle of this when his son Nahuel arrived; he'd come to the town on horseback, as calm as if he had never heard about the eviction.

"How can you be so calm, Son? Aren't you worried about the soldiers coming?"

"No," Nahuel replied curtly. "Something tells me that man, Liam, is lying. He is always finding excuses to meddle in our lives."

His father shook his head angrily, and they went into the house to talk. Nahuel Evans went straight to check the mail; Galensho's store also served as the post office. He bought provisions from his father and some scented soap for Pirenrayen.

A few miles away, the train was approaching at full speed. The soldiers were celebrating the engine's repair. Their commanders congratulated Liam for his admirable work in solving the problem. Everything seemed to be in order when a tornado descended without warning and began to furiously buffet the train cars. Liam had no idea that the tornado was in fact the *maulen*, the wind of justice evoked by the spirits as they rode in circles, summoned by my grandmother. Mounted upon invisible steeds were my ancestors, bringing the weight of justice to bear with all their might, determined to restore harmony.

Liam began to worry and headed toward the locomotive. He walked with difficulty through the cars. When he reached the engine, the engineer and the stoker were in a panic; they couldn't control the machine, and there was no way to reduce its speed. The wind seemed to be calming, but suddenly, as if blown in on a cloud of dust, hundreds of horses appeared before them, blocking the tracks.

The train derailed at a lethal speed at a bend in the track, plunging into a ravine. There, it caught fire, and some of the cars were destroyed. Many of the passengers, and all the men operating the train, were killed. Blood flowed from them as in a *trayenco*, a red stream traced across the terrain of their bodies.

Liam was thrown from the train. He could feel the wet, sticky blood as it clung to his skin. He closed his eyes, and the pain disappeared. When he opened them again, Wanguelen was watching him, luminous and beautiful.

"*Ñi chaw, ñi chaw*, my father, my father," the girl said. "Rise up and come with us; we're all waiting for you!"

Liam kissed her cheek and felt that it was warm. He reached out his hand, and the girl helped him to his feet. Broad smiles of happiness lit up their faces. They were all there: Fresia, Kalfurayen, Linkoyan, Chekeken, Longko Naweltripay. And among them, his father was also present. Many others he did not know were there. The horses were shiny and handsome. Wanguelen mounted one, and Liam another. Naweltripay beckoned, and they rode together, ascending to the wenu mapu.

In the same instant that Liam O'Sullivan's eyes closed forever, he arrived at Pirenrayen's house and found her feeding corn to the chickens. She stared at him in bafflement. Liam leaned against the horses' hitching post, and my grandmother went out to meet him.

"What are you doing here?" she asked, but he did not answer. She insisted, "Come in, and let's drink some matés."

Liam smiled at her tenderly, raised his hand, and walked away. At that very moment, there was a strong gust of wind, and Pirenrayen understood what was happening. Her legs weakened, and she fell to her knees with heartrending sobs, furious and suffering. That's how Nahuel Evans found her when he arrived home with the telegram bearing bad tidings.

The news of the tragedy shook Buenos Aires. Many members of the elite offered the widow their condolences. Sarah convinced Christine to have her son's remains cremated and scattered in Mapuche territory. The whole town waited for the ashes to arrive. Cabrera and Kawel organized the railway employees so that no work would be done that day, and everyone could attend the funeral. The widow, alongside her mother-in-law, presided over the farewell mass, which was held at the station. Then they boarded the train to scatter the ashes along the stretch from there to the next station. There were heartfelt speeches, and Roig Evans played the farewell song on his accordion. Everyone wondered why Pirenrayen was not there. Kawel played the *kul kul*, the wind instrument we often use as a call to fight. There were tears and applause.

The train departed as if it were Liam's last journey. On board were Lord Husprum, Christine with her son in her arms, and Sarah, who held the urn containing her only son's ashes. When the train had pulled out of the station, my grandmother appeared at full gallop, running alongside the train. She seemed to see her beloved there, reaching out his hand to brush the tips of her fingers, just as they used to when they rode together in play.

Sarah saw her approaching and was moved to tears. She rose and crossed the car to the aisle, where the wind rustled her dress. She opened the bronze urn that held the ashes and let them fly, so that Liam would finally be free in that land and with that people whom he had so dearly loved.

Epilogue

I have shared with you youngsters the story of the train's arrival here, and of the man who poured all his efforts into achieving it. I have shared with you a portion of the stories I treasure in my memory.

Many things happened later. The train also brought good times, though we would never have wished for the cost of that progress to be the death of the quebracho forests that gave us water, shade, and sustenance. The lands seized from all Indigenous peoples. My father fought for the nationalization of the railway, and many Mapuches became railway workers.

Today, only desolate plains, abandoned stations, death, and solitude remain. You will find no birdsong there, no animals frolicking, no trees providing shade. Nothing but rusted iron and gray concrete. If that is civilization and we are the savages, then let us be savages to protect what little remains of life in our mapu.

That is how the railway was built, piercing the soul of Indigenous nations with its iron. And when we adapted to that kawel made of iron and smoke, they killed it, too.

Today, I am here, speaking to all of you who have come to support our resistance against eviction. I see that many of you are young, that you are white. I see many women, and my heart rejoices, for we now live in different times. There is understanding between us. You also receive wisdom; you wish to walk the path of memory, embrace the truth, and establish justice.

I, Llankaray, have shared our story with you. Now, I simply say, *küme akuimun*, welcome! I have much more to tell you, but that will be for the next time we meet. Memories don't allow us to forget the suffering and the work of being alive. Remembering gives us courage and dignity.

It gives us the strength to demand what we truly deserve.

LLANKARAY'S FAMILY TREE

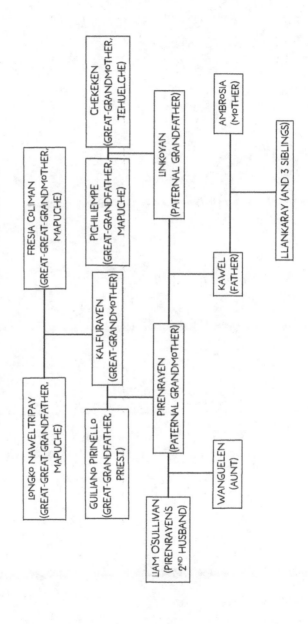

LONGKO NAWELTRIPAY (GREAT-GREAT-GRANDFATHER, MAPUCHE)

FRESIA COLIMAN (GREAT-GREAT-GRANDMOTHER, MAPUCHE)

CHEKEKEN (GREAT-GRANDMOTHER, TEHUELCHE)

GUILIANO PIRINELLO (GREAT-GRANDFATHER, PRIEST)

KALFURAYEN (GREAT-GRANDMOTHER)

PICHILLEMPE (GREAT-GRANDFATHER, MAPUCHE)

LINKOYAN (PATERNAL GRANDFATHER)

LIAM O'SULLIVAN (PIRENRAYEN'S 2ND HUSBAND)

PIRENRAYEN (PATERNAL GRANDMOTHER)

WANGUELEN (AUNT)

KAWEL (FATHER)

AMBROSIA (MOTHER)

LLANKARAY (AND 3 SIBLINGS)

About the Author

Photo © 2023

Moira Millán is a weychafe—warrior and defender—of the Mapuche Nation people. The daughter of railroad workers, she was born in the Chubut province of Argentina. She cofounded the October 11 Mapuche-Tehuelche Organization, which has recovered the territories of several communities and founded the Fight for Work movement. She started the March of Indigenous Women for Good Living, now a rights organization. In 2018 she organized the first Indigenous women's parliament. She continues to work on behalf of her people, the Earth, and the environment. Her activism has gained greater visibility in recent years amid ongoing repression in Patagonia. In 2012 she won the third DocTV Latin America contest as the cowriter of the documentary *Pupila de mujer, mirada de tierra*, directed by Florencia Copley. She won the Intercontinental Cry Indigenous Reporting Award with her article "Mapuche Motherhood in the Age of Benetton." *Train to Oblivion* is her debut novel, and she's now at work on the screenplay.

About the Translator

Charlotte Whittle is an editor, writer, and literary translator whose work has appeared in the *Literary Review*, *Los Angeles Times*, *Guernica*, *Electric Literature*, *BOMB*, the *Paris Review*, and elsewhere. Her translation of Norah Lange's *People in the Room* was longlisted for the Best Translated Book Award and shortlisted for the Warwick Prize for Women in Translation and the Society of Authors TA First Translation Prize. She has received two PEN Translates awards and has translated novels by contemporary Spanish and Latin American authors such as Jorge Comensal and Elisa Victoria, among others. She won the 2023 Queen Sofía Spanish Institute Translation Prize for her translation of *Papyrus: The Invention of Books in the Ancient World*, the international bestseller by Irene Vallejo. She divides her time between England and New York.